The Beautiful Love Songs Of Jenny Rennes

Robert Creffield

To those who value honesty and veracity
in our political leaders and the media
and to all those who understand the
virtue of a perfect pearl.

The Beautiful Love Songs of Jenny Rennes is written as a work of fiction; all references to political events and persons have been modified or contrived for fictional and dramatic purposes only.

Chapter One

Theo hated himself afterwards, facing the jury of his conscience, he was always found guilty of gross misconduct and sank into a broody melancholy, a short period of inescapable self-loathing.

Sasha stood at the mirror attaching the clasps of her black-laced bra with nimble finger work between her shoulder blades.

Every now and then she glanced at Theo lying on the creaky old bed blowing smoke rings into the stale air in estranged nonchalance. The shadows gathered and filled in the recesses of his unloved bedsit as the sun edged to the west in the cool June evening in Islington.

"You look miles away …" Sasha's face showed no real concern.

Theo broke from his reverie and examined her from his lowly supine position; this was a familiar ritual and he never ceased to be enthralled by the spectacle. How exquisite women are whilst preoccupied with their make-up and dressing. Where do they learn all the skills involved, the application of the creams, mascara, eyeliner, powders, and lipsticks not to mention the hair styling – all done so swiftly and deftly? It was one of life's true wonders to behold, this daily metamorphosis, from plain Jane to beguiling coquette, the eyes pivotal in this erotic transformation, painted to embellish all the carnal secrets designed to hypnotise you like a snake's stare before it strikes.

He watched her, gripped by the amatory routine, bunch her hair at the back with one hand and lasso it with a rubber band with the other to form a perfectly shaped pony-tail that she combed with the same devotion as a stable-hand brushing the mane of a thoroughbred horse.

"Penny for your thoughts …" She puckered her lips one more time as a finale to her performance in front of the mirror and started to put away her accessories into a well-worn make-up bag.

He stubbed out the cigarette. "I was thinking about the miners' strike actually – what do you think about it?"

"You're a strange one aren't you – I haven't got a clue. It's all those unions causing trouble eh?"

She bent down to pull up her white hipster jeans and as she stood upright tugging them into position a mauve-red scar was visible across her lower abdomen just above the pubic hairline.

She fastened the large stainless steel buckle to her yellow leather belt. Then she put on her pale blue T-shirt with the Kurt Cobain quote, "Better to burn out than fade away" printed on the front, and stood in the middle of the dingy little room sparkling like a flash of quartz in granite. She kept looking in the mirror as she did a half-turn to check her flexed bottom now hugged by the white denim and, satisfied with some pre-notion of its ideal shape, she gave it a gentle pat of approval.

She stood holding her purse with her shoulder bag resting by her feet like an obedient dog.

"So you have no opinion about the strike? Do you think the Government is right to take them on?" Theo moved over to the chair where his jacket had been thrown an hour before. He searched the pockets for his wallet.

"Don't ask me, I'm not bothered about it, why are you so concerned anyway?"

"I work in PR for the Government – it's my job to keep ahead of public opinion on such matters – don't you have any point of view at all?"

"I don't get involved in all that stuff – I don't understand it." She stood in heavy silence. A thrush darted up to the window, brushed a wing against it and flapped off in some distress.

"I could help you there – I've got the information you need." He looked at her sullen face void of curiosity. She looked at him with vacant eyes. He couldn't find the wallet.

"Na, don't bother, I really don't care one way or the other."

They kept gazing into each other's eyes until the differences between them became too complicated to resolve. A growing sense of impatience registered on her face.

"That'll be £10 then …" She opened her purse in anticipation.

Theo looked around for his wallet and eventually ran out of clues.

"Ah, I know, I left it down in the kitchen."

The phone rang from the landing below as he left the room.

Sasha went over to the easel in the corner of the room and its accompanying worktop strewn with an assortment of artists' items and other objects. She looked at each one with dreamy eyes – brushes, tubes of paint, pallet knives, a rag, a near empty bottle of linseed oil, two wooden pallets, sheets of blank paper, pencils, an ashtray, an opened packet of cigarettes, a notebook, a sketchpad with a drawing of a women's face, a stack of art magazines and a glass jar full of knick-knacks.

Along the wall were several paintings and prints including a large black and white reproduction of Robert Doisneau's photograph, *Beauty Is In The Eye Of The Beholder*. She looked at the subject of a boy standing in a Paris backstreet holding a large French stick of bread and counting his change. The boy was poor with cheap unclean clothes and dirty hands and knees; she was baffled by the picture and couldn't see why anyone would want to photograph the scene. She looked at the boy, the bread and the bustle of the surrounding street and completely missed the photographer's proposition that the boy's resilience to his lowly position and his daily struggle to get bread had a sort of beauty about it, the endearing attraction of those who never give up, whatever their circumstance.

Then she picked up the notebook and flicked through the well-thumbed pages; it was full of odd scribbles and random jottings – she stopped to read one:

After an argument tonight
went to bed and cuddled teddy –
turned over and lost teddy –
he had fallen to the floor forlorn –
said to myself "everyone's falling
out with me tonight."

She turned more pages and read another:

You want me to make you laugh
to be your toy clown
but I'm getting old and tired
and my batteries are run down.

She understood neither Doisneau's picture nor Theo's jottings and gave up trying. She put the notebook down and thought, 'You're a strange one Theo, very odd'.

Then she picked up the jar and held it to the bright evening sunlight streaming through the window – she could make out a single cufflink, some foreign coins, a small rubber tube of lighter fuel, some buttons, drawing pins and paper clips, a pencil sharpener, a dice and something shiny that caught her eye. She opened the jar and squeezed her fingers down to clasp the object pulling it out slowly and carefully. She could hear Theo's voice on the landing bringing the phone conversation to an end.

She examined the shiny object – it was a silver brooch of St Michael the helmeted winged Archangel with sword in hand ready to defend all believers against God's enemies. She was instantly taken by the small pendant, there was something strong and wholesome about the saintly figure, the protector of the good and virtuous standing defiant against corrupt and evil forces; she could hear Theo's footsteps on the stairs and something moved in her mind, an old forgotten superstition, an irrational belief ingrained within her DNA memory to do with gypsies and medieval folklore, about relics and the protection they gave against injury and disease – she heard Theo plodding up the stairs and in an instant dropped the brooch into her bag. She put the jar back onto the worktop and swiftly returned to where she had previously stood before the phone call.

Theo came in holding his wallet and stared at her with a solemn mien, "You ought to be careful Sasha."

The blood gushed to her head causing a dark pink stain of guilt to rise up from her neck across her cheeks.

"There was another attack in the Kings Cross area last night – seems someone's targeting women like you."

She released a tiny sigh like the last puff of air from a deflating balloon and the blush receded from her face back down her chest like ink through blotting paper.

"Women like me? What sort of woman is that then?" She looked at him with an expressionless gaze disguising the relief of such a near miss.

"Come on Sasha – you know what I mean, there's a nutter out there who's got it in for call girls – last night was the third attack in as many weeks – I'm just saying, you ought to be on your guard."

"Yeh well, maybe I'll hire a bodyguard – like one of the those huge bouncers over at The Black Cat nightclub? That might be interesting in more ways than one – anyway, no need to worry about me, I can take care of myself – but it's nice to know you care." She managed a rare smile.

He handed her the £10 and it disappeared into her purse like a rabbit down a hole.

She quickly put the purse back in her bag and said, "Thanks – I know one thing though, this tenner won't be worth £10 in a couple of months – not with all this inflation, I can't keep up with it."

She looked around the room to make sure she hadn't left anything then put a piece of gum into her mouth and chewed relentlessly, her jaws in rhythmic motion like cattle chewing grass.

Theo stood holding the door open as if he was letting a cat out.

She slung her bag over her shoulder, "OK, well, until the next time, just call the number, I'll look forward to it." She lied.

"Yeh sure, just be careful out there." He closed the door gently so as not to offend.

Sasha walked out onto the landing, her imitation paver shoes sliding lightly over the floorboards. She disappeared down the stairs leaving nothing but a hanging mist of Charlie perfume.

* * * * * * * *

It was early spring when Jenny Rennes had first met Danny on the platform at the Angel of Islington tube station. He stood by the stairs in an old cloth cap and a collarless shirt with waistcoat and brown corduroy trousers one size too big, busking a repertoire of popular folk songs with no less effect than if he had been an internationally acclaimed artist performing at the Albert Hall; he sang first to those alighting from either side of the City bound platform and then to those coming down the stairs in waves from the deep-shafted lifts. She had heard him whilst her lift was still gliding down the time worn concrete shaft and had bobbed to a stop on its shock absorbers, an echoing, haunting rendering of Ralph McTell's song, *Streets of London*.

She tarried standing close to him absorbed by his energy and the way he moved and strummed the guitar. He asked her for a cigarette following an announcement that the trains were delayed due to a fatality at Bank tube station. He had made a joke of how the recession must be serious if the bankers had started to throw themselves under trains. She laughed despite the harshness of his humour. They talked about music and lyrics and poetry. He asked her if she had been to the Thursday evening poetry session at The King's Head in Upper Street, and what a unique atmosphere the place had, and then asked her to meet him there the following Thursday; she agreed with a smile that beamed so bright it illuminated the prospects that such a proposal held in her imagination. A powerful stream of warm air pushed its way out from the black tunnel and along the platform spiked with wafts of old farts and cat piss to herald the arrival of the delayed train. The smile was still on her face as the train exploded from the tunnel out into open space and everyone stepped back squinting their eyes until it came to a halt. He spoke loudly over the din and said he was going to play his signature tune, *Danny Boy*, because it was mid-afternoon the time when the Irish navvies came back from work weary and full of pathos for the old country.

"They're always good for a few bob even though they're dirt poor."

She laughed and couldn't take her eyes off him, smitten by the gipsy in his blood and the love of life running through him like a rip current in the sea.

She went to The King's Head the following Thursday and got caught in the rain without an umbrella on the long walk down Upper Street. Danny seemed surprised to see her and took a few moments to recall who she was and where they had met. This disappointed her but she soon recovered as he introduced her to several people standing and sitting in the main saloon bar and like him they all had an artistic presence that seemed to be woven into their clothes and mannerisms and the atmosphere tingled with the promise of insights into London's hidden world of artists and musicians. The evening tripped along for her in a blur as time ran its course governed by a different law, an hour of casual talking and observation seemed to be no more than a few minutes but a short poem or song recital seemed to hang suspended in the smoky cavernous saloon long after it had ended. Down and down she tumbled like Alice in Wonderland all agog amongst the velvet jackets and velour jumpsuits, French terry cloth waistcoats, homburg hats, floral jeans, puffer vests, woollen dresses, sweaters and tunics and boots and sandals, patterned knitwear, and Ossie Clark style chiffon neckties and scarves, round and round she went dizzy and amazed with all the sights and sounds and offers of wine and Russian cigarettes and snippets of conversations pinging through the air about art and music; a woman in a pink crochet pull-on hat and yellow cotton dungarees came up to Danny and sat on his knee, puffing at his cigarette and earnestly engaged him about a painting she had seen at the Tate by Nevinson called, *The Soul of the Soulless City*. Danny kept leaning back and smiling as she spoke, stroking her hat as if he was stroking a cat behind the ears. Then a young Irishman who was known as Angelo of the Angel arrived looking like a gangster in a black shirt with white braces and a black fedora hat. He sat down beside her and asked her what she thought about the role of women in Victorian England. In the noisy clatter he leaned across to present his ear to her mouth before she had time to speak and she became tongue-tied.

"I'm not sure really, um, I reckon they had a tough time one way or the other, um, but they were stuck weren't they, in the convention of their day I mean, um, they had their obligations." She stumbled, her motor cortex temporarily malfunctioning.

Angelo looked up and stared at her as if struck by a Holy Intervention, "Well, Sweet Mother Mary, that's it for sure, my God you beautiful thing – that sums up the whole lot of it, from the top down to the toe perfectly, perfectly my dear girl." He leaned back and shouted out, "Yes! It's all about woman's obligations – yes, yes, sweet Mary so it is."

Danny and the girl in the pink hat looked over and laughed but no one knew what was funny and no one knew what Angelo was on about but it didn't seem to matter. On and on went the crazy night and she gave in to its random meander oblivious to time and worldly concerns, intoxicated by the music and the poetry and the wine and the characters all loopy and odd; she let herself drift along in the moment, her senses pulled and tugged by the giddy stream of surreal consciousness floating over the river of discovery like silver mist in her eyes.

Deep into the wee hours of the next morning, she laid down with Danny in his bedsit on Percy Circus near the Pentonville Road and embraced him with all her soul, giving herself totally to his warm blood filled body, bony and gnarled by frugal London street life and late night excesses. They met again and again in similar circumstances, once or twice in cafes during the day but mostly in bars at night and always finishing off at The King's Head. For a while Danny was a real friend and enthusiastic lover even teaching her how to play the guitar. Alas, hot passion cools and a lovers' bond fails if not properly charged with genuine love and a commitment to the same ideals.

One afternoon Jenny thought she would make a surprise visit to Danny's flat and so she skipped along with a bunch of daffodils she bought in Chapel Market. She arrived at Percy Circus at the junction with Prideaux Place and spotted Danny through the trees of the symmetrically fashioned oval garden in the middle of the square; he was standing on his doorstep kissing the girl with the pink hat who she had met that first night in The King's Head. She crouched next to a parked car on the corner but had clear sight of the entwined lovers and her eyes went straight to the pink hat that now sat lopsided on the girl's head; she looked on in a state of frozen disbelief as they kissed again and again until finally the girl walked off, a little wobbly at the knees, waving back at a weary faced Danny who closed the front door doing up his shirt buttons. Jenny shrank within herself and would have wept like a broken down-pipe in a storm if she hadn't felt such anger and betrayal. She walked wearily back to Pentonville Road tossing the daffodils into a dustbin that stood outside a car repair yard smelling of oil and greasy overalls.

He gave Jenny little thought and never tried to contact her again. As far as she was concerned it was a shattering end to her dream and she curled up in a ball of deep aching pain that lasted for three weeks before she could step out and face the world and a further four weeks before she smiled again. She kept away from The King's Head and never tried to track him down although she thought she saw him once busking on the Tottenham Court Road but she wasn't sure as the bus window was misted up in the damp rainy night. She did carry on practising the guitar and writing songs, that all featured women who had been treated cruelly by their lovers, but these laments brought little solace and if truth be known something died in her that afternoon on Percy Circus.

* * * * * * *

Two months passed and one Sunday afternoon Jenny sat by the open window of her bedsit in Packington Street off the Essex Road in Islington, the warm June air crept in and stifled her senses. She rested the guitar on her knee and struggled with the chords of the old ballad, *Come Ye Fair And Tender Maidens* that so aptly chimed with her mood. She sang with an intensity of meaning straight from the heart:

*"Do you remember our days of courting
When your head lay upon my breast
You could make me believe with the
falling of your arm that the sun rose
in the West."*

The chord changes were a struggle especially G to C to G, her fingers caught in a knot as they tried to slot onto the right spot on the fret-board. She played the verse over and over until the chord changes became easier. Then she sang the next verse with meaning so poignant it hurt:

*"If I had known before I courted
That love was such a killing thing
I'd lock my heart in a box of golden
And fasten it up with a silver pin."*

Concentrating on the chord changes tired her and the heat of the afternoon made her restless. She looked out the window as a bluebottle buzzed against the pane as if desperate to get inside the room and out of the sun.

"The irony of it ..." She thought, "The fly wants to get in and I want to get out. Whose the crazy one eh?"

She opened the window and leaned her head out to catch whatever cool air was passing by but there was none; leaning out she stared along the lonely Sunday Islington backstreet, a seemingly endless line of three storey Georgian townhouses each with the same six step stoop front doorstep beneath a pediment supported by two columns. Some were freshly painted, most were in various shades of off-white and a few were in need of repair, all led her eye far down the street towards the junction where more identical townhouses went off left and right, and then more junctions and more streets and so it went on to form a labyrinth where thousands of people lived out their private lives, known only to a handful of people and to God.

"How monotonous it all is." She looked back up the street towards the Essex Road that held a similar view. Someone a few houses down turned on a radio and the tune, *A Summer Place* floated out onto the street in the still air like velvet bubbles.

She thought, "Oh Lord, save me from this bloody heat – London makes me mentally ill in summer – the unbearable suffocation of it all, there always seems to be a sense of urgency to travel and wander, it's such a strain to be anchored each day to all this dreary routine." Her circannual cycle was a curse and summer always brought the same fidgety sense of unease and restlessness.

14

The sound of a bucket of water being moved on the pavement and the sloshing of a sponge against the windscreen of a parked car filled the air. A young man was washing his Austin Metro with the same rigor and concentration as if he was participating in a competition. The man's action, his earnest work engagement, gave her a quick mental image of her office desk in Camden Council where she worked as a Social Worker dealing specifically with the borough's homeless; a shiver ran down her spine as she envisaged the squalor and misery of her next batch of cases waiting for her attention on that rickety old desk.

Then a heavier thought weighed on her mind, the recent ignominy of losing out to Justine Bavington for the promotion to Head of Section. She had more experience than Bavington with an impressive track record in team leadership and demonstrable attainment results. Justine had not had the same length of experience neither had she dealt successfully with as many cases; what she lacked in value she made up with guile such as staying late to catch the attention of Mr Bates the Section Director and getting in early in the morning, bringing him coffee and pastries and gradually winning over his confidence to have cosy chats about her private life that she embellished with several fictitious accounts of unrequited love and other lies of broken romance.

Before long rumours flew around the office of Bates and Bavington sighted in back street pubs and bistros after working hours. The news that Bavington had been chosen over her for the Head of Section job made her feel under valued and sick to the pit of her stomach at the sheer injustice of it all. It was the first time she had experienced office gamesmanship and she had no answer to it, for she had believed that genuine hard work and competency was enough to get her the reward of promotion – the cruel reality that she was mistaken and that management could make unjust decisions crushed her motivation like a cartwheel going over a grape.

She bit her tongue remembering the office humiliation and looked up at the hazy sky and the relentless sun for some sort of redemption but only found the searing heat burning her eyes and boiling her brains. She murmured random curses under her breath like King Lear on the heath scene:

"Come on winter, do your worst – London's at peace with itself when it's grey and cold, the architecture makes sense and the fidgeting masses lose outline and shape – Monet knew that, he understood that London was at its atmospheric best in the mist and fog."

She went back inside and grabbed her guitar and black beret. "Sod this, I've got to get outside, get some air by the canal."

* * * * * * * *

It was 4.55 pm on Friday afternoon, the loose time of the week when time floats light and easy. Gilbert Penton-Fox looked over to Theo who was biting the end of his biro staring at his notepad deep in concentration that was only broken when he abstractedly gazed through the window at the two towers either end of St John's church opposite on Smith Square in the shadow of the Palace of Westminster. Penton-Fox placed his thumbs behind his navy blue braces pulling them out several inches from his chest before releasing them. The sharp snapping sound cracked the air like a film director's clapperboard. Theo did not stir.

"Come on Harrison old boy – it's nearly time to go and swim in the effervescent pools of Gordon's barely drinkable fizz."

"I suppose so."

Theo looked out again at St John's church standing white and solid in the late afternoon June sunshine slightly hidden behind two plane trees rich in new verdant leaf. A few commuters were scurrying across the square like a scene in a Childe Hassam painting. An elderly woman in a wheelchair was gliding back and forth at the foot of the steps trying to work out how to enter the church and finally went searching around the right hand flank with deep indignation palpable with each strenuous turn of the wheels. Theo thought of all the people who at that very moment were on their way to the church for the evening concert recitals of Handel's sonatas for oboe, violin and flute. How infinitely more civilised, he thought, than squashing nose to nose in Gordon's wine bar and talking forgettable trivia as the champagne was violated with contemptuous drivel.

Suzanne Trimmington-Smythe came over to Theo's desk and looked out the window at the sky speckled with threads of thin cloud lightly veined through the surrounding sapphire vastness.

"Ooogh, the weatherman said it would rain today – the liar! It looks fine. You can't trust the forecasts anymore can you?" She glanced down at Theo who resumed the earnest study of his notepad without replying.

"You are going for a drink aren't you Theo?" She had a glint in her eye and nodded as she spoke as if urging him on. She moved around his desk to obscure the view through the window and limit his distractions. She stood in front of him and visibly puffed out her breasts by gradual inhalations. For a few seconds his eyes were glued to the two heaving pouches of soft white flesh either side of her chest beneath her ballooning blouse each crowned with an acorn shaped summit.

"Yes I suppose so – but I have to see Tubby at five ..." He checked the clock sitting over the main door, " ... and that's now." He stood up, put on his jacket, grabbed his notepad and moved quickly towards the corner office. "I'll see you in Gordon's."

Toby 'Tubby' Trubshaw sat at his desk in earnest mode. The desk was antique and twice the size of modern office desks; even so, a spare space was difficult to spot and if there was a method to why a particular pile of papers stood next to another then it was known only to Tubby. This state of clutter had long since spread and infected all areas of his ample office where stylish furniture had been carefully placed in the early days of his tenure. Infrequent visitors were momentarily overwhelmed by the piles of books and pamphlets and charts and reports and miscellaneous papers stacked on every bookshelf, cabinet and side table all serving to give the impression that Tubby was a man who had either accomplished many things or a man with many things still to accomplish. Such impressions were carefully crafted by him to disguise a natural tendency towards sloth.

"Ah, Harrison my boy …"

Tubby looked up and his trademark chubby concertinaed cheeks and drooping jowls, that always reminded Theo of Alfred Hitchcock, wobbled like a strawberry jelly as he snorted the words through his nose. Theo had an urge to rush over and force Tubby to blow his nose into a tissue and thus restore order to the world.

"Sit yourself down why don't you." Theo moved some manila files from the particular chair at the end of Tubby's pointed finger.

"Well now Harrison, tell me what you think of this miners' strike business, in general I mean?" Tubby squinted slightly and the thinly disguised cunning in his question reminded Theo of Uriah Heep in David Copperfield.

"Well, I think it's a battle of wills and if you believe right is on your side then you will battle on and on – Scargill is fighting for the whole mining community and their livelihoods, but he's not getting total support because of the NUM's tactics of flying pickets …"

Tubby interrupted, "Yes, yes Harrison that's all well and good, but what does Mr and Mrs Porkpie sitting in their comfortable detached house in leafy Esher think of it all – those middle and upper class have-a-lots who consistently vote Conservative with the unflinching reliability of Big Ben, are they with the miners or with the Government on this matter – that is the question. You see it's got to make sense. What say you on that Harrison?"

Theo glanced at the picture of the Prime Minister on the wall behind Tubby's desk and was reminded of scenes in old films depicting colonial British outposts where the Colonel of the regiment always had a picture of the reigning British monarch on the wall whilst some hapless local native sat and worked a huge fan to cool the Colonel's sweaty brow.

Theo closed his eyes as if to help squeeze the statistics from his memory but the figures remained elusive. "Um, the last Gallup poll has those in sympathy with the miners slightly behind the National Coal Board – but it varies from region to region …"

"But what about the approval rating for the methods being used – the tactics, the flying pickets, trying to stop those miners who want to work from working, and of course, the violence – are we doing enough to shift opinion on the methods Harrison, the methods? It all has to make sense you see."

Theo suddenly remembered some figures. "Ah, well, let me see, yes, a big gap on the methods Sir – 15% approve and 79% disapprove …"

"Yes, yes, but what direction are the numbers going Harrison? It's the direction we're concerned with here, what?"

"Um …" Theo hadn't got a clue. He looked at Tubby with empty eyes, like a choirboy between hymns.

Tubby glared back at Theo with spikes in his eyes and his drooping jowls wobbled as he stamped out the words:

"Let me tell you that they have not moved much since the poll last month – and that's the rub – public opinion is a fickle thing Harrison and we have to be vigilant and prepared to pounce to nudge it one way or the other – it's got to make sense remember – and now we have all this unrest and brawling on the streets, well, the Prime Minister's office boys are getting themselves in a bit of a tizzy – they think it's getting out of hand, what with that fight up at Sheffield the other week, what was it, sixty odd injured, and then with that fracas outside the House last Thursday."

Tubby pointed in the approximate direction over the rooftops to the Houses of Parliament then he stared at Theo as if he was studying an information board at a railway station.

"And how many got arrested, tell me that?"

Theo flicked through layers of memory cells until he found the incident lurking in the swamp. "Um, about one hundred and twenty I believe Sir."

"Yes, yes, one hundred and twenty of the devils, would you believe it, one hundred and twenty of them kicking the police around like footballs, what? Well we can't have that can we, it just doesn't make sense, this is not El Salvador is it Harrison?" Tubby's jowls wobbled even more when he became excited.

"No Sir." A police siren went by outside with Doppler effect and the two men both peered at the window as if a striking miner was suddenly climbing through to vent his rage at them.

Tubby rested both thumbs behind his red braces and leant back in the extra padded armchair that masqueraded as an office desk-chair. He was growing weary of the conversation due to inherent limitations of concentration and the flickering visions of his waiting dinner darting through his brain, a large plate of sausages and mash with lashings of gravy and heaps of crusty bread.

He battled on. "And now, to top it all, we have this very day a miner killed picketing outside a power station in Yorkshire, killed by a lorry apparently, bloody nuisance what? Well, the Prime Minister doesn't like it one bit, she doesn't like the way it's looking for the Government, doesn't like the way the wind is blowing – too much opportunity for the miners to steal the limelight and get people's sympathy back, we have to be vigilant Harrison or else they'll come charging down Whitehall demanding some such nonsense, charging right through our windows, eh? And that doesn't make any sense does it?"

"I'm sorry to hear about the Yorkshire miner sir ..."

"Yes, yes, of course, but sympathy and tea is not the required response Harrison, we'll leave that morality stuff to David Jenkins our esteemed Bishop of Durham, he will give us all the sympathy that we can take I'm sure – no, no, the Prime Minister wants a new angle on this strike, a new way of looking at what's happening to push opinion around, a big heave-ho to make that approval rating gap even wider, the unions are the problem and we must get the people against them even more – she wants to turn the tide Harrison and get the polls totally against the miners, you know the sort of thing, 'Miners flaunt the law! Miners use excessive violence against the police! Miners determined to wreak mayhem and disorder across the land! Miners try to overturn democracy!' That sort of thing. It's time to use the old creative know-how and get the PR machine working Harrison, it has to make sense you see, do you get the drift my boy?"

Just then there was a light tap on the door and Eldred 'Cadgers' Cadgington stretched his devious looking face with pointed nose around it, "Sorry to disturb Sir but the latest Poll figures have come in, just a slight movement from last week with 16% approval and 78% against – thought you ought to know Sir."

"Yes, very good Cadgers, but they just confirm what I have been saying, the trend is moving in the wrong direction damn it!"

Cadgers withdrew his head like a tortoise and was about to close the door when Tubby shouted out, "Cadgers, tell me what you think of these miners, the NUM and their leader Scargill, what?"

Cadger's head popped back out again, "The NUM are anarchists Sir and Scargill is an extremist, a Trotskyist, whose aim is to destroy the Government and get the enemy, the Socialists, into power." His beady eyes glinted with cunning and guile. The door finally closed.

"There Harrison, there you are my boy, Cadger's has summed it up so well, no wishy-washy liberal nonsense, he'll go far, bulls-eye! And of course it makes perfect sense."

Tubby took a huge Havana cigar from a concealed box on his desk that only he knew was there and lit it up, releasing a plume of blue-grey smoke across to Theo that immediately infiltrated his olfactory receptor neurons as surely as if it was a potent biological chemical weapon developed at Portland Down.

"Well yes sir, but ... cooowf, cooowf." Theo's coughing bout was met with another salvo of cigar smoke.

"Now hear this Harrison. There's another mass picket planned for Monday at that wretched Orgreave Coking Plant near Sheffield or Rotherham or some such place – there's been one or two skirmishes there before but Monday's show is going to be big – I have it on good authority that some ten thousand miners will be on the picket hell bent on stopping supplies getting to the Steel Works at Scunthorpe – my information is that a bit of a ding-dong will take place at Orgreave on Monday and those miners will be given a bloody nose, enough said." Tubby tapped his little piggy nose with a stubby finger and leaned even further back in his plush chair, puffing at the enormous cigar and thought of his sausages and mash and gravy and heaved a sigh of impatience.

"Look – what I want you to do Harrison is get your self up to Orgreave for Monday's show and be our eyes and ears on the ground – I want you to follow the action, all of it, from beginning to end, and report back when it's over direct to me on my private line ..." He opened a desk drawer and pulled out a business card. "... there's the number – I want a summary and some suggestions of how we can nail these miners, some quick catchy phrases that the Prime Minister's speech writers can use to harden public opinion once and for all – have you got that Harrison, do you understand? Does it make sense Harrison?"

Tubby leant back once more and puffed at his cigar and Theo was reminded of J. Edgar Hoover's, 'The Mad March of Red Fascism' rant for some reason that he could not explain.

"Well yes sir, but …"

"I know it's short notice but that's the game when you work for Tory Central Office – it's a key assignment and I want effective results. I believe you're the man for the job Harrison, I've every confidence in you." Tubby lied, he had very little confidence in Theo and had become suspicious of his commitment to the Party's cause of late but had no other choice as the rest of the staff were all engaged on other projects.

"Good. And remember Harrison the old 'smear' technique honed so effectively by us Tory PR chaps over the years – when you talk about these miners don't forget to stigmatise them – so if they say they love their mother, you smear them as 'Mummy's Boys', if they say the Government should give more money for Welfare, you smear them as 'Socialists', if they say they want a fairer spread of wealth, you smear them as 'commies' – you get the idea Harrison, I want catchy phrases and any smears you can dream up – excellent, very good – it all has to make sense, now go see Imogen and she will set you up with your rail tickets and hotel – any questions?"

"Well sir, …"

Just then the door opened, as if on cue, and Tubby's secretary Imogen edged into the office looking straight at her boss with the same intense stare as she would give a burglar shinning up her drainpipe in the dead of night.

"Excuse me sir, but you remember I have to leave tonight by five-thirty?"

Imogen was an attractive but unimaginative, slightly dull girl whose upbringing by wealthy parents had ensured an immunity to hardship and stowed upon her bountiful privileges and favours that somehow had only hardened the blood in her veins and caused a blankness in her eyes.

"Yes of course – but first can you get Harrison those tickets for his trip to Orgreave on Monday. Excellent. That's the spirit. Good luck Harrison. Don't forget to call me on my direct number."

Back in her office, Imogen got together Theo's rail ticket and travel instructions into an envelope. She held a secret crush on Theo, something about the way he let his thick hair hang long and his watery grey-blue eyes that brought out a hidden mothering instinct to hold him and stroke his hair. She was also attracted by his aloofness and subdued tensile strength. She betrayed no hint of her secret as she handed Theo the envelope without a word spoken. Only her quiet, ruthless efficiency was evident but unbeknown to Theo she held a long and penetrating stare at his rear as he left her office.

Once alone she laid out flat on her back behind her desk. This unusual procedure was normally sufficient to ease the spasmodic back pain that had plagued her for several years; so despite the urgency to meet her friends she took ten minutes to lay still, like a log in a pond, with her head empty of any meaningful thoughts.

Meanwhile Tubby swivelled around in his enormous armchair puffing his cigar and staring out the window, the burden of his office bearing down on him and causing his flabby cheeks to redden with anxiety.

Outside across the square the early concertgoers were arriving at St John's church for the evening recitals of Handel's sonatas for oboe, violin and flute looking serious in silence.

* * * * * * * *

Theo descended the stairs from Villiers Street into the time-warped interior of Gordon's Wine bar crowded elbow to elbow with Friday night office workers intent on their brief alcohol induced escape from the rigours of work. He found his group sitting hidden in the furthest alcove in the gloomy back section with its damp wet walls and low vaulted ceiling that always reminded Theo of a medieval dungeon complete with dim candlelight and darkened shadowed recesses. Suzanne was giggling and staring into Gilbert Penton-Fox's eyes with dramatic effect as he poured her another glass of champagne.

"Ah Harrison, there you are, we were just talking about you, have a glass of the old Gordon's fizz – a bit more pricey since the last time we were here – all this inflation eh?" Penton-Fox chuckled as if the rise in inflation was simply an inevitable trifle without any serious consequences.

Theo squeezed onto a chair between two fellow public relations officers, Eldred 'Cadgers' Cadgington and Penelope Janners-Smith. "Thanks – cheers!" He sipped the wine slightly conscious of Janners's knee pressing against his leg.

Penton-Fox continued, "Cheers old man – so tell us what old Tubby wanted – don't say you've got a promotion eh? You'll be catching me up soon, Lord help us." His eyes swivelled as he sipped more wine and chuckled again. Theo wondered if everything seemed funny and frivolous to Penton-Fox, whether for him life was just a series of amusing incidents without feeling or pain. He thought, 'Is that what they teach them in public school, that everything is just a game and their money and power will guarantee they win, will always ensure they buy themselves out of trouble and treat every problem as a minor inconvenience?'

"Well, he wants me to go up to Sheffield on Monday and report back on some big shindig between the miners' picket at Orgreave Coking Plant and the lorry drivers taking the stuff over to British Steel in Scunthorpe – he reckons the police will be there in numbers and there's going to be a show-down."

Cadgers' face tightened with disbelief and jealously. He was the arch-stereotype public schoolboy, smart, quick, mean and ruthless; his eyes were set close together like an eagle and his nose was slender and pointed between two hollow cheeks that gave him a constant look of cunning and deviousness whilst his short-cut black hair was exaggerated by a sharp parting that gave hints of scholarship taking precedence over style and fashion for the effect of a superior moral advantage. It was widely known but never openly voiced that Cadgers had been gifted the job as a Public Relations Officer in Tory Headquarters by an arrangement hatched over drinks one Saturday afternoon at a London club between Tubby and Cadger's father, the owner of a huge Kent brewery and one of the Tory Party's more generous donors.

"What? Tubby has asked you Harrison to report on this – I can't see what difference it makes if you're there or not frankly – what does he expect you to do exactly, sort of bring them together and arbitrate as if you were the man from ACAS?"

Cadgers' eagle eyes gave the impression he was scheming some devious plot as he bellowed false laughter that was gilded with a platinum posh accent. "Has he mentioned this to you Janners?"

"Tubby hasn't said much to me since I gave him my report on the unemployment figures this week – not sure what he thought when I concluded that the latest total of three million-plus was a price worth paying for reforming the country and thinning down all those bloody nationalised industries – a few extra navvies chucked on the scrap-heap is neither here nor there – goodness knows what he thought of that – ha ha." The exertion of her laugh made Janners' knee press harder against Theo's leg; she was Oxford educated, keen and bright as a ferret but her knowledge of the world in general and the working class in particular was somewhere between 'little' and 'none' and had these qualities been a prerequisite for her job qualification she would have been rejected on the spot. She was not overall attractive but her large blue-green eyes, long mousy hair and ample breast were enough to distract the attention of men in her company who saw her as a good example of 'posh totty'.

Penton-Fox quickly intervened, "Now, now Janners steady on, unemployment is a bit of a problem and we still have to come up with something on that one – I think distraction tactics are called for and this miners' strike is pretty useful in that regard eh?" He paused and turned back to Theo.

"But tell me what he said Harrison, what does he want you to do up in Sheffield eh?" Despite three glasses of fizz going straight to his head and an irresistible impulse to be gay and frolicsome, Penton-Fox assumed a temporary serene and contemplative mood that he thought the subject deserved.

Suzanne looked at Theo and seemed to be stimulated by the attention he was receiving; she examined his dark brown hair, the way it fell mellifluously in random waves across his head and his large sad blue-grey eyes and bent Roman nose and felt an urge to touch him, to run her fingers across his cheeks and lips.

"Ooogh – I wish I was going with you to Sheffield Theo, sounds exciting. I've never been up north – what's it like? Ooogh." She squeezed the sound out through pursed lips to exaggerate the dangerous pleasure she thought going up north would entail.

"Yes, what's it like up north Harrison, gosh, I can't imagine it, do you actually need a passport to go there, eh what?" Janners' playful eyes glistened with contempt for the northern working class.

Theo ignored Janners' witless remark and gave Suzanne a quick glance and smiled. "It's more down to earth and honest in my opinion but you must make up your own mind Suzie."

He looked back to Penton-Fox and wondered how much information he should divulge. The truth was he hadn't fully understood what Tubby was expecting of him when he said,

'The Prime Minister wants a new angle on this strike – to push opinion along – a big heave-ho – the unions are the problem and we must get the people against them.' He thought the latest approval ratings on Government methods to tackle the strike were impressive; he couldn't see what all the fuss was about and hadn't had a chance to question the intent but was aware of a sharp sense of unease growing in his consciousness at the only logical conclusion.

"He wants me to observe and report back on how the miners behave – he is anticipating some big confrontation between them and the police and wants to up the anti and get public opinion ratcheted up against them – I said that the polls showed the public were very much against the miners' picketing methods but he says the Prime Minister wants to make sure the public are really against the miners – he wants them to be the out and out villains in the whole drama." He sipped the champagne and thought he had said too much on the subject.

"Well, that's a turn up for you Harrison isn't it? – all he's asked me to do is to put a gloss on the demise of the bloody Triumph motor car marquee – he reckons the public will be in a bit of a lather over it – been around for sixty years or so apparently – but I mean, who cares exactly, only a bloody car name, it's not exactly important is it?" Cadgers looked around the table for a sign of understanding and agreement but found none, "He wants me to come up with something that will put a smile back on Joe Public's face with this new Austin Rover 200 series – I mean, what can you say? Just another new car, big deal." Cadgers' thin spit-speckled lips sneered once again.

"Oh come on you lot, you'll have us all crying in our fizz in a minute – talking of which, we need another bottle of the old shampoo – who feels like trying to get through the teaming mass of the great unwashed?" Penton-Fox peered at the heavy throng of drinkers crammed together in all directions as if scanning the outer perimeter of a prison wall with a searchlight.

"I'll go – same again?" Theo clutched the empty bottle, eased himself out from the table and ducked into the scrum of drinkers squashed in the narrow walkways and massed in front of the small bar, "I might be some time …" He was heard to say as he disappeared into the crowd.

Waiting at the crowded bar that heaved and swayed like strips of kelp in the incoming tide, Theo's thoughts went racing ahead – there was something about this Orgreave assignment he didn't like, something dark and menacing hidden in what Tubby had said, what was it again, '…my information is that a bit of a ding-dong will take place at Orgreave on Monday and those miners will be given a bloody nose.' Theo kept mulling over the words and their implication and he balked at the idea of being complicit in some pre-planned trap to discredit the miners' cause and inflict hardship on them. He didn't care for the miners or their cause but he had his principles and sense of fair play and shrank at the idea of being used in some plot to use their struggle to benefit the Prime Minister's political advantage. He felt he was being used and the Orgreave assignment was devious and he loathed deceit and dishonesty. He felt the early stages of nausea towards his job and the people he worked with and knew the symptoms would get worse the more Tubby's scheme unfolded. He nudged his way to the bar and finally caught the barman's eye.

"Bottle of your house champagne please." The beady-eyed barman's forehead tightened with creases of disapproval as he quickly calculated the price of the champagne exceeded his hourly wage by a factor of four.

"That's eight pounds." Theo could almost hear the barman's silent curse as he pulled the champagne bottle from the refrigerated cabinet. Behind him the crowd pushed and nudged as if to signal that Theo's allotted time at the bar had now elapsed and his departure was overdue. Clutching the bottle and his change he eased his way back through the chattering horde.

"Excuse me ..." Theo crept gingerly through.

"Oh yes, we've been to see it, but why they wanted to spend a fortune on some silly Thames Barrier is beyond me – don't they know how many people are out of work – where's their priority?"

"Excuse me ..." Onwards he nudged.

"Went past it the other day, absolute disgrace, sooner they get rid of those layabout women camping out all over Greenham Common in their boiler suits the better, 'Women's Peace Camp' my arse - probably all lesbians anyway."

"Excuse me ..." Someone trod on his foot.

"Never liked Tommy Cooper couldn't see what was so funny in watching a bloke in a silly fez mucking up every trick he did – pity he's died though, but what a way to go."

"Excuse me ..." A young women leant forward guffawing and spilt some Liebfraumilch on his arm.

"What was the name of that policewoman who was shot by those Arabs? Oh yeh, Yvonne Fletcher, that's right, those bloody Libyans need sorting out, get the SAS on to 'em, they'll show 'em ..."

"Excuse me ..."

"What about Liverpool winning the European Cup for the fourth time – and the FA Cup and the League – what a club ..."

"Excuse me ..."

"Seen that new musical, *Starlight Express*? It's about some old steam engine called Rusty, can't see that lasting ..."

He arrived back at his workmates' alcove with the same sense of achievement as if he had reached Mount Everest's North Base Camp. He found Cadgers conducting a rendition of Harry Enfield's song, *Loadsofmoney Do'in Up The House*:

"Do'in up the house is my bread and butter
Me bird's page three and me car's a nutter
Loadsamoney is a shout I utter
As I wave my wad to the geezers in the gutter."

Janners' shrieks of laughter rose above all the din like a firework straight into the vaulted ceiling; she could not contain herself and practically choked with mirth. Wiping tears from her eyes she spluttered:

"Oh I love that bit about, 'waving my wad at the geezers in the gutter' – Oh that is just so hilarious ha, ha, ha." She let her head drop to the table whilst her body shook with convulsions.

Penton-Fox hurriedly took the bottle and popped the cork with gay abandonment up to the dank ceiling with no regard to where it might land, as it was, it ricocheted back down and pinged harmlessly off another table before setting off again and disappearing into the corner shadows. He quickly filled each glass waiting empty and silent before him and gave an impromptu toast, "Here's to wads of money ha, ha, ha …"

Theo tugged at his collar and wanted to feel cool air on his face. He needed to escape. The rest of the group fell about laughing once more, gulping the champagne as if it was lemonade. He felt increasingly detached from their way of life and slowly, bit-by-bit, his old problem of finding meaning and identity in a group re-emerged to blight his spirit. Within fifteen minutes of further relentless banter and distasteful quips at the plight of the poor and disadvantaged he announced he was going, made an excuse of being tired and bid his farewells.

Suzanne said she had to go too and asked Theo to wait for her. The two climbed the steep stairway and stepped out onto Villiers Street now only patchy with scurrying commuters in the evening June sunshine. They slowly walked down to the Embankment tube station and Suzanne seemed excited as she spoke quickly about the first thing that came into her head.

"Oh don't you just love London in the evening – and Oh look at the Victoria Gardens, gosh it looks so green and inviting, I wish a band was playing don't you Theo? And what about the Arches, I always think of that song, what's it called, you know, about sleeping under the arches?"

Theo gasped for air, "You mean, Underneath the Arches by Flanagen & Allen?" He gave a cursory glance to where she was looking at the Waterloo railway arches.

"Ya, ya that's the one – Ooogh isn't it all just marvellous, to think of those poor beggars sleeping over there all snuggled up warm and singing that song – so super-duper."

"No Suzie it was nothing like that – Flanagen wrote the song to the people in the Great Depression who slept under the arches of Derby's Friargate Railway bridge – they were hungry and homeless and miserable, there was nothing super about it."

The champagne, the sudden hit of fresh air and sunlight and the prospect of being alone with Theo sent Suzie floating high on the thermals of fantasy.

"Oh look Theo, look at the boat going by and all the people having fun, it must be one of those river dinner cruises – gosh, wish I was doing that, don't you? Oh, London is just so super, Ooogh." Theo gasped for more air and said nothing.

They arrived at the underground station. Theo glanced at the news billboard propped up by the wall between the newspaper seller and the flower vendor:

Record Unemployment –
3,260,000
Out of Work

"Don't you use the Northern Line Theo – so do I – we can go together – where is it you live again, Islington isn't it? Gosh, I live in Camden so we're practically next-door neighbours – gosh, fancy that! Actually Theo, why don't we go for another drink – have you been to the Hawley Arms in Camden, it's a great old fashioned pub, good food and there'll be music tonight – what d'ya say?"

Theo remained silent as they walked into the dimly lit station; a homeless man was sitting propped up against the wall with a tatty old straw hat turned upside down beside his knee displaying a few coins. The man stared at the ground with eyes empty of hope. Theo felt in his pocket and took out some coins then he dropped a shiny new fifty pence piece into the straw hat and the angle and force made it leap up and almost jump back out again as if embarrassed by its new home. The man's eyes did not move and he murmured in a low monotonous tone, "Thanks mate, God Bless."

They walked off down the long tunnels to the Northern line escalator. Theo breathed in the stale air and tried to focus.

"I'm a bit tired Suzie, thanks anyway, I reckon another pub scene will finish me off."

Her bouncy gay expression gave way to a look of disappointment. He paused and then relented for some irrational reason, contrary to his mood and better judgement.

"Well, you could come back to my place for a drink if you want?"

They got onto the escalator and stood perched still as it slowly wobbled its way down the yawning cavern to the tracks below. Suzanne's nervous posh little voice could be heard amongst the escalator's whirling engine cogs, "Ooogh Theo, that sounds super."

Meanwhile, back in Smith's Square a solitary office light shone from the otherwise blackened empty Tory Headquarters' building. Inside the dimly lit office Tubby sat in the spreading shadows with the phone pinned so close to his ear it practically fitted inside.

"Now do you understand Trubshaw? I want to advance this matter and move to a quick conclusion – your department has a vital role in the process – come back to me on Tuesday first thing with at least three good ideas – I want some powerful, quickly digested slogans we can feed to the public – we simply have to shift opinion over to us on this matter and Orgreave is the key, do you understand Trubshaw?"

The church clock struck eight o'clock as the doors creaked open with a sound reminiscent of a haunted house scene in an old Hammer horror film; people came out in twos and fours from the evening concert, their feet sharply clicking over the silent night pavement.

The shadows gathered more densely in Tubby's office. "Yes Prime Minister, of course, you can rely on my department's complete cooperation. I've put one of my best people on the case." He lied and it stuck in his throat. He put the phone down and thought of Theo let loose on the assignment. "My God, I hope I've done the right thing."

* * * * * * * *

Jenny sat on a rickety old bench by the Regent's canal and bathed in the blissful peace all around her. She was always surprised at the effect it had on her, it was such a secret place, undiscovered by the tourists and disregarded by the locals due to its run-down environment. There was the occasional runner and cyclist but mostly only long periods of silence and stillness, as quiet as dust in a church, broken by the odd person ambling along with no particular purpose. It was a marvel that such an oasis existed in the middle of London where only the sounds of nature and the distant murmur of traffic crinkled its tranquillity; she placed the guitar on her knee and resumed her practicing of the song that resonated so closely with her feelings:

"Come all ye fair and tender ladies.
Be careful how you court young men.
They're like a star on a summer's morning.
They'll first appear and then they're gone."

She paused and gazed at the water as if it might reveal the meaning of life's mysteries.

"Men are such bastards ..." She muttered to herself underneath her breath; it was a habit that went back to her childhood when she didn't have many friends and she discovered her other self, the voice within, that was always there to offer the other point of view, "...why do they lie and cheat and leave you in pieces, the bastards – they should all have samples of their sperm stored in fridges and then castrated at puberty – that would cure them, make them more human."

A mental picture of Danny came into her head like Banquo's ghost and she shuddered with the bitter memory of his loss. She looked up at the sky as a plane went over, droning like a distant lawnmower; she watched its slow descent into Heathrow and thought of the people on board sitting with their seats upright and trays back into position and urging the plane to land, to touch down on the solid earth once again, home and safe. A hot pulse of blood pushed through her veins as she felt trapped and restless, anchored to her position and routines, she longed for change.

A tramp who looked older than he was appeared from nowhere and shuffled by like a wandering dog sniffing drainpipes. He had matted long hair poking out from a bowler hat tilted on his head like Oliver Hardy and a thick beard that had transformed from a state of mild shagginess to extreme wildness without his knowledge. He went by with quick little movements of his feet holding some cardboard and with a fixed stare ahead as if he was late for an important meeting. She looked at his eyes as he passed but could not distract him from his purpose and on he went probably to some nook he had found for shelter beneath a bridge or a disused barge rotting away in a side basin. He was gone as quickly and silently as he had appeared, like a robin that suddenly lands by your seat and flies off in the blink of an eye. She sighed as if in pain and then placed her hands on the guitar's fret board and resumed practising the chord sequence again and again.

Time passed and the sun arched to the west enough to alter the light and change the sense of time. She finally stopped, stood up and carried on walking along the towpath. She had no set plan but was happy to keep strolling with the cooler air brushing her skin in the late afternoon.

The canal fascinated her in the same way as a large work of art might capture her imagination. There was something indefinable about it, the way it held the past so tangible she could almost see the bygone days evoked all around her. She marvelled at the sheer scale of the original enterprise and the enormous engineering feat involved, digging it all out foot by foot with pick and shovel and lining it with clay by hand, putting in place all the infrastructure of locks and steps and road bridges, tunnels, aqueducts, basins and towpaths, mile after mile across the country, along the valleys, over the dales, through the woods and meadows and all the earthly realm before it; those gritty navvies tough as flint working in all weathers to meet deadlines, working for little pay and no benefits to keep the wheels of progress turning, the relentless industrial wheels turning day and night producing coal and machinery and textiles, all having to be moved from the main towns and cities into the urban sprawl of London and its docks. Those unknown and unsung heroes, the labourers of the Industrial Revolution, hacking away at the soil and rock to build the canals and keep it all moving forward into that blind faith place known as progress.

She walked on lightly treading through the feather stillness and peace of the canal landscape. She was in awe at how it all just stood there suspended in time, the narrow boats moored alongside the towpath with an assortment of useful things sitting aloft, the odd bicycle and even a porter's trolley, wicker baskets, some logs for burning, jerry-cans, rope, plastic sheeting, TV aerials, tools of all kinds, potted plants for decoration and table & chairs placed aft or on the bow section for relaxing when time and schedules permitted, like having tea on a cottage lawn. The boats were home for thousands of people living on the canals up and down the country and Jenny was taken by their resilience at enduring such an alternative lifestyle. She walked on happy to be a visitor again in the silent world of the canalscape and the narrow boat users. She recognised some of the names, 'Pegasus – Derby' and 'Puddleduck – Worcester' and then the soft chug behind her namesake, 'Jenny Wren' the tour boat as she glided along to her mooring at the Wenlock Basin. The dark brown-black water held captive for many years and distilled in mystery, splashing alongside the towpath and gurgling beneath its concrete slabs.

Her mind was caught in the total magic of the place, the spiritual soothing balm of the genus loci, the serene stillness and sense of the past, the winding route through London's rarely seen backyards of side street dwellings and office buildings; on she strolled accompanied by the occasional flotilla of ducks on their silent forages between distant grassy knolls and columns of hardy hawthorns, alders and tilting willow.

Her musings were interrupted by the floating evocative notes from an accordion playing somewhere ahead. She recognised the unmistakable tune, *Sous le ciel de Paris*, and it immediately made her think of France. She stopped, spellbound by the music and the moment, the heat moving the air in looping currents, the buzzing drone of insects, the absolute calm of the canal-way and the ever present ghosts of its past all fused to anaesthetise her anxieties. She paused by the edge of the canal, her random thoughts zigzagging in different directions; she thought of Danny and wanted to share the moment with him, to walk arm in arm singing sweet love songs and pressing her hand in his; she thought of her parents at home in Folkestone, Dad tinkering with his kite and Mum sunbathing in the garden or dozing on the sofa watching an old film. Suddenly her mind was invaded with childhood memories of summer Sunday afternoons with her parents; she saw her mother with new eyes, someone who was young, not much older than her own twenty-four years, who made motherhood a vocation, something that was necessary and vital requiring all her attention – Jenny appreciated for the first time the enormous sacrifice her mother had made in this endeavour and the extent of the skills and competencies that the job demanded. Never before had she understood the difficulties involved in being a woman, a mother and a wife – the holy trinity of life – the sacred calling of young women to give their lives for the ultimate cause, the utter necessity of bearing children and bringing them up with love, knowledge and stability in order that they can cope and make good decisions and find a decent partner to propagate and keep the whole thing turning round and round in the endless cycle of life, with each cycle wider but stronger than the last. She stared at the dark treacle coloured water and imagined her mother's face peering back at her and smiling, 'Don't worry Jenny, it will be alright – you have to be patient, it will be OK, be strong, follow your dreams.'

She took out a penny from her pocket and tossing it into the canal whispered back at the apparition:

"Thank you mother, I know we have not always seen eye to eye lately but I hope you find love and happiness."

The small coin seemed to float for a second then turned and spiralled down into the dark murky water and was gone. A satisfying glow rippled through her and in that moment she felt a deep love for her parents. She thought of her Dad who had not been formally educated but had gained knowledge of people and the world that was beyond any curriculum – he had given her natural intelligence, street-wisdom and a broad sense of humour and she knew it was a priceless gift of incalculable value. She wanted to be with them again and chat about everything under the sun until it was late into the night; she longed to feel their love around her once more.

The accordion music seeped back into her ears, its darting notes circling around her imagination and weaving an irresistible web to catch her dreams, her dreams of travel and getting away from her routines and the stress of work – she suddenly had the thought:

"I must get away for a while." The accordion worked with her senses to draw inviting pictures of rural France. "I'll go to France. I'll go and stay by the sea for a few days, to get away from this stifling city and this broken country."

The notion filled her with a soothing comfort and she raced through a diary kept in her head and decided there and then to go off on the coming Wednesday and be back for the weekend, yes, she would strike whilst the iron was hot, just for the hell of it, sod the lot of 'em, sod the office, sod Justine Bavington, sod the Government's cuts, the work will have to wait – and she would visit her Mum & Dad whilst she was at it. It was an exciting plan and she smiled, almost laughed out loud, with the sense of adventure now waiting ahead.

Just then a cyclist came along, intent on getting to his destination as quickly as his legs could pedal, a silent weapon unheard and unseen by Jenny who stood with mind hopelessly adrift in whispery daydream oblivious to the living world around her. Her consciousness edged open to the sound of the cyclist's wheels whirling towards her, that she confused for a split second with the summer insects buzzing in the warm June air. Then the cyclist's shrieking yell:

"Watch out you silly cow – get out the bloody way you stupid bitch!"

Before her mind could assimilate what was happening she felt the jolting thud of the cyclist's hand hard on her shoulder as he swerved and pushed her out of his way from the path. She tried with all her might to keep upright but the laws of physics were against her and she toppled forward into the canal just catching sight of the cyclist's purple helmet as she plunged into the water. The words, "... you stupid bitch!" were drowned out as her ears filled with the peat coloured gloopy slop of the ancient canal.

* * * * * * * *

Suzanne's gay frivolousness, that had persisted throughout the journey to the Angel tube station and all along Upper Street, decidedly waned as she climbed the rickety stairs to Theo's dim attic room. Her reaction to the dreary garret and its state of threadbare penury instantly stifled her incessant garrulousness as surely as if Theo had opened the door to the interior of an igloo. She entered the squatty but homely living room in a state of speechlessness.

She stood looking around in the gathering shadows and finally said, "Ooogh Theo, so this is where you live – the inner sanctum of Theo Harrison – very snug." She lied and was amazed that anyone, let alone a representative of the Government's PR office, could live in such a dump.

Theo was aware of a prevailing odour of pilchards that caused a degree of sensitivity to the nose. He swiftly moved over to the room's single window and pulled down the sash letting in the evening London air with its accompaniment of monotonous droning traffic. He immediately felt weary as he always did when confronted with another human being that demanded his polite attention. He loathed these superficial preludes and wondered whether he should ask his work colleague to leave straightaway on the pretext of a sudden deepening migraine or just scoop her up and lift her over to the bed without bothering with the usual preliminaries and formalities. Alas, he was as capable of such precipitous acts as was his neighbour's cat to entertain a mouse for a cheese and biscuits supper.

"Please sit down Suzie." He pointed to the small armchair he had brought with him from his flat in Blackheath. There was no other chair. "Would you like a glass of wine – only got red, Rioja I think."

"Ooogh ya, thanks …" Suzanne was not in the mood nor was she capable of practising the finer skills of an oenophilist and would have accepted a cocktail of turpentine and Benzole if that was all Theo had to offer.

She put her yellow leather shoulder bag next to the armchair and sat down looking around her with eyes opened wide as a child looking out to sea. The small room was sparsely furnished with just a bed, a chair, a four drawer dresser, a single ancient wardrobe and a small table with a record player sitting on top surrounded by various books and papers; some vinyl records were stacked underneath. In the corner was an easel with a fresh canvas showing an outline of a young woman standing beneath an apple tree.

She became confused at all the tubes of paint and brushes and so many miscellaneous items strewn across the tiny side table. The aroma of paint and linseed oil now moved across the room displacing the dissipating wafts of pilchards that had been dominant for so long. There were several paintings and prints pinned to the walls but her eyes were drawn to one in particular.

"Ooogh, that's an interesting painting Theo – who is she? Did you paint it?"

Theo did not like to discuss his art, apart from regarding it as amateur he also thought it was personal, requiring explanations of his feelings that he knew were too abstract for common consensus.

"Yes – it's just a study of a girl I once knew – a long time ago."

Suzanne sensed she was trespassing on sensitive ground but the effect of the earlier champagne and her natural tendency towards the flippant did not prevent her from continuing.

"Well Theo, you are a dark horse – I had no idea you were an artist, gosh." She went over to the painting and studied it as if she would later be tested on its detail. "She's very attractive – what's her name?"

Theo winced at the question and was reluctant to be drawn any further on the subject and so busied himself opening the bottle of wine. He handed her a glass and went over to sit on the side of the bed but found it awkward and opted to squat on the floor instead. Her question hung in the air like a cobweb.

"The painting is called 'Angelina' and it's in the style of Arthur Hughes' *April Love* – do you know it?"

Suzanne sipped the wine and looked blank. "Ooogh, ya, I think so – not sure actually – sweet title …" She lied.

"No, it's not sweet, it's about the passing of a fragile love – Hughes' work is exquisite and sensual but the subject is sad, he's one of the most popular of all Pre-Raphaelite painters – there's a picture of it somewhere amongst those cuttings – I only wish my painting was half as good."

Suzanne ignored the reference to the scattered magazine cuttings and kept studying the painting with wide eyes and her glossed thin lips slightly apart as if she was watching a shooting star in the night sky.

"Ooogh Theo, what other secrets have you kept from us – I would never have believed it." She tilted forward slightly too far and spilt a little wine on the bare floorboard.

Theo felt the usual weight of boredom creep through his brain when engaged in the early stages of seduction and knew it had been a mistake to bring her to his lair. He pondered over the inherent weakness not yet corrected by evolution that prompted men to be so easily led by their genitals to a state of hopeless concupiscence. He changed the subject to the mundane.

"So what are you working on at the moment Suzie?" He looked over to catch her blank stare. "At work I mean …"

"Ooogh well, Tubby wants us to make more of this new breakaway miners' union, the Union of Democratic Miners, you know the one that's been put together by the Nottingham and Derby miners – well, he wants me to interview Ian MacGregor and put together a campaign to promote the UDM and use it to end the NUM's closed shop rule."

"In what way?"

Suzanne was not sure but didn't want to show it. "You know, now the UDM has been given official status the miners won't have to be members of the NUM to get work and negotiate pay – it's another way of breaking down their power and authority I suppose – anyway, I've got an interview with MacGregor next Wednesday to go over the press campaign, Ooogh lucky me ya?"

Theo changed his position on the floor to relieve the growing dumbness in his backside. "Do you like your job Suzie?" This was a question he had asked himself more and more of late and was curious if she too had doubts.

"Ooogh Theo, you are getting deep aren't you, ya, of course I do, who wouldn't like getting involved in all the important issues of the day and helping the Government stay in power, it's better than any other job I can think of, well, apart from being in films or on telly I suppose, ha, ha, or working at daddy's choc bar factory as a quality tester, or being a fashion model with a fabulous figure, ha, ha." Her expression brightened as she got carried away with the fantasies.

"But you don't get put off by the way we are meant to …" He tried to find the most appropriate word, " … by the level of mendacity expected of us?" He immediately regretted his choice of words as being too pompous and quickly said, "I mean by the way we have to present the facts?"

"Ooogh Theo, not sure I know what you mean, ha, ha." She gulped some more wine, far more than she needed.

A loud piercing sound came through the open window from the grunting traffic below on Upper Street as a bus driver and lorry driver locked horns over some minor territorial dispute.

Theo was losing patience, "I mean the way we are expected to bullshit and lie!" His emphasis on the last word was too strong and he examined her eyes for signs of disapproval.

"No, not at all. Old Joe Public is happy to believe anything we tell him isn't he? And what's wrong with that, he doesn't want to know all the nitty-gritty bits of detail, he's too busy. Take this miners' strike for instance, it's important we let them know how disruptive the miners are being, interfering with ordinary peoples' lives and trying to bring the Government down like they did with poor Edward Heath – that Scargill's a commie and an anarchist and we can't let him get away with it. I reckon we're doing the public a service ha, ha."

Theo felt his stomach ripple and his mind ache as his tolerance waned. He looked around his little room and felt cold and alone.

"But Suzie, have you looked at it from the miners' side, most of them work in small communities, often isolated places where the local collieries are the only source of employment – if you close the mines you take away their livelihoods and their communities, all the shops and cafés and pubs and social clubs and recreation grounds – it will reek havoc and misery far beyond the collieries themselves and it will cost the tax payers vast sums of dole money."

"Well, I don't know about that, but I know a lot of those mines are unproductive – we can't just carry on pouring money into them just because they support some remote community in some peat-bog valley – they got by before nationalisation didn't they? Privatisation will sort it out I'm sure."

Theo thought about the mining industry pre-nationalisation and the appalling safety conditions and low pay when miners were exploited for cheap labour as young as five years old.

"I wouldn't believe all you hear about privatisation if I were you, the miners were treated badly by the pit owners often with scant regard for safety and their life expectancy was below the average – privatisation was the problem then not the solution – the miners were always in peril, their job was dirty and dangerous, only the poor and uneducated would do that job, cheap labour for the toffs."

"Ooogh Theo you're sounding a bit radical – Tubby would be surprised to hear you talk like that – you sure your hearts in the job, you have to believe in the cause don't you, I mean, otherwise, what's the point – are you a bit of a leftie maybe? Cadgers thinks you are."

Theo suddenly thought of his old friend Sandy and all the arguments they had over the National Front in 1977 and the awful Lewisham riots. Sandy was convinced that Theo had become a Tory and now seven years later he was suspected of being a leftie by his workmates. He smiled at the irony of the situation.

"I'm not sure what is meant by 'leftie' or 'commie' – I just try and see the logic in any situation and work out what is right and what is wrong."

The room seemed to grow a little darker and a silence fell on them like the beginning of a snow shower. Suzie drank the rest of her wine in one gulp leaning her head backwards and letting it pour from her glass with as much finesse as John Mills' character Captain Anson downing his cold beer in the film, *Ice Cold In Alex*. Her eyes widened and her head started to roll to some imaginary tune buzzing in her brain. She darted her eyes up to the ceiling and then left and right around the room before finally coming to a halt at the stack of vinyl records. She got up and looked through them, her brain dizzy and her legs wobbly. "Ooogh let's play this – I love this song."

Theo put the stylus on the record and the quiet room was suddenly filled with Cyndi Lauper singing, *Time After Time*. The sentiment of the song ignited a sharp memory in Suzanne's mind and she came over to Theo, pulled him towards her with her arms around his neck, and began to smooch. The music gripped her senses and she started to mouth the lyrics like a hypnotic chant.

They first moved in small circles going from one foot to the other that Suzanne repeatedly misjudged nudging her even closer to Theo whose upright body acted as a cushion; then they came to a standstill and gently swayed from side to side to the haunting tune.

She held Theo even closer and started to press her lips against his cheek. Her blood surged and she began to lose all sense of time and place. She started to sing the lyrics out loud as she pressed her knee against Theo's crutch:

"After my picture fades and darkness has turned to grey
Watching through windows, you're wondering if I'm okay
Secrets stolen, from deep inside
The drum beats out of time … Time after time."

Theo withdrew within himself and any sensations that might have started to stir in the deep crevices of his loins immediately retreated to where they seemed inclined to stay. He thought of Sasha and how she knew how to work his feelings, how expert she was at drawing him out to give himself without commitment, to renew and complete him without an obligation. Since Angelina all those years ago he had never felt ready or willing to trust the love of another human being.

The record stopped and the silence of the room was harsh to his senses, he stepped back, "Look Suzie – I reckon I ought to turn in I'm feeling whacked out …" He lied. " … it's all this stuff at work and Tubby getting me involved with the miners' strike, I need to get myself prepared for the Orgreave trip – do you mind if we call it a day, sorry."

Suzanne opened her eyes as if she had been in a coma. She looked around and touched her cheeks as they lightly blushed. A small feeling of shame came over her like she had discovered someone secretly observing her getting undressed. Her consciousness turned a hundred and eighty degrees from steamy oblivion to clear cold reality and she trembled with an indelible guilt.

"Yes, Theo, of course, yes, that's OK ..." She almost stumbled turning back to the chair to pick up her bag.

He took her arm and steadied her balance. "I'll come down with you to get a cab – they come along Upper Street like flies round a jam pot this time of night." He pulled his jacket off the bed and checked his wallet. "I'll pay for the cab ..."

Outside she lurched towards the taxi, lost her balance and fell onto her knees then fell again spread-eagled with her arms and legs extended as if she was flying through the air. He helped her up.

As she got into the back of the taxi she turned and gave Theo a quick kiss that missed his lips as he turned away and landed on his jaw.

"Thanks Theo – I'm a bit smashed actually, must be all that Gordon's shampoo, ha, ha – we must do this again soon, properly."

The sound of a hiccup was just audible as he slammed the passenger door and the taxi grunted off, swallowed whole within seconds by the frenetic Islington Friday night traffic.

* * * * * * * *

Jenny walked back along the towpath dripping with canal water and clutching her guitar. The water trickled from every part of her like a sponge that has been soaked and then held up for gravity to take its course; it ran out of her hair, her ears and her nose and trickled over her lips and chin. She thought it tasted of engine oil and exhaust emission. She was angry and felt like crying but held fast as she had been taught not to show her emotions in public. So she walked with squelchy plimsolls and sodden blue cotton top and yellow jeans now several shades darker. Every now and then she checked the top of her head but her cherished beret was not there, lost in the melee of thrashing about in the canal and clambering back onto the towpath. She had bought the beret with Danny one Saturday afternoon as they strolled through Chapel Market; he had chosen it and put it onto her head making slight adjustments so it sat just tilting over to the right hand side like 'a true Parisian' he had said laughing at the effect. The beret was special to her and its loss was the one thing that hurt most in the whole sorry incident.

She finally arrived back at her bedsit and flip-flopped down the hall to the bathroom. Half way through the task of removing her heavy wet clothes she knelt down on the bathroom floor and cried, releasing the trauma of being hit by the cyclist as well as the ignominy of being knocked into the canal and the overriding sense of injustice that had filled up inside her like a water butt in a thunder storm. Returning back to her room she started to dress, relishing the simple luxury of dry, fresh clothes on her skin.

Once dressed she went down to the middle landing where the communal telephone sat on a small courtesy table accompanied by an ancient Tiffany lamp whose bulb had long since blown and never replaced. She dialled her parents' number and waited for their pick-up, the receiver pressing against her wet ear and making it feel soft and warm.

"Hello?" Jenny's father sounded startled as if something suspicious was implied by the act of anyone telephoning his number.

"Dad? Is that you? It's Jen – how are you Dad?" She felt the drama of the canal incident return and little tremors swelled behind her eyes as her tear ducts activated once more. Her voice could not disguise the shock she had experienced and she needed to bleed the incident from her mind.

"Jen? Are you alright my love, you sound different, is everything OK?" Like all parents Reggie had highly developed sensory antennae that picked up any hairline change in their offspring's demeanour.

"Oh, well, I had a bit of an accident Dad – got knocked into the canal by some maniac on a bike – I'm alright now, nothing broken, just shook me up that's all." She had to bite her lip to steady herself and hold back the tears from gushing.

"How did that happen for goodness sake – don't these cyclists have bells on their bikes - you sure you're OK? God, you never know what's going to happen next, I can't believe it."

He conjured up a picture of a London canal and narrow towpaths and his daughter thrashing about in the water slowly drowning with no one to help. "How deep are those canals anyway?"

"Really Dad, it's all OK, just a bit of shock, nothing broken, a graze on my knee trying to climb back onto the path – don't worry – got a bruise on my elbow too, nothing really, um, Oh the canals? I think they're about four feet or so, something like that – anyway, you know I'm a good swimmer, I can thank you and Mum for that."

"I can't believe it." Reggie picked up on the injustice of the incident and shared Jenny's anger.

Just then her upstairs neighbour, Maggie McGuire, started moving a huge wooden chest across the floor causing an ear-piercing noise to boom down through the ceiling, out over the landing and onwards into each room. For a few seconds it was impossible to speak. Finally Maggie McGuire's mysterious chore was done and peace restored.

"Christ Jen, what the hell's that? Is the roof caving in?"

"Sorry about that Dad, it's my flat mate Maggie upstairs, she's got this odd habit of moving a big wooden chest around every now and then, it's quite bizarre. Look, the reason I'm phoning is because I'm going over to France this Wednesday for a couple of days and thought I could stay over at yours Tuesday night to get the ferry to Calais next morning – would that be OK? Sorry it's short notice."

"Of course my love, you know your room is always here for you, always will be …" He had felt uneasy and affronted when Jenny had decided to leave home and live in London and kept her room tidy and ready for her return, " … but you won't get a ferry to Calais from Folkestone anymore, they switched the service just a few days ago to Dover, you can only go to Boulogne from here now."

"Is that right – wow, that service has been running for donkey's years hasn't it – everything is changing in front of our eyes, the country isn't the same anymore, it seems that profit comes before everything and peoples' needs are not important – Oh well, I'll go to Boulogne then, suppose it doesn't really matter, I'm just going for a short break." She quickly recalled her early memories of Boulogne and wondered whether it had changed. She started to feel hopeful again – it would be an adventure.

"Nothing stays the same anymore Jen – we're being led by a mean spendthrift shopkeeper – by the way, better get your ticket sooner rather than later what with all this inflation, you'll pay more in a few days time."

* * * * * * * *

Sasha lived in Somers Town in a single-room bedsit in Werrington Street near the Euston Road. The room was functional and served as a refuge whilst she went about her business in the surrounding area; she had no emotional or sentimental investment in the place and if the four walls of her little room held any secret it was only her discreet ambition to leave once she had saved enough money and move to Weymouth with her daughter Vana; she wanted to give her daughter the best opportunity to fulfil her potential using her talents and skills as well as giving herself a new start, some where clean and fresh, away from the London noise and frenzy, somewhere by the sea. The choice of Weymouth was based on the sentimental feeling she had towards the place from when she had gone on a school visit eleven years earlier and fell in love with its esplanade of fine Georgian and Regency terrace apartments, shops, hotels and guest houses. A fantasy of living in a grand Regency apartment overlooking Weymouth bay was often the last thought in her head before she drifted off to sleep at night.

She had built up her business from scratch starting as a streetwise twenty-year old from Romford. Her lack of education was compensated by a quick mind and steely determination. She was attractive in that way most men liked, embodying the classic features of a tart, with mousy blonde hair, narrow face with pronounced cheek bones, full lips and deep set lavender eyes, shapely legs, round bottom and a full bosom that signalled its presence from behind both summer and winter garments.

With such an inventory her decision to become a call girl was straightforward for she had the confidence to believe she would get regular work and be able to build up a clientele offering her remuneration far exceeding anything she might get from a nine to five office job typing and filing documents. She decided to organise herself as a business entity targeting her market within the A and B categories on the Social Grade model, that is, her clients should be professional types with plenty of money. She then applied these parameters to her local areas of Kings Cross and St Pancras, Camden and Islington, with possible options of Hampstead and Highgate.

Walking the streets at night or getting tied to some dodgy pimp was rejected. She would operate as a sole-trader and leave her card in hotels and boarding houses and selected telephone boxes in the more salubrious streets. It was necessary to make phone calls to other call-girls on the pretext of acting for male associates to find out the going prices for different services and from these she drew up a tariff that took the average going rate and added fifteen per cent for what she believed were her superior features. Under no circumstances would she entertain clients in her bedsit but operate a strictly call-out service; it was necessary to have a telephone installed with a cassette answer machine that had just come onto the market.

It took her only three months to establish a list of repeat-customers having rejected several that she considered too risky or perverted. She never revealed much about herself or allowed clients to get too close to her private life and so avoided intimate conversations, touching and kissing that was beyond the requirement of the paid service.

Each month she visited the local health clinic for a general check up. She kept her earnings in a metal box that she placed in a shoebox that she hid in her suitcase that she wrapped in a blanket that she kept under the bed and each night she would take out the money and count it and feel good about the rate by which the amount was accumulating. She reckoned that she would have enough money in two months to put down as a deposit on a modest apartment in Weymouth based on the average of her monthly earnings. Each evening she arrived back at her lonely room relieved she had encountered no aggravation or violence that day but was aware of the dangers involved in her work and the risks she took.

Friday evenings were one of her busy periods especially the time between ten o'clock and midnight. It was nine forty-five and she had already gone out on two calls to clients in Kings Cross and Russell Square. Back in her bedsit she had taken a bath in the communal bathroom down the hallway and was back in her room pulling up her favourite white hipster jeans when the phone rang. She jumped across the floor holding her jeans around her bottom as if competing in a school sack race and lifted the receiver.

"Sasha? It's Banjoko. How are you Sasha my dear? Can you come round, I wonder? I mean can you come round now, do you understand me?"

Banjoko was one of her recent clients whose wealth made her over look a worrying aggressive tendency he had. He was forty-eight years old, six foot two and well built, obese even, with obvious signs of over-eating and over-indulgence in general. He was quick minded but not quick footed and always opted to sit rather than stand. He was from Southern Nigeria belonging to the Yoruba people. He was a natural bully with an acute sense of self-importance topped with a super ego and showed no sign of patience with anyone who was slow to understand him or carry out his demands.

She had had two previous sessions with him that had both been an ordeal and given her reason to be concerned. During the first he had started to moan and curse in an incoherent way, as if he was shouting abuse at some unseen menace. Sasha had a stereotype image of an African witchdoctor dancing around a campfire thumping his chest and wailing to the gods. The second session was different in that he had only wanted her to use her hand that took an inordinately long time to finalise. During the climax he had tightly gripped her arms oblivious to the pressure he was exerting and the pain involved. For both sessions he had given her four times her going rate. She was torn between turning away such a lucrative client and exposing herself to further abuse and possible violence.

"Hello Banjoko, well, it's getting late …"

"Don't concern yourself with that my dear, everything is fine believe me, everything is fine. Come round now, it will be worth your while, this I can assure you my dear." Banjoko's deep voice was absolute.

"OK, but it'll take me half an hour at least."

"Don't worry about that my dear – I will be expecting you soon." With that Banjoko hung up.

Banjoko worked in the Nigerian Embassy as a high-ranking official, the details of which he never disclosed. He lived in a huge apartment overlooking Regent's Park. It was decorated to a sumptuous standard with fine antique furnishings complete with French chandeliers, a celeste, gilded wall mirrors and rare Turkish Ushak rugs. The air always seemed scented with lemon zest. Sasha was intimidated by the plush interior and felt cheap in its opulent expanse.

He grunted through his nose as he opened the door, standing in a peacock blue satin dressing gown with his bare legs just visible below the hem and nudged her inside by way of tilting his huge solid head sideways as if showing her some irritation to his skin below the ear. She brushed past him and made her way into the living room, the rug yielding to her soft slip-on shoes as if she was walking over a layer of duck and down feathers.

"Please my dear, won't you put your things over there and sit down just here." He pointed to one of the Edwardian armchairs.

As far as Banjoko was concerned, he was paying for Sasha's time and if the pressure building up in his loins was anything to go by there was no time to lose.

Sasha sat down and Banjoko remained standing in front of her fulfilling a plan he had imagined earlier.

"Oh yes my dear, that is just right. Oh I have always admired your lips and that colour you use, what is it now, tell me, Oh I know, let me see, it's burgundy rouge is it not? Such big juicy lips – made for pleasing a man is it not so? Let us begin."

He undid the cord to the dressing gown and pulled it open. "There Sasha my dear, you see I am ready for you tonight and there is no mistake about that right?" He snorted like a pig.

He leant forward and held her neck with his hand pulling her head firmly towards him. He regarded her head and lips and tongue merely as things to be hired for pleasure, like a ski-jet or speedboat; he was paying for her service and she was reduced to the workings of a machine, to be wound up and move to his demands, solely for his pleasure.

A clock struck eleven o'clock in Westminster chime somewhere in an adjourning room that gave the degenerate proceedings an aura of respectability.

A tremor of vulnerability jagged her nerves. She checked herself and thought, 'Come on Sasha, you are professional, you have to deal with situations like this – this is just part of your job, get on with it.'

She felt no desire, not even a trace of fascination, just a cold separateness that gave her the extraordinary sense of being outside her body and looking down on this other Sasha, the one who worked as a call girl, the one who went in to strangers homes to pleasure them mechanically and in silence, a dealer in the cold capitalist world of sex trading.

She worked her head up and down in steady rhythmic movement. He stood in front of her, his head leant backwards as if he was mesmerised by the ceiling's lavishly ornate plaster mouldings, that were indeed a thing of wonder, expertly fashioned in the English style with open strap work scrolls, flowers and fruits.

His bullet head started to turn in small circles like a boxer who had just been landed a decisive blow to the chin and was about to collapse in a heap. Within a few seconds a bass pitched groan came forth from his huge barrel chest, faint at first but then expanding to a deep continuous groan that seemed involuntary coming from rarely used cavities within him; it signalled the beginning of the end of the ordeal for Sasha and this at least encouraged her, for the speed of his imminent climax was in such contrast to the two previous sessions. She slowed down her action believing the end was nigh.

He had transformed into a brute that held neither respect nor interest in her feelings. "You bitch, don't you dare stop, you white bitch, don't stop."

The ugliness of his words and the threat they conveyed pushed her senses into the early stages of shock. He groaned deeper and deeper, leaning his head so far back his Adam's apple nearly pushed out through the skin of his throat. He increased the pressure around her neck with his hand and she quickened the action with her head once again.

"Ahh, don't stop, harder, harder now."

Sasha responded, her only thought was to finish the whole sordid ordeal and get away, to walk to the tube station in the cool night air, free and easy and a little richer.

"Faster, harder, keep going bitch – don't stop." He looked down at Sasha working away and his face was gripped with some terrible pain as if an inner demon was taking over and turning him into a beast; he squeezed her neck tighter, his eyes opened wide, bloodshot red, like a sick mad hound.

"Don't stop or I'll snap your neck …" He growled like a dog.

Sasha could not move – he held her clasped to the armchair with an iron grip; his face puffed out, his mouth stretched wide open like a yawning hippopotamus, the tribal ritual scars on his cheeks fanning out like the infrastructure of a leaf and his terrible devil eyes burned red scorch marks into Sasha's blue eyes as he buckled at the knees and tottered on his toes just keeping upright.

"Ahhhh …" He exploded and wailed at the crazy spirits in his head; he had morphed from Witchdoctor to Chief Warrior and beat his chest with his free hand. "Ahhhh – ahhhh …" The sinews and veins in his neck almost split as he swooned in deep primeval ecstasy.

He remained nailed to the spot keeping his grip around her neck as the sensation of his climax subsided, slowly and gradually like a wave drawn back into the sea. She felt the pain around her neck lessen as he loosened his grip and folded within himself, utterly spent and finished.

She took his hand with both of hers and pulled it away from her neck, releasing her own groan of relief but with no sexual pleasure attached just the gasping of a frightened animal as it breaks free from a snare of terror.

Banjoko gradually recovered and composed himself. He pulled together the dressing gown and took deep breaths.

"Oh yes, yes, yes – now that was something my dear, that was something alright." He had reverted back to the civilised Banjoko after the inner beast had subsided into the black devil heart of his super libido.

Sasha spat into a tissue and wiped her mouth. She had to get away; she had to feel the clean night air on her face.

"I have to go, I must get back ..." The terror she felt was palpable. She clutched her bag tight as if it was a lifebuoy.

"Yes, yes of course my dear, you must get back to your place in Werrington Street, of course my dear, of course – here, you must have something extra for tonight, here ..." He had gone to the splendid bureau plat writing desk standing proud by the corner window and taken an envelope from the top middle drawer.

Sasha took the envelope without opening it, her hand shaking and an acid bile reflux rising from her stomach up to the back of her throat; her knees did not seem connected to her legs but she somehow managed to walk to the door, slightly bent over like Groucho Marx.

"We must do this again very soon my dear, yes, it is good for both of us yes?" His big red eyes glowed like molten lava.

Sasha hurried from the apartment without saying a word. Ten yards along the road she knelt down bending over the gutter and released gulps of sick, spewing out her mouth, wrench after wrench, until there was nothing left but a thread of dribble dangling from her lips.

Chapter Two

Theo sat on the train examining the open three-day return rail ticket from St Pancras to Sheffield and the directions to the Royal Victoria Hotel for his two nights' stay that Imogen had arranged for him.

The train slowed as it approached the Knighton tunnel south of Leicester bellowing its warning whistle that cut the air and stopped all creatures in their tracks within a quarter-mile radius. The train entered the tunnel and the compartment receded into a dim yellow light from the two ceiling lamps that veiled the interior obscuring detail and definition. Theo looked out the window but could see only his face reflected back from the blackness like a ghost. Then the train swooshed back into the open silver light of day and he looked from passenger to passenger who all secretly stole glances at each other as if to make sure nothing untoward had happened, that everyone was still where they should be and the tunnel had not claimed a victim.

Theo's eyes grew heavy and the train's gentle rocking motion and accompanying rhythm of its wheels click-clacking over the points drew him into sleep like a lullaby. He thought again of Imogen held in his arms and burying his nose under her chin as he slid further down the tunnel of sleep, trailing his hand along her thigh, down he went, further and further, tracing the curve of her buttocks warm like sunned peaches and soft like a bird's feather-lined nest, down he went into the fathomless space of sleep and suddenly Imogen's face changed into Suzanne's who kept leaning back and gasping out, "Ooogh, Ooogh, Theo, Ooogh." Like a peahen returning a peacock's mating call, she pulled his hair and scratched his back with her nails frantically wanting him nearer, tugging him closer, coaxing him into the sacred apex of her open legs moist like rain drenched moss he slid between those white talcum-powdered thighs delicious in their sticky heat to cleanse himself at their holy temple gates – then Suzanne had gone and he was in a room full of paintings, canvasses, jars of linseed oil, brushes and pencils and there was Angelina, the long black-haired love of his life in blue denim dungarees leaning over him in her studio flat – it was Beckenham 1977 and he was crying in wounding gasps from deep within his throat, crying so hard it hurt his soul and Angelina was leaning over and letting loose a long line of spittle from her mouth dangling it into his worn-down, grey-blue eyes as if to cool them, as if to calm them and ease his pain and he raised his hand up to her beautiful chiselled chin to touch it and feel her warm blood once again, one more time, just to touch her one more time ... "Angelina, Angelina, my love ..." He softly whispered in his sleep.

Just then the train jolted as it pulled into Leicester station and Theo was shunted out of sleep as sure as if the train had hit the buffers. He lurched back into consciousness and immediately wondered whether anyone had noticed his open mouth whilst he had slept. He tried to swallow but his throat felt dry and rough as an old flannel. He sat conspicuous with inner guilt of his exquisite wicked dreams.

Everyone was busy with their own thoughts or so it seemed. A steward pushed a refreshment trolley along the corridor shouting, "Hot drinks, cold drinks, sandwiches, snacks."

Theo bought a black coffee and turned his mind to Orgreave; opening up his briefcase he took out the official Fact Sheet that was waiting there for such a moment.

Several people left the compartment leaving just two passengers and the newly formed stillness enabled him to properly engage his notes; his concentration was soon disrupted by a group of miners pushing onto the train and sending threads of conversation down the carriage that abruptly demanded attention of all those within earshot. The ambiance changed a shade darker as the truculent group stomped up and down the corridor looking for seats, imposing their presence as they went.

Within a few moments two young miners sat opposite Theo and continued their conversation that had began earlier on the platform.

Curly had thick black wavy hair and a face pinched at the cheekbones as if he had lived his life on a diet of cigarettes and beer with the occasional supplement of baked beans. He spoke in a thin voice and was quick to draw conclusion, having a tendency to force his will on others without due care of their position. He was busily engaged over-ruling his companion's observation.

"No Digsy, we've got to fight – we all know what the Prime Minister's game is, she wants revenge on what happened to Edward Heath in '74 – all this talk about only wanting to close twenty pits is rubbish, her real plan is to destroy the mining industry pure and simple, you wait, all one hundred and seventy pits will go, the whole lot, and all the miners, all two hundred thousand of them and their families and communities, all wiped out, ghost pits in ghost towns you'll see – it's all written out in that Ridley Report – she's following his blueprint to first provoke then smash the NUM."

Theo kept staring at his notes but listened with ears keen as a cat prowling the night for the faintest tic of a mouse.

Digsy was bright eyed with a round face, smooth and unblemished like milk that had retained most of its features from formative years giving an overall impression of a bouncy, cheeky schoolboy. Theo imagined him sitting there in a school blazer and cap on his head, rubbing his nose with his sleeve and sucking a gob-stopper.

"I'm not arguing with you on the wider point Curly, of course we've got to fight, but I'm talking about Scargill's tactics – he's played it wrong man, played right into the Prime Minister's hands, I mean, why the hell didn't he call a National Ballot, it's obvious what will happen next, she'll make it illegal to strike without a ballot – she'll beat us in the courts."

Curly's pinched cheeks drew inwards even further as he took a sharp intake of breath at Digsy's last comment. "Well, in that case Scargill will have to hold a National Ballot I suppose – but you've got to see where he's coming from, he reckons we should follow the Coal Board's tactics and they're closing pits on an area by area basis so he's allowing each mining area to vote for its own strike action as and when it's affected – that has to be the right way."

"But what does that mean, what's the reality of that strategy Curly – I'll tell you man, without a National Ballot miners in Nottinghamshire, Leicestershire – like where we are now – and parts of Derbyshire and Lancashire and North Wales have voted to keep working. We're seen as divided aren't we, some trying to get to work and the rest trying to stop them, it won't work in the long road." Digsy stared at his large boots that always looked dirty around the toecaps with imbedded grime and muck.

He continued, "And it's getting ugly what with that lad killed by a lorry on the picket last Friday over at Ollerton, Christ man, he was just a lad trying to stop the scabs from breaking the strike, there'll be more violence you'll see, and the press always concentrate on that and never the cause – you'll see public opinion work against us with the press egging it on …"

Theo stopped pretending to be reading and looked out the window as the train whirled across the vales and dales of central England humming through the village stations too remote to bother with, clattering over road bridges and the odd level crossing, panting and hissing its way up the country's spine to the far reaches of the North lying in wait all these years for his first gaze; he just made out the little village station sign at Quorn south of Loughborough as the train blurred past and thought he saw a public telephone box prominent on the platform proud as a red obelisk. On the train sped, chewing up the earth along its metal track past farms, cattle ponds, homesteads and hamlets dotted in the valleys and perched up in the rolling hills fingering the sky were stone church spires old as the local quarry and ancient as the flowing streams smoothing the gravel and rocks and tuning the gurgling eddies. On it went, solid and swift it sped past the flood plains and grazing lands with their idle herds and restless flocks trapped in the endless tapestry of pastures and their thorny hedgerow boundaries and spinney crested hills. On and on rattled the train pushing the air in a vortex out against the snug banks and cuttings bowing the stems of delicate red valerians, fanning the foxgloves and three cornered garlic and scaring the wits out of the common dog-violets surviving in the swirly tufted grass against all odds. On and on it went, puffing its mighty cheeks to blast its whistle out through the old oaks and fern leaved ash rooted firm in the lonely embankments refusing to budge and reluctant to sway but flickering their leaves as startled starlings un-perched fluttered forth in starbursts of flight.

He thought of the old England, the ancient England of his ancestors, and the closer he looked out across the land gliding past the clearer he saw that it had not changed but for the recent construction of highways and electric pylons it remained set in the same frame century after century, with its beautiful calm stillness, its smell of cattle and the rich dark earth renewed by wind and rain and the bubbling brooks; he felt a warm glow deep in his heart looking at this England passing by, in its bright blue and green summer gown, standing defiant and solid, weathered and still for so long but for the tilling of its soil and the harvesting of its crops – the great bountiful provider and sustainer of life, the precious Mother Earth – and there, somewhere out there, out of sight beneath the ancient earth were the mines, burrowed beneath the soundless passing countryside and daisy meadows, the pits laced the under-earth in a geometric grid of vertical shafts and horizontal tunnels concealing the men black with coal dust and sweat bent over with pick and fatigue longing for the light and rest.

He resumed the role-play of reading his papers. He was fascinated by this exchange of views from the two miners caught up in the dispute that was crippling their industry and realized they were most likely on their way to Orgreave to join the picket at the Coking Plant. The chance encounter could give him valuable insights into the miners' perspective and as he looked again at his papers he was urging them on with their conversation.

"But it's not just about the National Ballot mistake, his timing's all wrong too – why the hell couldn't he have started this strike in the middle of winter when coal stocks were low – he knew the Government was building up piles of the stuff, everyone knew it, what was he playing at calling the strike at the end of winter, makes no sense man?" Digsy's cherubic face seemed to growl like a child frustrated at some puzzle it failed to comprehend.

"Don't be such a defeatist Digsy – it looks like the dockers and maybe the railway lads will come out with us any day now – that'll take the smile off Thatcher's face."

"But we need the whole trade union movement behind us and that's not happening and it's been three months already, and even the dockers aren't a dead cert are they, they haven't voted for it yet, it could go the other way – and in the meantime we're all struggling with money." Digsy looked forlorn like a child who hadn't got his way.

Curly leant close to his companion's ear and whispered, "Shush man, you don't want to tell everyone about our pay and stuff like that, it's not for public knowledge, you don't know whose listening."

Digsy and Curly both looked around the carriage like two secret agents in an undercover espionage drama. They settled their gaze on Theo who could feel the effect like paper feels the rays of the sun beneath a magnifying glass. Despite the burning sensation on him Theo carried on with his pretence at reading.

An announcement came over the tannoy, "Loughborough station next stop. This train will shortly be arriving at Loughborough. Loughborough next stop."

Digsy lowered his voice assuming an earnest manner, "Well, it's getting hard to keep putting food on the table, what with the reduction in union pay and them taking away welfare benefits from our lasses, we can't live on nowt – air-pie doesn't fill you up man – and what with all this unemployment, what's the future Curly, what we going to do man when the cupboard's bare?"

"Shut up man, it won't come to that, stop being a namby-pamby, we're going to bloody win and beat the bastards like we did before, we're too strong for 'em, they've got no answer when us miners go all out."

Digsy did not respond and the two fell into an uneasy silence both staring out the window as if trying to discern the future from the tangle of Loughborough's backstreets.

At Loughborough the passenger next to Theo got off, as did the passenger next to Digsy and Curly. The three of them were alone in the compartment as the train pulled out of the station.

Digsy continued to be fascinated by his big dirty boots. Curly concentrated on Theo as if there was some mystery to be solved.

The close proximity of the three of them alone in the carriage dissipated the usual social barriers and Curly leant over to Theo with large open eyes full of curiosity.

"Hey man, just wondering like, are you a journalist by any chance, you know, one of those reporters?" Curly manufactured a gentle lilt to his thin voice to soften the intrusion and break from usual train passenger protocol of maintaining silence.

Theo shuddered and his stomach knotted as it had done all his life in such circumstances – right back to when his teacher would ask him to stand up and recite a passage or read out an essay. He loathed public gaze and attention and for a few seconds seemed to ignore Curly's question and kept staring at his notes for engaging argument on the Miners' Dispute; listed before him were some key bullet points:

- 75 per cent of British pits are losing money.
- The industry was losing £1.2 million per day.
- Interest payments amount to £467 million per year.
- The National Coal Board needs a subsidy of £875 million a year from the taxpayer.
- It cost £44 to mine a metric ton of British coal.
- America, Australia, and South Africa are selling coal on the world market for £32 a metric ton.
- Coal productivity is 20% below the level set in the 1974 Plan for Coal.

His eyes quickly scanned the bullet points and his brain felt numb with all the figures and their implications. He eventually looked up and met Curly's eyes and knew instinctively, as wild animals know these things, they were different in their kind with different stripes and different creed.

"No, I'm not ..." Theo could not think of anything else to add.

"It's OK man, I was just wonder'n 'cos of your notes – I thought maybe you're going to the picket at the Orgreave Coking Plant tomorrow – there'll be thousands of us there ..."

Curly paused as an express train thundered past and shook the carriage in a surge of vacuumed air and deafening sounds like crashing symbols and drums. The Doppler effect tailed off restoring calm to the half empty train compartment once again.

Theo replied before Curly could continue, "Oh really, is that where you're going then? You're a miner?" Theo's eyes went from Curly's mane of wavy black hair down to his hands resting on his lap; the fingers were rough, slightly swollen and discoloured, almost bruised, looking as if they had spent hours handling a shovel or pick. Theo then noticed the fingernails that were encrusted with coal dust or soot and wondered at the immense endurance and physical strength it took to toil for eight hours a day bent over in the mines. He felt so puny and weak at this difference between them, this difference of mental and physical strength.

Digsy, whose attention had been drawn to Theo's notes, wanted to take part in the conversation and said, "Hey, is that official Government notepaper you've got there man – do you work for the Tories then?"

Theo quickly put the Fact Sheet back in his briefcase. He felt caught out and embarrassed and was conscious of his cheeks flushing.

"No, I'm a teacher as a matter of fact and these are my student profile notes." He tapped his briefcase as the lie floated in the carriage like a bad smell. "So what are you hoping to achieve at Orgreave tomorrow – I mean, what's the plan, to stop people working or what?" Theo knew he was being too direct but he had always been hopeless at small talk and couldn't think of anything else to say. He glanced out the window and longed to be outside walking the rolling hills with the wind around him.

Curly said, "Well man, it's the Prime Minister whose the one trying to stop us working – she's the one who wants to close the pits, we're just trying to protect our jobs and livelihoods – pure and simple as that."

Digsy came in to show solidarity with his fellow miner, "Yeh, we're the ones trying to save our communities, she hasn't got a clue about the consequences, she's just after revenge on what happened to Heath, revenge for revenge sake, she couldn't care less about our mining communities – you know, when you close a pit you just don't close a pit – you close the butcher, the baker and the …"

"And the candlestick maker." Curly shouted out the familiar refrain with a wide grin and quickly looked between Digsy and Theo for recognition of his witty intervention.

"OK Curly, this isn't a joke man." He turned back to Theo more earnest than before, "No, closing a pit has a terrible knock-on effect, within weeks everything goes, the clothes shop, the carpet shop, the estate agent, the corner shop, everything, it all gets hammered and the place turns into a deprived area with all the crime and drug abuse that goes with it, when a whole community is on the dole – and think how much extra burden that puts on the taxpayer and the health service and police – it's not all about the profit and loss of one pit, it's about the whole community and what happens to everyone in it."

Theo had a vision of a mining town with its pit closed and men hanging around on street corners with no work and their children in ragged clothes and dirty faces and empty vacant eyes without the gleam of hope. He waited until his brain selected a reasoned argument, an irrefutable fact from his Fact Sheet. Finally he said:

"But can you expect the taxpayer to keep subsidising the mines? I mean, is it fair that £875 million comes out of the public coffers to keep them going when that could be spent on schools and hospitals …?"

Digsy came in anticipating the direction of Theo's remark, "Yeh, yeh I know, I've heard this nonsense a thousand times – look man, our mines are amongst the most efficient in Europe but yes they do require some subsidy but then so does the farming and fishing industries and no one's belly-aching about that lot are they?"

Then Curly chipped in just to add weight to Digsy argument, "Well the farmers and fishermen all vote Tory don't they, she don't want to upset 'em and lose votes. Did you know the Government has refused a European subsidy that would have helped to produce coal for the power stations at a cost way below the Polish coal imports – those Poles and Germans are laughing at us man because she's paying way over the odds to import their coal than to help us mine it ourselves."

The guard announced the next stop, "Nottingham station next stop. This train will shortly be arriving at Nottingham. Nottingham next stop."

Theo felt uneasy at the developing trialogue where his role was to stand up for the villain and justify something that he didn't really understand, only the crude economics put out by his department, the cold list of bullet points that ignored the human element and the wider financial consequences.

He looked at Curly then at Digsy, "Well, if that is the case, why do you think the Government is closing these pits if it's not about economics?" He hated himself for sounding so smug and indifferent but he could never ignore facts however damaging and unpleasant, that was his nature.

Digsy felt it was his turn to recite the well rehearsed riposte, "Well it's partly to revenge what happened to the Tory Government in 1974 the last time they tried to close our pits but there's more to it than that – it's being done out of spite to break the unions, the whole thing is political rather than financial. She could afford to pay out the subsidies what with all that North Sea oil money but she wants to destroy the unions and the NUM is the biggest union of 'em all, so that's the one to decapitate first." He looked at Theo to see if there was any sign of enlightenment in his eyes and thought he spotted a tiny flicker.

"Really? You really think the Government is going to these lengths just to break the unions – what would be the purpose of such a strategy, she would lose votes, it would work against her surely?"

Curly said, "Come on man, she doesn't rely on the working man's vote, she can take that hit and a bit more – no, she doesn't care about that, it's all about who has the power, it's always about power – she reckons to break the power of the unions so she can change politics in this country once and for all – her goal is to reduce the State, reduce public spending and welfare – she's said as much, you've only got to read between the lines of her speeches, it's all there, and we're in the front line, it's all out war and she's been planning this for months with all the stock piles of coal, and taking on all those extra road hauliers and converting power stations to burn oil – it's a clear plan to beat us."

The train slowed as it pulled into Nottingham station and eased to a halt. Theo was glad for the distraction and wanted the discussion to come to an end so he could close his eyes once again and free-fall into his subconscious. Doors slammed shut along the train as people boarded and looked for a seat in a preferred compartment; most passed by but eventually an elderly man entered and sat next to Theo who gave him a sideways glance as if he was checking an immigrant at a border control booth. The man was in his early sixties with an impressive mop of white hair that helped him retain a youthfulness but his eyes were large, dark and sad with a tinge of weariness. He kept his watery eyes open wide and stared at Theo and the two miners with a piercing concentration that suggested an unspecified abnormality. His presence changed the mood and a screen of self-consciousness descended in the compartment like fog.

Then Curly leant towards Theo and said in a noticeably lower voice, "Hey, man, why don't you come and join us on the picket tomorrow – you can meet our mates and help us with our cause – there won't be any trouble, nothing serious any road."

Theo ignored Curly's invitation and said, "But I don't understand ..." He checked the elderly man to make sure his comment was not intrusive, "... you say Thatcher's taking on the miners to break their power so it can go ahead and reduce public spending without strikes presumably – but why, there must be a bigger goal – she could reduce public spending anytime and a lot of people would agree with her?"

Digsy interrupted, also looking at the newly seated passenger as if that was now a prerequisite before saying anything, "Of course there's a bigger goal, she wants to privatise just about anything that moves – you wait, gas, electricity, water, railways, cars, post office, and the health services if she can get away with it – nothing will be spared, the Government will end up with nothing much to govern, be just like a small office tucked away in Whitehall counting the tax receipts – look man, they've already started with Jaguar yeh? Jaguar have just been put up for sale, who would have thought that, it's only a matter of time before the whole lot goes – and the reason why it hasn't is because of the unions – the Prime Minister has to defeat the unions and remove the only real barrier in her way so she can go ahead and sell the nation's silver – that's her goal man, clear as day."

The train slowly pulled out of the station in that silent soft way trains do, as if pulled gently along on floats. The silver haired stranger took out a banana from his holdall and peeled it releasing its pleasant scent around the carriage as effectively as if he had taken out an aerosol air freshener and sprayed it in all directions.

"That all sounds a bit far fetched." Theo was annoyed that the two country miners seemed to know more about Government plans and policy than he did working at its central headquarters.

"Surely it's just a matter of economics – doesn't it make sense to reduce Government spending which after all is our money, yours and mine, that's the bottom line – and some of these nationalised industries, well, like the mining industry, are over-manned and the work is awful back-breaking, unhealthy stuff isn't it – maybe its time for change – but I can't see all this privatization taking place, that's a different kettle of fish, I mean, for a start, we'll end up with thousands on the dole."

Curly said straight out, "Thousands more you mean – it's already reached over three million and rising every week – but we told you man, this is political, the economic argument is a camouflage, she has the money, billions of it from North Sea oil that could make a real difference to the whole country, can you imagine what could be done for our schools and universities and hospitals and housing with all that oil money, can you imagine what could be done to support jobs by investing in our industries, we'd be the envy of the world man – instead of that she'll blow it on her unproven ideology – on smaller Government and getting through her so called monetarist policy, her beloved free market economy – she'll do it too, she holds all the levers, she has all the equipment, the forces and the organization, and of course, most of the media who'll back her whatever, no matter what she says or does, they'll back her even if she stuck her bare arse out the front door of No 10 and farted *God Save The Queen*, they'd still back her up, they'd praise her virtuosity and her virtue of being so patriotic – you can't win man." Curly looked pleased with himself for his uncharacteristic imagery.

"And she has the will!" Digsy emphasised his friend's point by stabbing the air with his finger. Both the miners sat back as if the last remark was the coup de grace in the whole debate.

Curly said after a pause, "Yeh, come and join us man, what's the worst that can happen, we all end up in prison for fighting for our jobs, well, bring it on."

Theo had never considered these ideas before and was alarmed by them. Could it be true? He suddenly saw the possibilities of such a grand plan loom large in his imagination. He kept turning over in his mind the likelihood of the Government working out such a devious and convoluted strategy. A mental image of Tubby presented itself, puffing at his enormous cigar and growling at him, 'The Prime Minister wants a new angle on this strike – to push public opinion along – a big heave-ho – the unions are the problem and we must get the people against them – do you get my drift Harrison my boy?'

The elderly man put the banana skin on his lap and stared at Theo with eyes like Catherine Wheels and pushing his hand through his mop of white hair so he looked like the mad monk Rasputin he said:

"You speak of North Sea Oil, ah yes, that great natural asset that we have had so little benefit from – but do you know what Norway has done with its oil wealth extracted at the same time as ours – it's a different story for sure in Norway – over there it's all about, 'Prudent Resource Management' yes, that's what it's about – they used their oil wealth to set up a financial fund called, The Global Government Pension Fund, to invest their surplus oil money and attracted thousands of investors around the world, the more they put in the more it accrued – and do you know what the fund is worth today, just over 8,000 billion Norwegian kroner, yes, and what have they done with it you ask, well they have invested it for future prosperity and with the interest they have created the best welfare service in Europe, probably the world, and they spend it on schools and hospitals and infrastructure – that is what they have done with it, 'Prudent Resource Management' that's what." The old man stopped and looked out the window in silence.

The train purred along over bridges and rivers and the lush rich swathes of pasture and wooded vales. An uneasy silence took hold and finally Curly asked once again, "Well will you come along tomorrow man or not – we need all the help we can get?"

Theo sat mulling over what Norway had done with its oil wealth and how the UK had deliberately wasted its oil money; he saw for the first time the vast difference in spending priorities between the two countries and a shiver of shame shadowed his patriotism. Then he went over in his mind the various points Digsy and Curly had made during the past hour or so and realised his opinions were shifting by their own will in a way he would not have thought possible; he had not been prepared for these revelations nor the growing feeling of suspicion towards the Government they brought in their wake.

"I'm not sure, probably not, but I'll see how things go – how many do you reckon will be there, on the picket?" He remembered Tubby mentioning a figure of ten thousand.

Digsy said, "Who knows, a lot and that's for sure, several thousand – we have to stop that coke getting up to the Power Station at Scunthorpe – but we won't give any trouble man, not unless it comes our way, none of us wants trouble and we're not looking for it."

"And the police?" Theo knew he had touched the sensitive spot, the bit that hurt.

"They'll be all right man, just the usual bit of pushing and shoving, it's all a game really, we all know the rules and limitations, it'll be OK, nothing to worry about on that score."

Digsy's round schoolboy's face broke into a broad smile as if someone had just promised him a piece of treacle tart.

Theo wanted to close his eyes and be alone with himself, to move his thoughts around in his head unimpeded, without a judge and jury. He longed for solitude.

He closed his eyes to the gentle rocking motion of the train. His mind started to drift towards sleep.

The train continued shuffling along, sliding and rocking over the track, clickety-clack, sounding like a washboard in a skiffle band. Tubby's face appeared before him, staring straight into his eyes full of mischief and growling like a wolf:

"My information is that a bit of a ding-dong will take place at Orgreave and those miners will be given a bloody nose."

The train finally arrived at Sheffield station jerking Theo from his light dream.

Chapter Three

Sasha was returning from her appalling ordeal with Banjoko ashen and disturbed; she had recovered some of her composure and got over her nausea sufficiently to be able to navigate the short distance around the back streets behind Albany Street to Mornington Crescent tube station. She disliked using the underground late at night and usually got a taxi but as it was only one stop to Euston and she was feeling wretched she chose the tube. Besides, she figured no one could violate her any more than what Banjoko had done.

She positioned herself at the front of the train so she was near the driver's cabin to better attract his attention if she encountered trouble; it was a necessary precaution and sprang from the pit of vulnerability that Banjoko had plunged her into; she sat alone but for a few office workers returning home from their Friday night rendezvous in bars and restaurants across the capital and a couple of poor homeless men, with their bundles of belongings, on their way to ride the Central Line all night, round and round in an endless journey to nowhere.

Out onto the busy Euston Road she walked, the night air warm and clinging with a hint of a storm still in the offing. The traffic moved quietly, as if acknowledging the late hour, and was still busy with taxis and cars coming from the City and heading to the northern suburbs – a myriad of semi-detached homes spread along a labyrinth of intertwining back streets that make up London's northern outer circle from Uxbridge to Hackney Downs.

She immediately turned left onto Eversholt Street that led to her bedsit in Werrington Street. Away from the traffic and street lights she could hear her shoes clicking along the empty pavement beside the darkly shadowed terminus of Euston Station with its huge outer wall muffling the sounds from within its gaping space. She could just remember the old Euston Station with its Great Hall and the huge Arch outside clogging up the traffic – she had no romantic sense of its loss only a vague memory of the constant hooting of traffic and the grime and tawdriness of the station. Her parents sometimes took her to St Pancras to look at the steam engines puffing and hissing their way in and out of the pointed-arched train shed of iron and steel and her father romanticising that St Pancras was the King of Stations.

Her route was short but required the passing of several doorways and alleyways where the growing number of homeless people laid out on pieces of cardboard seemingly dead or in comatose with their empty cheap wine bottles left in the gutter alongside trails of their piss meandering to the nearest drain.

With her hand over her nose and mouth like a mask she was nearing Werrington Street when she became aware of footsteps behind her. When she turned there was no one in sight just a few shadowy figures pulling suitcases way back towards the junction with the Euston Road. She reached her bedsit, bolted the door and let out a long sigh, the sigh of a woman whose working day, spent in the anticipation of danger, is finally done and is home safe at last.

The ordeal with Banjoko had taken its toll and left her feeling dirty and physically abused; she pondered how she could cleanse her body but not so easily her soul. First she cleaned her teeth so hard her gums bled then she gargled several times so loud her neighbours might have thought a macerator had got jammed; then she washed quickly standing up in the communal bath and changed into an extra large T-shirt that she liked as it was loose and baggy and allowed the warm June evening air to pass over her skin and cool it like wisps from a fan of feathers.

She poured a glass of white burgundy wine she kept in the small fridge beside the table and sat back in the old armchair still exhausted but at last feeling back in control. She opened the envelope and took out several bank notes that she held in front of her for a few moments whilst she sipped her wine. There were ten £20 notes as crisp as the day they had left the press. She recounted to make certain. It was more than she had ever earned in one session and more than she normally made in two days. It astonished her and she kept turning over each note to examine it in detail. Then she added her other earnings for the day and counted the lot – the total was £290 and she gripped the notes as if to confirm her pleasure, more than most women of her age earned in a week. She sipped more wine and as it stimulated her thoughts she looked up at the ceiling to a series of images of what her life might have been like working in an office somewhere in the City, working eight hours a day for peanuts and commuting on a crowded train pushed up against some old pervert's chin and inhaling his spent mouldy sausage and bacon breath and discretely released poots. She gripped the bank notes again and her satisfaction was complete.

The terrifying session with Banjoko had graphically demonstrated how susceptible she was as a lone call girl. She poured more wine and drank slowly mulling over the emerging dilemma. Three more sessions with Banjoko at this rate of payment together with her other income would certainly get her closer to the money she needed for the Weymouth apartment in double quick time. On the other hand Banjoko was a slob whose temperament was unpredictable and who had shown an increase in violent tendency with each of her three visits. She cringed at the thought of his hand around her neck again and what he might do when he became possessed once more with his inner demons. He was not trustworthy and her life would be in danger if she risked more sessions. On the other hand he was so rich and paid handsomely – just three more sessions in say two weeks – just two weeks. It was tempting.

She took out the stash from under her bed, carefully unfolding the blanket and removing the shoe box from the suitcase and finally the metal box that contained all her hard earned cash. She needed £3,000 for a deposit on the apartment and have enough left to buy some furniture and kitchen essentials. She counted all the money. The total was just under £2,000 that left the best part of £1,000 to go – she made some quick mental calculations – without Banjoko, and based on her normal income of say £50 per day, it would take another month taking into account the added cost of living. On the other hand she could nearly halve that time just by having another three sessions with Banjoko – but could she risk being with that monster again, that was the question. She was not sure what to do because of the nature of Banjoko's erratic behaviour. It was not beyond possibility that he would slide further into depravity with say some bondage fantasy and God knows where that might lead, given his unstable mental condition that bordered on the psychopathic and his lack of control. She was used to pleasing men in all the orthodox ways but she could not handle any more physical threats like she had experienced that night. She decided it was not worth the risk and Banjoko would be struck off her client list forthwith.

She leant back in the armchair and felt relieved she had made her decision and that despite the awful scene with Banjoko she had at least moved closer to achieving the deposit. A glow of satisfaction warmed her heart knowing financial progress was steady and she was well on course. She thought of little Vana and how they would love being together at last in their new home by the sea – everything she did was to make that dream come true and nothing was going to stop her.

She put the money back under the bed, finished the wine, turned the light out and as she went over to her bed she pulled back the curtains by a few inches to span the street below. She did this little ritual every night before turning in and somehow it managed to stimulate her thoughts and concentrate her mind, like a moment of prayer. How still and hushed it looked, the dark purple night thickening the shadows and the orange street lamps casting circular rings of light across the grey black empty street. Somewhere a door slammed and a window opened just audible above the distant sounds coming from the station as trains shunted from the engine shed.

Her thoughts drifted to her humble parents' place in Romford where Vana was now lying in her bed asleep. She thought of her daughter, how beautiful she was and how she missed her. The paths she had taken when she was little more than an adolescent, lost and confused, suddenly appeared before her as if by way of a clearing in a forest of bewildering choices. There in front of her she could see her younger self at seventeen, poor with hard-up parents, limited prospects, a handful of GCE's and driven by crude romantic notions to go and help the underprivileged like herself. Then, still looking down the orange lit street towards Euston, an old memory flickered across her mind and the form of Yusuf appeared before her as real as if he was standing in the street below.

Yusuf had featured in her life all those years ago when she had gone to Somalia as a Voluntary Service Overseas worker in the southern coastal region between Mogadishu and Kismaayo. He was a local man who worked in the camp doing general maintenance work fixing the water pump system or the electric generator or de-blocking the waste disposal pipes.

He was young and handsome, spoke good English, and made Sasha laugh without much effort. She had fallen for him at first glance without a word exchanged between them. She worked hard teaching the local children English and arithmetic from textbooks the VSO acquired from the British Council's donations from educational publishers' remainder stock. When she wasn't teaching she was busy organising various sports activities and outdoor projects like clearing the ground for growing vegetables. She found it satisfying but exhausting work and come night time she always went to bed tired and lonely.

Her crush on Yusuf remained a secret and she did nothing to encourage him, indeed she positively kept her distance except where the need for his maintenance skills was required – but with just two weeks left before her contract expired and she was due to return to the UK she allowed herself to get involved and a brief relationship developed.

Yusuf pounced on the opportunity presented to him by the dropping of her guard and things accelerated rapidly. Within days she was meeting him at night in the storeroom to which Yusuf held a well used passkey. At first these rendezvous amounted to nothing more than kissing and cuddling and softly whispered exchanges of their life stories; then they drifted into closer encounters with less conversation and heavy petting. It was not until her final night during the farewell party in her honour that she gave herself completely whilst the music and dancing was still taking place across the yard.

The journey home the next day was emotionally painful with each mile grinding down her will not to turn around and go back; Yusuf swore blind he would visit her in the UK as soon as he was financially secure and could get away.

Within four weeks of returning home she discovered she was pregnant. She wrote to Yusuf several times but only her last letter got a reply – he wrote saying that he would take care of her and the child but needed time to save up enough money to get to the UK; he explained he had been involved in an accident when the jeep he was driving overturned on a sharp bend after an unusually heavy rainfall during Somalia's Xagaaye rainy season; he mentioned that the windscreen had shattered and a shard of glass had severed his left ear lobe completely; he said that the disfigurement made him embarrassed to face people and he was afraid she would find him ugly and reject him. Finally he said he was broke as he had lost his box of treasures in the crash – some cash and an expensive pearl brooch. The loss of the ornament had caused him great distress as it had belonged to his mother and the pearl was beyond value. She immediately replied, reassuring him that no physical disfigurement could lessen the worth of a person, as it was the inner-self and character that mattered; she commiserated with his loss of the heirloom but that pearls can take on different forms and that his life maybe blessed with replacement jewels of another kind. She was not sure of the rationality of her observation but did not know what else to say. She posted the letter hopeful that he would be encouraged to come over to the UK.

Every time the postman came to the door her heart missed a beat and she raced to see if there was a letter from him. She did not get a reply and her love for him only intensified by his absence.

She was nineteen coming on twenty, pregnant, jobless and living with her parents. The clouds gathered over her and her future looked uncertain. She was sick in her heart with worry and a sense of failure as well as bouts of debilitating morning sickness; she became pale and withdrawn with lack of sleep and loss of appetite.

Her parents guessed what was wrong and a family meeting took place one evening whereby it was agreed she would have the child and they would take care of it whilst Sasha went to London to find a job and save money for a place of her own. So it was that Sasha gave birth to Vana by Caesarean section – a sweet coffee coloured tiny bundle of joy with Sasha's turned up nose and Yusuf's huge brown eyes that made the bleakest of days quiver with love. She never did receive another letter from Yusuf despite writing him with her new London address.

The thought of Vana finally made her feel reassured as she stared out into the now dark blue night, her eyes tired and heavy and ready for sleep. She was about to close the curtains when she thought she noticed something move across the street behind the parked cars opposite. She rubbed her eyes wet with the strain of tiredness and the emotional drain of the session with Banjoko. She kept peering across the street and was about to abandon the vigil when suddenly the figure appeared again, quick as a blink, standing in the black night, dark and obscure, looking up at Sasha's window, silent like a hooded mannequin.

Her mind was confused and beaten by the day's extraordinary events and the memory of Yusuf and her VSO days. Her eyes felt like weighted beads heavy in their sockets with fatigue.

"Yusuf? Is that you Yusuf?" She whispered the question soft and incredulously to the blurred figure through the window misty from the warmth of her breath.

"Is it really you Yusuf?" Her voice lurched higher as she scanned the image to get clearer focus. She wiped the window with her open hand and craned her neck to get a better view, but the figure was gone. She looked left and right several times and finally settled her gaze towards the station and could just make out a small dark figure disappearing into the shadows by the railway arches.

Her weariness was making her doubt her sanity and she wondered whether she was hallucinating. She gently slapped her cheeks to reset her brain but everything remained the same; she sat by the window for another ten minutes, the adrenaline keeping her heavy eyes open and the mystery keeping her mind spinning with curiosity. At last she got into bed, softly, not wanting to make a noise, and pressing the back of her head into the pillow stayed rigid with her hands clasped together for comfort listening to the indistinguishable distant drone of London's symphony of midnight sound.

Chapter Four

Jenny sat in the backroom of her parents' house in Folkestone sipping tea that her mother always made too milky. On the coffee table was a huge Victoria sponge cake about six inches deep with two layers of thick butter cream and strawberry jam.

"Come on Jen, have some cake, you look like you need some nourishment and I made it special – here just a thin slice." Beverly cut a large wedge and handed Jenny the plate as if no further negotiation was required.

Beverly was forty-six years old but looked thirty-eight. The inevitable development of ageing, a few crows feet lines and some forehead frown furrows, only gave her an alluring mature quality and sex appeal especially when viewed with her slim figure and tresses of blonde hair that dangled loose over her shoulders. She invested much time and energy, not to mention a considerable amount of money, into looking attractive. She used the local swimming pool three times a week and was proud of her achievement to swim twenty lengths non-stop; she had also taken out a twelve-month membership to the newly opened leisure centre up near the Royal Victoria Hospital where she worked as a receptionist.

When Jenny left home Beverly sat down and re-examined her life and priorities. She regarded the moment as a keystone opportunity – she had devoted the best days of her life to her husband and bringing up her daughter and no one could accuse her of shirking her responsibilities for she had been singularly devout in the enterprise, an exemplary example of motherhood if ever there was one; in the solitary moments of inner reflection regarding her performance as a wife and mother there was one word that kept falling onto her tongue like a Holy Sacrament – 'sacrifice' – and she now wanted to reclaim something she believed had been lost, her youth.

She was secretly jealous of her daughter, envious of her vivacity and freedom of spirit. She decided to boost her vitality and regain her golden days before marriage and the commitment of motherhood, those wonderful days full of freedom, fun, friends and plenty of sex when she was the chief controller of her schedules. Of course, this new venture was to be a secret and as her plans gradually unfolded and she went through the transformation from tired housewife to blonde bomber she down-graded the outcome by telling her husband that she was trying to look her best for him.

Reggie was flattered by the explanation and for a while her new youthful look rekindled their sex life, although in that department Reggie had never exhibited the traits of a wild stallion, more a workhorse who did what it was told and never took the initiative. Eventually even Beverly's newly honed allure could not prevent their sex life slipping back into its old tired routine; the Sunday morning repetitious romp that Reggie never altered neither in style nor inventiveness, but just kept performing in the same way with as much free spirit as the beam of Newcomen's steam engine, up and down, up and down, until it was time to stop. Reggie was a kind, reliable and loving husband but he lacked imagination and without that golden nugget of human qualities he could as much infuse his sexual performance with daring acts of licentiousness as the Marquis de Sade could live the chaste life of a monk.

So it was that Beverly began a secret affair with a young man at work called Earl. He was all the things Reggie was not – he was unreliable, a cheat, and had a rogue's sense of fun and danger and in bed could perform more tricks than a trapeze artist. He lived in a run-down flat close to the hospital and he and Beverly went there twice a week at lunchtimes for sex and a sandwich; occasionally she invented reasons for going out in the evening for drinks with work friends just to see Earl and have more sex. She was smitten with him and intoxicated with the double life she lived and the thrill of danger the whole debauched enterprise gave her.

If Reggie suspected his wife of impropriety he did not show it but seemed to trust her implicitly to the point where an observer, knowing the facts of the case, would weep at his naivety. He in turn seemed content to go each day to the docks where he worked as a foreman overseeing the cars on and off the ferries; the work did not stretch his mind but it did not burden him with anxiety either and he could leave the job at the dock gates each evening and pick it up again the next day like a bicycle left on the railing.

In his spare time he read The Guardian newspaper from front to back and then switched to reading his latest book usually in the genre of English or French history. He was particularly fascinated with the French Revolution and what it must have been like to live during the Reign of Terror when the Government ruled by threat of the guillotine; he shivered to think how vulnerable ordinary folk were in that era and how anyone could accuse anyone else of being supporters of tyranny or federalism and sent off for execution just with a wink or nod from some miffed neighbour or acquaintance to the Secret Police – a crazy world where normal, everyday people were killing masses of other normal, everyday people. He always finished these reading sessions wondering how close England could get to becoming a similar tyrant state without law and order where the rabble ruled through ignorance and bigotry.

When he wasn't reading he worked on making his box kite, not a substantial project but one that required patience and moderate skills for cutting the different dowel lengths and cross-pieces and taping the plastic sails in the right way to secure the structure. It was an ideal task for his character requiring a steady hand and a tolerance of repetition. His aim was to fly it on Shorncliffe heights one windy Sunday afternoon.

Reggie was quite handsome in an old fashioned way, with his Brylcreem lacquered black hair, small oval face, piercing blue eyes and a stylish Roman nose that provided the perfect ledge for his reading glasses to nestle on. One of the women at work, Betty, who worked in the Admin Office, fancied him and always spent time chatting over a cup of tea when he visited the office to attend to some paperwork. Betty would ask Reggie on a Friday afternoon what his plans were for the weekend but he always answered factually and never interpreted the real meaning behind the enquiry. In truth, even if he had understood Betty's purpose he would never have taken it further as extramarital activity was strictly taboo for he took his marriage vows seriously and was blindly faithful, as a guide dog is blindly faithful to its blind owner.

Jenny nibbled at the edge of the huge slab of cake and peered at her mother. "You're looking amazing Mum – your hair and your face and your figure – what's going on, you haven't got a toy-boy have you, ha, ha?"

Beverly's eyes darted towards her daughter and their eyes locked for a fraction of a second, a frozen pause that hinted at some hidden truth – in that nano flicker of consciousness Jenny saw the guilt in her mother's eyes as if she had suddenly pulled a curtain and caught her committing a forbidden act.

"Oh yes, chance would be a fine thing – but how about you Jen, you're looking a bit strained, everything OK up there in the big smoke – how's that job of yours, what is it you do exactly, something to do with down-and-outs?" Beverly had quickly changed the subject but there was a discernible trace of blushing around her neck.

"Oh Mum, I've told you a hundred times, I work for Camden Town Council, as a Social Worker – the down-and-outs you refer to are the borough's homeless, I work for the homeless in Camden." As she stated her job title she felt a pang of pride as if she was doing something worthwhile, something real and necessary.

"Really? Can't see why the council has to spend money on that lot, why can't they sort their own lives out like we had to, nobody ever came knocking at our door from the council helping us out with benefits, we just had to muddle on and cope."

Jenny knew they had both stepped onto the familiar elevator – the elevator that would take them down floor by floor through all their differences and then down further to their prejudices and finally arrive at their different values and how they interpreted justice and equality; that was the basement floor, the rock bottom, the bottom of the rock that stood between them.

"Well Mum, some people aren't as resourceful as you and for various reasons need help to get them back on their feet – it's all about the cards you are dealt isn't it, some people struggle with a poor hand, they lose their job or their marriage breaks up or both and they can't afford the rent or food or both or they get sick or have an accident or whatever, there's loads of reasons why people find themselves homeless and I can assure you they are not all lazy scroungers not by a long chalk, that's just Daily Express propaganda, meaningless tosh that you should ignore – not many of my clients prefer homelessness as a way of life I can tell you that, who would? And remember, when your homeless you can't get a job, it's a Catch22 – you need a permanent address before you can get one and you need a job before you can get a permanent address – how would you cope I wonder?"

"OK Jen, don't get on your high horse, I was only making the point that we, my generation, looked after ourselves, we worked hard and never expected hand-outs, perish the thought, I would rather die than take welfare – it's got to be about commitment and planning ahead – I mean, look at all these schoolgirls getting pregnant, what's going on there I wonder – don't they teach them nothing at school about these things – and half the illegitimate kids are black aren't they – and where are the fathers I'd like to know, run off with another stupid girl no doubt and the whole thing starts all over – it's pathetic. Don't know what's happening to the country."

Jenny knew they had reached the basement floor but she winced at this new degree of prejudice now so apparent within her mother. Something had changed between them, love and mutual respect had diminished.

"It's not as simple as that Mum – but you're right to mention single parenting as a cause of homelessness."

"Did I mention that? Did I Reggie? She's putting words into my mouth as usual."

"Don't get me involved Bev." Reggie had kept quiet, happy to eat his piece of cake and sip his tea for he was well versed on these mother and daughter encounters and knew his place, "I just know this homeless problem is getting worse by the day – it's the economy behind it all …" He returned his plate to the coffee table and licked some strawberry jam from his fingers, "… it's always the economy – we're being governed by a mean hearted, thrifty grocer's daughter who knows the cost of everything and the value of nothing."

"Oh no, that's done it, now your father's up and away on one of his socialist flights of fantasy – watch out everyone! Ha ha – 'Is it a bird?' No. 'Is it a plane?' No, 'It's Reggie the Socialist Superman again.' Ha ha" Beverly chuckled to herself, a loveless nasty chuckle that was spiked and meant to hurt rather than spread fun. Reggie did not rise to the bait.

All three sipped their tea and a heavy silence fell on them like a fire-blanket.

"So what you up to Jen going over to France – bit of a holiday?" Reggie decided that in this instance discretion was the better part of valour.

"Well, just a short break Dad, to get away from things for a while – you know, to clear my head and think about where I am and where I'm going, that sort of thing." Jenny knew she sounded ambiguous.

Beverly still smarting interrupted more sharply than was necessary, "You should come up to the hospital and work there for a day or two – you'll soon get things into perspective Jen my girl." She drained her cup and then patted the back of her hair to make sure it was still holding its shape. "Right, well, I'll be off in a mo, going to see a couple of girls from work for a drink."

"Not another one Bev – don't know what you and your mates get to talk about all the time – and it's a bit early isn't it?"

Reggie glanced at the mantel clock and smiled as if he was joking but his smile remained fixed.

"No one's stopping you going out Reg – it's not my fault you prefer to stay in and mess about with that kite of yours." She stood up, adjusted her skirt as she walked across the room to the door.

Jenny looked at her mother's full profile closely. Her new fashionable clothes with the hugging black skirt and tight ivory silk blouse, the padded shoulders to her jacket, her vivid make-up that took five years off her age, her film star hair style and chunky jewellery all colluded to send a strong signal to anyone whose receiver was tuned to the same transmitter. Jenny kept looking at her mother as she moved across the room swaying her hips as she held her teacup and plate and knew in an instant what that signal was – she recognised someone who was dressed up for someone special and it was not for her father.

"Oh that's a pity Mum, I thought we could all go out tonight for something to eat or a drink maybe – but if you've already made plans?" Jenny was being mischievous as the thought of going out had only just occurred to her and she wasn't bothered one way or the other.

Beverly disappeared into the kitchen, put the cup and plate down and came back into the living room. "Um, well, not sure about that Jen, it's a nice idea but you should've mentioned it before – look, I won't be that long, a couple of hours maybe, then we could go to the new pizza place, Domino's, along the High Street." Beverly had no real interest in fulfilling this plan but knew when she was expected to show willing in such matters.

"No, it's OK Mum, that's too complicated, don't worry – me and Dad can go for a drink at the Lobster Pot – can't we Dad, and then get some fish & chips, how about that?" Jenny was deliberately overplaying the camaraderie card with her father to sting her mother.

The suggestion took Reggie by surprise but he always enjoyed his daughter's company and smiled, "Yes my love, of course, let's do that." He kept his eyes on his wife as she opened the front door without turning to say goodbye.

* * * * * * * *

The sun was going down and Sasha was mindful of her next engagement over in some cheap hotel on Argyle Street off the Euston Road; these were the places she hated most, the lonely backstreet hotels and their dingy dark cramped rooms smelling of cigarettes and burgers. The incident the night before with Banjoko and the mysterious figure appearing on the street below had unsettled her and for the first time her job made her feel threatened. She braced herself and concentrated on getting the apartment in Weymouth and the brand new life that awaited her there with little Vana. Just a month or so more and she would be free. A weak smile parted her lips as she took her bag, grabbed her key and denim jacket and stepped out into the evening twilight.

Half an hour later she was lying on a cheap creaky bed in the Angus Hotel with the Euston Road traffic droning through the open window and the sound of Eberhardt's huge stomach slapping against her as he heaved away to his own fantasy induced climax. She secretly chuckled to herself thinking of this large German man sighing and pressing himself against her with the name of Eberhardt; he had said that his name meant 'strong as a boar' and this definition tickled her imagination, picturing him as a fat hog foraging around with his large protruding snout.

She had never encountered anyone with a name so suited to their temperament and physique as Eberhardt, for he was indeed the biggest bore she had ever met, in every sense. If there was a Big Bore competition then Eberhardt would win it hands down. This huge mountain of a man was void of character and personality and seemed only to be concerned about his bodily needs – smoking emphysema-inducing numbers of cigarettes, eating enough beef to impress the Gauchos on the Argentinian Pampas, woofing back sacks of potatoes and vegetables, drinking barrels of larger and of course, the all important desire to satisfy his sexual appetites, that never seemed sated and always returned reinvigorated as day follows night.

He expected Sasha to deliver her full repertoire of sexual tricks and keep going until arriving at his favoured doggy-position that finally pushed him over the edge. He was not without wealth, despite his preference for the bleak Angus Hotel, and always paid £30 for the hour session that was way above her normal rates. It was nearly eleven o'clock when she left the hotel exhausted.

Back in her room she sipped a glass of wine as she finished getting ready for bed. She finally turned the light out and went to the window as part of her nightly ritual, staring up and down the street and letting her thoughts drift pleasantly with plans for the future; but as she looked out the previous evening's events came back to shake her from her sweet musings as if someone had poured a bucket of cold water over her head. She fixed her eyes on the vehicles parked opposite and for any sign that the mystery prowler was out there again. She shivered with the first sense that she was becoming obsessed with an unknown enemy. She studied each vehicle, each dark recess, each tree and shrub but there was nothing, just the slumbering empty street yawning for the morning routine to commence.

She turned the light back on and went and sat in the chair and drank some more wine. Then, to give herself a sense of comfort, she repeated her other nightly ritual of counting her money and thinking about Vana and Weymouth; these trusted routines to settle her mind and get her feeling tired did not work and she returned to her spot by the window, a lone midnight sentry guarding her sanctuary. She sat for fifteen uneventful minutes studying the line of parked vehicles and scanning the vast black night and the gathering clouds until her mind started to close down and the silent veil of tiredness began to fall over her apprehensiveness. Her eyes became heavier and smaller and her head was starting to nod when something caught her eye by a parked van opposite, a quick sudden flash of movement that even her sleepy brain identified as a human figure; her mind sprang back into alert mode as she focussed on the van expecting to see someone get into it and drive off but no one appeared. She kept her eyes glued in anticipation.

The night sky was a smooth pastel and veined with bright cream streaks from a shrouded moon like an Atkinson Grimshaw painting; then the moon was suddenly cloaked by cloud and turned black as the June night air dipped in temperature. A jagged fork of lightening split the sooty sky miles away towards Alexandra Palace and drops of rain the size of hazelnuts smacked the windowpane to herald the advancing downpour.

She remained motionless for another five minutes and kept staring at the van but still there was no movement or any sign of someone lurking behind it. She was about to give up when suddenly the figure appeared and stood still as a fence post between the van and a car; her heart missed a beat as she strained to see more detail – the shape was more male than female and she guessed he was wearing jeans and maybe a dark coloured sweater with a hood that had two distinct stripes going over it that made him look like a badger; the stripes appeared yellow but were probably grey or white it was difficult to tell in the dark orange light of the old sodium street lamp. The figure looked around and then up to Sasha's window, she could feel his eyes on her face and gulped down some caught phlegm in her throat, a nervous reaction as her eyes widened like a character in a Margaret Keane painting. She froze, her eyes locked onto where the stranger's face lurked inside the hood. For several moments there was no movement just the two looking at each other through the dark mauve night of Somers Town. The rain then fell hard and splattered the window like a drum beat as the figure turned slowly and walked back up Werrington Street silently with hooded head bowed.

She followed the shadowy shape as it disappeared through the rain leaving the torrential downpour to fill the empty space by the van as if the figure had never stood there, as if the small incident had never happened. But it had. Sasha kept looking down the street for several minutes convinced the episode was not over and the stranger would return; but nothing happened, all was still and restful like Christmas Eve, as the tiger moths in their kamikaze quest for lamplight were driven off by the rain.

With a troubled mind she got into bed and started to fiddle with her hair, curling it around her fingers and pulling at it, the habit was new and done involuntarily. Her mind was disturbed and racing with images and questions that made no sense. She could not sleep, not even slightly, and got up to check outside. She slowly pulled the curtains apart an inch or two and peered down onto the rain drenched street silent at the midnight hour.

She initially thought all was well as nothing stirred but for the distant purr of the ceaseless Euston Road traffic and the background hum of trains shunting in the sheds of Euston station. She was about to release the curtains and get back into bed when she saw him.

The hooded figure was there again standing behind another parked van. She couldn't believe her eyes; it was like a scene from a Hitchcock film unfolding in front of her. This time he was well concealed with only his head and shoulders just visible and almost obscured by the grey metal doors of a lock-up storage unit behind him. But it was him and no mistake. She felt her throat wobble and her stomach pitch at the danger threatened by this mysterious night prowler. She swallowed and steadied herself and tried to overcome her fear. Who was this man and what did he want? She looked through the curtain at the hooded head and the hooded head looked back straight at her. Once again it was impossible to make out the face as it was so well tucked within the hood. She kept her position as if her eyes were glued to the spot on which he stood. The stand-off seemed to go on for ever and she tried to match the shape of the head and body to anyone she knew but no one came forth as a definite match. She thought of Yusuf once again and tried to overlay his shape onto the figure below but her memory played tricks and the comparison was not reliable. As she stared out the idea that Yusuf had come to share his life with her and Vana momentarily made her heart skip a beat, the beat of longing.

Suddenly the mystery man moved around the van to the middle of the road and looked up in the direction of Sasha's window. The hood continued to obscure his face and if in that moment she could have reached down and pulled it away she willingly would have done so – but she could not, and the continuous uncertainty and apprehension only served to create anger out of fear. She thought, 'Who the hell is this creep standing in the middle of the road so late at night?' She wanted to unveil his disguise, pull off his hood and disclose him. She had had enough of this bizarre drama. She turned away from the window, quickly put on her dressing gown, slipped on her loafers and hurried downstairs gritting her teeth in steely determination to unmask the mystery man.

She opened the front door, clenched her right hand fist ready to jab and stepped outside onto the pavement still holding the door behind her with her other hand. No one was there. The rain splattered her face and soaked her gown. She stayed cemented to the spot peering up and down the street and across to the parked van but saw no one. The mystery man had vanished into thin air and his disappearance was worse than having the fiend staring up at her for she was braced to confront him and settle the matter. Now she was left with empty space and the mystery unsolved for another night. Her disappointment made her spit onto the pavement.

Back in bed she panted and breathed deeply shivering with fear. Twice more she got up to check the street but no one was there just the shadowed shapes of usual things misted by the rain. The night was heavy and long as she lay on her back searching for answers from the old lath and plaster ceiling stretched out above her. There were no answers and she fell awkwardly into a shallow sleep that was fraught with dark and threatening images. Outside the June night sky swirled black and troubled, menaced with distant lightening and rain relentlessly lashing the window.

The next morning she awoke early, bleary and perplexed about the mysterious person who had returned for a second night. Who was he and how did he know she was there peeping through the side of her curtain in the darkened room? With a troubled mind she got ready for her bi-monthly health check at the Camden Clinic behind King's Cross station. Just before she left her room she looked out the window to make sure no one was standing below watching her room.

Chapter Five

Monday 18th June was a bright sunny day with a few wispy clouds set high in the Sapphire blue sky.

Theo normally savoured the special calm that spread throughout a hotel in its Sunday guise when time seemed to hang still, light as a cobweb; however, the previous night at the Royal Victoria Hotel had been made unpleasant by the recent re-painting of his room that had left it with a toxic odour of solvents and resins that stuck to the hairs in his nose. The room had been too hot and opening the window only presented the alternative problem of pervading street noise that persisted all through the night by varying degrees. An early morning assault by the dustmen to empty the bottle bank positioned in the yard beneath his room had ensured further disruption.

Staying in hotel rooms always enlivened Theo's promiscuous thoughts, prompted in no small part by the enormous double bed that seemed incomplete with just him as its sole occupier; alone in its vast Waste Land he kept fantasising over the sexy girl on reception wishing she was there with him exploring the robustness of the mattress' coils and springs technology.

He got up at six-thirty, shaved, showered and dressed in a mild stupor before going down to the breakfast room.

He munched his way through an enormous breakfast as if he was a condemned criminal about to be led to the gallows. He relished the chance to tuck-away a full English breakfast that only hotels do so well. At a quarter to seven he was waiting for the Rotherham bus that would take him to Orgreave situated some four miles out of the city.

Despite the early hour it was evident from the amount of traffic and people heading down the A57 towards Orgreave that something big was in the offing. By the time the bus arrived the numbers of people walking towards the Coking Plant had turned into a crowd. They had made their way from mining communities all over the country in cars and coaches and public transport. The whole assembly crept along the main road via Wybourn as a procession interspersed with huge wobbling banners held aloft: 'United We Stand – Divided We Fall' and 'Coal Not Dole" and "Support The Miners'.

Women from the Sheffield Women Against Pit Closures group were amongst the crowd, and some of them had set up a roadside soup kitchen for those miners who had missed out on breakfast; but it was mostly men who gathered and they all seemed in jovial mood, chatting and laughing in that nervous way people do when they are committed to something they have no control over and are unsure of the outcome. The atmosphere reminded Theo of the times he had walked down the side streets of Charlton Valley towards the football stadium on a Saturday afternoon to see the home team play – everyone jostling along, bumping and butting in high spirits and hopeful anticipation.

The sun was eager to get into full glow higher in the sky and the temperature was rising by the minute; it was noticeable how many of the men were in jeans, T-shirts and trainers, casual attire for summer days, as they ambled along, jostling and bantering, their numbers swelling at each road junction where more miners joined the main throng, like a tributary pouring into the parent river at its confluence.

At the junction with the A630 Theo got off the bus and joined the huge plodding procession; he could soon make out the enormity of the Coking Plant with its series of spindly dark menacing chimneys poking into the clear blue sky, vast carbuncle-like gasometers, hissing jets of steam and zigzagging coal conveyor gantries. The whole complex looked like a scene from a Quatermas film set. The site seemed to grow in size with each step Theo took and his mind shook with the enormity of its scale made starker by its placement in an empty field outside Rotherham. An image of L. S. Lowry's bleak painting, *Industrial*

Landscape, flashed through his mind with its sense of industrial tundra, a landscape empty of hope and beauty.

The crowd grew denser under the rising sun and was constantly moving aside to make way for a flotilla of cars and coaches that were bringing miners in from all directions. The police were now lining each side of the road and virtually escorting them along. Theo arrived near the main gates whereced the hub of the picket was being directed to a side field already teaming with miners standing around in groups idly chatting and joking. He tried to assess how many miners there were but there was no way of knowing for sure – maybe five thousand. There was also a considerable police presence, crowding the area around the gates where the haulage lorries would come and go on their delivery duties to Scunthorpe Power Station, and many more lining the approach road and even more congregating in huge numbers at the bottom of the adjacent field. The numbers of police engaged on what was, in theory, just a regular miners' picket, was staggering and completely took Theo by surprise.

Although he was hemmed in by the irresistible flow of the crowd he tried to gather his thoughts and settle himself; he looked around for the best vantage point to observe proceedings. He had not reckoned on the police's pre-planned strategy of herding everyone into the field. He plodded along, without a choice, to the field now getting nearer and nearer and a sense of foreboding came over him as he saw it swelling with miners; it concerned him that at first glance there seemed to be no escape once inside the controlled gate. There was little doubt that the police's strategy was to trap the miners in the field. He needed more information but there was no one immediately available to consult, nothing but the horde of miners tramping towards the field like cattle. He cursed Tubby for such a poor brief.

The first section of police placements came within his reach as the crowd edged forward.

"Excuse me officer, what's happening? Why's everyone being directed into that field?" Theo was being nudged forward as he tried to engage the policeman.

"Keep moving along now …" The policeman was polite but decisive with just a hint of apprehension in his eyes, "Into the field, everyone move across into the field, everyone into the field, move across into the field now, move into the field."

He raised an arm as if on road traffic duty. The bobbing mass of miners had no choice but to creep towards the gate and squeeze through it like a turnstile at a stadium.

Two lads next to Theo joked, "Blimey, what's this, coppers being polite, that's a new one – they usually push us around – must be the warm weather."

Other miners chipped in, "Yeh, we came along the M1 and not a roadblock in sight – then we were practically escorted to the car park like VIPs – never known the Pigs to be so friendly – I don't trust 'em."

Theo had little choice other than to enter the field with the miners en masse. Once through the gate everyone dispersed and he had space to collect himself and look around.

The field was long with a steady 4 – 6% gradient; it looked as if it had been sewn with corn but was now heavily trampled down. The miners were loosely spread from the middle up to the top whilst the police were solidly congregated at the bottom. He weighed up his options and they were few; he could either go to the top of the hill and miss being close to any action that took place down near the police lines or go half way up, to get the perspective of the whole field. He decided on the latter but use the left hand side where a line of trees formed a natural border and offered him cover.

He walked on up the hill keeping behind the trees until he was approximately half way then lent his back against a tree and surveyed the scene before him. On his side of the field, from top to bottom, were the trees with a rickety fence behind them and several police and their Alsatian dogs dotted here and there; along the opposite side there were shrubs and small trees with more police dogs and at the top was a steep bank that went down to the railway line and a path leading to a narrow bridge that connected the field to the little town of Orgreave.

At the bottom, where the field flattened out, the whole area swarmed with police. The miners were still being corralled through the gate although the process was nearing completion; they continued to amble in a casual fashion, some towards the top of the hill whilst others stood or squatted on the grass slope. By this arrangement the police had three sides of the field well guarded forming a comprehensive barrier that ensured the miners had nowhere to go except over the narrow railway bridge at the top.

The temperature was getting warmer and many of the miners took off their T-shirts and stuffed them into their pockets preferring to go bare-chested. Time passed and an atmosphere of nervous insouciance spread over the field as miners chatted and joked amongst themselves; some sipped tea from thermos flasks whilst others preferred soft drinks from cans. Theo leant back against the tree looking up and down, left and right, and thought the scene appeared too easy going, like the calm before a storm. The clock was ticking and time dissolved into the warm June air bringing on a sense of suspended reality as if everyone was playing a part in an amateur drama. He moved a few feet down to another tree and resumed his watchful duties. He began to feel a little drowsy under the fierce sun as the first stages of dehydration took hold. Tubby's face appeared before him bobbing around like a balloon in the warm thermals. The balloon face hovered overhead, its small mean mouth opened and closed like a ventriloquist's dummy: 'My information is that a bit of a ding-dong will take place at Orgreave on Monday and those miners will be given a bloody nose.' He wanted to grab the balloon and put his fist through the small callous mouth, bursting it and making it disappear. He was feeling hot and faint. How the hell did Tubby know about a likely 'ding-dong' anyway? He wondered where the lines of command went from Whitehall to the police headquarters and who exactly was pulling the strings? He wiped the sweat from his brow and took deep breaths. He would have given a lot for a mouthful of cool water. The sun poured down through a clear blue sky, the birds were absent without leave, too scared to show themselves and embarrassed by what was taking place, and the charcoal sketch of a jet plane grew bigger as it descended to Manchester airport some thirty miles away through the heat haze.

Moments passed unregistered by time, he looked around the field again, nothing much was happening, just a drone of casual conversations and lively banter. He had no sense of any imminent mayhem as he surveyed the miners and so cast his eye to the bottom of the field where the police were earnestly making preparations for some unknown activity; their palpable energy and fretfulness was in evident contrast to the miners' casualness as they quickly grouped their ranks like extras on William Wyler's Ben-Hur film set.

Theo kept his attention on the police and within minutes their frantic movements turned into full-blown commotion as they were ordered to form phalanxes like Roman legionnaires getting ready for battle. The door of their mobile Command Post was constantly opening and closing as high-ranking officers went in for debriefing and the sharing of new strategies. As he looked he thought he recognised the elderly silver haired man from the train come out and disappear amongst the clamour of police – 'My God, is that really the old man on the train, he must be a an undercover agent-provocateur.' Theo had no time to ponder this further because over to the right of the Command Post was a squadron of police horses being made ready for engagement. Clearly a premeditated plan was being put into action unknown to the unsuspecting miners. By the gate police with dogs stood guard looking menacing as they pulled the leather leads against the powerful thrust of their dogs' neck collars to keep them from bounding off, snarling and bellicose, to find something to practice their flesh-tearing training on.

Outside on the road adjacent to the field, around the area close to the Coking Plant's main gates, something was afoot; a handful of miners who had avoided being forced into the field were now being pushed back along the side of the road. Then the sound of lorry diesel engines dominated the airways as a procession of thirty-five empty tip-up trucks came trundling along the narrow road to fill up at the Coking Plant – each one with a picket-defying driver behind the wheel. The twisting snake-like convoy bumped and rattled its way down the road sending its throaty engine revs across the fields alerting everyone to what was about to happen; this was the moment the mass picket had been waiting for, this was the moment they had discussed in living rooms and kitchenettes and over pints in pubs and social clubs and in the NUM operations office, this was when the six thousand strong mass picket would muster its combined strength to stop the lorries entering or leaving the mighty Orgreave Coking Plant. This was going to be the re-run of their famous victory at the Saltley Coke Works mass picket in Birmingham 1972 when their action led to the closing of that Works' gates and eventually to the NUM's victory and downfall of the Conservative Government in the 1974 election. The lorries roared forward and the chant of, 'Scab, Scab, Scab' could be heard rising up from the few miners standing on the side of the road.

Suddenly the miners in the field got to their feet as if a factory hooter had summoned clocking-off time. Up they got from their casual loitering, over they came from their dispersed locations to form a cohesive force moving towards the bottom of the hill – six thousand of them were galvanised and ready for action within minutes. The majority joined in the chanting of, 'Scab,

Scab, Scab' directed at the lorry drivers who were progressing towards the Coking Plant without obstruction.

As the lorries grunted onwards, the miners quickened their pace and surged downhill towards the gate to get onto the road and block the lorries from getting to their destination. At the same time the police closed their ranks and some five thousand of them squeezed shoulder-to-shoulder cordoning off both the exit from the field as well as protecting the Plant's entrance.

The two opposing forces came together as the miners pressed up against the police's front line that held its ground behind plastic shields; the miners pushed and heaved from behind like a gigantic rugby scrum, their front row using their shoulders like battering rams to wedge a gap through the police phalanx. But this was not Saltley and the police at Orgreave had been trained for this eventuality, indeed it was exactly what they had been expecting and they were prepared.

The miners continued to shove and thrust at the police blockade as had been their tactic in previous picket encounters from where this whole process had been honed into a kind of ritual – first the miners' show of strength, with their pushing and jostling, a few stones and the odd porkpie flung skywards towards the police who then retaliated by raising their shields and making their own counter-push against the miners – this well rehearsed tit-for-tat encounter, although bruising and potentially dangerous, usually amounted to nothing more than an eventual standoff without any major incident. Now, on this sunny June day at Orgreave, the police broke the unwritten pact and the miners were caught wrong-footed.

Then, by some disguised signal and without any justifiable provocation, the police lines opened up and from a few yards back a squad of eight mounted police cantered forward on their chargers wielding staves that were twice as long as standard truncheons, huge and menacing, they headed straight towards the miners who, quickly calculating the odds against them, turned desperately to flee, with some going over to the sides of the field and others instinctively preferring the higher ground.

Theo stood from his position by the trees watching the mayhem unfold in disbelief. The miners were scattering like ants all around him as if their lives depended on it. Some came over to where he stood but seeing the fence behind the trees and the police dog handlers guarding the area they abandoned that escape route and turned to run up the hill. Their previous light-hearted chatter that had descended that summer morning over the field like a soft blanket of sound wafting from a distant school playground, was now replaced with howls and squeals and the raucous warrior yells from the pursuing mounted police whilst the heavy thud of the horses' hooves pounded the hard earth giving a low bass accompaniment that seemed to make the leaves shake on the windless day.

The mounted police fanned out in pursuit of the miners with their staves held high ready to be brought crashing down indiscriminately onto a head, a shoulder or an arm. They each seemed to select a particular miner and with steely determination gave chase. The retreating miners had the hill against them and those who had led the initial surge towards the police phalanxes were now the nearest targets for punishment. What followed was nothing short of a rout. The fleeing miners straggling at the back were picked off remorselessly by the mounted police who thundered forward, each horse at least seventeen hands at the withers, lashing out with their long truncheons as coldheartedly as if they were tasked to strike coconuts from their shies at the local fair.

Theo stood riveted to the spot, looking on in dismay as blow after blow felled the unarmed miners struggling up the hill. One young lad, noticeable for his red T-shirt, was chased near to where Theo stood and fell exhausted onto his knees with his arms over his head for protection; a mounted policeman came up and lashed the defenceless miner with his truncheon across his body and his head. Theo's stomach quivered with nervous bile as the lad's flesh turned red with blood. After their first charge the mounted police circled around the field again and again picking off miners at random.

Then, by another signal, wave after wave of the police "snatch squads" in full riot gear came charging through the police lines at the bottom of the field. These snatch-squads were each made up of twenty officers, a sergeant and an inspector and had been specially trained in dealing with public disorder incidents. They burst out of the police ranks onto the open field rattling their short round shields with their truncheons, sounding like Zulu warriors at the battle of Rorke's Drift.

Their orders seemed to be simple and unambiguous – to strike down the first miner they came across and arrest them. Out they ran and carried out the order with disproportionate zeal and callous determination. One by one the miners were seized upon and if they put up the slightest resistance they were coshed to the ground, many were further struck even in that position, and then roughly man-handled with their arms pushed up their backs, kicked and pushed to the waiting police wagons below. Theo witnessed the snatch squads' brutal tactics and savage ruthlessness in a deepening sense of bewilderment and despair.

The heat and brutality made him feel faint and nauseous as the main body of miners was forced up the hill by the relentless assault; seeing this he decided to change position again and went stealthily behind the line of trees to the crest, looking around him, sideways and to his rear like a cricketer taking the crease.

The bulk of miners who had made it to the top of the hill were scrambling to get over the railway footbridge but the speed at which the police were closing on them and the logistics of getting so many across the narrow bridge presented a hopeless task; with the odds stacked against them the whole picket fragmented with some attempting to cross the bridge and others shinning down the steep railway embankment and gingerly stepping over the tracks. Some of them who had witnessed the police violence more comprehensively than others decided to take retaliatory action in a last ditch effort of defiance. They grabbed any object they could find and let loose a scattering of missiles down the hill towards the advancing police. A smoke bomb suddenly went off giving a theatrical effect to the whole melodrama. Some of the missiles, mainly stones, found their mark and there were police injuries but these were few and far between, for the miners in their T-shirts and jeans were no match for the mounted police's long batons nor the shields and truncheons of the well-prepared police snatch squads.

Theo's throat was parched and the heat had drained his energy; his light headedness was getting worse as he edged from the tree-line cover out across the top of the hill and crouched into a small gap overlooking the railway still within a safe distance from the main affray. From this vantage point he saw the police continue to charge up the hill clubbing and arresting the scattering miners at will. He noticed some fleeing miners clambering over the footbridge and many more crossing the tracks and disappearing into nearby Orgreave village. He was shocked at the awful over-reaction of the police and the grim intent of the snatch-squads in pursuing the hapless miners as they fled in all directions into the back streets of the village.

The relentless heat was making his dehydration worse and weakening his spirit; the violence of the battle raging around him made him feel bewildered and enraged in equal measure; nothing had prepared him for what he had witnessed and the whole incident had affronted his sense of justice and standards of human decency.

He backed out of his hiding place overcome by paroxysms of confusion and decided on the spot to get the hell out of Orgreave. He was physically and mentally exhausted and did not care whether he would be mistaken for a miner and arrested he just wanted to get back to some kind of normality, to peace and civilised behaviour. He set off down the hill behind the trees, stooping and leaning forward like a civilian dodging snipers in some war-torn ravaged country; towards the bottom of the hill he stopped and took another look around noticing for the first time the BBC TV camera unit positioned on the opposite side of the field.

There seemed to be no other option than to join what was left of the picket now rounded up and penned in by the police near the main gate. The battle was all but over and the miners were defeated, all they could do was to stare across the road to the Coking Plant and await their final humiliation – the lorries coming out through the gates with their loads of coke headed for the Scunthorpe Power Station. A handful of miners still running loose were yelling obscenities at the marauding police whilst others were being dragged to the police wagons like sacks of spuds.

He checked his watch, it was two-forty five, time seemed to have stood still and he had no idea where the last four hours had gone, they had just disappeared like bubbles in the air. In spite of his wooziness he suddenly thought about his job obligations, suppressed throughout the extraordinary events of the day, they suddenly hit him like a punch to the jaw. He searched inside his trouser pockets and pulled out Tubby's business card. As he stared at it, feeling heavy with fatigue, it seemed to go in and out of focus at the same time as Tubby's strict diktat became blurred, almost insignificant.

He tried to focus on Tubby's instructions that he had shouted across the office, 'I want a summary and some suggestions of how we can nail these miners, some quick catchy phrases that the Prime Minister's speech writers can use to harden public opinion once and for all – have you got that Harrison, do you understand?' He recalled the command and felt depressed. He had no idea what to say about the shameful unwarranted police brutality metered out to the miners.

The sun poured down reddening his skin and sapping his strength. The burden of his duties to deliver a report to satisfy Tubby's demands started to weigh on his mind like a migraine. It was impossible for him to come up with anti-miners slogans when the miners had been so harshly and unfairly treated. It was a matter of honesty and integrity and he knew he could not tarnish these imperatives with a bunch of claptrap lies for the Prime Minister's speechwriters or anyone else.

Then he remembered Tubby's final command to contact him directly when it was over. He looked again at the business card and Tubby's phone number. He stared at the lines of police hemming everyone in and thought, 'How can I do that penned in here, in the middle of no where – it's hopeless.' He absentmindedly cast his eyes over the group of miners and then focussed on a particular face just a few feet away to his right, a dejected looking cherub face with a cut and dark blue reddish swelling above the left eye. It was Digsy. He edged over to where the young man stood and tapped him on the shoulder.

"It's Digsy isn't it?" Digsy slowly looked around, his dark weary eyes scanning Theo's face.

"Oh, it's you, the gaffer on the train – so you made it after all?" Digsy looked dejected and beaten like a Second World War soldier waiting for evacuation from Dunkirk beach.

"So where's your mate, Curly?" Theo quickly looked left and right in a gesture to find Digsy's partner.

"Last time I saw him he had two coppers beating the shit out of him man – all he had done was walk thirty yards up the hill, they pounced on him like a pack of hyenas, kicking him and beating him with those long truncheons, then they arrested him and chucked him in the bloody van like a pile of dung."

Digsy was hurt in every sense, inside and out, and looked at Theo for some sort of justice, "They would have chucked me in there too but I ran off, not without one of the bastards clipping me over the head with his truncheon." He pointed to his damaged left eye to make sure Theo knew what he was talking about. The nasty wound was swollen with a jagged gash now congealed by over exposure to the healing sun.

"Yes, there was a lot of that going on wasn't there, I saw it all, I can't believe it." Theo was warming to the role of being an independent witness and assumed an air of being serious and earnest at the same time.

"They had no right, what they did today was wrong man, they had no right." Digsy was looking down and seemed to be talking to some invisible deity, a spirit diffused within the earth, a higher being, higher than mortal man, who would note all the wrongs and reek retribution on the perpetrators.

Theo repeated his previous line but with more sympathy, "Yes, I saw it all, the police just grabbing and bashing people at random …"

"Yeh, well, it may have looked like it was random, but it was all carefully planned man, wasn't it? Those bastards knew what they were doing all right – they'd never come down on us like that before man, not that brutal, just a bit of pushing and shoving on both sides, but this was different man, it was planned to military precision, they're Maggie's Boot Boys – no bones about it, it was all planned from above …"

"You think so? Who …" Theo was intrigued.

"Oh man, you know who, we told you about it on the train – it's got McGregor's dabs all over it, no doubt man, he and the Prime Minister have had the whole thing mapped out for months …" Digsy looked up and pointed towards the Coking Plant, "… all those lorry driver scabs for a start, all hired by the Government weeks ago, all picked for the job, all non-union men who don't give a monkeys about picket lines and all ready to move the coal around the country, anywhere they're told man

– like a mobile army in its own right – give those scabs enough money and they'll sell their own mothers down the river."

Theo was listening intently to the wounded, embattled Digsy who had sunk so low in spirit and was downcast with the heavy dejection of injustice. He felt once again the same sense of alarm come over him as he had done on the train, but now he had seen with his own eyes the real possibility that Digsy was right, there really was a plan to stop the miners at all costs.

Digsy saw Theo's expression change and pushed his point further. "It's all been worked out man, McGregor is their hired gunfighter, they got him from British Steel where the bastard shot down the workforce by half – and before that he had broken-up the United Mine Workers' Union in Wyoming – they knew exactly what they were do'n getting McGregor to run the NCB – you can imagine the job interview, "This is your brief man, get in there and smash the bastards to bits like you've done in all your other jobs."

"You think it was all a plan?" Theo still couldn't believe the Government was capable of deception and cunning on such a scale; what was dawning on him with ever more clarity was that he, himself, was part of it all, part of the plot to destroy the unions and change public opinion. He stood there dizzy in the heat and loathed himself for being nothing but a little foot soldier for the Government and a pathetic pedlar of their propaganda. The thought made him grind his teeth and clench his fists.

Just then a mighty roar of engines from the fleet of lorries swept over the field as they started up and growled to life from the Coking Plant causing all eyes to turn to the main gates like a weathervane caught in a sudden breeze. Everyone inched forward, their anger and frustration evident but impotent with nothing to vent it on.

"Wise up man, what happened here today was a big step towards the Government's plan to defeat us and the union movement in general – the Prime Minister has been brainwashed by Milton Friedman's cracked-pot theories of monetarism – but it's all theory man, none of it has been tested, just one big gamble and it's the union movement she's gambling with …" Bigsy's voice was suddenly drowned out as a helicopter chugged low over the field like a scene from the TV series, M*A*S*H.

Just then the Coking Plant's main gates opened and the lorries came out, one after the other, full to the brim with coke, they snarled and rumbled their way along the road heavily guarded on both sides by police three lines deep. The miners held in the field were powerless to stop them and could only bite their lips at what was happening under their noses. Some were silent, silent in anger, and others shook their fists and yelled abuse at the spectacle they had sworn would never happen. As a group they swayed back and forth, spitting out their disgust and shouting out, 'Scabs' and 'Scum' into the bright June afternoon sky like stones from a sling, shooting through the air, rising and falling unhindered, off the mark and with no consequence.

The miners' day was done, their famous victory at the Saltley Coke Works in 1972 had not been repeated, and they stayed penned in yelling and moaning and waving their fists at an opponent who had been too well prepared.

Theo had no choice but to remain standing in the afternoon heat with the miners, feeling dejected, tired and dehydrated to the point where his mind was beginning to wander off on its own. He kept seeing Tubby's damned face everywhere and hearing his strict commands ringing in his head. His heart sank at the responsibility to make sense of what he had seen but he knew he could never dream up any catch phrases against the miners from the deeply disturbing egregious acts of violence he had witnessed the police perform – it was immoral, like trying to put a positive spin on the Peterloo Massacre of 1819.

It was late in the afternoon when the police finally opened the gate and let the weary miners plod out of the field with nothing but the sickening memory of fully loaded trucks disappearing down the road to Scunthorpe Power Station to haunt them.

As Theo walked through the gate, his head swimming in a swoon of woozy dehydration and his eyes offended by what he had witnessed, he turned to give one last look at the mayhem around the police encampment at the bottom of the field; it was then something moved in his mind, lurching him to a new state of awareness, levering away an old boulder of creed from its tether of nurtured principle; he slowly walked on with clenched fists cursing Tubby and everything he represented, 'You bastard liar!'

* * * * * * * *

Jenny and her father sat in the Lobster Pot pub both with half-pints of beer and a packet of plain crisps in front of them. The pub was old and tacky, tucked away in one the backstreets near the docks mainly serving long standing local residents and those recently moved into the new council estate nearby. The snug bar was small and the air heavy with cigarette smoke, that never had enough time to dissipate before it was replenished by the returning drinkers on their endless cycle of lunchtime and evening sessions. Reggie was a frequent visitor and was well known by the landlady who found his quiet demeanour and civil persona a refreshing change from her usual band of rowdy regulars.

"So tell me about this change of service Dad – the ferries are only going to Boulogne now? What's that mean to you and your job?" Jenny could see the potential problem and worried about her Dad's employment prospects. There were so many changes going on, so many factory closures and job losses – the whole country seemed to be under a threat of redundancy. He was pushing forty-eight years old and would struggle to find another job with equal benefits and pay.

Reggie sipped his beer and licked his lips. "Well Jen, I reckon the ferry company just doesn't see any future operating out of Folkestone – it's all about profit projections isn't it, some little upstart sitting in the Sealink Stena office has done some calculations and doesn't think there's a profit to be had so they've cut the service. Don't ask me how they work these things out, but Folkestone to Calais is not the flavour of the month, it's all about Dover. No investment here and that's for sure. All we've got is the Boulogne route now..." He took another sip of beer, "... and don't bet the farm on that staying around for long."

"But haven't they had a meeting with you all and explained things Dad?" Jenny knew there were workers' rights and proper procedures to follow.

"Well, yes I suppose you could call it that – but I'm not sure I'm any the wiser – they just said it wasn't profitable and that was that – eight have been given redundancy notice but it won't stop there."

"Why, have you heard something, what will happen then?" Jenny felt the hopelessness of the ferry workers' position.

"You don't have to be a clairvoyant to see that the Boulogne route won't last – I give it another couple of years tops. Then this place won't run anymore ferries, just those bloody noisy hovercrafts that keep breaking down – and finally that Channel Tunnel idea will see off Folkestone altogether, you mark my words."

"You think the Tunnel will go ahead?"

"Yes, of course, they've been fiddling around with it for years but now they've got the technology and the political will it will kick-off over the next few years, no doubt about it."

"So, what about your job Dad, do any of those eight men given redundancy notices work under you?" Jenny had a vision of her father out of work making kites all day.

"Most of 'em actually, except Don and Hilda in Admin – all the others work with me loading and unloading the ferries." He gazed out the window to the back streets, the rows of terrace houses, the street lamps, the graffiti and some kids playing football using their coats for goalposts, and took a deep sigh. "I don't know Jen, it's all getting a bit depressing isn't it – have you seen the news on telly these days, they've actually put in a slot to show where the latest factory closures are, little flags on a map, and each day they pin on more flags – what the heck's going on?" He looked calm but in his eyes Jenny could see worry and resentment.

"But Dad – they haven't actually made you redundant yet?" She wanted to turn the conversation around and get him to feel more positive.

He looked out the window and seemed to be struggling with some thing, a heavy obstacle on his mind that he couldn't lift away, and he stumbled into a sudden state of fury.

He bit his lip. "They say they can't guarantee anything, they say we just have to make the Boulogne route successful, but no promises and no guarantees – that's Britain today for 'yer isn't it, they've changed everything with their clip-boards and time and motion studies and 'market economy' mantra, and all that tosh, but at the core of their new efficiency drives is self-interest – everyone wants the highest price when they're selling but the lowest price when they're buying, so how can everyone benefit I wonder, how does everyone win in that situation – they can't, the market economy serves the rich and powerful but it creates losers, it relies on someone's loss." He drained the glass and looked at Jenny with large bewildered eyes, like a man defeated by an irrepressible system.

"Well, it's supposed to give us cheaper prices by increasing competition, isn't that right – is it cheaper to go to Calais from Dover, if so, then the market economy is working isn't it Dad?" Jenny was not sure about her argument but felt she should act as devil's advocate.

"No, no Jen, they can manipulate outcomes if it suits their purpose, it's all about investment, they could have put money into Folkestone and made it compete with Dover, now that would have been more like a market economy, that might have pushed prices down in both places, but they don't want that, they've got a captive market and they can do what they like as long as a fat profit is the outcome – the bottom line is we're all dispensable, just little cogs in their free market experiment." He looked at his empty glass.

"Come on Jen, drink up, I'll get another one …"

"Actually Dad, I wouldn't mind a port and lemon if that's OK – here, let me get them …"

"No, no, I'll get these, port and lemon eh? Well, in that case I might have a Scotch." His wooden chair screeched against the floorboards as he got up and the three other customers in the timeless snug all jumped, suddenly shaken from their private meditations.

Jenny looked about the small bar and wondered how many people had sat in it over the years with their different stories of success and failure, with their moments of joy and sadness, of disappointment and jubilation. She thought about the role a backstreet pub like the Lobster Pot served in the community and how it was being affected by the recession, whether the redundant men drank more or stayed away under the constraint.

She looked up into the far corner and noticed a tiny fragment of an old Christmas paper chain still pinned to the ceiling and imagined all the past Christmases played out in this little room, and all the New Year's Eve celebrations, and big moments like VE day – all those times when the local people came together to chat and sing and laugh and dance, moments of joy shared in this squatty little dump of a place. She closed her eyes and tried to imagine the scene on Tuesday 8th May, 1945, with everyone dressed up in their Sunday best gathered around the old upright piano singing along to their favourite war time tunes like, *My Old Dutch* and *If You Were The Only Girl In The World* – the pathos and the booze and the flirty glances and the smell of tobacco and Lifebuoy soap permeating from floor to ceiling, distilling the memories like permanent ghosts forever enshrined within the cream and brown painted walls.

She sat all dreamy and distracted by the phantoms of yesterday tickling her imagination; the dreary little bar was a bastion for men during the daytime with the odd single woman venturing in from time to time hardened or oblivious to the nasty chauvinism dominant in the breed of day time male drinkers. Only in the evenings and especially at weekends did the doors open to couples who would sit often in silence or engage in fragmented conversation of light-hearted mediocrity.

Then she thought of the couples who used the back street bar as a hide-away, a den for those who were having affairs huddled in the shadowy corners drawing deep into their lovers' eyes the illicit images of the carnal pleasures waiting to be fulfilled. From no where an image of her mother flashed before her; she saw her as clear as a robin in snow sitting with her lover at the table opposite stroking his hand and staring through the pupils of his eyes into his soul, willing him to return the warm flesh touch.

She looked at the apparitions and sensed their presence as real as any living thing with a beating heart and felt sad; she knew by the special instincts woven into her genes that her mother was having an affair, she recognized the signs back in the living room seeing her dressed up like a tart and now she was certain. At that moment she felt like taking her father in her arms to protect him from the tawdry lie of his marriage and the harm and dejection that awaited him.

"You look miles away." Reggie put down the glasses, slightly spilling the port and lemon that had been over-filled by the distracted landlady. "Iris doesn't concentrate on what she's doing – it's not as if she's run off her feet with customers either."

They both sipped their drinks, Reggie looking down at his glass and Jenny looking up at her father.

"So how are things generally Dad – everything OK with Mum?"

Reggie's expression did not alter and he slowly looked up licking his lips.

"Yeh – of course, why shouldn't it be?"

"No, nothing Dad, I was just asking – she looks so different, she's really changed her style hasn't she? I reckon she's taken ten years off." She looked at her father for any sign of concern but there was none.

"Oh that, well, women like to keep themselves looking good don't they Jen? I mean, it's important to them isn't it – and I must say she's looking great these days, given her a new lease of life."

The door opened and two young men came in from a local construction site and plodded towards the bar, their heavy boots dotted with plaster and building site muck.

"And she's going out more too...?" Jenny was nudging closer to her real concern. "… is that OK with you Dad?"

"It's fine my luv, really, I'm happy if she's happy and she seems really happy these days and that's for sure." This was not true. Reggie had started to harbour a nagging fear that his wife was seeing another man. He couldn't help but notice the changes that Beverly had made to herself and the broadening of her social activities. He may have had only a secondary school education but he was no fool and as sensitive as the next man; he knew there was more to her make-over than just a mid-life crisis, he knew instinctively someone was lurking in the background and that someone was a man, there was no other explanation for the glossy rouge lipstick, tight fitting tops and uplift bras. He could not bear to confront the issue neither with himself nor with Beverly and especially not with Jenny. He knew his wife was lying to him and he knew he was lying to himself but for the sake of his marriage he intended to keep his thoughts to himself.

"So have you met these friends of hers from work – does she ever bring them home?" Jenny was aware that the conversation was turning into a cross-examination and that she was trespassing onto the private property of a marriage.

"No she hasn't – but then why would she, not much fun in that is there, they prefer to go out to the swanky pubs in town, bit more lively I suppose – look Jen, what's on your mind luv, don't you like your mother's new found youth?" Reggie gave a short laugh but it was false and fell flat.

"You trust her don't you Dad?" The question was sharp and pointed making the air go pregnant with possibilities. There was a long silence punctuated only by the occasional peel of laughter from the two builders propping up the bar and the noise of a motorbike with a faulty silencer being driven up and down the side street by the local James Dean lookalike out for a joy ride.

Finally Reggie spoke in a hushed voice, "I have to don't I? You have to trust one another Jen, what else is there?" He sipped his Scotch and slightly pursed his lips. "What else is there – we've only got trust, without that the whole lot falls down. Honesty is everything to me."

"OK Dad, that's fine, I didn't mean to pry." Jenny looked at her Dad and thought how vulnerable he was, this bashful unassuming man who wouldn't harm a fly was too trusting and blind in his love. She was struck by the notion that love was cruel and if not properly balanced could destroy you.

"So tell me about you Jen, you're going off to France for a break – is work getting you down my love?"

"Oh I don't know Dad, well yes, I suppose it is but only because there's so much of it, so many people are struggling with their rents and losing the fight, losing their jobs and losing their homes – they all end up in my department and we're run off our feet. We're the last line of hope before they're out living on the streets." She sighed and blew through her lips as if she was feeling faint with the weight of her burden.

"No chance of getting extra staff then?" Reggie knew the answer but felt the obligation to ask the question.

"Some chance, the Government's cut the budget and we're struggling to keep the staff we've got, I reckon some will have to go and then the wheels will come off and the whole service will come to a halt – but hey, this Government doesn't care about social services or any services or any public duty does it – I reckon they're deliberately crashing the whole thing to push it over to the private sector – privatise the whole lot, same with all the welfare services and the NHS won't be immune – it will all end up being run by some private corporation who hasn't got a clue how it all works and is only interested in making a profit out of it – makes you sick doesn't it, these Tories just don't get public services do they? The whole principle of everyone working and contributing for the common good is alien to them – if it doesn't generate cash and a profit then sell it and who cares about consequences, who cares that people will be faced with the burden of extra cost, who cares about the poor anyway, it's their fault isn't it, they shouldn't have had so many kids, should've worked harder at school, should be more responsible, should be more Tory in fact!"

She came to a pause and took a deep breath exhausted with the way everything was changing and the injustice of it all, the ever growing gap between rich and poor, the piles of unemployed growing by the day, the factory closures, the homeless, the child poverty, and all the latest news about the miners' strike and the pit closures, it all formed a collective negative tug at her sense of well being.

"Come on Jen, drink up and have another – we can't have all this doom and gloom, life's too short – remember, everything is a series of cycles, round and round it all goes, first it's this and then it's that, always turning and changing and reappearing – this Tory lot won't last forever, they'll have their day and burn themselves out then the people will want a change."

"Yeh, a change all right Dad, as long as it's not Labour, the establishment won't have that will they, over their dead bodies."

She finished her port and lemon and put the glass down too heavily as if to emphasis her point.

"Oh no, we can't have that can we – the Tory press barons and the Prime Minister all getting together over secret dinners in their Whitehall clubs to map out their in-step strategy – their coordinated front page attacks on Labour, all using the same lies and distortions, all the same sensational language, 'Reds Under The Bed' and 'Trotskyist Militants" – and the saddest thing of all is that the comfortable middle classes swallow it, time after time, no matter what the Tories throw at them, going around smashing the country up like Bullingdon Club yobs, they couldn't care a damn as long as they're left alone in their tidy, neat houses down leafy suburban streets gloating over their low taxes and big pension pots – they don't need welfare." Jenny picked up her father's glass and cursed the air as she got up.

"Oh sod'em Dad – what can you do? It's a loaded dice and you can't win – sod the lot of them – same again?" She swaggered over to the bar heavy with attitude.

Reggie thought about what his daughter had said and admired her pluck and spirit. She reminded him of himself in his younger days working on the railways as a shunting yard foreman, those carefree days before his job was axed and he was forced to take work on the ferries. He stared out the dirty window over to the docks and thought of his current job and how vulnerable it was and how he loathed it; a succession of faces paraded in front of him from the past, the men he had worked with back in the '60s on the railway, brothers in arms against Beeching's cold-blooded murder of the rail network. One by one his old mates appeared before him – Tommy Tiddles, Billy 'Boxer' Robinson, Mad Harry, Skip Troutman, Freddie 'Teacake' – all good men and wonderful company – where were they now, he wondered.

He thought of those days and warmed inside with a glow of love for the old pals who fought the bitter changes with all their might but to no avail – Beeching got his way and one-third of the country's seven thousand railway stations and five thousand route miles of track were axed along with his job.

The whiskey trickled slowly into his blood and through his brain and as it did he jerked with emotion thinking about the union meetings and the promises to stop Beeching's short-sighted butchery. He smiled at the memory of all the comradeship, the drinking sessions and the laughter, he had never laughed so much before or since, even through the misery of the struggle, all the men formed a bond and humour and goodwill were the glue that kept them together to keep fighting, never to give in. He looked over to the bar and stared at his daughter's back as she took money from her purse to pay for the drinks and thought, 'By God, you're the same as me, twenty-five years ago I was like you, the same spirit and the same sense of duty to fight for what's right.' In that single moment his eyes swelled and love poured out of him for his Jenny.

They raised their full glasses once again and said 'Cheers' looking at each other tenderly.

"You still haven't told me about this trip to France Jen – what's the real reason then?"

"Oh, you know, all that work stuff and then, well, there was this fella, Danny was his name, I met him in London, down the Underground actually, he was busking, he's a fine guitar player, much better than me ..." Her eyes misted over and her mind started to wonder. "… He was so attractive, I mean he was good looking but also his personality was just – well, so electric, he seemed so at ease, so carefree yet so wised-up to everything – he had a flat and loads of people knew him, it was a ride on a magic carpet Dad, flying around Islington for a few months with Danny, high as kites and loving every minute of it – but then, well you know how the story goes Dad I'm sure, I gave him my heart, all of my love, all of myself, and the creep two-times me, probably worse than that actually if the truth be known, caught him with another woman coming out of his flat – he just shrugged it off, as if it didn't matter – I wanted to think like that too, you know, like it was the way of the world, the world Danny lived in, where you just go with someone for pleasure in that moment and then move on, but I couldn't, I loved him – and now I go around with this pain just under the surface, like the shadow of a fish beneath the water."

Jenny drained half her glass in one go as the lingering wound of Danny's loss bled her senses and she needed to take the sting out of the pain.

"Men like that don't take the old road Jen, they live by different standards and girls like you always get hurt by them – so, you're going off to France to help forget about Danny, is that it?"

"Yes, that and the work pressure and the general situation everywhere, it's just a romantic notion really – when I was on that canal walk I heard this accordion playing just before that idiot cyclist shoved me in – it was so quiet and peaceful by the canal at that moment, the still water, the gentle sounds of a summer day, the special sense of solitude you get along a London canal – and the accordion playing far off – it all rushed to my head and made me think of France – I love France and knew in that moment I had to go there again, just for a few days, to get away from all the mess here and be in France, sitting in a Monet style poppy field or on a sand dune and writing folk songs." She smiled and emptied her glass – the port now tickling her nerve ends and rekindling her imagination.

Reggie smiled, a willing accomplice, "Me too – do you remember that trip we made to Beauvais and Chartres and Rouen – visiting those wonderful cathedrals Jen – you were only a young teenager but you loved those great monuments to God, your eyes stretched wide open as you entered them, you were gob-smacked at their vast spaces and the darkened silent interiors and the fact that they had been standing on the same spot for six hundred years with so many people throughout the ages sitting there, talking to God – do you remember?"

"Of course, how could I ever forget Dad – that was such a wonderful holiday, and how clever of you to think of it, travelling around Northern France in our old Austin Allegro. I loved Normandy and staying in that little cottage with wooden beams and outside stairs to the little bedroom and that huge orchard – you and mum got squiffy on cider and I was sick with so many of those yummy crepes, my favourite was the creamy coffee mascarpone ones, I was seriously hooked on those, ha, ha, Gosh Dad, those were lovely times, and you and mum were so happy then …"

The era of when her parents had been happy in each other's company came vividly back to her mind, those sunny holiday days when they held hands and sang songs and laughed at each other's jokes. "Yeh, you were so happy the two of you, back then …"

"Well, we were young Jen, love is never as real as it is when you're young – what did Wordsworth say …?"

She jumped in quick as the silver flash of a minnow in a sunlight pool:

"Bliss it was in that dawn to be alive - but to be young was very heaven."

They both smiled and Reggie said, "So you still remember?"

"I remember you making me read his Prelude and I didn't really get it at the time, it's a bit loose and complicated but later when I read Kerouac and Ginsberg I realised what a genius Wordsworth was and so ahead of his time in that spontaneous, free-style way he had."

"It was for your own good Jen, but looking back I was a bit of a masochist, I must admit." She tapped his hand with hers and they both laughed again.

"Dad, there was something else I was thinking about on the canal path that day – I was thinking about you and Mum and the sacrifices you both made bringing me up – and all the things you taught me, not just Wordsworth, but how to look at things, how to see, you know, how to feel and how to observe, I realised at that moment how important you both are to me and I wanted to see you again." She felt the pang of emotion grip her nerves once again as she made her little confession and she stopped as her eyes moistened.

Reggie looked at her, his deep dark eyes with their thick brown circles widened to show a rich seam of love. "You were a joy to bring up Jen, so quick to learn, so eager to discover and understand things – always getting hold of shells and flower buds and anything else you came across and examining them, turning them round and upside down and wanting to know how they were made, how they worked – we were lucky to have one like you – some kids, well, you know, they can't help it for sure, but some are just dull, some don't have that special thing you had, they don't have the spark of curiosity."

Just then, the two builders at the bar, who had been studiously reading their evening newspapers, broke into a rant over some of the news articles; Jason bellowed in a booming voice as if his mate was sitting across the room instead of just inches away on a barstool:

"Eh Pete, get this, the average house price has gone up from £28,000 to £32,000 in one year – that's £4,000– fat chance you and me getting a mortgage at that rate."

Pete was engrossed in his own sense of indignation, "Yeh? Well what about this, interest rate is now at 12%, yeh, that's right, 12%, oh, and did you know that repossessions are rising again and that 28% of children are living below the poverty line?"

Jason kept the string of headline statistics going, "Yeh, well 'Greed is Good' as they say Pete my son, and now the truth is coming out about all those privatisation deals – they're calling it the biggest electoral bribe in history, you know, selling all the family silver, all those shares being sold on the cheap, apparently most people sold theirs immediately and all those vital utilities were bought up by corporations – I wonder how many of those CEOs have friends in Government eh – it's all one big con ain't it?"

Pete and Jason kept up this exchange for several more minutes until they ran out of snippets at which point they both fell into serious contemplation of the sports news.

Reggie and Jenny sat listening to the comments flung out at random and left dangling in the air never properly examined nor discussed by the two half-baked dissidents. When it finished a sense of injustice and hardship lingered of a country being systematically bent out of shape by a Government vowed to reducing the State's spending at any cost.

"They're right Dad, that's what I was trying to say just now, it's all getting desperate out there, poverty, unemployment and homelessness everywhere you look whilst the top 10% of earners receive almost 50% of tax breaks – do you know how bad it is, all this unemployment amongst the sixteen to twenty-four year olds – it currently stands at 1,200,00 – and you should see what all this means, the detail Dad, I mean, the actual reality of it all – go and see all these kids and their parents sleeping rough on cardboard beneath the Canning Town flyover and in all the other pedestrian underpasses in London – I have to deal with all this, it's my job, I have to try and make sense of it and find them some real accommodation but it's practically impossible, all our funding has been cut and there's no spare properties – and there's thousands of empty mansions in Mayfair and Belgravia owned by billionaires just waiting for the insane London house prices to go sky-high before selling – there's no justice, it's just so wrong."

Jenny's own censor filter of what is acceptable social behaviour made her stop, her voice straining at high pitch and her eyes wide as a startled Lemur, she looked at her father for his reaction. Reggie returned her look and didn't know what to say, he felt helpless and ashamed of his country. He drained his glass and immediately went off to the bar, a little wobbly on his legs. He bought the same again and one each for Jason, Pete and the landlady.

He sat down, swallowed a mouth full of Scotch and started to tap the table top whilst he sang the old music hall classic:

"She was poor but she was honest
Though she came from humble stock
And her honest heart was beating
Underneath her tattered frock."

Jenny's eyes softened and she looked at her father in amazement whilst Jason and Pete both turned around to see where the song was coming from. The Landlady too was curious but happy that the Lobster Pot rang with song once again.

Reggie was unperturbed and continued at a higher pitch:

"But the rich man saw her beauty
She knew not his base design
And he took her to a hotel
And bought her a small port wine."

Jenny picked up the spirit of the moment and the poignancy of the song and wished she had brought her guitar along. With the port swirling around her head she leant over and clasped her fathers hands with hers, warm and soft she squeezed them with feeling as she joined him in repeating the timeless refrain louder with each line:

"It's the same the whole world over,
It's the poor what gets the blame,
While the rich gets all the pleasure,
Ain't it a blooming shame."

Pete and Jason put their newspapers down and looking across the little snug bar to where Reggie and Jenny sat hand-in-hand they joined the landlady and three ex-dockers looking across from the adjacent public bar to repeat the chorus of the famous working class anthem:

"It's the same the whole world over,
It's the poor what gets the blame,
While the rich gets all the pleasure,
Ain't it a blooming shame."

Early next morning with her bag packed, her guitar over her shoulder and her eyes puffed with their own black bags from the previous late night she said goodbye to her father, holding him close to her she whispered in his ear, "Take care Dad, be strong and say goodbye to mum for me again."

Reggie whispered back into Jenny's ear, "You too my darling girl, don't let the buggers get you down, and don't eat too many of those crepes."

She walked off in the direction of the port to catch the eight o'clock ferry to Boulogne. The journey should only have taken twenty minutes with a brisk walk but her bag and the awkwardness of the guitar slowed her down to the point where she had to stop to catch her breath before moving on. She stood panting on a side road that ran parallel to the main road and nonchalantly looked around whilst securing the guitar strap over her shoulder.

It was then she saw her mother three hundred yards further ahead standing on the corner of an alleyway that intersected with the road. It was unmistakably Beverly and she looked alluring and attractive even at that distance. She was standing next to a young man and they were talking up close as if they were saying their farewells and sweet nothings. Just then they embraced and then clasped each other in a long and meaningful kiss. The man then disappeared down the alleyway and Beverly walked away in the direction of the port where the main road veered off towards the hospital where she worked, her power-suit with its sturdy shoulder pads silhouetted against the morning sky.

Jenny could not believe her eyes and all her worst fears were confirmed. She had a vision of her father's sad vulnerable face appear before her. 'He trusts her so much, this will kill him, the rotten cow …'

A nearby church clock struck the three-quarter hour chime prompting Jenny to get a move on so she tightened her grip around the bag and guitar and hurried quick-step along to the passenger terminal, her heart heavy with incomprehension as she went.

Chapter Six

Sasha sat in the waiting room of the Camden Sexual Health Clinic feeling numb. The place had that effect on her. Never failed. Many times she had sat looking at the same light green distempered walls bare but for a lonely clock and a notice board on which was pinned a poster warning of the dangers of sexually transmitted infections.

Only a single circular window positioned high up on the exterior wall gave enough light to break the sense of pervading gloom. Her feet creaked on a loose floorboard as she sat impatient to get the routine health check over with. The clock ticked and the floorboards creaked and time dragged in this lonely place where so many had sat waiting to have their little private spots of trouble sorted out.

It never got busy in the secluded backstreet clinic and Sasha wondered if the appointments were deliberately spread out to avoid congestion and assist patients' anonymity. Every now and then the door opened and an orderly or nurse moved across the floor as if walking on air and disappeared in one of the two rooms, Clinic A for males and Clinic B for females. Sasha checked her bag for her outpatients' card and sat looking at the history of her appointments' record. She looked down the list of dates going back seven months. She had not missed one appointment not even the one that fell between Christmas and New Year when she had to make a special effort travelling back from visiting her parents in Romford and returning the same afternoon on restricted public transport. Only once had it been necessary to undertake treatment and that was for a mild form of chlamydia that was cleared up with antibiotics and she had kept a clean bill of health ever since. She was confident this success was due to her strategy of keeping to a group of known clients.

At twelve minutes past her appointment time the door of Clinic B opened and a short ginger-haired skinny girl no more than seventeen came out chewing gum and went clip-clopping across the waiting room looking bored in red high-heel shoes, short black skirt and powder-blue top one size too small, as if she had been made-up to look like a hooker on a film-set; she swung open the exit door heavy against the wall, and clip-clopped along the corridor, her little arse tick-tocking like a metronome to a three-beat bar as she went.

The familiar middle-aged nurse appeared a few minutes later, "Ms Phillips? The doctor will see you now."

Sasha sat down in front of Dr McNally's desk, the chair still warm from the ginger-haired girls' skinny bottom.

Dr McNally was in his early fifties with thin black hair he kept short and lacquered to his head and a narrow face with hollow eyes that looked as if he had witnessed everything nature could throw at him in his chosen field of sexually transmitted diseases. In every other way he would blend into a crowd and disappear with his ordinariness but for one striking feature – he wore a distinctive large black eye patch over his right eye that always reminded Sasha of the Israeli military leader, Moshe Dayan.

There was something mysterious and threatening about Dr McNally, as if he was concealing some dreadful secret, something that Sasha always sensed about him but could never identify; it evoked an irrational fear but it was real in its abstract form like knowing by the heightened tone of silence that a beastly predator was lurking somewhere in the undergrowth through which your path was going.

"Ah Ms Phillips …" McNally mechanically scanned Sasha's notes, "Nothing to report I trust?" He looked up and Sasha could see a dark sadness and despair in his left eye where hope should thrive. He studied Sasha's face with the same level of scrutiny as that of a t'ai chi ch'uan exponent.

Sasha knew the drill but what she dreaded most was tripping McNally into one of his rants about the Lord judging her sinful ways and pleading with her to repent and take a different path.

"No Doctor, I'm fine thanks, nothing to report." She tried to appear small and timid, almost invisible.

"Um, and how long have you been doing that?" He pointed at Sasha's hand as it entwined and gently pulled thin strands of her blonde hair around her fingers.

Sasha abruptly stopped the involuntarily newly acquired habit.

"I find myself doing it off and on these days, probably a couple of weeks now I suppose."

McNally continued to read Sasha's notes as if he was searching for some important information but couldn't find it.

"Well, it's most likely the start of Trichotillomania, an impulse control disorder that involves the uncontrollable plucking of ones own hair, it's a nervous reaction – you are under some strain at the moment I believe Ms Phillips?"

"Well, no, not really, well, yes, I suppose I am Doctor, bit more than usual at any rate." Sasha was flustered and felt herself blush wondering how the doctor knew about the strain she was under.

"Well, my advice is to go and see your GP and get some help otherwise you'll end up bald as a coot." He went back to studying Sasha's notes.

Sasha looked around the room, her eyes darting left and right whilst her head stayed still like an owl. The walls were painted in the same light green distemper as the waiting room but were adorned with an impressive collection of information posters covering all the key aspects of McNally's business: 'How to distinguish between gonorrhoea and syphilis', and one announced loudly, 'HIV Tests Now Available', others explained the dangers of unprotected sex, pubic hair lice, Herpes, rectum sores and vaginal discharge. Sasha marvelled at how anyone could devote their working life to these matters and stay sane but immediately checked herself realising that this very environment might explain McNally's strange and threatening personality.

Looking down from its lofty position on the wall behind McNally was a large picture depicting Jesus with a saintly bearded face, calm and reassuring, painted to arrest your attention and alert you to a sense of earthly inadequacy and base human degradation. His serene eyes stared into your soul emphasising the urgency to reform. He was painted wearing a simple white gown that a peasant might wear, he had no jewellery or anything that suggested wealth or possession, nothing but the single gown folded over his shoulder and chest; a series of coloured rings, brilliant gold, blue and red, emanated from behind his head like bands of a rainbow stretching out across the sky to heaven and eternity. Sasha was transfixed by the picture and its power to alter her mind to something preternatural and mystical, like a drug, it spiked her consciousness into the mystery and solace of religion that she had long abandoned. She kept sneaking glances at it and felt uncomfortable under its gaze, as if Jesus was judging her and weighing up the penalty for her sins.

"Please take off your skirt and underwear and lie back with your legs bent at the knee."

McNally nudged Sasha' legs apart and adjusted his head torch to get clearer vision. "Now I'm just going to examine you internally, would you prefer that the nurse attended at this point?" He looked at her with his expressionless face, hardened by so many years of carrying out these examinations, so many years of doing the same thing and asking the same questions.

"No Doctor, it's OK." She actually would have preferred the nurse to be present but balked at the negative view she thought McNally would have of this decision.

"Very well then ..."

She felt the special tingle sensation of another human's touch but it was cold and clinical and disconnected her brain from her body's internal pleasure dome of nerve-ends; she sought a mental distraction and started to think of Weymouth and her new apartment now just a few weeks away from being a reality.

"That's OK Ms Phillips …"

She closed her eyes and saw herself walking along the seafront, it was a brilliant sunny day, the air was warm and the sky blue as the bobbing sea. She sat on the soft yellow ochre sand grainy between her fingers and rested her head back as she welcomed the spirits of the sea into her soul now finally calmed by the peace of the seaside town she had worked so hard to reside in; she sat still and at peace with herself, a deep feeling of achievement came over her, she who had given so much to achieve her ambition, and now she had arrived, now she was in situ, finally free to relax and be herself.

"Nothing wrong here, everything's as it should be …"

McNally's rubber gloved fingers stretching and tugging in the final stages of his exact, well-trained examination.

"Now please turn over and I'll check your anus and rectum cavity – this will feel cold as I'm using a gel."

Back in her imagination at Weymouth the sea lapped up to her feet and the gulls squawked and dived happy to be alive as the sun tanned her back and a wasp jived on her ice cream droppings. This is what she had dreamt about for so long, this was her heaven on earth and now she could start again, new and unknown, she could be anyone she chose – she leant back with eyes closed and drifted out to sea, the soft moving waves of her dreams, gently out, out to where silence and peace wrapped around her senses, deep as the sea.

"Now sit up please and let's have a look down your throat." McNally removed his rubber gloves, washed his hands and put on a fresh pair that made the familiar smacking sound as he tugged them on. "Say arhh, arhh – please get dressed and I will take a small blood sample and then perhaps you can take this bottle and give me a little urine before you go?"

Afterwards Sasha stood up to leave and said, "Oh by the way Doctor, the next appointment will be my last, I'm off to pastures new, you remember I mentioned it before."

McNally looked up from completing the Patient's Examination Form. "Yes, you're going to Weymouth I recall?"

He continued to fill out the form seemingly having no interest in the matter but Sasha picked up the microscopic nodes of his mood suddenly altering.

She was surprised he had remembered her plan to move to Weymouth and offered more information:

"I'm buying a little apartment down there, a new beginning, I shall sort of start again, if you know what I mean?"

She felt the awkwardness of her words and how difficult it was to explain what she was doing in casual conversation. Then it occurred to her that most people longed to get away from their routine, yearned to be free of the repetitive cycle of work, ached to be carefree by the wild windy sea. She continued, "I'm looking forward to being there so much, to fulfil myself, to make my dream come true."

McNally's tired, strained face looked up with its spooky patched right eye, menacing and hideous, and Sasha knew with one glance he was flipping into his dark, terrifying Dr Jekyll superego.

"Ms Phillips, you know I have told you before, you should reconsider your position, both your mortal body and your eternal soul are in danger doing what you do, you should reconsider your options, it's never too late to redeem yourself, to change course and move towards the light – you should stop all this sinful carnal pleasure and debauchery – tell me you will change your ways Ms Phillips, before it's too late, tell me you will turn a new leaf in Weymouth."

This was McNally's coup de grace, when he filled her head with the dread of being condemned to eternal punishment in Hell. She loathed him for this aspect of his nature and the audacity to present it during regular examinations; she felt he was going beyond his professional remit.

"Really doctor, you have no right to speak to me like that, you have no right to judge me – I'm just doing what I can for myself and my child, it's not easy out there you know."

"We all have choices to make, we are all responsible for our actions – and where is the father I wonder – I wage you he's not part of this?"

"That's none of your business doctor, none of this is your business – I know what I'm doing, what I have to do, and it's nothing to do with you …"

"It's got everything to do with me Ms Phillips, I'm here to check your physical health and that means keeping an eye on your mental health as well – you should take heed of my warning, you should change before it's too late."

The spoken threat was like a bullet between her eyes and she reeled with its impact. There was a silence long enough to reload a gun but nothing more.

"Right then, hand this form to the nurse on your way out."

He handed over the form and immediately averted eye contact looking back at his papers.

Sasha sensed the distrust and loathing that he had for her and all women of her kind. She grabbed the form and walked out with his words, 'You should change before it's too late' ringing in her ears.

Walking out onto the driveway she met Gale who was arriving for her appointment. Gale was also a call girl who preferred to work alone like Sasha but with far less scruples about her clients. Her work philosophy was, 'Take what you can get for as much as you can get', and she went anywhere the work took her, from rich Arabs in bland Heathrow hotel rooms to black gangland gangsters in sleazy back street dives in Brixton.

Sasha had met her in a late-night café in Old Spitalfield's Market near Liverpool Street station soon after she had arrived in London and was grateful for her advice on different rates of services and other tips of the trade. She lived close by to Sasha off the Kings Cross Road and had suggested they meet up for drinks once or twice but Sasha had always made excuses preferring not to establish a relationship with her or anyone else. Their paths crossed frequently and Sasha had become aware of Gale's curiosity to find out more about her personal circumstances. Somehow, and it was the strangest thing, Gale knew about Sasha's plan to move to Weymouth.

"Hi Sasha – been to see the doc? It comes round quick doesn't it? How is the old fart then?"

Sasha was still reeling from McNally's extraordinary outburst.

"Watch out, he's in one of his high holy moods, virtually told me I was on course for being cast into hell and damnation if I carry on doing this caper – he's such a religious nut, it's getting worse I reckon."

"Tell me about it – he's tried to get me to say prayers and repent, right there and then on the bloody clinic floor – I couldn't believe it, put the fear of God in me, said my soul was in danger – you don't think he's finally tossed himself off into the loony bin do ya – one too many J. Arthur Ranks?" Gale rapidly moved her hand up and down to demonstrate McNally engaged in an act of masturbation, as she did so Jenny noticed her right eye twitch – an involuntary spasm of the eyelid brought on by a combination of stress, drugs and drinking too much alcohol, the unholy triad of the call girl's lot.

"I don't know about that, I wouldn't be surprised though – how are things with you Gale?" Sasha thought Gale looked exhausted – there was something not right behind those big brown eyes, something dishonest and threatening even.

"Oh you know, the usual, can't complain, had me ups and downs so to speak, ha ha." Gale forced a dirty laugh and then suddenly said, "I suppose you'll be moving off to Weymouth soon won't you, must be getting close?"

Another shiver passed over Sasha. Se had to find out how Gale knew about Weymouth.

"Gale, how come you know about me moving, I've never mentioned it, have I?"

Gale looked surprised as if she had been caught performing some minor misdemeanour. "No, it was him wasn't it …?" She pointed towards the back of the building in the approximate direction of McNally's clinic, "… he mentioned it one day – he was talking about how close-knit all us girls are, all living round the corner from one another, seemed fascinated by it actually, then he mentioned you and said you would be leaving soon, going to Weymouth. He's a funny one alright."

Silence fell between them as a passing cloud dimmed the sun.

"We should have a drink to celebrate you moving – blimey Sasha, you must be doing alright to afford your own place, wish I was raking it in, but I ain't – don't know where it all goes, just never seem able to save anything – 'ere, do you work more nights than day jobs, is that it, more night jobs yeh, is that it?"

Sasha knew where Gale's money went, it was evident in her dark heroine stained eyes.

Sasha moved quickly off the subject, "Yeh, but you look as if you're doing alright yourself." She lied straight faced, "Look at your lovely clothes and those yellow shoes look expensive, they're leather aren't they?" Sasha smiled and stepped forward to signal her wish to move away.

"Anyway, I'd better go, can't keep the customers waiting."

Gale called out as she entered the clinic, "Don't let appearances fool you, I'm skint and it's not for lack of trying."

She gave Sasha a side look from the corner of her eye that was sly and suggested deviousness like the look a tout makes as he places your money on a hopeless bet. Sasha hurried along the pavement without looking back.

* * * * * * * *

By the time Sasha arrived back at her bedsit her thoughts were swirling around like a washing machine drum. Her brief encounter with Gale had left her curious and suspicious. She kept wondering whether Gale could be the midnight prowler. The more she pondered the idea the more senseless it seemed – why would she lurk behind parked vehicles in the middle of the night – what would be her motive? Unless she was putting someone else up to it, a boyfriend or drug dealer maybe – no, she dismissed the idea and was annoyed at her deepening paranoia; in any case there was something about the gait and build of the prowler that suggested it was a man not a women.

As the day wore on her thoughts became clearer and she began to realise that the prowler must be one of her clients. There was no other explanation as she had not made any real friends, nor enemies, nor developed any social activities since her arrival in London.

She mulled over her regular activities and habits – by necessity she had to visit the launderette and local food shops but she avoided forming friendships with people whose routines coincided with her own or with other tenants that she met occasionally.

For such brief encounters she would just say, 'Hello' and smile, seemingly too busy to stop and tarry. She discovered the wonderful silent environment of the British Museum's library and how it satisfied her need for anonymity; she visited it on a regular basis, losing herself in its bewildering choice of wonders from around the world. There she would sit in the afternoon winter shadows as it turned murky outside, reading about the treasures of ancient Egypt and Greece, or the rise and fall of the

Roman Empire, or the anthropology of African tribes, and get carried away with her little discoveries that often made the return walk along Woburn Place towards the Euston Road regret her failures at the Romford Secondary School where no teacher ever inspired her nor illuminated the joy of knowledge as much as her visits to the British Museum's library.

She sat in her room with a cup of lukewarm coffee thinking about her clients, their shape and height and who amongst them could be the midnight mystery prowler staring up at her from behind the van. The problem was the hood. She never saw the face and only had the outline of the hidden head and the general body shape to go on.

Suddenly the image of Theo came to her mind. Could it be Theo – was he the right height and shape? Yes, he did fit the shape, but he was too broody and melancholy, aloof even – no, it couldn't be Theo, he just didn't care enough about her one way or the other.

She racked her brains going through the list of her clients checking their physique and personalities and whether any of them had ever given signs of infatuation or possessiveness. Then a client called Kevin came to mind who she visited twice a month over in Carnegie Street off the Caledonian Road; he was an Irishman from Tralee and was always waxing lyrical about the old country and the beautiful Purple Mountain and how one day he would return for sure. Kevin couldn't keep his hands off her and always wanted to take matters beyond the boundaries of a business arrangement, slobbering her with kisses and caresses that she forbade as too serious and personal. More than once she had to remind him of her 'statute of limitations' that did not allow for such intimacies but still he persisted, attempting French kissing and love-biting her neck. If any of her clients could become infatuated with her it was Kevin for he always suggested going out to dances and night clubs and wanted to know what she had been doing since their previous meeting; she thought about his body shape, tracing it over the image of the mystery man held in her mind's eye – but he was a bit too tall and chunky and walked more slowly and deliberately like John Wayne – no it was not a good match; in any case he was constantly telling her of his exploits at the local gym working-out on the body-building apparatus and boasting about the women he had picked-up and got into his bed, 'As easy as taking a rattle from a baby's pram.' She did wonder why he kept paying for her services if his conquests with women were so numerous. Then a picture of Kevin's nude body came to mind and she wondered how someone with such an impressive physique could ever feel inferior. Men built like that never feel small, far from it, they usually go through life with a swagger and arrogance, not needing to commit to anyone in particular, for they know their self-confidence is irresistible to women. No, all things considered, she concluded, it couldn't be Kevin, he just wasn't lonely or desperate enough.

She went through images of all her clients, as if looking through a police file of criminal mug shots, a parade of disparate men of various ages and sizes, colours and backgrounds, and tried to match them with their personalities; alas it was a hopeless task with too many imponderables. She thought of Banjoko and Eberhardt but they were both giants and plodded around slow and heavy like elephants. She did remember that Banjoko had let slip that he knew where she lived and that puzzled her, but he may have seen her in Werrington Street by chance or she may have mentioned it in some context. No, it was neither of those two Goliaths for sure.

Her thoughts eventually settled on Yusuf. It had been nearly three years since their fling in Somalia and she had only heard from him on the one occasion when he had written telling her about the accident in the jeep. She had written him several times and finally with details of her current address but he had never responded. Could the midnight prowler be Yusuf? No, it made no sense, his prolonged silence had to be due to his carefree lifestyle in sunny Somalia with its constant supply of women. No, it wasn't likely he would throw away all that for a shackled life of fatherly commitment in cold, rainy London Town.

Sitting in silent complexity, long enough for the light to darken the shade on the wall, she suddenly made up her mind. She was going to lay in wait outside, that very night, hidden behind the dustbins in the side alleyway. She would squat there for as long as it took and confront the mystery pest. She would settle things once and for all and pluck this cursed thorn out of her backside. She had one client later in the afternoon and two more in the evening. She would be back by midnight and then she would prepare herself and get into position outside. It was a drastic plan but she had a determined, obstinate nature that once pushed over the limit would turn her into Boadicea the warrior.

Her last client was in Camden, a middle aged Polish man called Nacek who had been obsessed with sketching her, Degas style, occupied with her ablutions de toilettes; he was particularly fond of seeing her undress and bending over an old wooden chair with her arse up in the air. He had made several charcoal sketches of her thus engaged that captured her beautifully formed bone structure as well as her natural alluring coquettishness. He showed her the sketches and she asked to keep one of her standing with her right hand on her right hip and her head slightly tilted to the left and her mousy hair draped down over her shoulders. He said it showed her inner mystery and strength. She kept staring at it enthralled at seeing her own image reproduced so professionally on paper. He said she could keep it in lieu of a twenty per cent discount to the ten pounds hourly session. She was flattered by the evocative sketch and agreed to the discount. The session was completed with her kneeling in front of him performing oral sex whilst he groaned, a long continuous throat rattling noise that shifted seamlessly from ecstasy to pain until it was over. Afterwards she felt nothing, it was cold, joyless work. She left Nacek's flat at twelve minutes past eleven and scurried back to her bedsit to carry out her plan to confront the prowler.

She arrived back in her room at eleven thirty-five fully focussed on her plan of action. She moved swiftly and within minutes she was dressed in black tight leotards and a black Lycra gym top, looking like a member of the elite Special Operations Forces, ready for her alleyway sortie.

By eleven fifty she was sitting behind an arrangement of dustbins in the shadows of the little alleyway that ran along the side of the building. She had left the front door ajar in case she needed to make a hasty retreat. Now it was just a waiting game and Sasha was good at waiting.

As she sat still and silent the hushed night closed in around her, gentle and soft, like slow rising mist across a moor, fanning against her cheeks as the distant sounds of the Euston Road traffic and the clanking of the great Euston railway terminal eased into their unobtrusive night-time mode. A door opened and closed, a cat meowed and two dogs barked insults at each other somewhere nearby. At one point she heard her telephone ring through the open window above.

By twelve-thirty it got quieter still, just the occasional car going by and a window being opened to let the cool June night air into some stuffy room close-by. She sat and waited. Her leg muscles became stiff with lack of movement and the ischium bone in her backside jarred with numbness. She changed her leg position at more regular intervals. The moon came out from paper-thin clouds pushed silently forward by a lazy western breeze.

It was about twelve-forty when she heard footsteps moving up level to her building and stopping. She moved her head slightly to the right, squinting through the gap between two bins, out across the road to the vehicles parked in their usual positions. Standing behind the favoured white van was the hooded figure, slightly crouched and mostly hidden but unmistakable. She felt as though she had caught a rat whose scratching noises had driven her mad for weeks. She took a sharp intake of breath and the adrenaline pumped through her blood causing her heartbeat to accelerate so much she could feel it pressing against her ribcage tightened by the Lycra top.

She kept her eye trained on the figure who kept staring up at Sasha's window. The moment had come. The night was as still as a clearing in a remote wood, so quiet that time seemed to stop. The scene was set. Sasha suddenly stood up, knocking one of the bins, she rushed out into the road. The hooded figure was taken completely by surprise and froze like a petrified body at Pompeii. Sasha came to within three feet of the figure and halted. Still she could not make out the face within the hood.

"Hey, what are you doing here, who the hell are you?" Sasha knew she could have shouted louder and with more aggression but for some reason exercised constraint in deference to the hour and not wishing to disturb her neighbours' peace; above all she wanted to pull down the hood and reveal the mystery figure's identity.

The figure had not moved but remained with its head slightly bent forward so the face was obscured within the hood.

She stepped slowly forward with one hand stretched out to pull up the hood but as she did so the mystery prowler raised his right arm and sent something hard like a cosh crashing against the side of her head. It was done as quick as a snake's bite and there was no time for defence or retaliation. She felt a needle of pain go through her head and then the shutters at the sides closed as her vision blacked-out and she collapsed onto the pavement, bent over like a pillow bolster, her head smashing against the edge of the kerb, the thud sounding like a cauliflower being hit with a hammer, and a thin trickle of blood seeped from under her head.

Chapter Seven

Theo finally got back to the Royal Victoria Hotel in Sheffield as the nearby clock tower struck six o'clock. He felt faint with exhaustion as he trudged across reception to the lifts, diminished by the day's extraordinary events.

Once in his room he immediately gulped down a small bottle of water left by his bed and then staggered over to the little table by the window and sat there in a semi-fevered daze, with his notebook and the telephone at the ready, waiting for the mental strength to call Tubby. His mind kept wandering as if he was nodding off to sleep but it wasn't sleep that closed in on him, more like delirium that was taking hold.

He looked out at the great Sheffield City landscape all around and felt its dark, bleak mood suppress his senses. He sat back feeling woozy and dejected, staring at the abandoned, decaying remnants of what was once the manufacturing centre of the world, and mourned the passing of its glorious industrial epoch. His weary eyes scanned the soot grimed cityscape, the disused office buildings and derelict warehouses and remnants of the steel works ubiquitous down the main street and side roads, all now empty, leaving just the ghosts of hell-fire smelters, forges and steel rolling works, the myriad of steel plants once engaged in refining and manufacturing, in making things of quality to supply the demand for specialised tools, drills and dies, for cutlery and ships and railway track and tramways and guns and cars and everything else that spat out from the furnace of the industrial revolution – useful, essential things of steel made with precision to a quarter of a thousandth of an inch in exactness; all the plant and all the workers and their expertise now gone and replaced with nothing that would last, nothing you could grip with your fist, just a faceless service industry that was little more than a soufflé ready to flop from the whims of market forces.

His eyes felt heavy and his mind was slowly closing down. Everywhere he looked, everything he saw, seemed to have a dark shadow over it, all the old order that had been established over decades was now vitiated and social deprivation and misery was impregnating every street and building like a poisonous gas.

The whole country was afflicted by a creeping malady and everywhere the tyranny of bad Government was turning it upside down with its inane ideology and its crass assertion that there was no such thing as society; but the biggest sin of all was the unpardonable indictment of one million and two hundred thousand youngsters with no work and without the life blood of hope. A nasty lump formed in his throat as he thought of Tubby, the Government and his role in propagating their mendacious claptrap that it was all being done for the good of the people.

He sat for some time staring out the window as the sun started its long arc down towards the western sky waiting with streaking pinkish orange tones in anticipation. His mind was becoming more erratic as it kept wandering back to the shameful scenes he had witnessed in the field next to the Coking Plant – the way the miners were herded into it like cattle, penned in and then set upon mercilessly by the police, bludgeoned without caution, baton-beaten to their knees just for staging their usual rendition of a slightly over-zealous protest.

The vile bloody scenes flicked through his brain – the thundering hooves of the police horses, the miners running in all directions and their reverberating screams bellowing out like smoke from steam engines, the wielded police truncheons bearing down again and again like piston rods, the marauding snatch-squads like crazed blood-hounds mercilessly pursuing their unarmed quarry, and the sheer misery of the miners, their hope stubbed into the earth like cigarette butts, all alone, dazed, puzzled and defeated.

He had always been guided by rational thought and an ingrained unquestionable loyalty to law and order but what he had witnessed at Orgreave turned everything upside down, all the pillars of his temple to fairness and decency, to civilized behaviour and justice had been splintered and scattered across the battle field like the miners' broken banners. He felt a growing nausea rising inside driven by an acute sense of shame; he was ashamed of the establishment that paid him to promote its corrupt versions of fairness and decency; he was shocked that it could commit such violent acts that were an affront to his creed of what is right and what is wrong. Right should always prevail over wrong, he had been taught it from the nipple, it was the marrow in the bones of decent folk and it mattered. Honesty, veracity and integrity mattered. He was embarrassed to be part of the sham. A nasty lingering vision was left in his mind and it would not budge – it was the realization that the whole despicable scene was all part of a well orchestrated plan involving the police, the NUM, the media and most alarming of all, the Government, his paymasters. He kept asking the same question over and again:

'So if the Government is part of it, how high up the corridors of power does it go?' He then thought again of Tubby's words, 'Those miners will be given a bloody nose.'

Tubby surely knew more than he had let on, there was an official agenda, and if Tubby had his orders then those orders came from the Government, they came from the very top. A sharp shudder went down his spine and he exhaled deeply to restore his equilibrium. His emotions were like a pinball pinging from one sensation to another without time to stop and reflect. Then the weight of responsibility pressed down on him and he put his head in his hands and gently squeezed his temples. He had to phone Tubby, it was time to make his report but his mind was lacking clarity, it was confused, almost frazzled, he felt hot and unsteady and he didn't have a clue what to say.

He poured a glass of warm Chardonnay from an inadequately stocked mini-bar and resumed his seat by the window but he could not focus on his report. He looked out the window once again, and the same dreary scene stared back. The wine exaggerated his senses and he started to feel angry – he closed his eyes and swore out loud, "You shit heads!"

He took another sip of wine and tried to concentrate on what he was going to say to Tubby. Instead an image of Imogen appeared before him, from nowhere, sitting on the bed with her icy blue eyes and beautiful pale face leaning back naked, a slender shape of pinky-white skin, soft and sweet like coconut syrup, speaking in that slow bored way she had, 'Come on Theo, come over here, I want to feel you, I want to hold your …' Her voice petered out as she leant back pouting her thin lips, her body arched and waiting …

"Fuck off Imogen!" Theo shouted at the empty bed.

He was feeling flushed and bothered and started to drift from reality to hallucination and back again; through the mire of mental muddle came Tubby's voice yet again, back through the smog of time and the awful events at Orgreave came his strict, no-nonsense command. His brain flickered and fell into early unconsciousness. There was Tubby sitting at his huge office desk with his enormous cigar held in his stubby little hand. There he was swivelling around in his ludicrously large chair and puffing out billows of bluish toxic cigar smoke between growls of anxious directives like Churchill in his war bunker during operation Overlord – 'Listen here Harrison. I want a summary and some suggestions of how we can nail these miners, some quick catchy phrases that the Prime Minister's speech writers can use to harden public opinion once and for all.'

He shouted at the image as if it was real, "Fuck off Tubby, you fat lying toad!"

He was entering into the early stages of delirium as he shouted at the ghost of Tubby appearing through the hotel room wall like a scene from Polanski's film *Repulsion*. There was Tubby's face before him real as a stubbed toe and he reeled at the horror of it – 'Do you hear me Harrison, this is important, I want you to follow the action, all of it, from beginning to end, and report back – have you got that Harrison?'

Theo saw Tubby for what he was, a key player in the establishment's cruel game to break the unions, a key player in the Government's secret scheme to bring in monetarist policies and the privatisation of industries – Tubby and his department were the mouthpiece, the tannoy to broadcast the official propaganda to persuade public opinion and transform society for ever.

Theo's mouth dropped and his jaw froze as the full force of this subterfuge hit his consciousness like a paperweight on his toe. He was part of the Government's Lie Machine, he was being paid to provide the slogans, the lies, his job was to lie, he was an official liar – it was all a lie and pulling the strings was the Prime Minister, she was the enemy with a smiling face and a posh power-suit, the sharp-toothed wolf in a cloak of respectability, the disguised dismantler of society's infrastructure and institutions that have stood for decades, she was the real enemy, the hidden enemy, the enemy within.

Angry, hot, confused and swaying with fatigue and dehydration he peered at Tubby's business card; he had to phone the direct line and get the whole sordid thing over and done with, he had to phone now, it was overdue. He dialled the number.

"Trubshaw speaking."

"Hello Sir, it's Harrison, me, Sir, it's me ..."

"Where the hell have you been Harrison, I expected your call this afternoon?" Theo could hear Tubby's spittle and he knew he was puffing on a cigar.

" ... everywhere, all over the field, you know, the field by the Coking Plant, all the miners, everywhere Sir ..."

"Yes, yes I know where it all took place – you should've phoned hours ago, whole office been left dangling in suspense, well, anyway, I've seen the first newsreel rushes from the BBC – what a rabble, a nasty mob of commies for sure, police did well to restrain them hey what?"

There was more spittle and some puffing from Tubby's end of the phone. "Well anyway, look Harrison, I've got to report back to HQ this evening, we need to advise the Prime Minister on what line to take, I've got a good idea from the newsreel but I need a catchy slogan, something memorable, a powerful strapline, you know, something to nail the bastards – what have you come up with Harrison? Give me some ideas." More sounds of spittle and some papers being shuffled.

Theo sank in the chair so his neck rested awkwardly on the back support whilst his backside was practically falling off the seat. " … long day Sir, so many terrible things, the police, they were – you know, the police were smashing the miners – knocking them around like skittles – Maggie's Boot Boys …"

"What are you mumbling about Harrison, you're not making sense, of course the police were defending the right of the lorry drivers to go about their lawful business, what were you expecting, a tea party on the lawn? What have you got?" Tubby's voice was now growling with impatience.

Theo's eyes were starting to blink and close. "She's changing everything isn't she, pulling it all apart, the threads and stitches of society are coming undone, never be put back again, like Humpty Dumpty Sir, pieces can't go back again, she's the one isn't she, the one pulling the strings, pulling you and me, she's the enemy Sir, the enemy within …"

Theo was hot and his eyes heavy with the will to finally close, the room was moving around like a slow turning carousel at a fun fair.

"I can't make out what you are saying Harrison, have you caught the sun or something, what the hell are you muttering about – but I get your drift about the enemy, now that's a powerful image Harrison, yes, I'm getting that very clearly, yes, yes, 'The Enemy Within" yes, I can work on that – it makes good sense."

Theo continued in a sort of semi-conscious stupor, " … we mustn't allow it Sir, she can't get away with it, she's the silent enemy, she doesn't share the values of the people she serves, she's forcing her way against their wishes, she's going against parliamentary democracy – she's undermining the rule of Law, we mustn't allow it Sir, have to stop her and her cabinet …" The room was a fairground and he was on a merry-go-round, riding on a wooden horse to the sound of a steam powered organ.

"Harrison, this is a bad line, sounds like you are talking gibberish, remember it has to make sense, but I'm picking up on some good ideas, yes, there's some good leads here, I've just got to pull it together, now give me a second …" A large puffing sound replaced Tubby's voice and his cigar smoke almost oozed out of Theo's phone.

"Yes, yes, how's this Harrison, 'Giving in to the miners would be surrendering the rule of parliamentary democracy to the rule of the mob', or how about, 'The rule of Law must prevail over the rule of the mob' – how's that sound Harrison? Makes a lot of sense eh what?"

Theo was dipping in and out of consciousness as he whirled around, up and down, to the fairground Wurlitzer, sliding ever nearer to the edge of the chair.

Tubby went on, "And oh yes, that bit about the enemy, let me see, yes, we must get the people to see the union leaders as 'The enemy within' who don't share the values of the great British public – that's good, I'll work in something about the Falklands, always a winner with the public, something along the lines of, 'We had to fight the enemy without in the Falklands – we now have to fight the enemy within' bla bla – yes, yes

Harrison that's quite promising, I know she will be pleased with that – it makes sense, anything else?"

"... not right, the police – the police violence, sudden, awful, everywhere, the police, to blame, the police, right to the top, a conspiracy ..."

Theo was fading out as round and round went the bloody pictures of Orgreave, getting smaller and smaller, like water swirling down a sink – round and round went the fading images, the police baton charging, the miners felled to the ground, blood in hair, blood on faces, everyone running in all directions, the snatch-squads, truncheons smashing against flesh, more blood, misery, all planned, a conspiracy from the very top. He was feeling fainter and through the window Sheffield's bleak empty industrial landscape was fading, round and round went the images, his eye pupils dilated as the lids blinked rapidly to close.

"You know Harrison that really is quite good, 'The Enemy Within' – really quite good." Tubby was in his own dream world. It makes sense Harrison, you know it has to make sense."

" ... a conspiracy Sir, I don't believe it, any of it, the police had their orders, must have been planned, must have come from the top, from her, planned for weeks, miners were lambs to the slaughter – I don't feel too good Sir, got to close my ..."

"Yes, yes Harrison of course, have a nap, take the rest of the week off, you've earned a break – get away from it all, come back next Monday, let Imogen know ..." Tubby hung-up.

Theo slid off the chair flat out on the floor. With his nose against the carpet he could smell the distilled essence of the room's recent history, all the previous occupants, their perfume and after-shave, their shower gel, their leather shoes, their sweat, their sex, and all the minute components picked up from the teaming mass of humanity down in the streets. He slowly closed his eyes to narrow slits like archers' openings in castle walls and remained still, peering at the table legs and the green floral wallpaper styled on William Morris' classic designs. The air was still with tiny dust particles floating in random pattern like minute Chinese lanterns and behind, out through the slightly opened sash window, the purr of road traffic gently hummed away like a lawn mower idling on low revs. His eyes closed.

He slept for two hours spread-eagled on the hotel room floor by the window. He awoke to find the telephone in his hand and several questions in his head. Light rain pattered against the window as if it was falling to cleanse the land. Then he gradually remembered his disjointed report and the extraordinary phone call to Tubby.

"Oh my God, I was talking rubbish – he completely got hold of the wrong end of the stick."

Then the key phrases came back to him, smashed back into place in his thick head like rivets pounded by a steam-hammer: 'The Rule of the Mob' and 'The Enemy Within.'

He held his head as if to keep it steady, to stop it falling off with guilt and shame.

"No, no, he's got it wrong, I never meant it that way – Oh shit."

He undressed and showered, a long lingering shower to revive and purge him of the callous violence and brutal injustice he had witnessed. He stood motionless for several minutes to let the warm clear water run through his sweat-knotted hair, over his face and shoulders and down his body to cleanse him of any traces of the foul day, a day that upset the natural order of things, a day that disturbed the balance of his mind.

He was hungry and decided to go and have dinner on expenses. He flicked on the TV whilst he dressed.

Into the room came a special BBC's news bulletin showing images of the miners' plight at Orgreave that very day; the reporter was calling it, 'The Battle of Orgreave.' Theo stopped putting on his socks and sat on the bed to watch – the film showed the miners throwing missiles at the police who then charged them on horseback in what looked like plausible retaliation. Theo finished the glass of wine in disbelief.

"It didn't happen like that, that's not right, it was the other way round." He shouted at the TV, puzzled and shocked.

"It was the other way round, the police charged the miners first – that's what happened."

Then an image of a miner being beaten over the head by a police officer quickly flashed onto the screen but it was deliberately shown following the altered sequence of the police being attacked by stone throwing miners as if to justify the level of police violence, as if to say, 'Look, under such violent provocation when the police were set upon by a bunch of out of control trouble-making rioters, it was completely reasonable, they had to retaliate with force.' Theo could not believe what he was seeing and yelled at the TV:

"This is the BBC for Christ's sake, not some tin-pot banana state broadcasting propaganda bullshit – what the hell's happening to this country?"

The news bulletin continued with a succession of images showing miners apparently "rampaging" about, shouting and punching the air, depicting them as a pack of fierce, anti-social extremists; other images showed the police in an apparent stance of self-defence, hitting back at the miners with their truncheons and then more scenes of exhausted looking police officers, bent over double and injured in some way, whilst there were only one or two images of miners bleeding from their wounds. The whole news bulletin had been carefully edited to show the police acting in a noble and courageous response to a wild, anarchist mob.

The news report finished with images of some miners being arrested and pushed into waiting wagons. Then the cameras moved over to the road to show the fleet of lorries leaving the Coking Plant on their way to the Scunthorpe Power Station, triumphant and unhindered.

"A victory for the police, for the people and democracy." claimed the news presenter.

Theo stood in front of the TV wearing an unbuttoned shirt and one sock whilst holding the other, in a state of utter disbelief. He kept staring at the TV screen with his sense of decency and honour crumbling piece by piece.

Then the Assistant Chief Constable of South Yorkshire Police was talking to the camera in stern and serious tones, exact and precise like a military commander trotting out statistics:

"I had 4,600 officers from 18 different forces at my disposal, including 186 police support units, whose role is to break up public disorder." He was asked about the snatch squads and he said, "There were 345 men in riot gear including short, round shields and truncheons – the first time they had been used on British mainland. It was also the first time that police in riot gear with the long, plastic shields had ever been deployed in South Yorkshire."

Then, as he spoke, as if to reinforce his final statement, repeated images of missile throwing miners beamed out. He continued:

"This was a battle and the police were the victims of violent rioters and responded only proportionately. It is everyone's right to engage in peaceful protest and demonstration but what happened here today went beyond that and the police had to deal with anarchy and violent factions of the far left hell-bent on causing maximum disruption to those going about their lawful business of providing energy to the country and maximum violence to the police whose purpose was to keep law and order. No one looking at these scenes today can say the police did not respond reasonably and with great constraint, I applaud my brave officers for their fine work."

The news bulletin finished with a final picture of an injured policeman being helped to his feet by three fellow officers. Theo turned off the TV and stood looking at the blank screen for several seconds thinking he might still be hallucinating.

He finished dressing in a state of perplexity at the twisted BBC's news bulletin transmitted into every home in the land. He sat staring out the window, tired and disturbed, his mood dark-blue indigo like the fading sky and oncoming night outside.

Just then the telephone rang. "Yes? Hello?" Theo whispered the half-hearted salutation.

"Theo? Is that you? It's Imogen. How are you? Tubby said to give you a call to make sure you were alright – he said you sounded a bit odd before – hello, Theo, are you there?"

Theo said in a feather-soft voice that might have gone straight past the average person's eardrum undetected, "Imogen? What's wrong?"

"Is that you Theo, can hardly hear you – nothing wrong this end, well, not really I suppose, apart from Cadgers going around earlier today, when Tubby was getting in a bit of a funk over not hearing from you, making mischief, you know Cadgers, he's always ready to put the boot in if there's an opportunity, it's part of his breeding isn't it?"

Theo had a stream of surreal images flash before him of Cadgers and Tubby doing a sort of Red Indian war dance, hopping from one foot to the other, from one office to another, holding imaginary tomahawks, and chanting as they patted their lips with their fingers, 'Woo woo woo woo.'

"What are you saying Imogen, what mischief was Cadgers making?" Theo's head was beginning to hurt again.

"Oh nothing really, you know Cadgers, he was saying that he should have done the assignment at Orgreave, that he would have had the report in on time, I'm sure it was all harmless fun really."

"Doesn't sound like it – what did Tubby say?" In his mind's eye Theo could see Cadger's face turn purple and his eyes pop wide open as he squeezed the bastard's throat with one hand and tightened his grip around his balls with the other.

"Oh Theo, I shouldn't really be telling you all this, I only 'phoned 'cos Tubby told me to – well, at first Tubby kept pacing up and down as the afternoon went by and the more it went by the more he paced up and down, I must say, the names he was calling you in the end would make a sailor blush – kept saying none of it made sense, you know how he keeps saying that about everything …"

"What else, carry on Imogen, it's OK."

Theo imagined Imogen cuddle up to him as he put his arm around her, her soft hair nuzzled beneath his chin warm and silky and her large eyes staring out, vacant and signifying nothing – he mused how odd it was that simple minded women hold such fascination with men.

"Well, Cadgers kept talking out loud, you know, as if he was talking to the filing cabinets, just mouthing off to himself really, about how he should have had the assignment and how unreliable you are, not the right man for the job, that sort of thing – said something about you being a commie underneath it all and your heart not in the job, can't think what he meant really, we all thought he was out of order, just an opportunist taking advantage of your situation, whatever situation you were in, none of us knew exactly you see, that was the problem really – can you tell if someone's a commie I wonder, underneath it all, I mean, does it show, you know, like you can if someone's a Jew, he, he, he – sorry that was a bit naughty wasn't it, he, he?"

"Don't be ludicrous Imogen, just tell me what else he said?" Theo's impatience was clear.

"Sorry Theo, but all this business is making my back ache again, you know how I suffer with my back – anyway, Tubby heard Cadger's rant, most of it anyway, he must of done 'cos he kept coming out and pacing around, but he didn't say anything directly to Cadgers, just that everything had to make sense and it didn't, in the end Penton-Fox told Cadgers to shut up – then we heard Tubby's phone ring and it was you – can't tell you what a relief that was – we heard him talking to you but couldn't work out what was being said, sounded disjointed, none of it made much sense actually, no, I mean it really didn't, but Tubby was happy afterwards, he kept saying you've 'nailed it', over and over again, 'Harrison's only gone and nailed it', he kept saying. Then he sat down with me and dictated some copy for the Prime Minister that I had to type up and get over to No10 straightaway by bike – it was all a big to-do. Cadgers didn't say anything after that, looked a bit disappointed actually."

Imogen stopped to take breath, surprised at how much her brain was churning out considering she didn't know what she was going to say when Tubby had told her to make the telephone call.

"I see, what else? What was it Tubby dictated?" Theo dreaded confirmation of what he knew was going to be the substance of Tubby's advice to the Prime Minister.

"Oh I can't remember it all, something about 'The rule of the mob' and 'The enemy' doing something or other – not sure." There was a long pause that suggested a degree of introspection at both ends.

Then Imogen said, "Are you still there Theo? Are you alright? Tubby said you were not feeling OK, are you alright now?"

"No, not really, I feel a bit rough, look, was that it – is there anything else you can remember?" Theo didn't know which was greater, his hunger or his tiredness. There was another long pause.

"Oh, Suzie was asking after you, quite a lot actually. Are you sure you're OK Theo, you sound a bit odd, not your usual self?"

Imogen's voice never altered its tone, not by a single quaver, to accompany the different levels of concern she expressed.

"Actually Imogen I feel sick, sick of it all, so much dishonesty behind everything, got to go, I'm really hungry, I'll phone you –

Oh, by the way, I won't be in for the rest of the week, Tubby's idea, back on Monday, thanks for calling, I'll be OK, mind your back, bye."

Theo hung up. He was confused and knew he had some important decisions to make about his job and his life, he didn't know which way to turn and felt lost.

"Sodding little Cadgers, sodding Tubby, bunch of bloody liars the lot of 'em."

Determined hunger pangs were rising up from his stomach and sending out clear orders for curry chicken madras with garlic rice, mango chutney and a chapatti. He licked his dry lips cracked by an afternoon under the Orgreave sun.

He grabbed his wallet and bag and was about to leave the room when by some instinct he switched on the TV again. The same news channel appeared and the Prime Minister was talking to the camera solemnly and earnestly about 'The Battle of Orgreave' – a tag that she had now adopted as the official description.

"This is unacceptable, what we have got is an attempt to substitute the rule of the mob for the rule of law, and it must not succeed. There are those who are using violence and intimidation to impose their will on others who do not want it – the rule of law must prevail over the rule of the mob."

Theo's eyes opened wide as a tunnel. " My God – they got her on there quick enough, bloody unbelievable– and all that stuff about 'the rule of the mob' is mine, taken out of context from my rant to Tubby."

The Prime Minister continued, "We had to fight the enemy without in the Falklands – we always have to be aware of the enemy within, which is much more difficult to fight and more dangerous to liberty – this is mob violence by anarchist elements – violence and intimidation are unacceptable and an affront to both our civil and criminal law – we cannot allow the hooligan mob to beat us."

Theo couldn't take his eyes off the screen as the Prime Minister's words trotted out as if she was reading a cue-card held up by Tubby off-camera; every word he had mumbled to Tubby was now dropping out of the Prime Minister's mouth one by one like pellets of regurgitated bile.

On and on went the Prime Minister, "Scargill's shock troops cannot succeed – the miners' leader was making the country witness an attempt at preventing democracy."

Then the screen switched to the Chairman of the Police Federation, who was earnestly praising his gallant and brave police officers, going about their dangerous work to protect society's decent and law-abiding public from, "the militant miners." There seemed no end to the establishment's shameful conspiracy and their tissue of lies.

Theo could take no more and turned off the TV.

He felt sick at heart. The country was being manipulated and drip-fed lies. The Prime Minister was lying, the Police hierarchy was lying, the BBC was lying, Tubby was lying, Cadgers was lying – the whole rotten lot of them was a cesspit of lies and distortion, it was invidious and corrupt, its lack of integrity glaring like a boil on the end of a nose.

This sudden realisation that he was part of a disreputable Government made him feel shabby and dishonest and in that moment he loathed himself nearly as much as he despised the remit of his office; his resentment gnawed away at his nerves as he banged the door behind him, clenching his teeth, his mind full of doubt and his stomach empty as a sock.

An hour later he was leaning back in a comfortable padded chair in the Akabar Indian restaurant on a side street in the City Centre, sipping a glass of Cote de Rhone, listening to the dream-inducing voice of Lata Mangeskhar beaming out of two wall speakers, his throat tingling with sparkling spices and flavours from his meal.

He resolved to accept Tubby's offer and take a few days off, to find a place away from it all, somewhere different from all the lousy familiarity and detached from all the sordid lies and deceit that crept from underneath everything – he would go on a short break to France and find a little hotel near Boulogne or Calais just for the hell of it, to try and restore some peace to his mind.

He suddenly had a vision of staying in an old fashioned hotel in a little seaside French town where time stood still, peaceful and undemanding, gulls squawking on rooftops and the smell of fresh bread and Gaulloise cigarettes riding on soft sea sprayed breezes. He drank some more wine and his thoughts began to glow in a more positive direction. He had made his decision.

Tomorrow he would return to his London bedsit, spend the day organising himself and getting ready for the short break to France – he quickly ran through in his mind the key things he needed to do – sort out his laundry, pack a bag, check the train and ferry times, dig out his road map of Northern France, exchange some cash for French francs – the decision had been quick and impetuous but it excited him and anyway he didn't care a damn about anything. The days' extraordinary events had changed him in a fundamental way and he knew he couldn't stay working as a press officer for the Tory party for much longer, he just couldn't square it with his conscience, the job demanded his soul and that he would not give. He would sit by the sea in France and sort out his future. With his mind made up he finished the glass of wine and for the first time that day a sort of contentment smoothed his creased senses as he stared vacantly at a wilting rose in a glass vase on the table.

On the way back to the hotel he bought a bottle of Cote de Rhone having got a taste for it at the Akabar. Once in his room, he turned down the lights and sat in the chair by the window drinking the wine and mulling over the day's events one more time as he stared at the cityscape now draped in its nightgown below; then he turned his imagination to his visit to France and wondered what adventures lay ahead.

By midnight he was more than ready for bed, got undressed, did a strip-wash at the sink and started to feel horny. Something to do with the warm soapy water, he could not tell, but the sensation caught him by surprise and he mused over this odd unpredictable urge that was peculiar to man, the beast that could strike from the shadows at any moment night or day. Then, as he put his T-shirt on he thought of Sasha, the goddess of sex, the provider of carnal pleasure without commitment. The wine had removed any remnants of common sense that had survived the day's ordeal at Orgreave and now he was sitting on the bed by the phone, horny, sozzled and irrational.

He convinced himself he had to speak to Sasha and arrange to see her back in London, before he went off to France. It was rash and lacked good judgement – normally his hallmark, but this was no ordinary day and it was late and he wasn't thinking with his head but with something lower down his body. It was an impetuous plan but the beast was demanding and impatient and reason didn't come into it.

He got a direct line and dialled Sasha's number, it rang several times and finally clicked with Sasha's voice at the other end sounding soft and sleepy.

"Yes? Who is it?"

"Sasha? It's me, Theo, now to see you, tomorrow, on my place, tomorrow evening, got to …"

"Theo! It's late, what are you doing, I was asleep, couldn't you have waited until the morning? You sound pissed." She was annoyed and it showed.

"Ah, good observation, I shouldn't imbibe so copiously should I? But don't get cross Sasha, you know I care you loads of, worried about you, in there out of it, you living hand to mouth so to speak – he, he, he, get it, hand to mouth, he, he."

"Stop being silly Theo and go to bed."

Theo felt disappointed, his impulsive plan was dissolving like ice cubes in the sun, together with his wits, "Yes, I suppose, but so much has happened today, all the bastards, pack of lies all of it, I've been thinking of you long and hard, ha, ha, get it, long and hard, ha, ha, no, I mean, when I think of you long and hard ha, ha – I must see you – what there was it like tonight, no, I mean, what was it like there tonight – sort of – but Cadgers' little prick, no, Cadgers is a little prick, you're right, mustn't cast nasturtiums I mean aspersions …"

"Theo, you're drunk, I can't understand you, call me tomorrow." Sasha hung up leaving him unfulfilled and embarrassed.

He got into the big lonely double bed and sighed, "It doesn't matter I suppose, nothing really matters." Then he was gone, sliding away from the turmoil of the long tormenting day, down the tunnel of sleep to nothingness.

* * * * * * * *

Next morning Theo somehow managed to catch the eight-forty train to London and arrived back at his Islington bedsit at eleven-thirty. He felt groggy from a hangover but with his better judgement restored, and the prospect of a short break in France ahead he quickly got into his stride. The rest of the day he spent organising his trip and found time to get over to London Bridge station where he bought advance return rail and ferry tickets to Calais via Dover as well as some French francs from a Bureau de Change kiosk on the Charing Cross Road – at six o'clock he was back in Islington, showered and dressed and feeling moderately excited about getting away from everything and having time to think things through, about himself and his future. He was conscious however of a splinter of remorse sticking in his memory over the inappropriate phone call he had made to Sasha the night before; the more he remembered the ludicrous conversation the more he wanted to hide away in shame.

"I'll call her later maybe, yes later."

Just then the phone rang and he hurried off to the landing to answer it.

"Theo? It's Suzanne – how are you – been missing you in the office, but you're back now from that place up north, Sheffield was it – must have been ghastly, you poor thing, all those miners fighting everyone, Ooogh."

"Suzie? Well this is a surprise – what's up?" Images of his last encounter with Suzanne paraded before him – her writhing body pressed against his whilst they smooched around his room.

"Wondered what you were doing tonight – I'm in The Hawley Arms in Camden, ghastly place, full of dirty old men who read The Guardian, sitting here all by myself – fancy a drink?" The truth was that Suzanne had been stood-up and had had one too many glasses of wine as she waited in vain for her date.

"I thought you liked The Hawley Arms? Look Suzie I'm not good company, had a rough time up in Sheffield …"

"Oh come on Theo, you can tell me all about it over a drink – things have been happening at the office too, come on, just one drink, or two, ya?."

"No Suzie, really, I'm knackered and feeling a bit low, besides I've got to be up early in the morning – I'm off to France for a few days."

There was the distinct sound of wine being slurped at Suzanne's end, then she said, "Just one drink Theo – come on, rescue me from this tedium." More slurping sounds.

"Not this time Suzie – besides, don't you have your interview with MacGregor tomorrow – you will have to have your wits about you for that, better get an early night, that's my advice, there's a time to play and a time to work Suzie, that's what my old Mum used to say." Theo really wanted to know more about what had been happening in the office.

"Ooogh Theo, that's so sweet, you talking about your old Mum like that, gosh, sounds like something from Oliver Twist Ooogh – not sure whether Mummy would ever understand me calling her 'my old Mum' Ooogh – anyway, what's that you say about MacGregor? Oh you know about that do you? Well, look Theo, thanks to all your good work and the Prime Minister's statements, the public can see that the problem with this pesky strike is with the miners isn't it, look at all the press coverage we've had over the past twenty-four hours showing people how violent the picket lines can be stopping ordinary miners going to work – MacGregor is very much behind this breakaway union, the UDM, in fact I happen to know he will recognise it in future wage negotiations and he wants to make sure it's treated equally with the NUM membership as a condition for employment – and that will end the NUM closed shop Theo – brilliant tactics don't you think? – Ooogh." The mention of MacGregor seemed to give Suzanne some focus and clarity of mind.

"You think MacGreggor was behind the set up of the UDM?" Theo was suddenly interested in the conversation.

"Oh Theo, that's a bit dramatic. No I didn't say that, but I wouldn't be at all surprised if he didn't encourage it in some way, he's certainly not against it, in fact he wants me to get the press to shout its praises – you know the sort of thing, front page splashes everywhere showing how the UDM members are just trying to keep the country going and resist the bullying of Scargill and the violent NUM miners manning their pickets – it's going to be easy Theo, like falling off a log, the press will have a field day promoting the good 'ole Nottingham and South Derbyshire miners and their brand new patriotic union, they'll make sure the public see them as heroes – Ooogh – but look Theo, never mind all that, why don't you come over here for a drink, we can talk about it then if you really want, you're a bit of a dark horse aren't you Theo?"

Theo could hear the sound of more wine being poured into a glass.

"I don't think so Suzie, but tell me about all these things that have been happening in the office since I've been away?" He was beginning to wish he had a glass of wine at hand as his expectation and curiosity enlivened his imagination.

"Oh that, well, Tubby suddenly held a department meeting first thing this morning – thought it was going to be to congratulate us on our efforts, and yours of course, getting all this fantastic news coverage for the Prime Minister over that ghastly punch up by the miners on the police, but it wasn't, it was about changes he's making to the department, apparently Cadgers is being promoted to Senior Public Relations Officer, can you believe it, he's only been there five minutes and let's face it, he's not much good is he, bit of a creep too, but there you are – Janners, you and me will all report to him – what do you think about that Theo, Ooogh. Life's a bit of a hoot at Tory HQ eh what? Ooogh."

Theo was shocked, he couldn't have been more shocked than if he had woken up sleep walking through a minefield.

"Why? What's all that about? We don't need another layer of management – and how does Penton-Fox feel about it, sort of diminishes his role doesn't it? I can't believe it!"

Suddenly Theo loathed his job even more than he had done in the wake of the Orgreave debacle.

"What the fuck is the justification for that little private school twerp becoming our Manager? I thought Tubby believed in meritocracy, he's always spouting on about it, one of his bloody mantras, it's all a load of bullshit isn't it, just the same old pile of nepotistic bullshit, the old-boy network bullshit, I can't believe it!"

"Oh Theo, I like it when you get angry! Look, it's about who you know, and who your parents know – that's how it works Theo, nothing to do with merit you silly boy – you know Cadger's father puts pots of money into the Party's piggybank and he knows Tubby, they go to the same London club – went to the same school, enough said, it happens all the time, come on, get over it won't you, I'm getting lonely and some old tramp at the bar keeps winking at me – my God he actually rolls his own cigarettes, would you believe it?"

"And when was I going to be told I wonder? Or am I just an after-thought?" The shock news was tightening his stomach with the bile of resentment and the acid of humiliation.

"Don't know Theo, I think Tubby said he was going to talk to you when you got back – you being away and everything – look, why don't I come round to your place – we could carry on where we left off the other night ya? Ooogh."

He could practically smell her rising hormone. "Look Suzie, I've really got to go, something's come up, don't forget, 'Early night for Suzie' not 'Late night for Suzie' – bye for now." He hung up before she could slurp another word.

He spent the next half an hour packing a bag, running the iron over a decent looking shirt, putting creases in his shorts and slacks and then panicked when he couldn't find his passport. He searched everywhere, turned out drawers and cupboards, through pockets and between piles of clothes, under the bed and even the bathroom medicine cabinet, but the elusive little blue booklet was nowhere to be found. This new frustration together with the angst of Orgreave and the extraordinary latest developments at the office piled up on his nerves and he started to curse out loud:

"Bloody sodding bastards, fucking shitty bum-holes."

It was then that he noticed the pile of art magazines on the table next to the easel – he went over and lifted them up, and there sitting alone and out of place was his passport.

"Fuck me, there you are, you bleeding little arsehole – what the fuck are you doing hiding there?"

He grabbed it and pressed it to his chest with a deep and satisfying sigh of relief as if he had found a lost puppy. He finally finished packing and a brief moment of calm descended before his equilibrium once again went out of balance thinking about Cadgers' promotion. He looked around snarling at the ceiling and walls, "His old man must have pulled old Tubby's strings for sure – everything about this crappy mob lacks integrity – where's the sodding integrity then Tubby eh?"

He passed the rest of the evening in a semi-daze, beginning with a snack of pilchards on toast and then gobbling up the last few scoops of some ice cream he found dying in the back of the freezer; he then opened a bottle of wine, put on Cohen's latest album, *Recent Songs*, and relaxed thinking about the coming days and his trip to France. After a while he went over and stood by the window looking down like a kestrel onto the scurrying relentless traffic – as he gazed out the wine skipped his thoughts and his imagination skidded into a stream of consciousness:

'God almighty, all this dirty diesel shit invisibly spraying everyone, the silent assassin ignored by the authorities, all the people being poisoned as they glide along, as if on wheels, through the June night air, to and fro along Upper Street they go, some this way and some that – over there someone jumping in a puddle, the pure joy of jumping in puddles, should make it part of mental disorder therapy – all these faceless figures bound up in this endless pursuit of something intangible, scurrying and rushing, this way and that, everyone preoccupied with living and everyone busy dying, this state of dying concealed within, every moment it creeps forwards beneath the skin undetected – Oh Lord I'm not ready for it, too many things not done – but it's people who ruin beautiful things with their crude habits and limited intelligence, look over there, the pub door, four men carry out some drunk, each holding a limb, out to a waiting taxi, off along the purple road it goes out of sight, get rid of the evidence, ignorance is the enemy of enlightenment, we should all be taught to sing hymns at the gate of enlightenment on this solemn earth bloodied by the struggles of our fathers, we should all learn the sacred incense rituals to ward off ignorance and stand defiant before the candescent glow of truth and honour – Matisse said never get rid of your mistakes, I can't give mine away – Oh Lord the children, the poor little bastards, at least we hide the awful truth from them, get them believing Father Christmas is watching, can't tell them life is pointless and the horror of old age is waiting like an executioner, poverty is a child without an education, tell that to the privileged few tucked up tight at boarding school – I remember shivering with fright in class, the ghastly smell, sent home with a knot in my tummy, the dawning fear of the adult world, like fog rolling in from the sea – Heraclitus said no man ever steps in the same river twice, pity it's not the same for dog poo – it's all so bloody pathetic, at least Tchaikovsky understood and left us his *Pathétique* Symphony, his lullaby to the sensitive and deranged, poor bastard botched his suicide, the canal only three feet deep where he jumped in ..."

Just then a jet plane whined above as it came in low on its way to the City Airport and he looked up at the cloudy evening sky for some sort of sign, something to believe in, some reassurance that evolution will bring a fairer society, a nobler mind, some sort of saviour stepping out of the shadows – he gazed deep into the sky disappointed by the silence – then Cohen's song, *The Window* softly climbed above it all and he got lost in its haunting imagery:

"Now why do you stand by the window
Abandoned to beauty and pride
The thorn of the night in your bosom
The spear of the age in your side?"

"And come forth from your cloud of unknowing
And kiss the cheek of the moon
The new Jerusalem glowing
Why tarry all night in this ruin?"

It was about ten o'clock when he decided to phone Sasha, mainly to apologise for his drunken call the night before, but the thought of getting her round for a late visit was lurking behind his intentions. He went carefully down the stairs to the dimly lit landing and dialled her number.

There was no answer. He sat there for a few minutes listening to the monotonous ringing tone and wondered where she was at this time of night – he whispered to himself, 'With a client somewhere most likely, in some hotel room or apartment, performing some sexual act from her extensive repertoire.' The phone finally clicked onto message mode that caught him by surprise. He fumbled and garbled his message:

"Oh Sasha, it's Theo – look, I'm sorry about last night, didn't mean to frighten you, um, I'd like to see you, tonight, I know it's getting late, but I've got to see you, want you to ease my troubled mind – I'm lost and bewildered Sasha, I've got such terrible thoughts, want you to squeeze the doubt and pain from me …" He accidentally pressed the receiver down and disconnected the call.

Back in his room he decided to call it a day and got into bed, laying on his back staring at the ceiling, letting all the events of the last forty-eight hours untangle themselves from his tired and cluttered mind. Out they all came, the train ride to Sheffield with Digsy and Curly, the shocking scenes at Orgreave, the bloody rout of the miners and their sickening humiliation, his incoherent phone call to Tubby, the TV news bulletin and the Prime Minister's condemnation of the miners using his slogans re-worked by Tubby, the unforgivable editing of the BBC newsreel, the meal at the Akaba restaurant, his decision to reassess his life and take a few days off in France, the news that weasel Cadgers had been unjustly promoted – all the key moments came tripping across the ceiling with all the characters in tow, like hand shadow puppets, each having their moment in the limelight; his eyes grew heavy and started to close on these dramas, taking him down and down the wooded path to the little cottage hidden in the undergrowth of his subconscious – he glided off with a verse from *Abide With Me* soothing his mind like a prayer:

"Swift to its close ebbs out life's little day.
Earth's joys grow dim, its glories pass away.
Change and decay in all around I see:
O Thou who changest not, abide with me."

Chapter Eight

Theo closed the front door and headed off down Upper Street to the Angel Underground Station conscious that he had only forty minutes to get to London Bridge for the eleven-thirty train to Dover. A few dirty clouds gathered low in the sky and some drops of warm rain made large spots on his denim shirt as if he had been hit several times with a water pistol. The news placard by the station entrance read:

> Maggie calls the miners –
> 'The Enemy Within.'

He emerged from the lift some ninety feet below ground onto the famous 'Island' platform as a southbound train came screeching in and ran to board it, brushing past a young busker in a tatty cloth cap and a collarless shirt with waistcoat and brown corduroy trousers singing Ralph Mctell's song, *Streets of London*, the two caught each other's eye in that split second.

At 4.30 pm he arrived in the pleasant little town of Wissant just over ten miles down the coast from Calais. The choice of Wissant was random having pencilled it on his map of the Pas-de-Calais for no other reason than it was roughly halfway between Calais and Boulogne and was by the sea. So when he got off the Calais-to-Boulogne bus he had no idea what to expect from the small provincial seaside town.

As soon as he alighted in the central square he knew he had chosen the right place by the grace and favour of serendipity; all around was a sense of calm and stillness that always seemed to permeate French villages no matter what time of day. This is what he wanted, somewhere away from the chaos of London and the lies behind everything; somewhere far from the scheming and conniving that goes on in the higher echelons of Government like King Henry VIII's court, all the servile sycophants manoeuvring for recognition and advancement, all the blatant dishonesty and distortion trickling down to street level where the proletariat squabble over parking spaces and garden fence boundary disputes. He wanted to purge himself of all the mess in his head, all the demons and sleep denying spirits troubling his mind, and the cursed image of Tubby perched over his bed like a vulture. He wanted to experience the peace of France's rural life – la paix de la campagne – somewhere he could lay out the pieces of his life and rearrange them in a better order. It felt great to step off the bus and be in France once again.

The June sky was scudded with strands of thin cloud as the sun stepped west in its late afternoon stroll. He took his bag and walked a short distance from the square down a narrow side street to a bridge by a river. Standing prominent on the corner plot was the Hotel de la Plage with its reddish brown and cream shuttered windows and wooden beamed walls in the Normandy style crowned with Terreal Barrel tiles more at home in the Mediterranean Provinces than the Nord-Pas-de-Calais-Picardie region. Theo knew instantly this was the right hotel. An aura of fascination and charm surrounded it echoing ancient tales of knights and maidens, of enchanters and sorcerers, of magic and wonder.

The girl on reception with a ponytail and large dark eyes, who introduced herself through a fixed smile as Thérèse, led him up the creaky stairs to a generous sized corner double room overlooking the river with far reaching views across the low lying town one way and out to the silent waiting sea the other. It was perfect. The peace and stillness stood there like a stage backdrop. The room was laid out in a simple but tasteful design with light blue stained wooden furniture – a huge poster bed, a chest of drawers, a wardrobe, a writing desk with chair and an armchair beside a standard lamp. In the corner was a small sink and kettle on a shelf next to a selection of tea, coffee and biscuits. On the little table next to the bed a lamp and a bottle of water with two glasses waited to be used. Thérèse's permanent smile, fixed both on her lips and in her eyes, accompanied her report that the town was busy this time of year with British tourists on their way to the ferry ports.

"Some go Calais oui? Some go Boulogne oui? This hotel is the 'milieu' oui, comme ci, comme ça?" She used both her hands to emphasise the position of the two ports, as if Theo looked as if he needed simple explanations.

She went on to say it was regrettable that the ferry service from Folkestone to Calais had stopped operating and this had caused financial problems for hoteliers and restaurateurs in the area. Then she said, as if anticipating it would eventually become an important issue for Theo, that the Hotel had an excellent restaurant on the ground floor – she pointed down through the floorboards and her smile widened so much Theo could see her tonsils. Just as she was leaving she turned and said:

"Ah, there are the problems in Angleterre oui?" She clenched both fists and moved them quickly up and down as if she was sparring in a boxing ring, "The Grandes émeutes et des victimes de la police, non?" Seeing Theo struggle with the translation she said, "The fighters in the mines oui? The police with the, how you say, the 'contusions et des coupures', the cuts and the splits, non? I see with the TV, oui?" Then she said, "Oh la la, le même partout dans le monde eh? OK – Mr A'arrison enjoy the stay oui, and you speak to me when you ask something oui?"

With that she left and Theo heard the sound of her dainty little feet fading away down the corridor towards reception.

Theo poured a glass of water and thought as he looked out the window towards the Channel, "Fuck me, the lies about Orgreave have reached France have they? Is there no limit to Tubby's PR bullshit?"

He laid out on the bed, the fresh cotton pillowcase and sheet pleasantly soft to his touch. The exquisite silence of the room recaptured its peaceful ambiance holding it in a frame of countless past occasions. He looked around and wondered how many visitors had gone before and done the exact same thing, lying where he was and scanning the walls and ceiling in dreamy nonchalance. His eyes grew heavy in the heat of the afternoon and sleep beckoned as his muscles and mind relaxed. A waft of warm air crept through the open window and softly touched his hot cheeks. Outside two mallards squawked at each other over some minor dispute and then flapped their wings in annoyance whilst a light aircraft's piston engine chugged lazily in the endless sky as it headed out across the Channel. He closed his eyes and an image of Sasha suddenly appeared before him, combing her long blonde hair naked by the mirror and smiling as she caught his eye.

Theo slept for half an hour and would have gone on longer but for a racket outside when someone dropped a tray of crockery. He was sure he could make out Thérèse's voice in the commotion, sounding fiercer than she had been earlier. He got up and looked down to the courtyard. Thérèse was no where to be seen but a young man was picking up pieces of broken cups and saucers from the patio area where customers took afternoon tea and cake by the river. A small pool of milk was making its way to the surrounding flowerbed as if being cheered on by the rows of Sunflowers standing proudly to attention in their yellow, orange and gold regalia.

He looked out towards the sea and scanned the vicinity for the quickest route to reach it. There was a path on the other side of the river that disappeared behind a row of shrubs and small trees and then hurried along the edge of a field before petering out at the foot of a high ridge of sand dunes – the final frontier between him and the beach. It appeared to be no distance at all and he calculated it should only take him ten minutes to reach it. He took out his small shoulder bag from his suitcase and put in his notebook, pencil and the biscuits and bottle of water from the side table; then he put on his shoes, his straw hat, grabbed the door key and went off down the rickety corridor to find the sea.

Thérèse was behind the reception desk and she smiled her best smile as he passed by.

"Ah Mr A'arrison, "Voulez vous Dîner ici ce soir? Um, the dinner place tonight, here in our restaurant oui? Very nice for you, the table to see the river, oui?"

Her aggressive attitude he had overheard during the crockery melee had been replaced once again with a synthetic customer-pleasing persona that was designed, by those responsible for her training, to put guests at ease and radiate an air of harmony whilst showing a willingness to satisfy their smallest pleasure. She kept her programmed smile on Theo without flinching and turned up the glow in her eyes that reminded him of an Olympic synchronised swimmer. She kept staring at Theo dazzling him with her display of white teeth and sparkling eyes.

Theo stopped and was caught in her trap as if tranquilised by a poison dart. "Well yes, maybe – but I may find …"

Thérèse interrupted, knowing the script better than he did, "This the best one without the doubts, all guests say this was true oui – the food, the river, the ambiance most pleasuring oui? I reserve you the table oui? Seven clocks OK?"

"Yes OK, why not? See you later." Theo hurried out and Thérèse's smile was swiftly removed as she made a note in her dinner reservation book.

* * * * * * *

The ambulance sped down Werrington Street to the University College of London Hospital's Emergency Department just around the corner on Gower Street, opposite Euston Square tube station, its blue light illuminating the surrounding night.

On board the paramedic attended to Sasha who was laid out on a stretcher unconscious. She had two head wounds, one over her left eye and down across her cheek and the other above her right temple. The paramedic checked her pulse and heart rate, both were faint. He checked her airways and loosened her blood stained top. The wound to the left-hand side of her head had already closed the eye and a deep purple bruise spread downwards from the forehead to the cheek like a squashed raspberry. He gently felt the cheekbone and knew instantly it was fractured.

The wound to the right-hand side of her head caused most concern. The edge of the kerb took the full impact of her head as she collapsed. A deep cut across the top part of her forehead over the temple was bleeding profusely. The medic felt the pangs of panic flutter in his stomach as he examined the wound. Blood kept seeping through his gloved fingers as he gently touched around the gash to see if any object was lodged inside.

The ambulance continued into the dark purple London night and a church bell chimed two o'clock somewhere in Somers Town; it arrived at A&E with a jolt, the urgency palpable in the beam of its headlamp, and the waiting emergency team wheeled Sasha on a trolley through doors and down corridors. Neon strip lights flickered above her as she was pushed along. A persistent smell of bleach and lemon infiltrated everything as night cleaners worked their rounds. Sasha's blood pressure had dropped. A saline bag and two hundred millilitres of blood was quickly fixed to the trolley and hoisted to begin the transfusion process.

She arrived at the Emergency Room oblivious to the scurry of activity as medics whirled around like disturbed wasps in a nest, each with their own well-rehearsed duties to perform. She was undressed for the accident trauma Consultant to conduct his examination. He studied the two wounds and then looked over the rest of her body front and back. He noted the mauvered scar across her lower abdomen. The wounds were cleaned and stitched. Her head was examined and x-rayed. It was confirmed that the left cheekbone was fractured. The Consultant was concerned about the extensive swelling on the right side of the head and possible clotting on the brain. Her blood pressure and breathing were low and kept under close surveillance. She remained unconscious and was finally taken to an Intensive Care Unit. A police constable arrived and wanted to interview her but was told to wait. The wall clock read 02.18 am and looked tired from all the attention it receives from anxious relatives night and day.

Meanwhile the police called on each flat in Sasha's digs on Werrington Street. Her five neighbours were quizzed about their whereabouts the previous evening and in the small hours up to 01.30 am. No one knew anything nor did they see anyone apart from Mr Robarts who had found her on the pavement. Sasha kept herself to herself and no one ever remembers seeing visitors. She was a loner but never any trouble, in fact no one was aware she was there half the time. The police team painstakingly searched every square inch of Sasha's bedsit, the cabinets, the cupboards, the drawers, the toilet cistern, the tin of coffee and the wooden tea container, the pillows, the window ledge; they went on their knees to check for loose floorboards then they stripped the bed and looked under it where they found the suitcase wrapped in a blanket and inside the shoe box and inside that the metal box with Sasha's savings rolled up with an elastic band. Detective Sergeant Whithers counted the wad of notes and declared, after giving a short whistle, that there was almost three grand in all, mostly in £20 notes, some tenners and a few fivers. The other officers raised their eyebrows and one whispered, "Blimey! Well, whoever did her in didn't do it for the money then." The other officers stood silently calculating that the metal box contained a quarter of their annual pay. Whithers corrected the officer, "She's not dead, not yet anyway, and let's pray it stays that way."

"Sarg – look at this, found it in the biscuit tin, looks like an address book – there's a lot of men in there Sarg, you don't think she was on the game do you?"

Whithers flicked through Sasha's address book several times, stopping every now and then to look closely at a certain name. The majority of entries only contained a Christian name and a telephone number, some had an address and Whithers noted they were within the Kings Cross, Camden and Islington area. Intriguingly some of the entries had a note written beside them but they were difficult to read.

"Sarg – there's something else here, by the telephone, looks like one those answer machine things."

"Well don't just stand there lad, play the bloody thing."

"Not sure how to do that Sarg, never used one before – don't want to break it or anything."

"OK, unplug it and bring it along for the tech boys down the station. Anything else before we go? Have you checked her clothes, inside her shoes – I want everything double checked, is that clear?"

Outside two officers scanned the road and pavement around the area where Sasha was found lying by the kerb. They both shone torches as they walked slowly, three feet apart, going in straight lines across the street and back again. It was 03.40 am, the dead of night, even the cats had gone back indoors, just a faint sound of a taxi or car going along the Euston Road every now and then and some diesel locomotives working in the marshalling yard by Euston station. The officers were getting tired and beginning to hallucinate with images of tea and toast back in the station's canteen when suddenly an object almost hidden in the gutter caught their eye. One of the officers bent down and held up something round and shining in the rays of his torch – it was a silver pin, for a tie or lapel, with a strange emblem welded to the middle with sharp edges, like two silver wings.

* * * * * * * *

Theo found the way to the dunes easily enough and laid out in a secluded recess that afforded a view out across the mass expanse of the wide open beach to the sea on one side whilst giving shelter and privacy on the other three sides by the towering dunes stacked all around like weather worn pyramids dappled with tufts of grass. At first his mind was full of scenes from the days' train and ferry journeys; then, as these cleared, he thought about the reprehensible events at Orgreave and the extraordinary media lies and distortions and was stung once again with the realisation that he had been manipulated by a discreditable boss and the Government offices he represented. He reeled with the appalling sense of injustice sticking in his mind like a spike. He lay flat out on his back with the late afternoon sun tingling his skin and gradually gave in to the exquisite peace, the soft sounds of lapping waves dissolving into the sand, the occasional squawk from a gliding gull and the warm salty sea air smothering him and renewing his spirit; he yearned for a kind of rejuvenation and laying there in the momentary hypnosis of the sun, sand and sea he started to feel his equilibrium return and gradually unclenched his fists as anxiety drained away.

He lay for twenty minutes or so caught in that twilight mental state where time stands still between semi-consciousness and dream. Every now and then he opened an eye to peer out to the scene below, as if to remind himself that there was still a reality and a live universe with a beating heart all around him. There below was his new reality far from the nightmare of Orgreave. Out on the horizon a broken line of ferries and container ships inched their way along the busy shipping lanes of the English Channel whilst nearer to shore a small squadron of yachts zigzagged across each others' bows like playful butterflies in the sunlight, their sails fluttering like wings against the blue sea.

He was reminded of Monet's painting, *Terrace at Sainte Adresse,* and thought how little the busy seascape scene had changed in just under a hundred years. The sun was beginning its inevitable slide down towards its western exit but still carried powerful rays of heat that would burn the skin if unprotected; most people had left the beach but a few remained scattered around, lingering late in the day to soak up the last of the sun and swim in the sea, their heads bobbing up and down with the incoming tide. Two children, probably brothers, dug holes and filled them with water; a solitary father was finishing building a sandcastle lost in his own creative world; a few women eked out the sunbathing opportunity, daring to go topless now the crowds had left but laying on their fronts for decency's sake; an elderly couple snoozed in their beach chairs, their heads back and mouths wide open; along the water's edge and down the promenade a handful of young lovers strolled, hand in hand, longing for the playful night to fall.

He surveyed the scene from his sand dune ledge and marvelled at the human need to restore itself by the healing balm of the littoral. His gaze eventually settled on the fidgeting, jittery sea with its inexhaustible line of waves moving forward to the shore, measuring out time and mortality forever more, finishing their journeys exactly where the land comes to a halt, that unique place in time and space where sea and land fuse to form the beginning and the end of themselves, the eternal circle of perpetual motion, defined and complete.

He stretched his legs out a little more and dug his heels into the sand – he felt so much better, the magical elixir of the seaside induced a sunnier disposition that had been absent in his life for so long.

Just then a woman's voice lifted high over the dunes and up into the crisp, sharp sea air cutting through it like a pistol shot.

She was singing a sad heartfelt song with such a pleasing melancholic tone that Theo was totally absorbed on the spot.

He laid out on the dune enthralled by the mystic beauty of the song as it looped around the dunes like a sand martin curling in flight:

"Come all ye fair and tender maidens
Take warning how you court your men
They're like a star on a cloudy morning
First they'll appear and then they're gone."

He was spellbound by the woman's beautiful voice and the haunting elegiac song. The pain behind the lament was real and moved him like a heartfelt eulogy. He let the pure pathos flow through his senses and evoke old memories of lost love still sensitive to the touch of time. The image of Angelina appeared before him just as it had done on the train three days before, always there ready to haunt him when he was slipping into dream or tormented by loneliness, caught unawares by a vision or a sound, provoked by the intensity of a fleeting moment, something beautiful and natural, something deep in his inner self, a valuable, priceless gift lost for ever, a part of him now missing, like the sky without the sun.

The song continued to float above, its notes like butterflies dancing in the sun lit air:

"Oh don't you remember our days of courting
You told me that you would love me the best
You could make me believe by the fall of your eyes
That the sun rose in the west."

He closed his eyes and went drifting off to the fateful afternoon in Angelina's flat in Beckenham in 1977 when he lost his one true love, when he had virtually caught her with Max having sex. He had interrogated her like a tedious bourgeois and he hated himself for it. What had she said when he had questioned her to the limit, 'It's only sex Theo, only sex - it's not important – just enjoy the moment we have together, here and now.' But he wanted her for himself; his love had no room for sharing her with another. His love for her was all consuming, like a drug, he wanted her complete and whole for himself and if not, then he would have to live without her, lost and void of feeling, going through the daily round like a zombie, there was no other choice for the character he was, for the sensitivity and limitations ingrained in his personality like sinews through flesh:

"I wish I was a little sparrow
And I had wings and I could fly
I'd fly right home to my false true lover
And when he'd ask, I would deny."

In his mind's eye he gazed back at that eclipsing moment when he lost Angelina, at the way he had let her slip away, caught in the web of his own restrictive conditioning and lack of worldliness, losing precious love through immaturity and ineptitude, held close one minute and gone the next.

The lovely song seemed to end but then, just as the gentle sound of the sea returned, it started over with the same rich haunting voice echoing around the dunes and out onto the beach:

"But I am not some little sparrow
I've no wings and I can't fly
So I'll stay right here with my grief and sorrow
And let my life pass me by."

Theo was seized by a powerful need to track the singing to its source, to discover the sorcerer of this magic spell, to follow each note like Hansel & Gretel following the beautiful white bird to the clearing in the woods, to the little cottage made of gingerbread and cake.

He got up and lent an ear to the sky. The voice was so clear, so sharp, so enticing, each word danced around his mind and pirouetted into his senses. The singer was close-by as the nuance of the rendition was discernable against the hum of the sea and the few people still using the beach. He grabbed his bag and made off along the narrow twisting paths over and around the dunes to his right-hand side away from the direction where he had entered. As he clambered up and down the song grew louder as if the singer was but a few feet away.

He reached the top of a dune, turned to his left facing the sea and there she was below him sitting on a yellow towel, upright with a guitar resting on her thigh. He gazed down mesmerised by the young woman seated with her back towards him singing her seductively sad song so alluringly to the sky and the sea. He waited for the last verse to finish and then using the sides of his shoes he slid down the dune towards her commando style.

His dramatic entrance startled the young woman and she turned clutching the guitar close to her chest peering at Theo with frightened eyes.

"Oh – you made me jump." She kept her eyes on Theo as if he was a wild animal capable of sudden movements.

"It's OK, sorry, the dunes give no warning, my fault …"

He slid down to the sandy alcove where she was sitting and looked at her with the softening early evening light catching her face in clear definition. He was drawn to her dark-brown eyes that were round and prominent and charged with an energy, a glossy powerful life-force energy that signalled awareness and intelligence and delivered with understanding and compassion.

He could not stop staring into her amazing eyes that sat huge in a small oval shaped face like sea caves, dark and mysterious.

"I heard you singing – such a sad song – you have the most beautiful voice – it sounded mystical, coming over the dunes so clear like an echo in the mountains." Theo moved his right hand in an arc above his head to indicate the huge expanse of the dunes.

The woman kept looking at him as she ran her hand back through her long black hair knotted by the sand and sea breeze searching for clues about his character, for signs of danger or warmth.

"I'm glad you liked it, but I can't really play or sing, I'm just a hopeful amateur." She studied Theo's eyes as he stared into hers and some powerful transmission took place, almost numinous, a spiritual transcendence that both relaxed and moved her.

"You play great, as much as I could make out any way."

"No, no I don't, I can assure you – I'm still learning, it takes a long time to master the chord changes – I can just about get by with the three basic chords – and the song demands more than that – do you know it?" Her large dark eyes were now relaxed and warm as she spoke.

"It's familiar, didn't Joan Baez do a version? You sound a bit like her actually." Theo frantically searched the music files in his brain to recall Joan Baez's rendition of the song.

The woman's eyes grew even larger, "Yes, she did, so you do know it, hers is the best I reckon, she sings it so beautifully, as you say, so sad, even better than the original version by Maybelle Carter – do you know that one?"

Theo didn't bother to go back into his mental files, "No …"

"Oh well, now Maybelle's version is really tricky, the guitar playing I mean, she came up with what is known as, 'The Carter Scratch' and it's so difficult to master."

She repositioned the guitar on her knee to demonstrate, "Maybelle used finger and thumb picks, like this – one to play the melody on the three bass strings and the other to strum out the rhythm on the treble strings – done simultaneously, I mean, how do you do that?" She attempted to play the opening chords using the Carter Scratch method but got it wrong. "You see, it's so tricky – I botch it every time, but I don't use thumb picks, just my long nails." She held up her right hand to show him her fingernails and laughed at herself as she did so – he loved her humility and lack of self-aggrandisement.

He warmed to her and smiled spontaneously, loving her open honest nature that worked like a sedative to his bruised and anxious character.

"I see what you mean – I saw John Williams at a concert and he does pretty much the same thing, except he plays classical pieces – I was knocked out by his rendering of Bach's Flute Suite – the way he transcribed it for guitar was amazing."

"John Williams! Well he's in a different league, the man's a complete genius – he can make the guitar sound as if he's playing a duet with someone – so you like John Williams and Joan Baez – you're obviously a music lover?" She moved her position slightly to avoid the evening sun shining in her big dark eyes.

"Music's important to me, the special art form – that song you were singing, it's about a woman losing a lover isn't it – you sing it with such …" He patted his breast with his fist, " … passion, you sing it like you feel it." He glanced down to the beach where the sound of two chairs being folded up by the elderly couple chinked his ear.

"It's a song about a woman in love and giving herself to a man whose feelings are not true, he deceives her, he's basically a liar who uses her to get his way and then dumps her – same old story really, down the years the path is littered with women cheated on by their lovers – women can be so vulnerable, and men can be such creeps." She looked at him with her big searching eyes for his reaction.

After a pause that hung too long he said, "Not all men, luck of the draw I suppose, it's all chance isn't it?" He shuffled from one foot to the other and was beginning to feel conspicuous standing and talking whilst she sat.

She sensed his discomfort and said in a softer voice, almost pleading, "Please, won't you sit down, there's plenty of room – my name's Jenny by the way, Jenny Rennes – I know, you wouldn't believe it would you, my mother's little joke – what's yours?" She gestured him to sit close by as if she was inviting him to sit down in one of her armchairs in her London flat.

Theo sat down feeling warm and alive, sitting next to the long black haired stranger on the dunes by the sea with the sun casting its glittering straight line path out to the horizon, never ending, the illusionary path forever leading to the vanishing point across the ocean, ad infinitum.

"Hello Jenny, I'm Theo – I think your name's great – where's it from?" Sitting down closer to her he was struck even more by her alluring eyes, they seemed to draw him in like Aphrodite, the goddess of Love and Beauty, beckoning him into the sea from where she came, born beneath the waves, the daughter of the sea-nymph Dione, he was slowly being held captive by her eyes and their effect on his imagination.

"Rennes? Oh it must be French I suppose, there's that city called Rennes isn't there – infamous for being the headquarters of the republican army during the French Revolution when they fought the royalist insurgents – must be where I get all my anarchist tendencies from – ha, ha."

Her laugh was contagious, a wonderfully melodic, cheeky laugh that had hidden tones of friskiness and backroom frivolity.

"It's all a bit odd, there's absolutely no French in the family as far as I know, although my mother's turned out to be a bit of a coquette, ha, ha." She changed the subject quickly, "So what about your name, sounds Greek …"

Theo didn't have a clue about the origin of his name.

"Probably – that would explain a lot, everything seems Greek to me, the whole lot of it." He raised his hand up to the sky to gesture the extent of his bewilderment.

They both laughed and Theo realised it was the first time he had done so in months.

"Would you like some wine?" Jenny shuffled around in her large canvas shoulder bag, "I got a couple of those small bottles on the ferry this morning."

"Ah, that sounds good – and how about some biscuits to go with it?" He pulled the packet of shortbread biscuits from his bag. "Well, we're a couple of swells." They both laughed again.

He sat leaning his back against the dune and sipped the warm merlot wine from the little bottle. Out on the Channel a ferry was reducing speed as it glided into its final docking zone outside Calais harbour and high in the sky above an old Piper piston-engine aircraft purred effortlessly on its straight-line course to Shoreham airport. The early evening light was warm and soft and licked everything with a coat of yellow-orange illuminant. A profound sense of calm spread through him slowly but surely like a wave easing across the sand before it finally stops.

"So you caught the ferry this morning? I got the two o'clock – I always forget how long that walk is from Dover station to the ferry – are you staying here for long?"

"No – I didn't go from Dover, I was staying with my parents in Folkestone last night and went from there to Boulogne – they've stopped the Folkestone-Calais service apparently – another bit of our old way of life gone – I'm only here for a couple of days, back on Friday and back to work Monday, urrgh!" She shrugged her shoulders as if the very thought of work gave her goose pimples.

"Well that's a coincidence, I've only come out for a few days too – in the back of my mind I have this secret thought that something adventurous might happen, like being press-ganged into the French Foreign Legion..." He smiled at his own imagination.

She said, "Well, something exciting might happen, you never know." She looked at him and returned his smile. "Are you staying in Wissant?"

"Yes, just over there, the Hotel de la Plage – nice old fashioned place, creaky floorboards and a huge poster bed – lovely and quiet, just the sound of the clock ticking in reception and the sea humming in the background – exactly what I wanted."

Just then the church bell boomed out over the dunes like it had done for hundreds of years. They both looked up to the sky as the great bell chimed as if they might spot the gongs flying past. "Ah, yes, well there is that little matter to contend with, I must say that bell was designed to be heard for miles, can't be far off the mighty Carolus – you know, the great Bourdon Bell of Antwerp Cathredal?"

She looked baffled. "If you say so – but it certainly is loud, kinda demands your attention – I've checked in at the Les Trois Burghers which is just off the square on the other side. It's small and quiet and clean but doesn't have the river outside, in fact it doesn't have anything outside, just the back of someone's house."

They both sipped their wine, nibbled a biscuit and looked at each other with more thoughts flickering between them than messages on the Wells Fargo telegraph wire.

"When I heard you singing I had to find out who it was, the song is so hauntingly sad and you sing so well Jenny. Does the song conceal some personal experience, some emotional hurt maybe – an unrequited love?"

She studied his eyes as if she was trying to see the outline of something distant, a shape shrouded in mist across a field.

"You're very perceptive Theo – yes, that and all the rest of it – I'm getting away from the aftermath of being dumped by some creep, some brilliant, amazing creep who led me on and then went with someone else – or did he already have the someone else and lead her on – I don't know, all too complicated – and there's all the other stuff, the job, the routine, the Government, London, my family, the whole bloody mess, ha" Theo thought her right eye was slightly watery.

"What about you? Are you getting away from something?"

He was fascinated by her sad dark-brown eyes and kept seeing different aspects of her character in them, together with warmth and kindness, they beckoned him and he fell into them like falling backwards into a pool.

"Well, yeh, there's a lot of junk building up in my life, had to get away and sit by the sea, take a deep breath and think it all through, maybe start again, possibly, it all depends."

"What do you do – I guess you're a teacher maybe, you communicate well and you have a certain intelligence in your eyes."

Theo had never felt intelligent in his life – he had grown up baffled by everything and the older he got the more confused he became.

"I work in PR – you know, those invisible manipulators who try and make you believe black is white and convince you in the virtue of something, even though there's very little virtue in anything – it's a form of trickery at best or lying at worst, aimed at the stupid who can't form their own opinion, usually to get them to buy something they don't need or vote for someone who is incompetent."

She leant her head back and laughed, "Ha, ha, I like that – so where do you practice this wicked witchcraft I wonder?"

He sipped the wine and thought about his job and all the chicanery, lies and deceit that ran through it like a cancer, contaminating all the vital organs and squeezing the life force out of it, reducing it to a dysfunction, a disease of the truth, like the disgrace of Orgreave, a discredit to the integrity of decent minded people – she was right, he practised witchcraft and Tubby was the witchdoctor, the lying cheating witchdoctor who conjured up harmful potions for society, the corrupt witchdoctor who would distort your opinion and debase your values if it furthered his party's political interests. He sighed as the wilful misrepresentation of the events at Orgreave pushed their way back to the front of his mind. He looked out across the beach below and the marine-blue lulling sea beyond and felt the hatred towards Tubby and the whole establishment he represented come trickling back into his veins like black poison.

The two boys digging in the sand started to argue about their accomplishment – they pushed each other and wrestled over ownership of a futile hole in the sand.

"I work for the Government, in its central HQ, I help to convince the public that what its doing is right and worth voting for – but I've seen through it, I can't take the deceit and the lies any more, it's too much, the lies are just too much." He felt strangely buoyant, almost relieved, to have made this statement like a confession to a priest.

Jenny sensed the weight of the moment. "So what brought on this disillusionment?" She asked the question with warm concern that softened any resilience he may have had to go further.

"Orgreave!" He let the word hang in the air like a bad smell.

"Orgreave? What? You mean you were there on Monday, at Orgreave?" She looked at him with knitted eyebrows and a scrunched up nose to convey astonishment.

"Yes – although it hardly seems like two days, more like a lifetime ago – strange how the mind can distort time when you get out of kilter with your daily routine."

"Wow, so you were at Orgreave – right in the middle of all that fighting? It looked pretty bad on the news, all those miners beating up the police …"

"No, no Jenny, that's my whole point, what you saw was a lie, it was the other way round, I was there hiding behind the trees, as an observer, I saw it with my own eyes, the police had it all planned, they herded the miners' into a field and basically beat the shit out of them – if you pardon my French, which I suppose you can seeing as we're in France." He smiled, a rare smile, like a diamond on his lips.

She looked at him with her eyebrows gradually unknitting, "I like it when you smile, you look so different, a bit cute." They both sipped the wine and kept staring at each other as if their spirits were bonding, silently like the tide seeping into the sand, something passed between them and glowed in their eyes. "So all those TV reports and bits of film were wrong?" Her eyebrows curved upwards again with puzzlement.

"Yes, absolutely – unbelievable isn't it, but I witnessed everything, the BBC distorted their own footage to show the miners charging at the police and throwing stuff – it wasn't like that, it was the police who charged at the miners first, on horseback, and whacked them senseless with those huge truncheons, cracking their heads like coconuts. The whole thing was contrived by the Government and the police to turn you against the miners – it was undemocratic to put it mildly."

She seemed to quickly understand the key concepts, "So that's what went on – a collusion between the BBC and the Government – is that what you're saying, and you were part of the commentary team or something?"

She was intrigued with his story and this pleased him, for he felt only kindred warmth and no judgement between them; she made it easy for him to reach out and share his feelings. He continued soft and easy as if he was alone in the woods talking to the natural world around him.

"It's worse than that, I was the one that provided the Prime Minister with those ridiculous comments she's been chucking all over the media – you know, that stuff about, 'The rule of law must prevail over the rule of the mob' and 'The Enemy Within.' I can't believe all the lies that I've heard bleating out across the airwaves in the past forty-eight hours – it beggars belief – are we really a democracy when the newspapers and the BBC work with the Government to distort the truth – that's why I had to get away, came straight here, just to clear my head and work out what I should do next."

Her large dark brown eyes now widened like two huge disks through her lovely loose black hair falling across her face. "This is like something from a John le Carré novel – it's unbelievable– but it makes sense, I can see that, the Prime Minister has to beat the miners, not just for revenge on Edward Heath back in the 70s but to beat the unions, that's her goal isn't it, beat the unions and then she can bring in the real changes, changes to state ownership, banking, housing, education – privatise the whole bloody lot – that's her game I bet."

Jenny finished her wine with a decisive swig that saw her leaning her head right back and emptying the bottle through her lips like a sailor in a tavern at closing time.

He leaned towards her, the muscles around his eyes taut with astonishment, "Wow, that's very impressive Jenny, I'd say you have a remarkable talent at grasping the facts and seeing through this charade – you're bang on."

All around them the early evening light-blue pastel sky, the choir of the swooping gliding gulls and the lake-like sea syncopated into a Debussy symphony in his mind, touching his spirit and his soul, a soft caress.

"You fascinate me Theo – you're a mechanic working for the Tory propaganda machine yet you don't seem very Tory to me – not a true blue Tory any way – you're a sheep in wolf's clothing, how come?"

He looked within himself, down the well of his past and saw someone who had never been blindly faithful to any political party – his key concern had been to understand the reason behind things, if he could not understand the reasoning he couldn't believe in the principle; he had only ever wanted politicians to care for the people, to forge policies that would distribute as much wealth and benefits as could be afforded; for him, Government economic policy should principally be about the sharing of wealth, and Government vision should be about creating a fairer, more egalitarian society.

"I wasn't bothered about whether or not I was a true Tory, it was just a job opportunity that came along when I needed a change in my life …"

"Another change? But the Tory Party? Any port in the storm eh? Really? … ha, ha."

Her wicked laugh was sardonic but her smiling eyes were warm with understanding.

He felt relaxed in her company; an easy simpatico mood embraced him, an old almost forgotten emotion in his brain disused for so long now flicked back to life again, like Frankenstein's muscle ligaments receiving their first electrical charge. There was something about her that made him drop his guard and speak spontaneously from his heart.

"I never really understood much of what was going on, growing up was a complete puzzle, my Dad leaving us when I was just nine, the blackboard jungle of school, the arbitrary choice of a career path, the un-meritocratic workplace riddled with unjust favours and nepotistic promotions, the vanity obsessed complexities of relationships and now this awful reality that our Government is nothing more than a lying, manipulative spreader of propaganda, masquerading as ideological social engineers pretending to be working for the good of the people – forcing unproven free-market monetarism on us, un-regulating financial services to make casino capitalists out of East-End barrow boys in pinstripe suits and promoting this awful greed ethic, as if that's what life is all about, as if that's why we're here for God's sake, and all at the cost of public services and high unemployment – this is serious bullshit, serious because they mean it and they will bulldoze society as we know it, right down to the ground, flatten it, change the landscape forever, just to achieve their ends – what's that they say to justify their social vandalism, 'If it does not fit with our long-term strategic vision – get rid of it, sell it' – that's dangerous Government, but they don't say it straight, they lie and deceive, they wrap it up as some sort of phony benefit, like they're acting solely for the people, they're nothing more than false prophets the lot of em."

Jenny got hold of her guitar and rested it on her knee once again but instead of playing she gently stroked the strings with her fingers, as if she was pacifying it, like a mother stroking a sobbing child's head.

"It's true, we should expect more from our leaders but they always lie – it's par for the course just to get elected – 'tell them what they want to hear then go ahead and do something else' – it's like a code of practice for politicians – under their banner of 'ideology' they get away with murder."

"It shouldn't be that way Jenny should it? Honesty and integrity are important qualities – those are the values behind the law, education, the church, the pillars of a decent society, they are passed on from generation to generation through our mother's milk, they are our sacred creed, and they matter, they really matter."

She started to pluck the bass string slowly like a bell tolling danger. "It's difficult for the average person to work out what's real and what's not – most of 'em are preoccupied trying to make ends meet – they don't have time to analyse all the detail – they just want a fair share, a decent return for their labours, food on the table, a roof over their heads and a chance to improve their lot for themselves and their kids – they will believe you if you tell them to vote for X if he or she says all the right words, if they appear to know how to identify with ordinary people's problems – it's all about mimicking the right sentiments isn't it, and presenting the right image, these politicians will lie straight faced to get your vote, there's no morality, with them it's all about winning, getting into power, the end justifies the means – meanwhile the poor get poorer and the rich get richer, at least they do under the Tories, it was always thus."

Theo listened to her talk and loved her Joan of Arc spirit that seemed to strengthen his resolve; her nature was a magnet to his and their feelings and interpretations of the world around them were similar, the nuances forged on the same anvil of experience and sensitivity. Suddenly he saw his old friend Sandy appear in memory and all their confrontations over the rise of the National Front and the effects of immigration back in the mid-70s came flooding back – how he regretted losing touch with his old friend and how he ached to sit with him once again to sift through all the issues of the day.

"You remind me of an old friend – he thought like you, definite and on the side of the underdog – I was a million miles behind him back then in the 70s when we argued all night over the National Front – I thought I out-reasoned him but I didn't, I just saw everything in shades of grey, so to speak – always been a problem of mine – I have to reason with all sides of the problem before I can truly believe in the solution." He looked at her and became nostalgic for something dear and lost but possibly found again, on the sand dunes of Wissant.

She filled with empathy for him, "Don't blame yourself – the way we see the world is a core learning faculty and it takes time, years, sometimes a life-time, to see things differently – but we can learn from experience, it's a good teacher but often only in retrospect." She looked at him with her beautiful dark eyes and his feelings for her moved imperceptibly, measured by grains of sand, towards a kind of love.

"So where is he now, your old adversary friend? By the logic of you working for the Tories he should be working for Neil Kinnock, or Robert Maxwell ha, ha."

"We left on bad terms, I was completely screwed up and he was hopelessly in love – last I heard he'd moved to Australia – beginning to see why now, although I'm not convinced any one country has produced a utopia – in the end they all fall into the same trap, they sell you the work ethic so as to protect the elite power structure – they don't want you getting too smart and upsetting things, they have to protect the one-per cent club at all costs."

She laughed, "Ha – the one-per cent club? What's that? Sounds a bit naughty."

"You know, all the nation's wealth is owned by one per cent of the people – it's feudal and goes back to the Middle Ages – the Barons who hold the wealth, the power, will do anything to keep it that way – the vassals, the workers, you and me, are made to feel thankful for our basic comforts and modest pleasures – the one per cent allow a few plebs to climb their ladder every now and then to make it look like there's opportunity for all – it's bullshit – and to rub salt in the wound they never pay their fair share of tax – the tax burden always falls onto the poor and middle class – the one per cent have got their tax lawyers to show them the loopholes, it's big business avoiding tax – and the one per cent have a powerful weapon, they control the media and get all the commanding jobs, because of their privileged parents they get into the best schools and end up judges and civil servant mandarins and high level bureaucrats, the advisers and law makers – from there they can manipulate the serfs, especially in this country, into accepting all sorts of hardships and injustices like insufficient housing, insufficient work opportunities, child poverty and inadequate workers' rights by pulling the teeth from the trade unions – which is where my job comes in – but not for long, can't do the lies any more …" He paused and looked confused.

"I know Theo, I know how you feel, it's all about trust isn't it – when the trust goes, well, it's time to go – but what will you do, if you leave your job I mean? So many of us are feeling lost right now, what was it that Ophelia said, something about, '– we know who we are but we don't know where we are going' – that's about it right?"

He had been asking himself the same question since leaving Orgreave and hadn't come up with an answer. He loved this easy way of being with her, this frictionless flight through turbulent air like two birds weaving around and across the same thermals, attuned and telepathic, content just to be flying in the same direction.

"I used to work for *The Rainbow* magazine, handling the publicity and doing a bit of artwork for the cover – looking back it seems exciting now but at the time I got overwhelmed by the pressure – the deadlines were always coming at you, like slings and arrows, I suppose I could go back into magazine publishing, but it would be a bit like warming up cold fish & chips."

"Or you could take your skills into another sector altogether, flip the coin, play to your strengths but without the commercial bullshit."

He looked at her with a flush of excitement and anticipation tickling his senses as if she had found a key he had been looking for, "What are you thinking of?"

"Go and teach – you'd make a good teacher Theo, you have an authoritative demeanour, you're clear and concise and I bet you're good at what you do – teach marketing or PR or graphic design – or all three, there's a growing number of marketing courses popping up in Further Education – go and research it, might be just right for you, marketing is the future yeh? It helps sell more stuff, good for all those greedy Barons, and the one per cent club yeh? Ha, ha."

He felt a streak of light enter his brain and a path open up through the tangle of hopelessness that had choked his geniality for so long, like the sudden lifting of a migraine.

"Yes, you may have something there, I'll check it out – I've never seen myself as a teacher, an old lecher maybe." They both laughed, looking at each other, something alive and exciting moving between them, a natural energy.

"Play some more music Jenny – play that song again, I love the way you sing it." He closed his eyes in anticipation.

She repositioned the guitar in readiness to play. "No, not that one – how about a bit of Leonard Cohen, do you know, *Hey, That's No Way To Say Goodbye?* It's one of my favourite songs." She started to sing before he could answer:

"I loved you in the morning, our kisses deep and warm,
your hair upon the pillow like a sleepy golden storm,
yes many loved before us, I know that we are not new,
in city and in forest they smiled like me and you,
but let's not talk of love or chains and things we can't untie,
your eyes are soft with sorrow, Hey, that's no way to say goodbye."

She stopped and looked at him as he opened his eyes, "Isn't that just so beautiful – the words go straight to the heart."

"When you sing I feel a sort of peace come on, a stillness, it almost sends me to sleep, and that's the mark of any great song." He felt a strong urge to touch her long black hair, to feel it through his fingers, but resisted.

The sun was taking tiny steps downwards as if bored with the now near-deserted beach, the last stragglers having slipped away as dinnertime beckoned, and just two solitary horse riders cantering along a stretch of harder sand, their heads bobbing up and down in unison as they grew smaller against the vast sky and sea.

"Theo – why don't you sing something, anything, but not too complicated, I should be able to do something with three chords – what do you know?" She looked at him with her beautiful eyes that held no trickery or deceit – just warm pools of intrigue and calmness.

"No really Jenny, I don't sing so well." He was taken by surprise and wilted under the sudden spotlight.

"I'll not take no for an answer – come on, look, there's no one around, just me, and I can't sing for toffee."

Something about her radiated a sense of familiarity and ease and he was hopelessly trapped in the fine web of her allure. He wanted to please her.

"Well, I know a few Dylan songs, let me see, how about *Love Minus Zero* – do you know it?"

"Yes, I'm a big Dylan fan too, come on, …" She started to strum the opening few bars peering into his eyes as if willing him to sing.

And so it was that on that early June evening on the sand dunes of Wissant Theo sang in public for the first time in his life, albeit to an audience of one; as he started to sing a squabble of seagulls swooped low over the dunes above them engaged in a heated argument over possession of a piece of pilfered cake; He waited for the fracas to pass:

"My love she speaks like silence
Without ideals or violence
She doesn't have to say she's faithful
Yet she's true, like ice, like fire."

"People carry roses
And make promises by the hours
My love she laughs like the flowers
Valentines can't buy her."

Still looking into each other's eyes Jenny joined in:

"Some speak of the future
My love she speaks softly
She knows there's no success like failure
And that failure's no success at all."

Their singing petered out as they didn't know any more words and there was silence, a deep silence that rang sweet like Tibetan monastery gongs, soothing and soulful through their minds, healing each others' wounds, replacing pain with love. The beautiful silence did not need any more words.

Finally Jenny put aside the guitar and almost whispered, "Do you fancy getting together for dinner Theo?"

His eyes were almost dancing in their sockets, "Just what I was thinking – come to my hotel …" He pointed over the dunes in the direction to where the Hotel de la Plage stood out of sight, "I've got a table booked, at 'seven clocks' as the concierge so charmingly put it."

Back in his room Theo turned on the TV and tuned it to BBC 1 then stepped into the bathroom to wash. The BBC's six o'clock news programme came on with a photograph of the Prime Minister filling the fuzzy screen followed by the news presenter reading one of her quotes regarding the miners' action at Orgreave that was still making headline news. Theo could just make out some of the words as he stood at the bathroom sink washing his face:

"What we have got is an attempt to substitute the rule of the mob for the rule of the law."

He finished washing and went back into the room, bending down to put on a pair of clean underwear, when the news bulletin changed to show the Prime Minister's policy advisor sternly speaking out against the miners, his language acerbic and his judgement severe.

"These miners are Scargill's shock troops – their violence and intimidation, on the scale which we saw at Orgreave, are unacceptable and an affront to both the civil and criminal law – what happened at Orgreave had been mob violence".

Theo put on a pair of white linen trousers and cursed, "So Tubby's really turning the screw, bringing on the Prime Minister's policy advisor to coordinate the message, and of course the same message will be plastered all over the Tory press tomorrow – people will be swimming in all the lies and bullshit – the bastards."

The news bulletin finished with a statement that the miners arrested at Orgreave would be charged with the serious offence of, 'Riot' rather than the lesser one of, 'Public Disorder'. Theo said out loud, "That's right, first lie through your teeth then kick 'em in the balls – those lads can't afford hefty fines, they'll end up in prison, their families will suffer – the bastards, still pulling the wool over the public's eyes – bet Tubby's rubbing his fat tummy with glee."

He finished buttoning up his casual shirt, grabbed his wallet and door key and left the room. Walking down the narrow passageway to the stairs he passed another room with its door wide open and the TV left on; as he walked by he heard fragments from a London Local News update:

"There has been another brutal attack on a call girl in London's infamous Kings Cross area – in the small hours of Wednesday 19th – she remains in a coma in the Intensive Care Unit – Police are investigating her whereabouts prior to the attack."

He was concentrating on the evening ahead and dinner with Jenny and if truth be told he was more than a little nervous – the TV news announcement therefore went in one ear and out the other and he missed the photograph of Sasha that appeared on the screen as he passed the door.

* * * * * * * *

Detective Chief Inspector Tonks sat in the incident room a little agitated, as he leaned back in his old swivel chair stroking his rough unshaven chin with his eyes half closed in a squint. He was a veteran London cop and over a career spanning thirty two years had seen just about every vile act one human being can inflict upon another together with the plethora of petty crimes and minor misdemeanours that occur every day across the vast metropolis, much of it just 'dirt down the drain' as he often described it. He had been put in charge of the King's Cross call girl case to catch the elusive culprit and stop the attacks from escalating.

"Right, first of all, the news from the hospital is that Sasha has a fractured left cheekbone from a blow by some object or other and extensive swelling and possible clotting on the brain on the right-side of the head caused by her falling and hitting the edge of the kerb – she remains unconscious in Intensive Care – her condition is said to be serious."

The other members of the Serious Crime Team looked on in sombre mood befitting the severity of the crime.

Tonks continued, "So, what we got so far?" He levelled his gaze on Detective Sergeant Whithers and lifted his eyebrows as a cue for the report to begin.

Whithers dutifully went over to the display board on the wall and pointed at a photograph of Sasha.

"Sasha Phillips, twenty years old, of 22 Werrington Street King's Cross – found unconscious on the pavement outside her digs with serious head wounds at 01.56 am Wednesday 20th June by one of her neighbours, Mr Robarts, who was returning from a night out in Piccadilly – she was wearing black leotards and a black Lycra top – we don't know how long she had been lying there but forensics say, as a reasonable guess, about an hour due to excessive blood loss and the degree by which her wounds eventually congealed. Sasha's been working as a call girl for the past seven months, originally from Romford, Essex where her parents live. Works alone and keeps herself to herself, none of her neighbours know much about her, just 'hello' and 'how are you' is all they get from her. She is strictly 'call out girl' and never entertains her clients in her digs. We have her address book and it contains thirty one names – only Christian names, except two, all with telephone numbers except three, all are within the Kings Cross, Camden and Islington area." Whithers paused and looked around the room as if he was expecting some reaction to this basic introduction.

Tonks grunted as he cleared his throat, "Is that it Detective Sergeant?"

"No Sir, there's a bit more – we have spoken to Sasha's parents and they tell us she has a child from a Somalian gentlemen, Yusuf, whom she met when she was out there doing voluntary work with the VSO – that was a year ago. As far as the parents know Yusuf has never seen nor made contact with Sasha since her return from the VSO." Whithers stopped again looking closely at his notebook as if it was difficult to read his own handwriting.

"Anything else?" Tonks's voice contained a hint of impatience.

"Yes Sir, the parents are looking after the child, Vana, whilst Sasha earns enough money to buy a place of her own, in Weymouth actually, for herself and the kid – they didn't know she was on the game, came as a big shock – they said that Sasha had told them she was close to getting the deposit money, about a month away according to them." Whithers kept peering at his notes as if there was something hidden that he couldn't find. The sound of a door closing down the corridor and a phone ringing in the next room exaggerated the delay.

"Yes, yes Detective Sergeant – what else you got there?" Tonks was impatient like a man held in a queue for too long.

Whithers looked nervous and out of place at the front of the room by the display board as if he was waiting to be taken to the top of a scaffold and publically hanged.

"Well Gov, there's the silver brooch found in the gutter near where Sasha was attacked …" He took out the pendant from a plastic bag and held it up with some tweezers. "… not sure what this design means Gov, the lab boys have checked it out for prints and I'm waiting for their report – of course it may have nothing to do with the incident."

Tonks eyed the brooch closely, "Yes, let me know what the lab boys say straightaway – anything else Detective Sergeant?"

"Yes, um, we found £1,950 under her bed in mixed notes, must be that deposit money for her Weymouth place I reckon, then there's the answer phone machine – we have had our tech boys go through the tape with a fine tooth comb and the vast majority of the messages were just incoming calls from her clients to arrange meetings but there were one or two interesting exceptions – one was from a man called Banjoko that was timed at 11.31pm Tuesday 19th June – that's just over two hours before Sasha was found unconscious on the pavement – Banjoko's message is difficult to hear, he has a strong Nigerian accent, but it's clear he's angry with her for not answering his calls, really angry – there are two previous calls from him made throughout Tuesday but for some reason Sasha does not pick up or call back – checking her address book we can see that Banjoko's name is crossed through – there must have been a falling out somewhere along the line Gov." Whithers was now more relaxed and getting into his stride.

"Yes, yes, carry on Detective Sergeant, who was the other message from?" Tonks was now visibly curious and interested in the unfolding evidence.

Whithers continued, "Then there was a message from some one called Theo – made at 10.08pm Tuesday, that reads, "It's Theo – got to see you, want you to ease my troubled mind – I'm lost and bewildered Sasha, I've got such terrible thoughts, want you to squeeze the doubt and pain from me." We've phone-traced Banjoko's and Theo's addresses and both are within a fifteen minute tube ride from Werrington Street, so either one could easily have got round to Sasha's place that night." Whithers looked around for some sign of appreciation from his colleagues.

"Very good Detective Sergeant – do we know anything about her last client before she was attacked?"

"Yes Gov, her last client according to her answer machine was a Polish gentleman called Nacek whose appointment with her was at 10.15pm – Nacek lives in Camden and a neighbour confirms he saw a woman fitting Sasha's description leave Nacek's place at approximately 11.10pm, wearing a short blue skirt and yellow top." Whithers turned the pages of his notebook and then said, "An interesting thing Gov, we found this charcoal sketch of Sasha in her room signed by Nacek."

Whithers held up the sketch and there was a slight murmuring amongst the officers as they took in the full splendour of Sasha's nude image.

The blank expression in Tonks's shadowy brooding eyes went darker still and then half closed to form his favoured squint as if his eyesight was suffering from cataracts.

"What are the similarities between this case and the other three?" He kept squinting his eyes as he looked at Whithers as if his thoughts were causing pain.

"Well, just that all four involve call girls operating in the Kings Cross area and all were assaulted outside or very close to their abodes and all were bludgeoned by a blunt weapon but forensics can't confirm it was the same one used in all four attacks, they say it was most likely a cosh or some sort of heavy stick or club – none of the other attacks have been fatal and there is reason to believe the assailant is wanting to punish the victims rather than kill or maim them – all the attacks occurred late at night, no robbery involved …"

Just then the door opened and the Desk Sergeant stood with a piece of paper in his hand looking intense.

"Just heard from Peters at the hospital Gov – Miss Phillips is still in Intensive Care, still unconscious but her breathing has become erratic and causing some concern."

Tonks leapt out of his seat as quickly as if he had just noticed a Blue Krait crawling up his leg. "Thank you Sergeant – right lads, it's time for action – I want Constables Miller and Pace to go and bring in Banjoko and Constables Bryce and Swan go and fetch that Theo character here pronto – both for questioning – I don't care what they're doing, just bring 'em in asap – off you go – Oh and Detective Sergeant, one more thing, did you notice any bedtime casual wear on Sasha's bed, pyjamas, T-shirt, any loungewear of any sort, sweatshirt, joggers, that sort of thing?"

Whithers, who had almost left the room, stepped back inside and reopened his notebook, "Um, no Gov, I didn't note anything."

Constable Bryce called out, "Yes Gov, she did have a floppy T-shirt lying on top of her bed, looked like it had been thrown across it, across the pillow actually – I remember 'cos I was the one that stripped her bed – it had 'Weymouth Sands' printed on it in big gold letters."

The meeting room emptied as quickly as a sink of water with its plug pulled.

Tonks went over to the display board and looked hard at the picture of Sasha, "So this geezer didn't break in and take your money – he attacked you on the street outside – what was the motive, and what were you doing out on the pavement at that time – if you left Nacek's just past eleven you would have got home at 11.30pm latest – if you were found at 01.56am when were you attacked, it couldn't have been when you got back from Nacek's because you were found wearing lycra gym clothes, not presumably your working clothes that your wardrobe suggests are much smarter, what with all those tailored suits, jackets with padded shoulders, roll-neck sweaters and sexy short skirts – so why were you wearing those gym clothes I wonder - were you awoken by someone prowling outside and you went to investigate – but if so, why did you change clothes, why not just lean out the window to look – or did you arrange to meet someone for some reason? There's something odd about this case – it looks like a random mugging but it's not and there doesn't seem to be any motive."

He stood for some moments peering at Sasha's photograph and started to stroke his chin again, "I've got a funny feeling about this one." With that he squinted his eyes one more time.

Chapter Nine

Theo and Jenny sat on the Hotel de la Plage's outside terrace in the soft late twilight with the exhausted sun just departed and the emerging three-quarter moon getting ready for its show; the terrace radiated with a sense of tranquillity in the thin half-light with mauve and blue undertones and the breeze hardly moving on the warm balmy night, just enough to rustle the surrounding lime trees.

They sat in preferred silence accompanied by the amplified sounds of the bobbing, summer-slow river as it ambled down its channelled route to the expansive sands on Wissant beach. After dinner they had chosen to vacate the old fashioned dining room, pleasant though it was, and sit out the rest of the evening on the terrace with its, soirée romantique à l'extérieur and extra river feature. Several other guests had made the same decision and the terrace was dotted with couples and one or two family groups, mainly British, sitting in pools of flickering orange light from each table's identical glass candle holder.

"I can't believe it Jenny – you live in Packington Street off the Essex Road? That's incredible, what a coincidence, I live in Upper Street, how about that? Practically around the corner from you – that's truly amazing." Theo's face kept changing colour in the lambent candlelight.

"Upper Street goes on forever – where's your place exactly?" Jenny drew on a cigarette that she had saved for such an exquisite moment.

"I live above that old shop, the one with the Jewish name, Schram and Scheddle, you must know it – it used to be an old tailor shop with a sewing machine in the front window? It's donkey's years old, still got the original name sign though."

He looked at her hoping she knew what he was talking about.

"Of course I know it, everyone knows the Schram and Scheddle shop, it's legendary – well, well, that is amazing, you really are so very close to my place – you must come round for Sunday tea sometime, ha, ha."

They both made quick mental assessments of the implications of living so close to each other, searching for any possible negative aspects but could find none.

"I like that idea." Theo had a vision of himself dressed up in his Sunday best strolling round to Packington Street for tea with Jenny and felt strangely excited about the prospect.

"Can't tell you how many times I've walked up and down Upper Street, must have passed your place dozens of times – I met this chap, Danny, and he used to hang out in the Kings' Head in Upper Street." The sudden sharpness of this memory altered the cadence of her speech and even in the shadowy candlelight he could clearly see the change of expression come over her lovely oval face and dark eyes.

He poured her another glass of wine from the bottle she had chosen at dinner, a crisp Loire rosé that tasted of ripe strawberries. He knew this was the time to bleed her emotions.

"Tell me about Danny." His voice was soft and gentle accompanied by the lazy moving river and the unmistakable music of Stéphane Grappelli's violin playing *Stardust* drifting out the dining room window from Thérèse's concealed record player.

She looked wounded, a deep cut, her eyes were full of pain. She drew hard on the cigarette making her cheeks go hollow.

"God, I loved that man, I would have gone to the ends of the earth for him, and he knew it, but it was hopeless, I was just a narrow minded innocent little twerp up from the sticks, from Folkestone actually, practically straight from school, and couldn't compete in his world – he had this way about him, he kinda gave the impression he knew everything just with his eyes, he had a natural gift of the gab too, I mean he'd convince you black was white – or like that song says, 'You could make me believe by the fall of your eyes that the sun rose in the west' – and you stood there gazing into those bewitching eyes and believed him, he was a busker by day, and a sort of Falstaff at night, holding court in the Kings' Head with all his cronies, dressed in his old velvet jacket and jeans and plimsolls and long hair and homburg hat and those eyes of his, they could cut right into your soul with one look. He smoked Russian cigarettes, recited Wordsworth at the drop of a hat, taught me to play the guitar, ha-ha, said I was his muse, like Yeats' Maud Gonne, he introduced me to a world I knew nothing about, music, poetry, art, politics, topical argument, social issues, yes and of course, sex – he made out we were, you know, 'together' and for a while it looked like that, we spent all our time in his room in Percy Circus near the Pentonville Road or in the Kings' Head – he was like a King to me, and I was his Queen, it felt good – but it all came crashing down, as quickly as it had started, I caught him with another woman, same old story, I wasn't his Queen, I wasn't even his Courtesan, more like a mistress or a slutty concubine tart." She emptied her glass and refilled it puffing quickly at her cigarette as she did so.

"Some men can be awful like that ..." Theo didn't want to interrupt her flow but thought he ought to throw a pebble into her stream of memories just to show he was attentive and sympathetic.

"Ah, but it's not just the men, I'll give you that, the women can be liars and cheats too." The wine and the moment, the lovely warm evening, the fading light, the music, the river, the background drumming bass notes of the sea against the dunes, the delicious meal still flavouring her mouth and the proximity of Theo, it all conspired to exorcise the demons building up for so long inside her.

"Then there's this latest thing I've discovered, my mum's having an affair right under my dad's nose – would you believe it? She's forty-six years old but looks much younger with new hairstyle and clothes – and it works, she looks fantastic. I saw her with her new man as I was going off to the station this morning – Christ, was it really just this morning, feels like days ago – they were down this back street, kissing each other goodbye – goodness knows how long its been going on for, she keeps going out dressed up to the nines and telling my Dad she's seeing her girlfriends for a drink – all the bare-faced lies, hundreds of them – I think my father knows something but he's turning a blind eye, probably hoping it will fizzle out and everything will be alright again – he's such a lovely man, gentle and kind and caring, he'd do anything for my mum, she doesn't deserve him, I hope it all goes wrong for her, but that would mean it all going wrong for Dad too – Oh God, it's such a big mess." She lit another cigarette and looked curiously at ease with herself despite the emotional revelations.

Theo poured the last of the wine into his glass and looked around for one of the staff but they were all inside, probably sitting in the kitchen eating dinner whilst the guests digested theirs.

"Do you fancy a ciggy Theo?" She held out a packet of Gauloise cigarettes with one or two protruding from the opened corner.

He looked at the smooth round temptresses beckoning his touch just as a whiff of smoke from her cigarette curled through the air making a beeline for his nose like a snake slithering off to a hole in a rock. "Yeh, actually I would." She leant over the table with her lighter.

He leant back with a fag in one hand and a glass of wine in the other looking for all the world like a stereotypical university lecturer in a campus bar trying to impress his students.

"One of the last things my father told me just before he left us, up in our lonely twenty-two storey block in Depford, when I was nine, about living with my mother, he said, 'We just can't carry on any more – it doesn't work – it's difficult sometimes Theo, you'll see when you get older, it's not easy, relationships are not easy, you'll find out, nothing is perfect.' Perhaps this whole marriage thing has run its course, I mean, from a strictly anthropological, evolutional standpoint, it's probably defunct – only promoted as an ideal to keep us in check, stop us from anti-social behaviour, fornicating with our neighbours and loading society with too many abandoned babies – bad for the economy, bad for state control, bad for effective Government – much better to have everyone banged up with a big mortgage around their necks and a bunch of kids they feel morally responsible for – you're not inclined to be a rebel when the system has you manacled financially and ethically, ha ha."

"Blimey Theo, you're quite a nonconformist behind that bourgeois suave exterior aren't you – I love it!"

"Oh don't mind me, it's these Gauloise, get me every time, one puff and I turn into Sartre – 'just like that' …" He flicked his hands over mimicking Tommy Cooper.

As they burst out laughing Thérèse appeared as if on cue in a West End theatre farce.

"Allo Mr 'Arrison, "J'espère que vous avez apprécié votre repas, oui?"

"It was lovely Thérèse thank you …"

"Ah bon, et la nuit est jeune oui?"

"Well, yes but the old legs are feeling their age – been a long day."

"Ah Mr 'Arrison we must hold on to the youth oui? One minute it is here …" Thérèse held up a clenched fist, "… and then it is gone oui?" She then unclenched her fist and puffed into her palm as if she was blowing something away that was light and delicate, like a petal.

"I cannot argue with your observation Thérèse." Theo finished his wine.

"Mr 'Arrison – please permit me to give the cognac - gratis, sur la maison, avec mes compliments oui?"

"Thérèse – that is beyond my wildest dreams, merci!"

"Also for Mademoiselle oui?"

"Yes Thérèse – thank you."

Thérèse went off in the direction of the dining room stopping to speak to a small family group on the way.

"Gosh Theo, you're quite impressive with the old French lingo – I love the language, it sounds so romantic and sophisticated, and hey, I'd forgotten I was a 'Mademoiselle', sounds a bit young actually - and what's that she calls you – 'Mr 'Arrison' – is that your name, ha ha?"

Theo smiled. "My surname is 'Harrison' but the French have trouble with 'H's' – but somehow she makes it sound more interesting than plain 'Harrison', that's the wonder of foreign accents isn't it?"

Night was closing in fast and the moon changed hue to a deep rich cream radiating faint rings of warm light in the clear night sky.

"So Theo, you're fed up with your job, with all the dishonesty that goes with it and here I am fed up with relationships and all the lies that go with them – we're a right pair!"

Theo was slightly stung with the mention of his job; the sharp definition of all its recent horrors had receded since arriving in France barely ten hours ago. He changed the subject:

"Tell me about your job Jenny – are you a counsellor of some sort or a therapist maybe?"

She looked at him and laughed seeing something profoundly funny in his question. "What do you mean Theo Harrison, like a marriage counsellor or sex therapist perhaps – in your dreams my boy! Ha, ha."

They both leant back and laughed so loud the other guests stopped talking and looked around. A brief silence descended on the terrace.

She continued in a softer voice, "Um, well, you've given me some ideas, ha, ha – no, nothing so interesting, I'm a Social Worker for Camden Council mainly working with the borough's homeless – it's a bitter-sweet job, I love it that I have in my remit the scope to help people, all those down-trodden ordinary people that for one reason or other find themselves, or themselves and their families, without a roof over their head – but my work has become a living nightmare under this Government, they've cut the budget just when they've pushed up inflation and unemployment, we're overwhelmed with cases and the truth is, we just can't cope, it breaks your heart to see these people, their little kids, poor and helpless, with no where to go …"

She took a sudden intake of breath and looked up at the sky, keeping her damp eyes from his gaze. After a few seconds she regained her composure and continued, "You should see the mess we're in Theo, no where to put them, most end up sleeping rough, have you seen the underpass at that roundabout near Waterloo station – there's a sodding town down there, they practically have their own bin collections, you should go see it Theo, it's a real eye opener – this Government has a lot to answer for – of course their newspaper chums keep quiet about it all don't they, heaven forbid they show you a bit of reality of working class life under all these Tory cuts, all the unforeseen social consequences – and if that's not enough, I have to contend with office politics would you believe, I recently lost out for promotion to Head of Section – the Section Director gave the job to some recent upstart who doesn't have any where near the same experience or attainment results as me – of course he's screwing her on the side, so that's alright then – who cares about the merit and justice of it all, mind you, she played a canny hand I'll give her that, performed every trick in the book to get his attention, Christ she practically threw herself at him – why are men so easily manipulated, one tweak of their willy and they're like putty in the hand, so to speak – it's got to be fair hasn't it, that's what we're taught, but it isn't, fairness and justice have nothing to do with it, it's morally corrupt."

Theo was moved deeply by her words. There was something natural and honest about her and he felt at ease in her company, easy in his soul, easy to speak and easy to be silent; he leant over and held her hand, feeling her warm blood moving through her fingers, trickling along and through his, joined in the moving flow of their life blood shared. He gently squeezed her hand tighter and felt the strong pulse of their life blood pass between them – their souls attracted like magnets, something soft and fine like silk thread entwined them – he had never trusted his feelings before, never sure what he had felt was the same as the other person's feelings for him, never certain it was a true match, but this was different, he could detect the signals coming back from Jenny, powerful bleeps traced on his mental sonar screen, clear as the June night air, in that moment he felt the love flow between them, sparkling and new, precious like a pearl and crisp like a freshly picked apple.

Just then Thérèse appeared with their drinks and two gratis chocolates on a small silver tray, "Alors voici vos boissons." She carefully placed the small glasses of cognac onto the table disturbing a couple of moths dancing around the candle flame.

"Ooo la la, there is more news with the mineurs de charbon oui, the Prime Minister she is on the TV now and she is saying the mineurs, they are Mr Scargill's shock troops, and they bring the violence and are, how you say, affront, yes affront to the law, and the mineurs who is arrested oui, they be charged with the riots and the riots mean life incarcérés, you say, in the prisons oui, life in the prisons for the riots – it is a big price to pay oui?"

"It's all lies Thérèse – rien que des mensonges – the Prime Minister and her media puppets spread lies or manipulate videos, and then ride out the repercussions, if there are any, but by that time the damage is done." Theo held up his cognac to the candlelight and then sipped the dark brown liquid, slowly, savouring each drop. "Oh that's wonderful Thérèse …"

"Merci monsieur – puis-je vous obtenir autre chose?"

"Yes Thérèse – we'll let you know if we need anything else, merci beaucoup."

He studied Jenny who was eating her chocolate as if it was a tingling erotic pleasure, closing her eyes with delight as she slowly savoured the sumptuous dark chocolate morello cherry liquor that burst with tangy Kirsch flavours in her mouth.

"God, is there no end to all these Government lies and distortions – where's the integrity, why isn't it important?"

Jenny finally opened her eyes from her brief moment of ecstasy working her tongue around the inside of her mouth and through her moist lips making little smacking sounds.

"The Prime Minister doesn't have any, she's decided that to get her way, to change the country's working practices and attitudes, to bring about the biggest subjugation of the working class ever witnessed she will have to adopt military tactics – to know your enemy and its weaknesses, to know where and when to attack, to set up decoys, snares, distractions, smokescreens, anything that gives her advantage, and most importantly, to have a well oiled propaganda machine working away night and day giving out exaggerated false accounts and generally tarnishing the enemy's character and image – and then voila! Once she has the rest of the country believing all the gobshite she can bring about her new brand of economics and social reform – job done, trade unions without teeth, then the rest of the country, the malleable middle class, the well off and the one per cent will go around singing her praises, especially if she's tossed them a few quid in tax deduction. The clever bitch!"

Theo sipped his cognac that had already tripped a dopamine rush. "Don't remind me, I know I've got blood on my hands …" He held up his hands and put on a Lawrence Olivier voice:

"What hands are here? Hah! They pluck out mine eyes.
Will all great Neptune's ocean wash this blood
Clean from my hand? No; this my hand will rather
The multitudinous seas incarnadine,
Making the green one red ..."

"There, that's all I remember, my best rendition of Macbeth, now I feel lighter despite my sins, ha."

"Wow, very good, I'm almost impressed, ha, ha.'

She kept staring at the silver tray and the remaining chocolate liquor sitting forlorn and abandoned.

"Have you thought any more about your job Theo?"

He couldn't evade the subject any longer, "Sort of, I know I can't continue putting lies into my bosses mouth so he can put them into the Prime Minister's or one of her Cabinet donkeys – I have to strive to be better than that, I shall leave, I have to for my own peace of mind, my resignation will be an act of atonement and that's the best thing to do, otherwise, I shall sleep no more – Theo doth murder sleep."

"So will you do that straightaway or what – If it were done when 'tis done, then it's well it were done quickly' or something like that."

"Ah, so you took Macbeth for GCE too?"

"Of course, we all did, great play – but seriously Theo, it's best to have something else lined up isn't it?" She took a sip of cognac. "Um, that goes so well with the cherry liquor."

He continued, "There's no point hanging around – my mind's made up – I'm not sure what to do next though, I've got some savings so there's no real rush – it all seems such a big deal, such a burden at the moment, my work, the miner's strike, this bloody recession, rampant inflation, public spending cuts, poverty and homelessness everywhere, inequality, all the lies, lies, lies and this ghastly Government induced selfishness, so much wrong and so much to put right – she can't win again can she? Not after all this mayhem, she can't win again in '87 surely not, she won't have bloody Argentina to save her next time."

She moved her fingers through his hand wrapped around hers, "Things will change, you have to believe in the future – there's a limit to how much shit the people will put up with – even the smug English middle class will change their attitude in time – it will just take someone not too unlike them, someone they can trust to stand up for their way of life and offer a better deal for ordinary people and they will put their cross in a different box – even if that means not voting Tory, but that person hasn't appeared yet, they're waiting in the shadows, but there will be one that nudges out into the crowd, just a matter of time."

A rich silence fell around them and as the night had deepened it amplified the unmistakeable rumble of the incoming tide from across the dunes – a melody of symbols and bass drums, booms and splatter mixed together in a jazz of brawling sea.

"Do you hear it Jen? The great sound of the ocean – inimitable and powerful like something supernatural – the Cornish have a word for it – Mordros – the sound of the sea."

"I love it – you can hear it in those conch shells too can't you, how strange that is." Her eyes beamed with the memory of putting her ear to a conch for the first time when she was a child.

They both remained silent listening to the Mordros that was made more sweet by their state of comfort and pleasure sitting on the terrace; then she looked above at the night sky vivid clear without its cloud companion and wondrous with its layers of pulsing stars. She became mesmerised by the immensity and the demanding mystery of it all, the utter unfathomableness of its vastness and incalculability of its depth.

"Theo – look, right over there – do you see that milky blur of stars all grouped together – over there, to your right –that's the great spiral Andromeda Galaxy our nearest large galaxy – it's the most distant object you can see with your naked eye – and there, do you see that bright star close to it, that's the Schedar in Cassiopeia, it's the constellation's brightest star, and it points to Andromeda. Look at Andromeda Theo, it's so small from here isn't it, a small bright spec really, but just think, it contains about one trillion stars and a hundred million galaxies – it's mind boggling isn't it, can't get your head around it, it's about two and a half million light years away – and it's there right now, as we look, hundreds and hundreds of stars, some dying and others being formed, the cycle of life and death even in the heavens – who knows whether there's life amongst all that, I wouldn't bet against it, and then when you look around here at this little planet Earth, that you wouldn't even see from Andromeda, you start to get true perspective on these petty problems that seem so important to us right now, but actually they're not, when you hold them up against the night sky they're nothing really are they – everything just pales into insignificance."

"Well, yes but that's no 'constellation' to our problems right now, ha, ha." His deliberate malapropism shook her out of her galactic profundity.

"Very droll Theo …"

They both laughed again peering into each others' eyes.

"Seriously though, aren't you fascinated by space and the stars and all the unknowns up there?" She again seemed to disappear somewhere secret within herself as she continued to gaze upwards.

"Of course …" Theo put on a sober tone to his voice that he thought the subject required, "… I just so love that painting, *Starry Night* – the way the night sky seems to swirl and move like the sea – full of mystery and a touch of menace – Van Gogh said the stars reminded him of death but they make me feel alive, alive with curiosity – a sort of promise that there is something else, beyond our knowledge, that awaits us…"

She looked at him with wonder in her eyes, "Exactly Theo – you've summed it up pretty well …"

There was a warm silence between them that moved and pulsed with depth and infinite possibilities like the firmament.

Then finally she said in a gayer tone, "Actually Theo, you know you believe in the general principles of equal distribution and sharing of wealth for the common good – well, do you mind if I have your chocolate?" She quickly grabbed the solitary cherry liquor from the tray.

"Umm, that's so yummy – you may be a champagne socialist Theo but I'm a cherry liquor communist – ha, ha."

"That's a brilliant idea, let's have a glass of champagne to finish the evening – as an excuse to celebrate my big decision to leave work – no more tangled webs we weave, no more dishonesty, no more distortions, no more deception, no more working for the Prime Minister and all her lying cohorts – a new future."

She leant over the table towards him, practically resting her forehead on his and started to sing:

"I ain't gonna work on Maggie's farm no more
Well, I try my best
To be just like I am
But everybody wants you
To be just like them
They say, "Sing while you slave," and I just get bored
Ah, I ain't gonna work on Maggie's farm no more."

In that moment a new love passed irrepressibly between them, flowing through their veins and tingling their nerves, they both felt alive again and renewed. He inched forward feeling the warm, sweaty pad of her forehead and sang along with all his heart. Above them trillions of stars studded the black velvet sky, shining for the here and now, for love and youth and life.

Chapter Ten

Theo arrived back at his bedsit in Islington late Friday afternoon, tired and exhausted by the journey from Wissant and Dover, his head full of images of Jenny and the time they spent over the last couple of days exploring the countryside around Calais and Boulogne; his heart raced as he recalled their goodbye kiss that morning as she boarded her bus to Boulogne in the main square in Wissant with those last whispered words as she pressed a small piece of pink paper into his hand:

"Don't forget to phone me, as soon as you get back tonight, don't forget, I'll be waiting …"

Her words wrapped in hot breath still purred in his ears as he sped along in the bus to Calais; he saw her lovely face superimposed on everything that went by, making the journey pass in a sort of surreal dream – he felt renewed and alive, his future ablaze with exciting possibilities.

He had no sooner put his bag down when the front door bell rang.

Police constables Swan and Bryce stood on the doorstep stiff and straight like two newly painted lamp posts on an army parade ground. Swan had a narrow weasel face whilst Bryce's head was like a large baking potato; they both stared at Theo with grim set eyes especially trained for solemn occasions.

Bryce stood upright with his small mouth opening like a robot. "Mr Harrison? Mr Theo Harrison? This is Constable Swan and I'm Constable Bryce from Camden Police Station."

Theo's mind spun like an engine's flywheel trying to guess what had happened, some bad news about a relative no doubt, but which one?

"Yes, that's right, what's up officers?" Theo's expression was suitably grave and serious as befitted the melodrama.

"We believe you are an associate of a one Sasha Phillips of 22 Werrington Street, is that correct Sir?" Bryce looked down his bent nose into Theo's eyes as cold as a polar bear as it sinks its teeth into a seal's throat.

A now faded vision of Sasha flicked through Theo's mind, her hands and eyes and naked body all tripped through like a 16mm film running through a cine camera's shutter.

"Yes, I know Sasha, what's happened?"

Swan quickly interjected, "We need to ask you some questions down at the station concerning your recent engagements with Ms Phillips – can you please get your things and come with us, we have a car outside."

"I've literally just come in, been travelling up from France all day, can't this wait until I've sorted myself out, I could come along this evening?" He knew his plea did not sound convincing.

"No Sir, we need to question you straight away, can you get your things now please." Bryce's icy eyes made it clear what Theo should do next.

"Well, OK, but I could do with something, some refreshment."

At the police station Theo was searched and his pockets emptied with all his stuff put into a clear plastic bag, these included: a wallet containing twenty two French francs and forty centimes and a twenty pound note, a packet of Gauloises cigarettes, a disposable lighter, a notebook and pencil, a Travelcard, a clipped rail and ferry ticket, a door key, a pocket-sized packet of tissues and a small piece of pink paper torn from a diary with a telephone number written on it in pencil next to the name 'Jenny'. He was then told to fill out a form giving all his personal details, after which he had his fingerprints taken.

Finally he was led into an interview room by Swan and Bryce where Detective Chief Inspector Tonks sat going through some papers and photographs.

"Sit down Mr Harrison please – do you know why you are here Sir?"

"I've got no idea, something to do with Sasha – but I haven't been given any details, how is she, what's happened exactly?"

Tonks pushed a photograph across the table, "Do you recognise this person?"

"Yes, of course, that's Sasha – looks a bit younger there – what's happened to her?"

"All in good time Sir. Can you confirm your relationship with Sasha Phillips please?" Tonks sat poised over his notebook, with pen in hand.

"My relationship? I don't have a relationship, not in the sense of being a relative, or a lover, or …"

"In what sense would you say then Sir, given that Ms Phillips' occupation is, how can I put it, a 'visiting prostitute'?" Tonks' dry squinting eyes looked as if there was absolutely nothing in the world that could make them shine with joy or astonishment.

There was a loud silence in the interview room.

"Well OK, yes, I saw Sasha from time to time, but it was strictly business – not a relationship – I saw her when I got, well, lonely." Theo felt pathetic and ashamed, like an adolescent caught playing with himself in the shower.

"Yes, quite so Mr Harrison, I notice you are not married – do you have a partner, a steady girlfriend?"

"What's that got to do with anything, no, I don't have a partner, I'm not running a business consortium for Christ's sake."

"And when was the last time you, um, shall I say, had an appointment with Ms Phillips?" Tonks was writing in his notebook as he spoke stretching out the word 'appointment' as if it was pulled from his mouth like chewing gum.

Theo tried to remember but a thick fog was seeping through the alleyways of his memory.

"I don't know, probably a couple of weeks ago – I can't remember exactly, the week before last sometime I think."

Tonks looked up, "Can you tell me where you were the evening of Monday 18th June and the evening of Tuesday 19th June between midnight and 2.00 am?"

Quick flashes of the events at Orgreave came immediately to his mind followed instantly by disjointed memories of the extraordinary events back at the Sheffield hotel.

"I'm not sure, it seems ages ago, let me see, I went up to Sheffield on Sunday, the 17th, on business and returned to London on the Tuesday, the 19th and went off to France on the 20th …"

"Hold on Mr Harrison, not so fast, let's put some detail into this shall we – now, tell me why you went to Sheffield, how and when you got there, where you were staying, how and when you got back to London and then the details of your trip to France, please take your time …"

Theo's mind sank into a quagmire, he was tired, hungry and thirsty and just wanted to shower and have a meal in peace.

Laboriously he picked his way through the details, outlining his trip to Sheffield and the subsequent visit to France. Tonks, a seasoned note taker with his own version of shorthand, scribbled quickly into his notepad.

"I see, so you work for the Government's Public Relations office, um, that's very interesting."

"You may think so, but I can assure you it's not the word I'd use – look, do you have a cup of tea or something, I've been travelling most of the day and I'm tired and thirsty."

Tonks looked across to Swan and moved his eyes in a sideways direction towards the door. Swan got up and left the room.

Tonks took a deep breath as if he was about to plunge under water. "Well of course we can check all that with your office

Sir." He looked through his notes again until he found a particular entry.

"Now tell me about the night of Monday 18th if you don't mind, when you got back to your hotel room from, ah let me see, what was the restaurant name, oh yes, the Akabar – when you got back from the Akabar did you make a telephone call?"

The crazy midnight call to Sasha jumped into his memory like a large slab of concrete dropped into a secluded woodland pond.

"Yes, I believe I did, to Sasha actually, it was a bit silly ..."

Tonks interrupted, "Yes, well, we'll be the judge of that, what did you say?"

"I was drunk and phoned her late, must have been about midnight, I wanted to see her, I wanted to arrange a time for the next day back in London – I woke her up, she was annoyed, she told me to phone her in the morning and hung up – the whole thing lasted about a minute, it was stupid of me."

Tonks was looking straight into Theo's eyes with his squinting stare, "And did you phone her in the morning?"

"No – I phoned her later that evening, about ten or thereabouts, but she wasn't in, so I left a message."

Tonks pulled out a piece of paper from the pile on the desk, "Yes, we have the transcript here Mr Harrison – it's amazing this new technology isn't it, got everything anyone has ever said on that answer machine of hers – this is what you said Mr Harrison ..." He read out Theo's message:

'Oh Sasha, it's Theo – look, I'm sorry about last night, didn't mean to frighten you, um, I'd like to see you, tonight, I know it's getting late, but I've got to see you, want you to ease my troubled mind – I'm lost and bewildered Sasha, I've got such terrible thoughts, want you to squeeze the doubt and pain from me.'

"What were the 'terrible thoughts' I wonder?" Tonks looked like a chess player who was gaining the upper hand.

Theo started to lose his temper. "Look, I want to know what this is about, you've dragged me here virtually from the boat train, I'm exhausted, hungry and thirsty, you've not given me any explanation and then quizzed me over some drunken phone call I made late at night nearly a week ago – what the hell has happened to Sasha?" Theo's voice rose in pitch as he spoke finishing almost in a restrained shout.

"OK Sir, steady on. I will tell you what this is about, but I was trying to understand the circumstances of your recent communications concerning Sasha Phillips – well now, there was an incident concerning Ms Phillips, she was brutally attacked outside her place at 22 Werrington Street, King's Cross."

Tonks found another photograph and placed it in front of Theo.

"Here, you can see, she was found unconscious on the pavement with serious head wounds, one to the left-hand side fracturing the cheekbone and a more serious wound to the right-hand side probably where she fell onto the edge of the kerb – causing a deep cut and extensive swelling with likely clotting to the brain – she is still unconscious in Intensive Care…" Tonks paused to let the information sink into Theo's mind.

Theo stared at the photograph of Sasha in horror, "Oh my God, the poor thing …" He was genuinely shocked at her injuries and his heart filled with concern for her. "What hospital is she in?"

"She's in the UCH but as I say, she's still in Intensive, no visitors – right, so Mr Harrison, what were these 'terrible thoughts' of yours that you wanted to share with Ms Phillips?"

"Look, I'd had an extremely long and emotionally draining time in Sheffield, as an observer to the events at Orgreave, with the miners and the police and everything, it was awful, I just wanted someone to talk to – but it doesn't matter does it Officer because she wasn't at home and I was in my flat, so what are we talking about?"

Just then Swan came in with a mug of coffee and a plate of biscuits on a tray together with a document that he handed to Tonks. Theo could hardly stop himself from stuffing two biscuits in his mouth at one go.

Tonks read the document as he said to Theo, "Well, we'll check all these details of course … um, that's very interesting, very interesting indeed." He studied the document for a long time and then peered at Theo like someone who was aware of a secret.

"You have my rail and ferry ticket – that should be enough." For the first time Theo saw the ignominy of having his name openly dragged through all the public enquiries linked to Sasha and the call girl case.

"Mr Harrison, I'm just a humble servant of the people, trying to keep the peace and keep villains off the streets, I want to know if you went round to Sasha's place after you left the telephone message on Tuesday 19th June, after your message at ten o'clock, yes or no?"

Theo gulped the coffee so fast he slightly burnt his mouth. "No, I did not go round to Sasha's – I went to bed, I had to be up next morning to go to Calais – actually, I've never been to her place, she always comes to mine, she's a call girl after all, not a socialite, she's not bloody Lady Ottoline-Morrell for Christ's sake is she, her job is to call on customers not the other way round, she didn't answer my call, she must have been out – she always picks up if she's there, have you checked who her client was at that time – you'll see the timings match with what I'm saying …"

Tonks retorted sharply, "Of course we've checked, and someone bearing Sasha's description was seen leaving her last client's address at approximately eleven-ten that means she would have been back at her digs around eleven-thirty – so the question is Mr Harrison can you account for your movements between your phone call at ten o'clock and when she was found at one-fifty six Wednesday morning?"

"Well, no, because there weren't any movements, I was in my bloody bed wasn't I?"

Tonks looked at the document once again allowing a devilish grimace to reshape his mouth.

"Tell me Mr Harrison, is this silver brooch known to you?" He pushed across the table a photograph of a pendant.

Theo could hardly believe his eyes as he instantly recognised his silver brooch of the helmeted winged Archangel St Michael with his sword in hand. It was unusual and he had never seen another like it. There was no doubt it was his but he couldn't imagine how or why it was related to the brutal attack on Sasha.

The fact was he hadn't seen it, or thought about it for months and wouldn't have known where he kept it – his mind went blank, he was baffled by this sudden turn of events.

"Well Mr Harrison, what is your answer?" Tonks leaned over and squinted so much his eyes balls all but disappeared.

"Yes, that's mine, it's very special, my St Michael charm, my mother gave it to me years ago, but, I don't understand, why, I mean, what has it got to do with anything?" His astonishment was so acute even the Police Station's cat would have raised its ears at the sight.

"Ah well, that's interesting, very interesting indeed – this silver brooch was found in the gutter right next to where Sasha was attacked and your fingerprints Mr Harrison are on it – that links you directly to the scene of the crime – now, perhaps you would like to think again and tell me if you visited Sasha after your phone call eh?"

Theo drank some more coffee and tried to think clearly – the only explanation was that Sasha must have stolen the brooch but he could never prove it.

"Look, this is ludicrous, I have absolutely no reason to attack Sasha, there simply is no motive is there, far from wanting to harm her I was desperate to see her, you know, for the comforts she offers – I was run down with everything at work, with the experience of Orgreave – I just wanted to be with her – she knows how to please you, how to relax you, she's good at what she does believe me." He thought how inept his words sounded and regretted saying them.

Tonks didn't seem to hear what Theo had said and spoke slowly to indicate his growing frustration.

"So Mr Harrison, tell me what you meant when you said, and I quote, '…want you to ease my troubled mind – I'm lost and bewildered Sasha, I've got such terrible thoughts …' Isn't it the case Mr Harrison that you were not in your right state of mind, you were in some sort of frenzy to see Sasha and you went round there, knowing she would be returning shortly from her last client, to persuade her to let you in – and when she did not, because maybe she was just too tired or perhaps she was put off by your, shall we say, over-zealousness, you lost your temper and struck her there and then on the pavement and in the struggle you lost your lucky charm – then you panicked and scarpered off to France, to disappear for awhile – isn't that what happened Mr Harrison – look, I'm a man of the world and I've seen a lot of things in my time, I reckon you probably didn't mean to inflict the terrible injuries she got when her head hit the curb, but nevertheless, it was you that went round there and struck her, isn't that what happened Mr Harrison?"

Theo felt overwhelmed by Tonks' persistence, his persuasive account, and the high level of probability it presented. He was feeling frayed from his long day travelling back to London and strained by lack of rest and proper sustenance, his nerves were shot out and he even started to imagine that he might have gone round to Sasha's place after all and struck her, such was the state of his confusion.

"No, no, that is not what happened, I didn't go round to see her, I went to bed – you'll have to believe me, I went to bed …"

Tonks lined up some photographs of three women in front of Theo.

"Do you know these young ladies Mr Harrison?" He pointed at each photograph in turn with a finger stained with nicotine, "…this one, Ms McDonald, this one, Ms Tyler and this one, Ms Patcham?" He spoke slowly and methodically as if Theo had learning difficulties.

"No, never seen them before – who are they?"

Tonks leaned back in his chair, "They are call girls, and they all work in the same area as Sasha, or thereabouts, and they have all been subjected to late night attacks, outside or near to where they live – fortunately they all survived but were badly beaten up – Tyler's got a four inch scar across her temple and a bit of ear missing, McDonald's half blind and Patcham's jaw doesn't work properly 'cos it was broken in two places – take a close look please Mr Harrison and tell me if you've seen any of them before."

"I've told you, I don't know them and haven't seen them before, although I have heard about the attacks, everyone's talking about them."

"I see, OK, well I will tell you what we're going to do – we are going to detain you for further questioning – Constable Swan here will be asking you some more questions and after that you will be put into one of the cells …"

"You haven't charged me therefore I'm free to go …" Theo was desperate to get back to the comforts of his bedsit, to the freedom of his life, "… and why don't you check with these three women – they will know it wasn't me that attacked them – and another thing, have you checked whether Sasha's fingerprints are on the brooch – I bet they are, she must have stolen it from me."

Tonks got up from the table, "Everything in good time Mr Harrison, everything in good time – but I'm afraid you're not free to go, not yet, we can keep you for questioning up to twenty-four hours if need be – there's a lot of circumstantial evidence linking you to this crime – I want you to think very hard about your movements on Tuesday 19th after ten o'clock." Tonks left the room and Swan took charge of the interview.

It was then that Theo checked his watch, it was nearly half past eight. He had lost track of time. Something was hidden in his memory, clouded over by all the dramatic developments from when he had arrived back from France, by all the sweet memories of being with Jenny during the past couple of days – something was there waiting to reveal itself, to emerge suddenly like an underwater swimmer slowly resurfacing, startling his numbed senses. Then he remembered, he had promised to phone Jenny, she was at home waiting for his call, the evening was slipping away and he had no means of contacting her.

Meanwhile in an adjourning interview room Banjoko stood up from the table and addressed Detective Sergeant Whithers, and Constables Miller and Pace seated opposite, in a voice that was pitched to show controlled superiority:

"Gentlemen, it is with regret that you did not listen to me earlier, we could have saved ourselves all this time and effort. Most unfortunate. I have given you absolute assurance of my preoccupation elsewhere around eleven-thirty last Tuesday night and right through to Wednesday morning – it would not be acceptable or diplomatic however for you to pursue this matter any further."

Withers looked at Pace who looked at Miller and Miller looked back at both Pace and Withers and they all disappeared into a hazy conundrum.

Withers said, "Are you saying Mr Banjoko that the Swedish lady you claim to have been with all that time cannot be approached to verify your statement?"

"Gentlemen, that is most precise. The lady works for the Swedish Embassy and I work for the Nigerian Embassy as a high-ranking official – we are both exempt from further scrutiny and protected by Diplomatic Immunity as defined in International Law and practised on a reciprocal basis by the UK Government, my Government and the Swedish Government – besides, any further investigations would prove most unfortunate for her marriage."

Banjoko's large watery red eyes gazed at Withers and Pace and Miller like an old hunting dog waiting to be sent off to collect the game.

"Gentlemen, I think you agree yes, we have concluded our business here tonight?"

With that Banjoko got up and slowly departed and there was nothing Withers nor Pace nor Miller could do about it.

* * * * * * * *

When Jenny arrived back at her bedsit in Packington Street she made a coffee and collapsed into the armchair feeling tired but elated at the same time. Her short stay in Wissant had given her a new lease of life and she felt more positive than she had done for months. Thoughts of Theo kept flicking through her head – his voice, his penetrating eyes, his thick wavy hair and distinctive bent nose presented an image that would not readily shift from her mind; but what attracted her most of all was his quick and abstract sense of humour that was reticent and subtle at first but came on more spontaneously as they relaxed in each other's company.

She sat reviving over a mug of coffee reliving the time spent together exploring Wissant, swimming in the sea, taking the bus to Ambleteuse ten miles along the coast and eating Moules à la Marinière and crusty bread in a restaurant close to the huge Fort by the river Slack, sitting on the dunes, holding hands and the first kiss that sealed something precious starting to grow between them; then the dinner in Wissant on the last night in a little bistro off the central square when she chose the Confit de Canard and he the Oysters Mignonette and how they laughed at their stereotypical choices of what the English are expected to eat in France; and she recalled his natural curiosity in what the waiter had to say about the old harbour town and its historical connection to Thomas Becket – how the Archbishop had returned from exile by ship from the little port early December 1170 and was murdered twenty-eight days later in Canterbury Cathedral; there followed some discussion about why he had been killed and how his knights may have taken Henry II's words too literally when he had said in a moment of agitation – 'Will no one rid me of this turbulent priest?' She recalled how Theo was fascinated by this likely theory of misinterpretation and how it reminded him of the way his boss had so empathically misinterpreted his report of the events at Orgreave.

Then the memory of being back in his hotel room washed over her like the Cascade du Casteu waterfall, invigorating her and cleansing her senses; that exquisite moment in the dark making love on the four poster bed, sharing their precious gifts with each other, complete and whole, it had sealed something exquisite and priceless, a treasure of love that bound them forever. She sat tingling with these memories and the insights into Theo's character and with each revelation her love for him deepened. Her heart yearned to see him again for there was no doubt that every time she thought of him her eyes glowed bright with an inner intensity that could not be explained in medical science whilst a soft tender smile revealed a dimple on each cheek.

She unpacked, washed and had just put on clean shorts and a bra when the phone rang. She bounded down to the middle landing and picked up the phone expecting to hear Theo's voice.

"Hello Jen – is that you, it's Dad here." Reggie's voice was toneless and flat signalling a disturbance lurking somewhere.

"Dad? What's up? You're very quiet."

"She's left me Jen, your mother has left me, gone off with some one from work, Earl or somebody."

Jenny screamed within herself, 'You bitch Mum!' as if she had anticipated this development; then after a pause she said, "Oh Dad, that's awful, I'm so sorry for you, but really, I'm not surprised, it was obvious something was going on, just by looking at her, she didn't make herself up like that for her mates did she Dad?"

She knew she was being harsh but she was astonished her father had not been suspicious long before this final blow, and in any case she had instantly slipped into the role of being a fair and balanced arbitrator and reasoned observer.

"Yeh, I knew alright, but I didn't want to admit it, I didn't want to confront her 'cos I knew it would bring everything to a head, I was afraid of what would happen – and now it has." His soft single pitched voice came from someone broken and small.

"Oh Dad, when did this happen, Christ I only saw you a few days ago?" Jenny recalled the evening they had spent together in the Lobster Pot just three nights ago when she brought the subject up but he had dismissed it.

"She told me Wednesday night, the day you left for France, she came home, cooked dinner and then packed an over-night bag and told me as she was leaving, that she'd be back for the rest of her things, just like that, as brazen as you please – my God there's no love left in that woman and that's for sure – all those years we had together – I trusted her Jen, it's the broken trust that cuts me deep – and all the blatant lies."

"Look Dad, I'd prefer to have this conversation face to face but as you've phoned, well, look, I would have told you, but I saw Mum that morning when I went to the ferry port, I saw her by an alleyway kissing some bloke – must have been Earl – I had my suspicions before but seeing them together knocked me out, so brazen – but what did she say Dad, I mean, is it definite, maybe it will pass over, in time?" Jenny was getting lost in her own emotions and the sense that nothing could be done for her hapless, beleaguered father, like a bird with a broken wing cornered by a fox.

"I just don't know Jen, who knows? God I feel so let down, it's this feeling of, well, this feeling of treachery, of being lied to, being cheated on – makes you feel hurt and empty – no, it won't pass over, I can tell she's got it bad for this Earl – it's a big thing to chuck in your marriage, she means it – said she's coming back for the rest of her stuff over the weekend."

"Oh Dad, what will you do? Shall I come and stay for a while maybe?"

"No, no Jen, it's OK – I've got to sort it out, got to carry on, actually, I told someone about it at work yesterday, a friend of mine, Betty in Admin, we've been having little chats for some time now, and today she asked me round to her place for dinner tomorrow night – would you believe it, that's kind of her isn't it, but I don't know about going for dinner, it's a bit sudden, can you imagine the conversation, I'll be a bundle of laughs won't I?" His natural voice tone had recovered and he sounded more sure and confident.

"Really? That was quick. What the heck, I would definitely go round to Betty's for dinner Dad, that'll take your mind off things won't it – what she like this Betty?"

"Betty? She's a sweet lady, a widower, I've always got on with her, for chats and putting the world to rights, we see eye to eye on things, said she would like to see my kite actually, that's funny ain't it, didn't think of it that way, ha, ha – no seriously, she's thoughtful and she's got a caring nature, but it's a bit sudden isn't it – maybe another time, I said I'd phone and let her know, I must admit I'm tempted …"

"Dad, you've got nothing to lose and right now you need a friend – promise me you'll phone her and tell her you'll see her tomorrow night – phone her now Dad promise me, you'll have loads to talk about, what with Mum and her telling you about her husband."

"Yes, maybe I will – but how was France my luv? Did you get things sorted out in your head, with work and everything I mean?" His equilibrium seemed stable and he sounded his old self.

"Oh Dad, I had a lovely time and met this fantastic chap, Theo, he lives just around the corner would you believe it, literally five minutes away – I'm waiting for his call right now actually – can't wait to see him again, we just hit it off straightaway – God moves in mysterious ways does he not?"

"Go grab the opportunity my luv, with both hands, trust your judgement – true love is more precious than all the money in the world, grab it and keep it close if you think you've found it."

Just past midnight Jenny finally went to bed having stayed up all evening in her room waiting for Theo's phone call that never came.

* * * * * * * *

A significant development occurred at twelve minutes past midnight and Detective Sergeant Whithers and Constable Miller were sent out to investigate.

A young woman had been beaten unconscious outside her flat on Britannia Street off the King's Cross Road. Constable Pace was already at the scene guarding a man in handcuffs as a small group of people gathered despite the late hour; an ambulance was in attendance, standing still and ominous with its back doors closed whilst the paramedics worked on the victim inside. Several drops of blood stained the pavement and a single yellow leather shoe sat upside down in the gutter.

"What's going on Constable – and who's that?" Whithers looked intently at the handcuffed man then up and down, left and right across the street, as if he was on a secret mission behind enemy lines.

"Young lady Sarg, another call girl, attacked as she arrived back at her place." Pace pointed to the building they were standing outside, a dilapidated old three-storey Georgian town house, typical of the area north of the King's Cross Road that somehow had avoided Hermann Goring's 1940 Luftwaffe blitz.

"She was badly beaten around the head and was unconscious but the paramedics have got her back with us thank God."

He pointed at the ambulance with its blue light flashing across the street and reflecting in every surrounding window.

"This is the suspect Sarg – tackled to the ground by those two young men over there as they came out of the Hotel Alhambra across the street."

"Really? Well I'll be damned. Right, let's get him and the two witnesses down to the 'nick – Miller, you stay here and wait for news from the medics and see if any one else saw anything – have a look around the pavement area too but don't touch anything until forensics arrive – then report back as soon as you know what the score is – we'll need a statement from the victim too, if she's up to it."

Later that morning, at 4.00 am sharp, Tonks began a debriefing meeting in somewhat jubilant mood.

"Right, well, it looks like we may have cracked this call girl case at last." His eyes were wide open without a hint of his trademark squint as he strutted around the incident room like a cockerel watching over its brood of hens. He moved over to the display board pointing at a photograph of a young women with a face marked by purple-mauve bruises and a nasty gash over the left eye.

"This is Gale Edwards, a thirty-two year old call girl who lives at 5 Britannia Street off the Kings Cross Road. Like the other four victims Gale works on her own and has clients across London – you might say she is not particular in her choice. She was attacked last night at around 11.30 pm outside her digs but fortunately the attack was stopped by these two men ..." He pointed at two photographs on the display board, "... Nigel Crow and Benjamin Noads, who happened to be leaving a nearby hotel where they had been playing cards – they managed to hold the assailant and call 999, Constable Pace was on foot patrol nearby and was notified by radio. Gale was bludgeoned with some sort of cosh type weapon and knocked unconscious but has since recovered and is being treated at the UCH – she has eight stitches above her left eye but is OK physically apart from that – she is suffering from slight post traumatic stress but was able to confirm the identity of her assailant and has signed a statement to that effect. We also have statements from Crow and Noads."

Tonks was in a lively mood considering the late hour, aided by a couple of drams of whisky he had taken with his colleagues to celebrate the arrest. He couldn't resist a smile, almost half-heartedly, as he puffed out his chest and proclaimed:

"Excellent news boys – we've got the bugger!"

A loud cheer dinned the clammy confined space of the incident room. He raised his hand as if he was directing traffic.

"Now then, what do we know about the attacker, what have we got Detective Sergeant?"

Whithers normally resented these tiresome debriefing meetings and being asked to explain everything to everybody, he was by nature a silent sort who preferred to just get on with his job without public scrutiny; on this occasion however, the successful conclusion to the Kings Cross call girl case was sufficient to both lighten his burden and give him a position of celebrity, albeit in a minor role, amongst his peers. Buoyed by this gush of vanity and a fool's sense of self-importance, he proudly joined his boss by the display board, beaming from ear to ear, to claim his brief moment of fame.

"Well Gov, he's a doctor, Dr McNally, he works at the Camden Sexual Health Clinic where all five victims go for regular check-ups – he knew them all, intimately, in a medical sense I mean. Gale said how awkward he made her feel – going on about the sins of debauchery and how she should give up her immoral work and repent her ways – we've checked his flat and its full of religious paraphernalia, there's a picture of Jesus in all the rooms, and by his bed there's a crucifix and rosary and several prayer books, he's completely obsessed and delusional – I interviewed him this morning Gov and he's confessed to the attack on Gale, said he happened to come across her walking down Britannia Street, said he couldn't sleep and was out for a stroll – although he lives in Highgate, said when he met her he just wanted to talk and make her change her ways and repent her sins, that he didn't mean to hurt her but she started to hit him and he retaliated – he denies attacking the other girls, said it wasn't him, said it was someone else, just a coincidence, but he would say that I suppose, wouldn't he?"

"Can any of the other girls identify McNally?" Tonks went straight to the bottom line.

Whithers' face went blank, "No Gov, none of them saw their attacker so we can't prove it was him – and he's got alibis left, right and centre. But there's a lot of circumstantial evidence what with him being the same build, wearing a dark coloured hoodie and of course being their doctor – and they all have their own version of how he lectures them at the end of each medical check-up on the depravities of the flesh, and how they should change their ways or 'pay the consequences' as Gale put it – it's obvious he's a religious fanatic who has put himself on some private mission to rid the streets of 'these fallen angels' as he calls them, and stop the spread of what he sees as an obsession with carnal pleasure – fortunately no one's got killed, and it's likely his real intention was just to scare them but the attacks were getting more vicious and who knows how things would have ended up if we hadn't stopped him…"

Tonks butt in, "Quite so Detective Sergeant, but we need proof to nail him to all five attacks…" A blue-bottle had flown through the open window and was buzzing around the ceiling's florescent strip in an aerobatic display that included nose dives, loop-the-loops and barrel rolls, "… well, we'll have to work on that – meantime, book the bastard for the attack on Gale." He suddenly stopped and squinted his eyes as if a painful picture had just resurfaced in his memory.

"How's the other one getting on? What's her name, Sasha, how is she?" Tonks looked genuinely concerned like the father of a grown up daughter that he was.

Whithers too changed his expression to show due respect for Sasha. "No change yet Gov, she's still in Intensive and being monitored round the clock – they're worried about the clot on her brain and reckon the next twenty-four hours are critical."

"Poor sod – keep me informed. Now then, what about our friend down in the cells – Theo Harrison, he's pretty much off the hook isn't he?" Tonks looked around the room with his penetrating squinting eyes.

"Yes Gov – it turned out that Sasha's fingerprints were on that silver brooch – she must have nicked it at some point – he just got caught up in it all Gov, wrong place at the wrong time and all that …" Whithers had lost interest in Theo knowing he had no relevance to the case.

"Right, well, go and do the paperwork and release him Detective Sergeant – we don't want him hanging about do we?"

"What now Gov? It's twenty past four – shall we wait until the morning proper?" Whithers couldn't be bothered with Theo one way or the other.

Tonks walked over to the window and looked out onto the dark mauve London skyline with streaks of yellow-cream light beginning to fan across the eastern sky heralding the advancing dawn and a new day.

"Go and release him Detective Sergeant."

The whisky had worn off and the long night was beginning to dampen Tonks' lighter mood.

"And then there's our friend Mr Banjoko – that ran into a dead-end too didn't it Detective Sergeant?"

"Yes Gov – he's covered by Diplomatic Immunity – but Pace and Miller checked his alibi nevertheless and it turns out to be kosher – he did indeed spend the night with a Swedish lady, a diplomat Sir."

"We can strike that one off too then … how sordid it all is."

He yawned, a deeply excavated exhalation that came from the pot-holes of his weariness, gradually filling up over the past twenty-four hours, charged by all the worry and responsibility of his office – a wholly satisfying yawn that is known only to those who labour without rest and whose job is nearly done.

* * * * * * * *

After the phone conversation with her Dad, Jenny sat around in a coalescing state of disquiet stirred by a deepening annoyance with her mother's behaviour and growing frustration over Theo's silence. It had been a long day and she was exhausted; she gave up listening out for the phone and went to bed just past 11.00pm with the memories of her time with Theo at Wissant still dominating her thoughts and calming her nagging anxieties.

The following day she busied herself with clearing up her room, going off to the laundrette, ironing and tidying up the kitchen area.

Still the phone did not ring.

Early evening she went through the motions of getting ready to go out; she stretched out the routine of choosing which clothes to wear, placing several coloured tops on the bed and matching them with various styles of slacks and shorts.

Still the phone did not ring.

She spent longer than was usual washing her hair, putting on make up and choosing suitable earrings and necklace, the subtle and tasteful taking precedence over the loud and brash.

Still the phone did not ring.

At 08.00pm she opened a bottle of wine and sat in the armchair by the window thinking of Theo and her parents in equal measure of torment and disappointment. So many questions kept buzzing around her head it ached with uncertainty.

She stared out the window over the rooftops of Packington Street and saw Theo's face everywhere; she thought of their first kiss on the dunes and how she had tingled at the touch of his lips. She sipped a little wine and the heart wrenching memories intensified.

"Where the fuck are you Theo? Why don't you call for God's sake?"

Then she thought of her Mum walking out on her Dad for her lover-boy – she sipped some more wine and became angry staring out at the evening sky gathering cloud in the distance.

"You bastard Mum – how could you treat Dad like that, like an old rag you can't be bothered with anymore – just chucking him away as if he was nothing, just worthless rubbish, where did the love go Mum?"

After a while she poured herself another glass of wine but this seemed only to heighten her sense of pity for her Dad and turn the anger she felt for her Mum into white rage. At the end of the second glass she was delivering a bitter diatribe to her mother as if she was sitting opposite.

"And all those lies you told, how could you do that straight faced? One made up story after the other, about going out with your friends – yeh, right, dressed up like a sailor's tart you shameless hussy – how could you do that, right under Dad's nose, lying and cheating all the time, going out under false pretences and coming back late at night no doubt smelling like an over worked whore – rubbing Dad's nose in your filthy mess, your dirty filthy lies – how could you do that Mum?"

Another half glass of wine and the pathos started to run riot around her brain like a virus. The love and admiration she had felt for her mother so strongly that day walking by the canal had been ripped from her affection like a bough from a tree in a storm.

"Dad loved you so much, he adored you, would have done anything for you, and don't think he didn't know, don't think your dirty little game wasn't known to him – Oh, he knew alright, but he went along with all your lies, pretended everything was OK, 'cos he didn't want to lose you, didn't want to force you, to turn you away – you bitch!"

Her eyes were fierce and her teeth clenched as she stared out the window once again shouting at the sky, at the spiteful, merciless gods:

"Bloody lies, nothing but lies, you can't trust anyone, bloody lies all of it …"

Then she shuddered as she thought she heard the phone ring but it was just a similar tone floating through the open window from across the street.

The sound altered the focus of her diatribe, "Where the fuck are you Theo? Was it all just a game – didn't it mean anything to you – why are men so bloody fickle?"

She leaned forward studying the carpet, her eyes wide open, mean and bitter, her rancour growing imperceptibly like pus in a boil. She had reached a state of despair and the next stop on the line was self-destructive atrabiliousness. She got up and shook her head like a dog coming out of a river.

"Sod this – I'm going for a walk." She threw the empty wine glass down and as it rolled over the carpet she strained to hold back her tears.

Outside the cool June evening air worked with the wine to trip her brain into a state of super consciousness; she glided along the pavement as if the soles of her trainers were cushions of air. The clouds had gathered whilst she had sat in her room and a fine drizzle had eventually got through to sprinkle over her as she walked along.

"Ah, the sweet summer rain …" She slowly opened and closed her eyelashes to catch the soft droplets in her eyes.

It was 08.45pm and Upper Street was in that unreal state of calm when most people had already arrived at their meeting places in pubs and restaurants or were settled in the recently refurbished Screen On The Green cinema watching Sergio Leone's *Once Upon A Time In America*; even so, the pull of Saturday night was strong enough to keep the pavements busy with strolling lovers and hesitant newly met couples and groups of mates full of banter and hedonism whilst a myriad of bedsit rooms down every side street murmured to the sound of dinner party chatter inextricably changing gears from the cautious and polite to gay abandonment in a matter of hours.

Jenny's sense of singleness made her feel self-conscious and nauseous as she fell victim to the fever of Upper Street on a Saturday night; the fresh night air and the alcohol molecules diffusing through her blood stream induced a mild hallucination; she succumbed to a sort of voodoo, bewitched by sorcery and spirits, she began to see Theo at every turn, sometimes disappearing into a restaurant or coming out of a pub or laughing in that contagious way he had when clowning around.

She came up to the Schram and Scheddle shop and stood opposite mesmerised, observing every detail of the building as if each brick and window frame held the answer to the mystery of where he was and what he was doing. As she stared from across the street in a reverie, the building seemed to have a sense of being, a living thing that could communicate and explain why he hadn't been in touch. As she stared at the ancient tailor shop's sign she tried to recall what he had said about the location of his bedsit – was it on the right, or on the left, or was it directly above the old shop? Even in the overcast evening sky she knew the building was empty – a spreading shadow veiled the front and whispered to her, "I'm out, don't know when I'll be back."

She crossed over and checked the nametags on three doors to the left and three doors to the right but there was no mention of a 'Theo Harrison' although two tags were blank. Her confusion and disappointment fused with the rain shower, now falling steadily over her hair and changing the hue of her light summer clothes, to weaken her resolve.

She felt her heart tug her chest and clamp her lungs so she exhaled deeply and blurted out to the lifeless building, "Where the fuck are you Theo? Why aren't you here?" The rain started to drip off her nose and she reflected, "This pain is not drizzle – it's hard rain!"

She stepped back across the pavement and gave the building another scan for any sign of life but there was none. Standing there in the rain her spirit buckled with disappointment – she ached to see him again but this impulsive evening mission was fraught with distress and weakened her will; she felt empty and alone and fuelled only by bitter frustration she walked on aimlessly heading north along Upper Street.

On and on she strolled in a state of cogitation, oblivious to the rain, on and on past the solid white stoned Town Hall, the endless line of shops, boutiques, cafes, restaurants, on and on she went past the fire station and the red bricked Church of St Mary the Virgin with its white tipped spire disappearing into the ashen sky, on and on until the rain stopped and the sun made a half-hearted entrance between puffs of scattered cloud and there standing opposite was the King's Head sharply defined in the fresh evening light, winking at her, teasing her to enter, testing her will, tempting the fates in her weakened state of mind.

She crossed the street as if being reeled in by a hook and line and stood outside one of the huge bowed windows between two brown-red marble columns. The main door opened and an old man came out, staggered past her, his head down, back bent and legs bandy, smelling of old raincoats and chip fat; the door stayed open dispersing a cacophony of raucous bar room hullabaloo out along the street and diffusing amongst the traffic din.

She peered through the large window into the tightly knit throng of people clustered together, standing nose to nose, mouth to ear, back to back, side to side – one big heaving conglomerate of different types grouped together in a swaying and bobbing mass like strips of kelp in a riptide. She scanned the faces for someone familiar and thought she recognised Angelo of the Angel wearing his famous black fedora hat but wasn't sure as the figure disappeared behind a pillar before she could get a proper look.

The throng seemed to swell even more as the audience from the back room theatre swarmed out at the interval of Mia Nadasi's play, *Permanent Transit*. She kept staring into the bunched mass, searching for something or someone – a distant faint memory of her former self back in early spring when she spent so many hours in the bar transforming, like a form of metamorphous, from naïve jean clad Folkestone girl with fresh cheeks and the wind in her hair to a fully fledged London hipster with green velvet waistcoat over yellow jumpsuit, pink sneakers and gothic face make-up.

Then she saw him almost hidden leaning against the wall by the Gents – the unmistakable shape of Danny pinned against a young women, his hands clasping her cheeks and opening her soul with his devil eyes as if they were dancing a flamenco, so deeply did they peer into each other's eyes, 'Truly deep, deeper than all the wells and oceans of the world', as the poet Federico Garcia Lorca had once observed. A warm flush crept up her throat and over her face at the mere sight of him, like an intractable orgasm, then a sudden reverse, a cold stream of consciousness swept away the fantasy as she saw through the fake Danny in an instant, the charlatan imposter out flirting on a Saturday night in his favourite haunt – snaring another unsuspecting prey with his bewitching charm and honed hubris. She saw herself in the smitten girl, the way she wilted in his arms and pressed her hands behind his waist, completely besotted and spellbound, made Jenny want to go and pull her away before she succumbed further to his Lothario spell. Then she switched her gaze onto Danny, this potent dandy fop, playing out his part so well, leaning back against the wall with a Russian cigarette loose on his lips, pretending to be James Dean, Danny the great method actor delivering another fine performance mostly with unintelligible grimaces and silent gestures Rudolph Valentino style, seducing another gauche dumb-arse with his carefully crafted phoney intensity, on course to notch up just another disposable conquest, his trade-mark one-night stand melodrama back in his grotty bedsit on Percy Circus, it was so easy for him, like picking a low hanging ripe plum, it was all an act, a well rehearsed deception, a big lie. She closed her eyes and sighed.

Then she turned and walked back along Upper Street feeling cleansed from a dirty spell that had constrained her for months; a sprinkling of fine rain like mist returned and washed over her face once again, cool and fresh, she strolled along light and easy free from the clinging monkey of Danny finally off her back.

She thought of Theo and longed to hold him and feel his warm blood against her. She neared the old Schram and Scheddle shop once again but the building was still in darkness and her heart sagged. It was now a day and a half since she had last seen him and he hadn't phoned and wasn't at home – he had disappeared without trace. She gave the old shop front one last look thinking that at any moment a light would go on and his face appear at a window. She kept looking until her eyes strained in the fading light but there was nothing but eerie shadow covering the building like a shroud. She moved off, trudging back to Packington Street and her lonely little flat, dismayed and bewildered, lighter with the ghost of Danny finally exorcised but heavy with the loss of a new love, abandoned before it had began, stillborn and lifeless.

As she walked through the drizzle the bells of St Mary the Virgin peeled out the beginning of evening Vespers – a time to pray and give thanks for the day but the chimes, like bats from the belfry, dissipated and scattered into the night, lost and gone.

She bit her lip to cauterise the pain, the bloody burning pain of losing Theo and a line from a Rimbaud poem crept into her mind where the Vesper bells did not reach:

"A thousand dreams within me softly burn."

Chapter Ten

Theo woke up late Saturday afternoon from an anesthetised sleep deepened by the stresses of the previous night's drama played out at Camden Police Station. He sat on the edge of his bed staring down at the floor with his head in his hands reminiscent of Van Gogh's painting, *Old Man in Sorrow - On the Threshold of Eternity*. He tried to piece together the different acts of the drama, its plot and the main characters, but his brain was befuddled and he couldn't assemble all the fragments nor the sequences involved. He slowly got up, grabbed a towel and plodded off down the hall for a shower.

Later he sat at his desk with a cup of coffee, his mind a little clearer, and emptied the plastic bag of all his personal stuff handed back to him when he left the police station in an early morning daze. There in front of him was his wallet, cigarettes and lighter, his notebook and pencil, Travelcard, rail and ferry ticket and packet of tissues plus a copy of the form listing all the items.

He lit up one of the Gauloise cigarettes, sipped some coffee and stared at his things strewn in front of him. Then he opened the wallet and took out the two ten French franc notes and squeezed them between his thumb and fingers. Gradually the memories of his wonderful time at Wissant with Jenny came drifting back through the smog of the previous dreadful night when the police had practically accused him of assaulting Sasha.

He puffed the cigarette and thought of her photograph and appalling injuries, 'The poor thing – hope to God she's alright.'

Then he remembered the St Michael's silver brooch, 'The crafty hussy stole it – she bloody stole it from under my nose.'

He peered into the plastic bag, turned it upside down and shook it as if he was trying to dislodge some nasty insect caught inside. Nothing came out, the bag was as empty as a tin can on a

Bombay refuse dump. He looked down the checklist but the brooch was not listed. 'Right, you'll be hearing from me Detective Chief Inspector Tonks – that's my sodding brooch.'

He stubbed out the cigarette and finished the coffee as a warm breeze wafted through the opened window. Looking at the various items on the table triggered his memory once again about Jenny and sitting with her on the dunes at Wissant, that dot of a town in Northern France that was now so cherished by him, its genius loci held forever dear in his heart like a place of worship; he kept looking at the different objects and each one stood as a testament to that wonderful moment in his life that had moved him as powerfully as any biblical miracle – for he had been smitten by love there on the dunes and there was no greater miracle than love striking you down and changing your life in a blink of an eye. The full force of these sweet memories hit him like a lead weight on the forehead and he could feel and smell her in his mind tangible and real like flowing blood. The urge to see her and hold her again pushed against his will and he got up, agitated, and walked around the room searching for something that was missing in these recollections.

'Her telephone number! Where's that sodding piece of paper with her telephone number?'

He went back to the desk and made a forensic search for the small piece of pink paper, examining each and every item, he turned his wallet and the plastic bag inside out, then he checked the cigarette packet and notebook but the elusive piece of paper was missing. He got out his travelling bag and all the clothes he had worn whilst in France, checked every pocket and inner pocket and lining, but still he did not find it.

The effort of searching and the disappointment of not finding Jenny's phone number exhausted him and he laid flat out on the floor staring at the ceiling like a boxer waiting for the count. All the events of the last week compounded to form a potent insulin to his sense of well being. He laid out on the floor and tears began to trickle down his cheeks.

'You fucking bastards – all of you, nasty fucking bastards.'

He remained in this state of supine misery for several moments whilst the storm of self-pity defeatism spent its course and he slowly regained his composure. He started to piece together some positive plans – he would go back to the police station and retrieve his brooch and get them to check for Jenny's missing telephone number, then he would visit the library to research the process of becoming a college lecturer in marketing – that idea from Jenny had been an excellent one and he would pursue it – then on Monday he would have a meeting with Tubby and hand in his notice to be rid of all the dishonesty and corruption that he had discovered was so embedded in his job – he would start again, purged of the lies and deceit that blemished his sense of decency.

He got up, feeling better on this newly sketched out path stretching before him. He went over to the window to expand his vision and take in the afternoon air. There below was the usual frantic scene of Saturday afternoon Upper Street, people hurrying this way and that, an illogical obsession with materialism and an irrational preoccupation to be seen actively engaged in mindless consumerism – there they were, people scurrying like ants busy doing something or busy doing nothing, it mattered not, as long as they were seen to be busy.

He looked up at the deep blue June sky and thought of the infinite and mysterious firmament that was there, all around, a constant mystery, offering the ultimate puzzle, a competition open to all, free to enter, to explain that wondrous interaction between the earth, the moon and the sun and where it all begins and where it all ends. He was reminded of the last time he had gazed at the sky, that wonderful evening on the hotel terrace with Jenny – he recalled what she had said about our petty earthly problems, 'When you hold them up against the stars they're nothing really are they – everything just pales into insignificance.'

Just then a sudden thought bolted through his memory like a shooting star – 'Packington Street, Jenny lives on bloody Packington Street.' He bent over and held his knees shouting at the floor, 'You stupid idiot, she lives on Packington Street, just around the corner, you imbecile.' The fact that he had no idea of Jenny's address did not bother him nor dampen his ecstatic response to this sudden recollection, for the pulse of love is strong indeed and yields not to logic nor to reason.

Outside a weary pigeon landed on the window ledge, returning from its regular jaunt to Trafalgar Square to torment the tourists, it stood peering into Theo's room mystified to see the normally staid tenant skipping and punching the air with his fist yelling out, 'Packington Street' over and over again.

Half an hour later he was dressed and freshly groomed, with an endearing confident smile and a gleam in his eye, he bounded off down Gaskin Street towards the Essex Road and its junction with Packington Street in the hope of finding Jenny. The clock on the side of the Church of St Mary the Virgin was about to strike five o'clock.

* * * * * * * *

Reggie opened the front door just as Beverly was about to step out with two suitcases full of her clothes and personal belongings. She looked fresh and attractive with her hair loosely tied-up with a pink ribbon that contrasted well with her blonde hair giving her a rustic appeal, like someone who works on the land and who has more basic things to consider than what they look like.

"Bev?" Reggie was genuinely surprised. "I wasn't expecting to see you here." He was taken aback by this new casual looking Bev standing in front of him. "You look, um, well, different …"

"Do I? I'm a bit of a mess, been swimming at the leisure centre." An awkward silence fell between them. She put the cases down as the weight was straining her arms.

Reggie stepped inside and closed the front door. "Won't you stay for a coffee Bev? We've got things to talk about, haven't we?"

Beverly stared at him with the probability of agreeing or disagreeing going from eye to eye in an instant.

"OK, but just for a moment, I have to get on." She left the suitcases in the hall and went into the living room. Reggie went into the kitchen, the dutiful husband to the end, and made coffee like he had done so many times before.

They sat facing each other in the silent room with rays of sunlight passing through the opened curtain straight into Reggie's eyes. He moved across the sofa to avoid the glare.

"Look Reggie, I don't want any trouble, I've met someone else and that's that – it's just one of those things, it happens."

They had done this before, gone straight to the chase, it was their way, honed over many years of squabbling and settling disagreements.

"Does it? Why did it happen – I thought you were happy here?" He looked hurt and his voice strained with an emotion that is reserved for an unbearable loss.

"Now don't get upset Reggie – you must have noticed I was not happy, well, not in the last year or so, you must have seen that."

"No, I didn't see that – why didn't you say something, why didn't you flag it up so we could work it out?"

Beverly tried to sip her coffee but it was too hot even with the extra rouge gloss smeared on her lips like distemper.

"Look Reggie, this is bloody awkward, you're a lovely decent man and we've had some great times together, and what with bringing up Jen and everything, those times were special and we both share them, always will – but as you get older, well, you must have noticed, you change, inside of yourself, you start to see things different, you must know what I mean?"

She sounded as if she had rehearsed the speech but forgotten the ending; she peered at him like he was a stranger in a bus queue who didn't know when the next bus was due.

Reggie suddenly thought about the early days of their relationship, how it had all seemed new and exciting, the simple joy in everything, like children playing in the woods, they found happiness in adventures and discoveries.

Then flashes of their honeymoon went through his mind. He looked at Beverly almost pleadingly.

"We used to be happy, we never stopped laughing on our honeymoon did we? Remember that funny little hotel in the back streets of Montpellier, what was it called, The Sabot D'or that was it, I looked it up didn't I, it means 'The Golden Hoof' or some such nonsense, we laughed about it didn't we, I mean, who would call a hotel 'The Golden Hoof'? There wasn't a horse in sight. And you remember that noisy bloody flyover right outside our room? No wonder it was so cheap. And what about that other guest who got so drunk in the restaurant, the staff kept calling him, "Monsieur Little John' cos he was so big, remember he fell off his chair, just collapsed like a sack of spuds right there in the middle of the restaurant, it took two waiters and two men from the kitchen to lift him up and the Maitre D' kept shouting, 'No, no, put him out the back, not there, out the back.' And that couple above us, blimey, one minute they were at it 'ammer & tongs, we thought their bed would break and come crashing through the ceiling didn't we, then they had that almighty argument, remember Bev – we heard her shout out, 'Don't you dare touch me …' and then she started throwing his things out the window, trousers, shoes, towel, and most of it landed on our balcony – they left next day didn't they, he had a bald head and was wearing dark glasses, and they never spoke a word to each other all through breakfast, not a single word."

He stopped the unscheduled flow of reminiscences and stared out the window lost and bewildered as if awakening from a dream.

"We were happy then, weren't we? So what went wrong I wonder?" Outside on the lawn an angry seagull was squawking at a blackbird over a dispute concerning a small morsel of food no bigger than an acorn cup.

For a brief moment Beverly too was reliving these edited highlights of their honeymoon but she snapped out of it remembering her decision to leave Reggie and start a new life with Earl.

"I said didn't I that we've had some good times together, but it's over now – I want some excitement in my life, I want to feel young again, I want to feel like a woman again."

"So, this is about sex is it? You want sex with someone younger is that it Bev?" His sorrowful eyes pleaded with her, big and sad, like a furry pet waiting to be stroked.

"Oh come on, it's not just about sex, why do men always reduce everything down to sex?"

"Because it's behind most things we do and think isn't it, except prayer I suppose, even when we don't know it's there, it is …"

"What are you talking about Reggie? I've met this man …"

"I know, it's Earl isn't it? He's younger, he works at the hospital, and he makes you feel young again right?"

He took short little sips of his coffee and stared at Beverly, right into her eyes. "And he's great in bed right? And, now don't tell me, he makes you laugh, is that it Bev, this Earl you're leaving me for, he makes you laugh and he's good in bed, have I summed it up?" The sad furry pet was now bitter and angry.

She put her coffee down on the table. "If you're going to be like that I'll be off ..."

"Just tell me, am I wrong then?"

Several thoughts passed through Beverly's mind at once – the sex with Earl was good, there was no mistake about it, he was more virile and imaginative than Reggie who treated sex as a necessary routine, a marital obligation. But Earl didn't make her laugh, he was a broody, serious sort who kept his thoughts to himself. She shared no history with him and didn't really know him at all when she thought about it, not his ways and habits anyway. She suddenly saw the reality of the situation, she had fallen for Earl because he was not Reggie, he had sex appeal and represented an adventure, an ephemeral moment of pleasure, like getting drunk on a Saturday night.

"I'm not getting drawn into a big analysis of whose doing what and for what reason – just accept it Reggie, it's life, Earl makes me forget the time, he makes me forget who I am – but he's definitely not a funny man, he doesn't have a sense of humour actually, not like you anyway, and yours ain't that good."

"Really? Thanks for that anyway ..." Reggie now felt empty but in control of his senses, cold and inwardly reflective.

"Funny old world ain't it Bev? You meet someone, get married, have a family, go to sodding work all day, save up to buy nice things, and all the time you're getting old, bit by bit, like grains of sand dropping through the glass, bit by bit, poco a poco, imperceptibly, you look around one day and you realise you're old, a bloody old git whose bits don't work so well any more – and then, pow, the wife trades you in for some younger dude with a bigger nob."

"Shut up Reggie, stop thinking that way, that's not how it is – we can't explain everything can we? Sometimes things happen out of the blue, there's no one single reason, they just happen, as if they're meant to be – and you can't do anything about it." She looked at him and a surge of pathos crept up from within her, like a belch.

"I'm sorry Reggie, I really am, but what can I do? I don't want to leave with bad feeling and accusations flying in the air, but maybe you could've tried a bit more, you know, noticed me more, little things, noticed what I was wearing, and if my hair style had changed, whether I was happy or sad, Christ Reggie, you never noticed anything did you, it was all so mechanical, so routine, it choked the living breath out of me, you in your role and me in mine, and all that bloody regularity, choked me to death it did, I wanted more, I wanted someone to – well, someone to touch me, feel me here in my heart." She crossed her arms and pressed them against her chest. A gaping void opened up between them that offered no future. Reggie felt he was strapped in an electric chair and was about to be executed.

She continued in a softer, sombre voice as if she was mouthing a confession to a priest. "Then there was that moment, that moment after Jen was born when you said you didn't want any more kids – you were definite weren't you, so we never did, you never thought about me did you Reggie, did you stop to think about my feelings, fuck the hell you did, not once – something dried up and died then, something between us, it was only Jen that kept us going this long, you know I'm right don't you?"

Another silence fell between them, cold and still like snow, then he said, "All I know is, you have to work hard at relationships, you have to keep working at them, it's never easy, but you don't just chuck everything in when things get difficult."

He thought about the long years bringing up Jenny and how settled and content he had felt then, "You and me were OK weren't we – all those years watching Jen grow into a woman, we were happy – you were a fulfilled woman then weren't you Bev – and a great mother?"

A small shudder made her twitch her eyes and goose bumps pushed up the fine hair on her arms. "Yes, yes alright, they were good days, I'm not saying they weren't – and I wouldn't change them for anything, but they're over now aren't they, Christ, I hardly know Jen anymore, she's almost a stranger, not on the same wavelength, not like you and her anyway."

She looked at him with eyes vague and motionless like stones concealing nothing but dry earth, "You and me were just kids ourselves weren't we, playing at Mums & Dads, just kids." She stared at him for some kind of response but only the long terrible silence deepened, like the silence before a firing squad takes aim.

Then he finally said in a half whisper, "I only said that, about not having any more kids, because of you – I thought you couldn't manage another one, all that pain, when Jen was born, it nearly killed you, I couldn't stand seeing you in all that pain."

He sat with eyes opened wide as manholes without their covers, where all the dirt and regret of yesterday gets washed away out of sight.

"Well that was stupid – don't you know anything about women – we're made to feel that pain, we cope with it, it's part of being a woman – anyway, you should have said something, that's part of the problem isn't Reggie, you've always kept your feelings to yourself, like it was a bloody crime to share them – that was a crucial moment and you botched it."

"I can't help the way I'm made, I find it difficult to open up, it's the way I was brought up, not to show my feelings, to grin and bear it – it's just the way I am." He bowed his head in some kind of shame.

"You're just like your dad – never knew where you stood with him neither …" Her face showed no expression, just a coldness that drew the blood out of him.

"Well at least I was constant, you knew all about me before we married but you still went ahead – it was you that changed, like your mother before you, she chucked your father out too didn't she?"

"Shut up Reggie, that's got nothing to do with it, shut up!"

They sat looking at each other for several seconds, both reassessing their own positions and the weight of their feelings.

Finally, she said almost in a whisper, as if not to wake up someone else in the room, "Look Reggie, it's not fair to carry on with you as if nothing has happened, because it has, and I don't want to live a life of lies anymore – I hate all the lies, and I don't want to fight with you – we'll still be friends, won't we?"

She got up and moved slowly to the door. There was nothing left in her to say or exchange, she had said too much and now she wanted to go and leave her old life behind.

At that moment Reggie loathed her, a deep powerful scorn that severed the umbilical chord of his love for her and all the supply channels of truth and honesty that he had relied on throughout his marriage. He felt cheated, used and rejected.

Bizarrely, he suddenly saw the image of Betty through the French doors standing on the patio beckoning him to join her. The apparition changed the axis of his mood towards hope as it filled the room with colour like a glowing sunbeam, pointing to a brighter future.

"I suppose so." He said with a hidden smile on his lips like a man given a stay of execution.

Chapter Eleven

Sasha lay in a coma in the intensive care unit positioned at the far end on the ground floor of the University College Hospital. It was the last door along a spur that went off at the end of a long central corridor; its location was deliberately secluded and if one feature rose above the rest in its priority of essential environmental objectives it was the overwhelming need for silence, and this had been fully achieved, broken only by the continuous bleeping of the respiratory monitor similar to a submarine solar tracing device. Indeed, if you stood inside and closed your eyes you could easily imagine you were a submariner one hundred fathoms down in the deep silent ocean.

The murky interior was set in a thin veil of shadows punctuated only by a series of green, orange and red lights from electronic terminals along the back wall and from various monitoring equipment around Sasha's bed. Above was a panelled ceiling that emitted the softest of timid grey light as if sketched in charcoal tones. The blinds on the solitary window high up on the end wall were kept firmly closed.

Three tubes were attached to her, one for draining fluid from her right temple, the second was a feeding tube to her upper right arm; her face was still badly bruised but the huge swelling on the traumatised right side of her temple had receded and her blood pressure had improved. The potential deadly clotting to her brain had not materialised. The third tube was from the ventilator, left on its lowest setting, acting just as a precaution in case of sudden deterioration. The compresses to her fractured left cheekbone had greatly assisted in reducing the nasty swelling around that area of her face. The critical status of her condition had been reduced from Level 3 to Level 2 but she was still constantly monitored and remained under close surveillance until she was conscious and stable.

It was impossible to know what was passing through her comatose brain in the form of thought or dream or if she was suspended only on a long thread of disconnected sub-consciousness, an immeasurable black hole of time that held no sense of space and movement but just hung indefinitely and incalculably, black and still like a dreamless sleep.

She had been held in this marbled statuesque posture since her head had cracked against the side of the kerb outside her bedsit in Somers Town, felled by the mysterious hooded man who had lurked in the shadows opposite her front door. The consultant had said she was lucky the temporal artery had not been severed; nevertheless he was concerned at her state of stubborn coma.

Every half an hour the ICU nurse came in to check that she was comfortable and for any changes that may have occurred; but she continued to lay in sweet oblivion and no one could be certain whether her mind was relaying encouraging glimpses of her future, finally rid of her sordid call girl life, freely walking along the beach at Weymouth with little Vana, licking ice cream cones and throwing pebbles into the glassy sea. No one knew exactly how the cinematography worked in the unconscious brain; no one had the science or could prove how the pictures came and went, charged along by the wondrous synapses. Only the constant low-tone bleeping of the ventilator gave evidence of any form of life in Sasha. On and on it went, monotonous but deadly serious, it cast its weighty significance around the room, the sound of life measured in electronic pulses, echoing from wall to ceiling and worming the ear like a church bell summoning the Sunday flock to worship, to renew their hope and restore their faith.

Sasha's eyes were closed, her face serene and not a muscle moved nor a nerve twitched, she lay in a state of grace, like the medieval tomb effigy of Eleanor of Aquitaine, at peace with herself and her faithful dog silent at her feet. What images flickered like reels of film through that shutter behind those still eyes no one knew; possibly it was scenes from her early childhood, the hypnotic trickling of the fountain in St Cecelia's dappled churchyard where she passed through to the shops with her mother on Saturday mornings, or playing on bombsites with the local kids, or walking ankle deep in rivers on hot summer days, scrumping pears in Romford's better off neighbourhood, gazing through classroom windows and day-dreaming her schooldays away, dressing her new dolly on Christmas morning, learning to plait her hair, and countless hours just roaming the local woodlands with her friends, climbing trees, making daisy chains, picking bluebells, turning stag beetles upside-down, playing hide & seek and wide-eyed curious about discarded durex in the shelter on the common, poking them with sticks; or maybe it was extracts from her adolescence, Saturday afternoons with her best friend Ginny, dressing up in her mother's old mini-skirts and rolled-neck tops, mascara and lipstick, beads and ear-rings, singing songs into the tape-recorder, talking about boys and exaggerating her feelings, walking the suburban streets with nowhere to go, feeling exhilarated, lost and sensitive as hormones changed her mood and awakened sensuality, her imagination alert and curious, checking the size of her breasts in the mirror, longing to be grown up and admired by boys, her first casual sex with Ginny's older brother, her first cigarette, a badly made roll-up that singed her nose, the bitter-sweet period pain that heralded her adulthood, parties, dancing, flirting, kissing and more heavy petting in the woods by the scout-hut; her mind a kaleidoscope of shape and colour, her eyes turned upwards as with the last seconds of life, the final moments before oblivion and nothingness, looking up to heaven for thanks and gratitude, little Vana placed in her arms bloody and sticky from her surgically opened womb out into the light, through oblivion and into the light, her struggle with the fathomless obscurity from whence she came, into the grey light,

O Magnum Mysterium, where the act of sex and birth are a reversed mirror and the struggle for life and death are but the same.

A beam of sunlight found its way through a tiny crack in the venetian blinds pulled tightly shut by strict regulation. The sunbeam pierced the sanitised air of the ICU like a laser straight over to a photograph of Vana placed on a shelf beside Sasha's bed. The light lit up Vana's face highlighting her subtle curiosity and innocent defiance as she stared at the camera on that important moment when she was dressed ready for her first day at infant school. There she was, little Vana, bright eyed and strong, looking out onto the world with new eyes, announcing to everyone that she was ready for life's fantastic adventure, ready to fulfil her destiny and succeed in the eternal struggle, never to give in, just a thin beam of light, enough to illuminate her determination and extraordinary prescience.

Then, suddenly, in that intensive care unit late on Saturday evening, something changed, a scintilla deep within Sasha's brain stirred then rose like a surging river during a storm pressing on the flood gates, the gates of consciousness, something moved, succumbed and broke free, the gates opened and the water gushed through; the bleeping of the ventilator changed its pitch to a slower, measured tone. The nurse hurried into the room and leant over Sasha, taking her pulse and studying her eyes with a torch as they slowly opened, persistent tiny pulses of energy forcing them open, like a chick cracking its egg from within to be free from the endless blackness, the irresistible, incandescent force of life opened Sasha's eyes and the soft grey light of consciousness poured in once again.

The nurse squeezed Sasha's hand to reassure her, almost like a congratulation whilst Sasha's brain moved steadily back onto the rails of awareness – but all the while she kept her eyes fixed on the photo of little Vana and her magnificent defiant gaze keeping watch over her mother.

Chapter Twelve

Theo arrived at Packington Street excited by the proximity of Jenny living and breathing somewhere in one of the houses that stretched out in front of him. The sun came out from behind renegade clouds that drifted slowly across from the west and the white fronted houses seemed to merge in a long line of repeated form and shape without clear definition.

He walked slowly along the pavement looking up and then across, then up again, staring at every window, squinting as the sun flooded his eyes. On he slowly trod, preoccupied by his mission to find Jenny, and every movement that occurred, someone closing a front door, or moving behind a window, or climbing a stoop, or strolling towards him, received his close scrutiny whilst his heart raced in anticipation that it was her. But the street was long and the houses many and despite walking the entire length and back again the other side he found no sign of his newly discovered love. He stood at the junction with Essex Street and waited for twenty minutes on the off chance she would appear from one direction or other. He was desperate.

Saturday was beginning to fade and fold into that interim space between afternoon and evening, when it alters from the light stillness of the endless stretch of day into the kinetic tingle of expectation that is heightened by the prospect of another Saturday night fluttering through the airwaves like sparkling confetti. All around him Islington was getting ready for another Saturday night; everywhere there was an air of gathering expectancy along the busy streets as the advancing evening heralded a myriad of rendezvous or chance meetings.

Theo finally turned and walked attentively down Packington Street once more conscious that his persistent patrolling of the same street could be misconstrued as deviant behaviour. His eyes darted left and right, up and down, but still there was no sign of Jenny. His frustration mounted and he briefly considered embarking on a door-to-door campaign to find her but abandoned the idea as impractical. He heard a phone ring through one of the opened windows and thought the woman answering it sounded like Jenny but it was too faint for him to be sure.

"If only I had that sodding piece of paper with her telephone number – it must still be in the police station."

The weather was showing signs of changing as the evening was taking over its duty from the daytime shift. He looked up at the sky and sighed, "There will be rain." Then he took one more glance around him and down along the line of houses, "Sod it, I'm going to sort this out with Tonks."

Twenty minutes later he was at Camden Police Station and a chill went down his spine at the familiar interior with its dark brown-varnished doors and furnishings and its odd smell of polish and fear everywhere.

He rang a bell on the counter and the Desk Sergeant appeared from a backroom.

"Yes Sir, can I help?" The Sergeant studied Theo's face as if it was the central feature on a Wanted Poster.

"Oh, I was expecting Chief Inspector Tonks, I'm Theo Harrison, I was held here last night, to do with the assault on Sasha Phillips and released early this morning."

"Yes Mr Harrison, of course, I recall, Chief Inspector Tonks is off duty, how can I help you Sir?"

"Well, when I got home and checked my personal belongings I noticed a couple of things were missing."

"Really Mr Harrison? Well, you should have been given a form to sign by the Duty Sergeant that all your items had been returned to you."

"Yes, I was, and all seemed OK at the time but I was tired and I didn't realise a couple of things were missing." Theo realised his excuse sounded inept. "I know I should have checked more thoroughly but I had missed a night's sleep and I wasn't thinking straight."

The Desk Sergeant rubbed the end of his nose with his index finger, "Um, well, a bit irregular – so what is it you're missing Mr Harrison?" He moved over to a filing cabinet and pulled out a file.

"I'm missing a silver brooch, it's fairly small, just a bit bigger than a penny, it's in the shape of a St Michael, a helmeted winged Archangel, with a sword in his hand, quite distinctive and very special to me."

The Desk Sergeant checked the file in controlled silence and slowly read the case report.

"Yes I see, well that item is still being used as evidence in the case Mr Harrison, it was not part of your personal belongings taken from you on arrival here early yesterday evening …"

Theo interrupted showing clear irritation, "No, I see that, but nevertheless, it belongs to me and I would like it back."

"All in good time Mr Harrison, the brooch will be returned to you after the case involving Ms Phillips has been concluded, but right now it is still on-going – you will be notified in due course Sir – and what was the second item?"

"Ah yes, the second item …" Theo was beginning to regret the whole venture to the Police Station and wanted to get out.

"It was a small piece of paper, a small piece of pink paper actually, torn from a diary with a telephone number written on it in pencil next to the name 'Jenny' – the telephone number is important to me and it's the only reference I have of it, and yes, that was certainly part of my personal belongings Sergeant."

"Um, well, it's not listed on the Item Sheet that you signed off – no mention of any small piece of diary paper I'm afraid Mr Harrison." He continued to look through the file as he spoke, his grim expression giving no hope of a successful outcome.

"Damn that, I was banking on it being here."

"Sorry Mr Harrison, can't give it to you if we don't have it, and we don't have it Sir – maybe it's still in your pocket or bag, it being a small fragment and all." With that the Desk Sergeant turned and went back to the filing cabinet, signalling that the matter was closed and no further communication was required.

Theo stepped outside with his tail between his legs and walked along Camden High Street feeling miserable. By the entrance to the Underground station a man and a woman sat with their backs to the wall looking exhausted, dirty and hopeless. A small plastic pot was placed in front of them with a few pennies in it and a piece of paper, the back of an old used tote's betting slip, that read, "Homeless and Hungry, Please Help". Theo put a pound coin in the pot as he entered the station.

He made a sudden decision to go to The Archduke on the Southbank to listen to some jazz and allow a glass of wine to distract his troubled mind. He took the Northern Line to Waterloo and made his way to the fashionable wine bar via the pedestrian underpasses beneath the Bullring roundabout close to the station.

Light rain fell as he hurried along that gave the London air that rare fresh tang as the rain mingled with warm pavement dust. The evening light faded as he descended into the huge expanse of the underpass and his eyes struggled to adjust to the shadowy gloom. A pungent smell of piss and other excretory matter snagged on the hairs in his nose as he gingerly made his way diagonally across to the Southbank exit. All around him, set in an eerie silence, were the irregular shapes of makeshift cardboard homes, a vast hopeless landscape of some two hundred flimsy dwellings cramped together to form an asymmetrical mass like a hastily erected refugee camp. He recalled Jenny's reference to this human hellhole spread out around him but even her pre-warning could not lessen the shock of its eye-staining awfulness.

The prime sites were by the walls or against the supporting pillars whose flanks offered the illusionary sense of protection and security; for the majority however the only option was to pitch up close to a neighbour out in the open expanse of cold concrete. Theo held a hand over his nose as he walked through the neglected, unwashed throng and his stomach heaved with the sickening bile of disgust. Here it was, the shocking reality of the Government's monetarist policy, here was the effluent emission from the sewer of capitalism, here was the living proof of its failed austerity policy – resulting in over three million unemployed workers across the country and represented by this ragged, abandoned commune, superfluous to society's needs, a festering boil suppurating below the frenzy of London traffic, a smelly refuse tip of trashed lives driven underground and out of sight, an appalling testament of an uncaring Government.

He squinted as he went through the dimly lit subterranean cavern where the sun was embarrassed to enter, to catch the faint outline of those huddled down on their cardboard beds waiting for the night to drift in when they could venture out on the prowl for scraps of food and half-decent cigarette-butts; here they gathered like a herd of stranded seals, dispossessed, disenfranchised and discarded, snorting and farting, burping and coughing, men and women, old and young, living out this tormented life of helplessness down this huge drain in central London, barely compos mentis between binges on cheap cider, sherry and meths to ease their miserable lives and nullify their brains, pressed beneath the pavement slabs like ugly insects out of sight and out of mind, a collective, spent force hanging on without hope between despair and sorrow in London's discreditable Cardboard City.

Back up into the sweet open air the rain had stopped as he walked the short distance to The Archduke; his mind deeply troubled with what he had witnessed, so many poor sods paying the price of the Government's stubborn callousness and spiteful turpitude.

He entered The Archduke and his spirits were immediately lifted by the juxtaposition of smooth jazz wafting around the open-plan interior from the combo of piano, double bass and tenor saxophone coming from the first floor balcony. It was busy with that early evening mix of merry wandering journeymen, those stopping off on their way out and those stopping off on their way in to the great capital.

He found a seat in the corner at the back where an opened door led to a small patio and sipped a glass of Rioja as the cool evening air breathed on his face. He sat back and let the sensual music lift him out of himself, out from the strains and anxieties of the past few days beginning with his trip to Sheffield and the awfulness of Orgreave, the brief escape to France and the chance meeting with Jenny on the dunes with the surge of new love that caught him unawares and stunned his mind, the return to London and the prospect of a new life with Jenny only to be snatched by the police in connection with the brutal attack on Sasha, being locked up in the loathsome Camden Police Station cell and then the early morning release back to his bedsit and the discovery he had lost Jenny's phone number.

He sipped the red wine and let the parade of characters from these dramatic scenes parade in front of him as the jazz continued to ease his soul – first there was Penton-Fox and all the clowns in the office, Janners, Cadgers, Suzanne and Imogen, all parading through his mind like a troupe of circus performers, awkward and amateur, and led by that crass sycophant ringmaster Toby 'Tubby' Trubshaw, complete with top hat and cane, pirouetting amongst his inept team of truth alchemists and lie-peddlers who clap and cheer him as he bows to his supreme commander peering down from her private box, the Prime Minister, that big deceiver, quasi social engineer and economic theorist experimenter; then along came Curly and Digsy and the long line of dispirited miners walking single-file from the field at Orgreave like gassed soldiers at Passchendaele; the jazz wafted on and on, rocking his thoughts like a cradle in a tree-top, on and on went the parade in arbitrary sequence, Detective Chief Inspector Tonks with bent back and hunched shoulders and orange nicotine fingers followed by Constables Swan and Bryce and Detective Sergeant Whithers all looking ghost like and surreal as if in a Giorgio de Chirico painting; then Sasha appeared wearing a bandage around her head like the Invisible Man and he reached out to her but she vanished into thin air as the music stopped and a faint sound of applause came from the balcony above.

He sipped some more wine and his mind grew lighter. The jazz trio started up again, led by the tenor sax, he recognised the cool, soft melody of *Body and Soul* by Johnny Green; the hypnotic music and the infusion of wine cast him off, out over the sea, out, out across the deep blue rocking sea to Wissant, Northern France. There she was, the mysterious Jenny, sitting like a mermaid on the dunes, as if waiting for him. He closed his eyes and drifted with the music, a warm glow of love spread through him riding on the nectar of wine, it brought the image of Jenny up close, almost within touching distance, he could see her and feel her presence, "Oh God Jenny I want you so much." He squeezed both his upper arms with his hands as if he was caressing her like he did that last night in Wissant in the shadows of his hotel. He swam in the warm flow of this special memory gliding along its current and buoyed by its surging force. The saxophone blew deep, slow notes out into the clammy air and he was healed of all the ugly things he had seen and witnessed, all the lies, the distortions and the unforeseen consequences, all the poverty and abandonment of hope that had stung his eyes was now anaesthetised, replaced with a love for Jenny constructed in his heart with Tungsten steel girders. He opened his eyes and looked around the ground floor bar;

there before him was a small sample of London café society, the well-heeled chattering classes – close by four lads already half pissed were laughing at everything and nothing, nervous and gay, their young lives full of frivolity; next to them a middle aged couple in earnest conversation and over there a group of five women in their thirties sat in serious mode discussing a play they had seen – Theo could just make out they were talking about T.S. Eliot's troubled first marriage and guessed the play was Michael Hastings's *Tom & Viv*, one of them, a self-appointed leader of group outings and instigator of general conversations, sat with the chair reversed back to front, like the famous photo of Christine Keeler sitting nude on the Arne Jacobsen designed chair – she constantly looked around the group and nudged the conversation on, asking questions and elaborating on half-hearted answers, like a conductor of an amateur orchestra, she was hopelessly inflated with a sense of her own importance; next to them, behind the large potted Areca Palm, sat a younger couple in their early twenties, probably on their first London date, she nervously touching her hair and he keeping a cool expression as if he was always in control, they kept looking into each others' eyes oblivious to their surroundings and the magical jazz, they existed there and then just for each other, closing out the world around them.

Theo marvelled at the young lovers, he finished his wine and sat staring at them, how their love seemed new, fresh and clean, the moment was theirs, their love sharp like the sun in late June, they swam in each others' eyes, those pools of deep hope and infatuation – he whispered to himself as if in the place of the young man staring at his beautiful young companion:

Her eyes had tiny patterns in them,
Slithery and watery and floating faint,
Mystery and intrigue they contained
Something vague, like Rothko's shapes.

Just then a large group came in, three middle aged couples, dressed for dinner and the theatre and immediately gathered around the bar in dominant mode. Theo could hear them chattering over each other like squawking parrots and caught the odd comment here and there:

"No, Harry, it's called *Wild Honey*, not *Wild Sex* darling …"
Hoots of laughter.

"Who did you say wrote it, Mike Fry?"

"Not Fry, it's Michael Frayn, not Fry, you're thinking of chocolate again aren't you Ducks?"

More hoots of laughter.

"Didn't Checkhov write it, or was it Pasternak, I'm sure I read Checkhov somewhere?"

"It's based on Checkhov's *Platonov* – straight Checkhov would be far too much for today's youngsters, simply lack the intellect, I blame all these education reformists, none of them are properly educated, too much tolerance of the mundane."

Quieter hoots peeled out.

"Oh, and aren't you just bursting to see that Ian Holm, I mean, talk about class acting – did you see him as Lenny in *The Homecoming* – now that's what I call a real thespian."

"He's not in it Gerty, wrong one, it's Ian McKellen – please keep up old girl …"

Hoot after hoot rang out as they took their drinks from the bar leaving a hole in the air that the jazz filled searchingly.

Hearing the lively banter Theo mused at how we all revert to being naughty teenage pranksters once we are removed from the constraints of our regular homely routines and placed amongst trusted friends with drink in hand and the evening adventures waiting ahead. He sat mesmerised by the group, almost infatuated with their personas and quick throwaway comments, and it was then he saw him – the unmistakable shape of Sandy leaning against the bar alone in the opposite corner.

"Sandy? It's me, Theo. By God, I haven't seen you for, well, what is it, seven years now – I can't believe it." He went up close and put his hand on his old friend's shoulder. "How are you?"

"Theo? What the hell …" Sandy was dragged out of deep inner reflection, his eyes almost popping out of his head as he studied Theo closely, "You haven't changed, a bit older around the eyes maybe – what are you doing here, I can't believe it's you."

They ordered a bottle of house red and sat at Theo's table by the opened door to the back patio. The cool air fanned their faces and refreshed them from the clammy atmosphere of tobacco, perfume and armpit sweat building up inside as the popular venue filled close to its Saturday night peak.

They both sat momentarily in silence from the initial shock encounter and scanned each other's face, their brains rapidly recalling all stored data of the other held in deep memory.

"This is unbelievable Sandy, I only popped in here for a quick drink …" He looked around the bar, "So where's Mavis, didn't you both go off to Australia?" He couldn't remember where he had heard that piece of news all those years ago but he could still feel the sting of it, such a desperate and impulsive thing to do he had concluded at the time.

Sandy looked tired and something else was hidden in his eyes, he looked worried. "Mavis? Oh, I'm meeting up with her later, sort of killing time, she's visiting her Mother – anyway, never mind about that, how are you, what are you doing with yourself these days, do you still live in Blackheath, where are you working, tell me everything." Sandy's warm and genuine interest in his friend helped Theo loosen the nervous tension rippling through his stomach.

"That's a long story Sandy, the quick headlines are, I live in Islington, I'm still single, I work in PR for the Government over in Smith Square, but that's going to change soon – and how about you?"

Theo kept looking at his friend as he spoke and was sure he had lost his sparkle with some sadness hidden behind his dark blue eyes showing through like a cloud covering the sun.

"You look very tanned, life in the Antipodes obviously suits you – you did get to Australia didn't you?" Theo tried to force his eyes to be warm and caring as he started to recall those awful days back in 1977 and the riots in Lewisham that had caused such a rift between them.

Sandy was not his fluent self and something was holding him back, "Yeh, me and Mavis got down there in the end, bit of a hassle but I eventually got a visa thanks to my Public Health qualification being on their Skilled Occupation List – I knew all that bloody hard work would come in handy one day."

As if by some quirk of biology, practically in the realms of Dr Jekyll and Mr Hyde, Theo started to change his persona and revert to the character honed all those years in the regular company of his old friend, a cold, precise assessor of the facts.

"You mean you exchanged your job here in London as a Public Health Officer to the same job in Australia – you sort of just changed the scenery? Didn't that become boring in the end too?"

This abrupt reappearance of Theo's old direct self that had infuriated him back in the 70s reignited his irritation but, for the sake of their reunion, he remained measured and calm, "No Theo, I was never bored with my job over here, I was a Junior Public Health Officer if you recall, but I was sick to death with the way this country was leaning to the right – that's why I was keen to join the Lewisham march against the NF – that was quite a day back in 1977 one way and another."

They both continued to study each other, their memories of that amazing day, Saturday 13th August 1977, forever seared on their minds, now rekindled and throwing out hot embers of images of their own personal experience; the old stone, kept so long in shadow, had been turned over and Sandy wanted to know more about all the creepy-crawlies now exposed under the glare of daylight.

"So what did happen to you Theo – you never did get to New Cross that day did you?"

Theo took a large gulp of wine, more than was required. "I suppose I was having some kind of breakdown – nothing seemed real to me, I could never feel, honestly feel, all that stuff about left and right, the fascists and the commies, I could never really believe it, what you and the rest were feeling, it felt phoney somehow and I was all screwed up over Angelina – God, how I loved that woman, but it was hopeless, like trying to tether a free spirit, just couldn't hold her down in a conventional sense, impossible – you know I still see her in my dreams or some ghost of her appears in the darkness when I'm laying down, flying over my bed like a bird – frightens the life out of me ..."

"Really? When you're pissed most likely! So what happened?"

Sandy's tired eyes looked serious but acutely interested as if he had come across an old photo album that contained clues to a long hidden secret. "I remember that last phone call – you seemed totally out of it, I was concerned about you, about your mental state, about your safety."

"Yeh, you were right, I was down and out, near the edge – what happened? Let me see, I left the march at Lewisham and went back to Angelina's place in Beckenham – practically found her and Max at it, not quite, saw him walk off as I arrived and it was obvious from the state of her and her bed what they had been up to – it cut me in two, and she was just so abject and placid, as if she had no real feeling for me, or anyone or anything, everything was just inanimate, objects without feelings, to be used and castoff at her will, it broke my spirit ..."

"But that wasn't the end of Angelina was it? You saw her again didn't you?" Sandy looked puzzled as if something he had believed in was now proving invalid.

"What do you mean – no, I never saw her again – she destroyed my trust and once that happens I'm done, there's no way back, it's part of my make-up, I'm stubborn like a bloody donkey."

"But I spoke to her afterwards Theo, I met her in Beckenham, a couple of months after the Lewisham riot, just before me and Mavis went to Australia, she was so sad, kept saying how she missed you and what a mess she made of things, I thought she was going to contact you, she said she would …"

"What? You met her? But she didn't know my number or where I lived, she couldn't have contacted me – my God, after all these years, I never knew that, it all looked so hopeless that last time I saw her, she made it clear, very clear, she didn't want commitment, she got annoyed with my questions and bourgeois attitude towards Max, she made me feel the difference between us, in our natures, and it all looked finished and over – my God, can't believe it, she said she missed me, is that right Sandy?"

Sandy knew he had pulled back a curtain that had remained closed for seven years and put a spotlight on a long lost treasure, the lost jewel in Theo's life, and how he might have regained it had the curtain been pulled open long before.

"Yes Theo, I kid you not, I would have contacted you myself, but, well, you know, we weren't talking and anyway I was preoccupied with getting off down-under, starting my new life, and how was I to know she didn't have your details, she never asked for them come to think about it – I feel awful about this."

"It's not your fault is it?" Theo drank more wine and sat back staring up at the first floor gallery as the musicians started up again with a slow jazz rendering of, *I've Got You Under My Skin*.

He kept seeing Angelina's face looking down on him, with her beautiful shy smile and her paint stained dungarees and her amazing intellect shining through her dark eyes. Then he recalled the pain of the last encounter, her dishevelled bed, the sex dank bed smelling of Max's awful aftershave, and her attitude, that carefree, loose, free-spirited Bohemian way she had of detaching sex from the conventional lovers' gift and treating it as something mundane, like a kiss on the cheek. He stared at her image hovering above as the lyrics of the tune got into his ears:

"I would sacrifice anything come what might
For the sake of havin' you near
In spite of the warning voice that comes in the night
And repeats - how it yells in my ear:
Don't you know, little fool, you never can win?
Why not use your mentality - step up, wake up to reality?"

He snapped back into consciousness. "It's OK Sandy, just wasn't to be, it's all past and gone, buried with all the other trash in my life back then …" He filled their glasses and sipped more wine. "So, let's change the subject before I slit my wrists once and for all, are you happy in Aus, any regrets? You have to watch out for those Redback spiders eh?"

Sandy thought he noticed a slight glaze in Theo's eyes. He leant over and rested his hand on Theo's arm.

"I'm really sorry my friend, I can see that was a bit of bum news for you …" A silence fell between them and the moment became heavy with reflection. Then Sandy spoke again as if picking up a passage he had previously been reading.

"Yeh, right, the old Redback, or the Black Widow as some call it, yeh, you have to be careful of those little bleeders, highly venomous, most of the houses have built in space underneath the ground floor and nets all along – you have to be on your guard, you get used to it I suppose."

"Yes, I suppose we're all adaptable." Theo's eyes were beginning to wander, rolling down the river of wine.

"Theo, tell me about this job of yours, did you say you work in PR for the Government?"

"Yeh, I'm right in the control centre of the Government's big Lie Machine – but not for long, I've had enough, I'm chucking my notice in Monday, adios, finito benito, au revoir, Good Night Vienna." The wine, combined with the adrenalin impulse from the unexpected meeting with his old friend, shifted his position on the seven stages of drunkenness from euphoria to confusion.

This big news flash did not move Sandy in any discernable way and he asked calmly, "Really? So what's brought this on?"

Theo was disappointed and thought his news deserved a more dramatic reception. "That's a big question Sandy – it's complicated, but in a nutshell my friend, I've suddenly seen what my office and my colleagues really stand for, they are nothing but Government agents, paid to perpetrate lies, to put a spin on any event so it either boosts the Government's image or deflects their mistakes onto someone or something else – let me tell you what happened up in Orgreave last Monday …"

Theo gave a brief resumé of his experience at Orgreave and his involvement in the drama on the miners' picket. Sandy bowed his head forward as if he was listening to an official Government radio announcement of national importance.

"I saw with my own eyes what happened at Orgreave, those miners did not, they certainly did not, in no way, start the violence, it was the police who kicked it off, they had obviously pre-planned the whole thing – they were like a bunch of South American militia – used maximum force – bludgeoned the miners – trying to turn public opinion against their cause – this is all about killing off the miners' union, and unions in general, they don't give a shit about their jobs, their pits, their livelihoods and their communities, this is the Government at its callous worse, it's a form of social engineering in a sort of amateurish, brutal way." Theo's disjointed summary concluded with a suppressed hiccup.

Once again Sandy showed no surprise, "Well Theo, I'm not sure what else you expected working for their Central Office PR – deception and misrepresentation would seem to be the main tenets of the job – perhaps you were a bit naïve – and I'm not up to date with this miners' strike business but what I can make out, just walking about London these past few days, it looks like the old country is in deep shit, never seen so much poverty and homelessness everywhere, and you, Theo Harrison, are right in the firing line, part of the Government's propaganda offensive, well, well, who would have believed it – and now you've seen through all the lies, a sort of 'Paul's conversion on the road to Damascus' moment eh? Better late than never I suppose, well, 'seeing is believing' but 'blessed are those who can believe without seeing' as Grasshopper in Kung Fu might say – so what are you going to do now, stick to PR or go back into publishing?" Sandy was distracted by the middle aged group who were now finishing off their third bottle of wine and laughing at anything or anyone who appeared on their radar.

"Phew – that Scargill's a nasty piece of work though isn't he? But he's losing the battle against Margaret, bitten off more than he can chew there, nothing but a tin pot dictator lording it over a rabble of left-wing commies – you can tell he's rattled though seeing the amount of hair he's lost, ha, ha."

The whole group bent over and practically split their sides with laughter.

Theo looked angry, the wine emboldening his newly acquired spirit of allegiance with the miners and their cause.

Sandy noticed the ire in his friend's eyes.

"Forget it Theo, wine and ignorance is a heady brew, just ignore the idiots."

Theo looked back to his friend, "But there's the real problem Sandy, a perfect example, the comfortable middle class' opinion emphatically manipulated by, well, actually by me and my department – we are responsible for those clowns' view of the world, we know they are too dumb, or complacent, preoccupied or just disinterested, to reason with all the carefully prepared digestible chunks of garbage we feed them – and they swallow it every time, it's like they have string attached to them and we sit around in Central Office and just keep giving them ready-made opinions, we pull them this way and that, like bloody puppets, it's all so easy, and of course we have all the Tory newspapers to help us reinforce the message, like taking candy from a baby."

Theo released another hiccup.

Sandy looked distant and disinterested as if Theo was preaching to the converted, "Well, I won't say 'I told you so' but now you understand why I got out – Australia isn't flawless but Bob Hawk's Labour Party's doing a reasonable job and it all seems more honest somehow, less media controlled than over here – the Aussies are a difficult bunch to push around and they wouldn't stand for any of this Thatcher bull shit."

The hypnotism of the bar's heady atmosphere increased as the jazz ensemble played, *Look of Love* and the room bellowed with the clatter of Saturday night chitchat and cheap throwaway jollity.

Sandy spoke a little louder over the soft undertone of dreamy music, "So Theo, my little born-again socialist and freethinker, what are you going to do now – go and work for Michael Foot?"

Theo looked miffed, "It's Neil Kinnock now, not Foot – no of course I'm not going to do that ..." Something else was seeping into his consciousness, something more powerful than politics, "... you know I've met this wonderful girl Sandy, came across her in the sand dunes near Calais, sitting there singing Joan Baez, it was practically love at first sight, her name's Jenny, she's amazing, everything I've always wanted in a women, she's strong and independent, creative and sensitive but has understanding and empathy, she's sort of attractive, you know, she's not a beauty but she has amazing eyes and hair, can't stop thinking about her but now I can't find her, she's out there somewhere, I know her sodding street but not her address, isn't that stupid of me, how do you find out where someone lives exactly? Anyway, it was Jenny who suggested I try teaching, marketing or PR or graphic design – there's a big demand for marketing courses in Further Education apparently and they need more teachers, so, watch this space."

"Really? – You a teacher, good luck with it Theo – you've always been good at explaining things, making difficult things easy to follow, I suppose that's why you ended up in PR – you know, I was always envious of your job in publishing, it seemed so much more glamorous than mine – but what's this about not knowing where Jenny lives? You're kidding? That's twice now isn't it, history is repeating itself – I always thought you were the Filofax king, you should keep a note of important things – so, you've lost her address – but don't you have her telephone number? Have you tried the telephone directory?"

Sandy went through the motions of being concerned but the truth was he remembered quite clearly the many times his friend had fallen in love so quickly and deeply, with Katrina and Angelina and a string of women before that, and he couldn't take this latest episode seriously.

Theo briefly considered telling Sandy about Sasha but thought better of it. "Yes, tried the telephone directory but she's not listed, the phone must be registered under the landlord's name – I keep wandering up and down her street like a prowler but she never appears, what else can I do?"

"And she doesn't have your number or address?" Sandy checked his watch and thought about his arrangement to meet Mavis at eight o'clock.

"No, I never gave her my phone number – I did mention the name of the shop I live above on Upper Street but she may have forgotten it." Theo noticed his friend's distraction. "So where did you say Mavis was, with her mother? Are you two OK?" He sensed something was not right with Sandy.

"Oh, we're meeting up at eight o'clock over on Goodge Street, at the Spaghetti House, I've got to watch the time."

Theo looked hard at his friend, "You never had kids then?" Even after seven years it was uncanny how they could both pick up on each other's sensitivities, their mental antennae finely tuned to each other's thoughts.

Sandy sipped more wine and then leant back and finished the glass in one go. The jazz trio started up again with, *Maybe You'll Be There* and a sharp aura of expectancy hung over him as if an attic door was about to open onto his hidden inner self.

"We've been trying, but it never worked out for us – we've looked into IVF but it's expensive, what with the ovulation induction, the first IVF cycle and subsequent cycles, the freezing of embryos and sperm and so on, it's all broken down into carefully contrived stages and the costs add up at each stage so we keep putting it off – then we thought about adoption but it's not the same is it, not like having your own child, so time goes by and I know it's eating away at Mavis more than me, and it's pretty bad with me."

Theo had absolutely no knowledge of Sandy's problem but knew instinctively his friend was hurting. "I suppose you've had tests, I mean you must know whether it's a sperm or egg problem right?" He regretted the question and the direct way he framed it, its pointed harshness hung in the air between them like dog poo in a car.

Sandy looked at Theo with blank eyes, smitten by his friend's trademark pragmatic attitude.

"Yes Theo, we've had tests, I have a low sperm count, but knowing that doesn't solve the problem does it?"

"No, it doesn't, of course not – well, you're going to have to save up for the IVF treatment, it's the only way – can you get it done under the NHS over here?"

"We're just about to take up Australian citizenship so we won't qualify – it's a bit of a bummer as they say down under – yeh, you're probably right though, we have to save up, but it's going to be a long road and no guarantee of success at the end of it, and now I'm not sure it's worth it anyway."

With that Sandy got up and went off to the toilet leaving Theo to ponder his friend's predicament. He looked around the crowded bar, at those talking and those listening, all compressed into the confined space and lulled by alcohol, music and the quest for love or sex that permeated everything.

He thought, almost muttering under his breath, 'It's this sense of being on a conveyor belt that gets me, this process society has ordained as being necessary and imperative, there waiting for us, handed to us as a fait accompli, a common life style, first we have the formative years with our parents where we copy their bloody nasty habits and mental defects, followed by school and all the indoctrination that goes with it, to be uniform wearing conformists, to toe the line, not to run down the corridor or ask awkward questions and appear too smart, or speak too loud, or act differently, then the struggle to get qualified and find work, then the ludicrous mating dance to find the right partner, then the mortgage and finally the need to feather the nest with a brood of kids – ah, Lord above, save me from this humdrum monotony, this damned sameness, this killer of the human spirit, save me.' He drained the glass and sighed.

Sandy returned still looking serious and glum as if he just had a quick session with a fortune-teller who had drawn the ace of spades with its kiss of death on his future.

"Sorry Theo but I've got to go, pity we can't make a night of it, so much more to talk about believe me, anyway, hope you find Jenny." He looked around then breathed in deeply, "It's been great meeting up again …"

Theo thought Sandy was bringing their unexpected reunion to an abrupt end.

Theo remained sitting. "Can't you stay a bit longer?" He checked his watch. "It's not quite seven thirty yet, time for one more glass surely?" Theo's head was whirling with headlines and front-page news articles from the last seven years of his life, rolling off his memory press in an urgent need to be read and examined by his old friend.

"Sorry Theo, but there isn't time ..." He moved away from the table and pushed his chair in.

"Well, when are you going back to Australia – can we meet up again?" Theo felt gloomy with some sort of defeat that he could not define.

"Not really – we're flying back on Tuesday and there's so much to do – but look, here's my address and phone number, keep in touch please Theo." He handed his business card to Theo who sat forlorn holding it in his outstretched hand.

"Goodbye Theo, hope everything works out OK, write to me and let me know how you get on with the teaching job and Jenny, and don't lose my address, bye ..."

Sandy turned and was about to depart when something stopped him in his tracks, something he felt obliged to divulge to Theo, something weighing on his mind for so long that it had soured his spirits. He turned around and leaned against the table with one hand indicating that the reprieve to his sudden departure was only temporary.

"Theo, I'm so sorry about all this, I'm not myself as you may have noticed, fact is ..." He hesitated at venturing into the span of wilderness that spread out in front of him, the unknown territory of revealing his innermost fear, "... fact is, Mavis has cancer, sodding bloody cancer."

He gulped at saying the word, as if its bitter acid taste stuck in his throat like a ball of fish bones.

"That's the real reason why we're over here, she's seeing a specialist Monday morning at The Royal Marsden, a specialist in ovarian cancer – I'm so frightened and she's being so fucking brave, it's all unbelievable, you never know what's around the corner do you – death comes on slowly by tiny steps, hidden out of sight, I'm not ready, not ready to lose her, too many things unsaid, too many things to put right, too many unfulfilled moments."

He bent further over towards Theo. "Forgive me Theo, got loads on my mind, I often thought how it would be if we ever met again, but it should've been better than this – hope it will one day, got to go."

He put his hand on Theo's arm and gripped it strongly as if conveying some profound inner feeling, and then he turned with noticeable urgency into the bustling throng.

Theo felt the numbness of sudden shock and had no time to think or reply. He called out to his friend in a state of panic as he edged out of sight, "Christ Sandy … I had no idea …"

He poured the remaining wine into his glass and looked at Sandy's empty chair and felt the huge weight of loss and surprise each clamping one of his temples.

He muttered under his breath, 'Fuck the shit, you poor bastard Sandy, you poor, poor bastard – why didn't you mention it earlier?'

He held out Sandy's card that read, Sandy McLochlan: Deputy Chief Public Health Officer, 524 Pacific Avenue, Bondoola, Rockhampton, Queensland, 4703, Australia.

The sharp contrast of Sandy's obvious success with his own flagging career progress hit him like a snowball in the eye and he shivered with uncertainty and the dull thud of failure.

"Excuse me mate, OK if I take the chair?" Without waiting for an answer Sandy's chair was lifted away and taken off to an adjourning table.

He sat there alone finishing the wine. He could just make out the tune, *Maybe You'll Be There* still being played but muffled amongst the Saturday night racket. A bout of maudlin self-pity encapsulated his mood as he recalled the song:

"Someday if all my prayers are answered
I'll hear a footstep on the stair
With anxious heart I'll hurry to the door
And maybe you'll be there."

A spontaneous outpouring of emotion swelled up inside and filled his eyes with tears as he thought about Sandy and Mavis and the pain of doubt that was crippling them. He thought how generous Sandy was to give him time, to go through the last forty minutes showing interest in what he was doing and not letting on, until the very last, about the huge hole of uncertainty in his own life and the prospect of Mavis' death. He pondered:

'People do not battle against deteriorating disease, the pending doom, the horse-drawn hearse waiting around the corner in black drapes and black feather plumes, scraping its hoof on the road snorting with impatience, no, what they fight against is the giving up of precious life, the giving up of colour and light, they battle against the unknown beyond death, the hidden horror of the nothing void.'

He stared absent-mindedly into the empty glass, his senses numb and hollow, when suddenly a vision of Jenny appeared before him once again, smiling from the bottom of the glass, her large bright eyes sparkling with love and hope.

Chapter Thirteen

Detective Chief Inspector Tonks sat beside Sasha in the ICU recovery unit exuding an air of calm concern and dependable authority. His face was lined with deep creases, channelled from years of too many late nights and early starts, cigarettes, whisky and the regular exposure to evil and dangerous people. Sasha was still weak but the nurse had helped her sit up for the Chief Inspector's visit.

"Now let me get this right Sasha, you first spotted this man prowling about in the middle of the night outside your place on the Friday 15th June, then again the following night, the Saturday, and again on Monday night, and on each occasion you never made contact, nor could you see his face behind the hood he was wearing?"

Sasha looked like the *Invisible Man* from the TV series with her head heavily bandaged with slits for her eyes, nose and mouth. Her left eye was bloodshot and her mouth dry from dehydration.

She whispered, "Yes officer, that's right."

"And on the Tuesday night, 19th June, you decided you had had enough and you went out to lay in wait for him, to find out who he was and scare him off?"

She spoke slowly and without varying pitch, "That's right."

"And that explains your change of clothes, you put on those black leotards and a black Lycra top so not to be noticed – it was premeditated – is that right?"

Her voice was soft and small, "Yes, I planned to wait, to hide in the dark, so I dressed in black …'

Tonks became conscious of his own voice and so lowered his tone in a show of sympathy, "Tell me, I'm just curious, but what did you think you would do when you got face to face, when you actually confronted the prowler?" His eyes squinted tightly.

"I had to know who it was, I just wanted to pull his hood up, to unmask him – I felt strong enough to do that, I was so annoyed with him, messing me about like that, he wasn't a big man, just a bit taller than me, thought I could handle him, didn't think it would get nasty."

"Had you not heard about the other attacks on ..." Tonks checked his language, "On other women of your profession?"

"Well yes, but all that seemed a bit remote, going on somewhere else, that it wouldn't happen to me, I suppose I wasn't thinking straight." She leaned over and took the glass of water sitting on the bedside cabinet, sipping it and then holding it on her lap, glad to occupy her hands with something.

They both looked at each other in silence, then Tonks said, "One of your clients is a man called Banjoko – why did you cross him off your list?"

Sasha's eyes closed, clearly visible through the bandage slits, "Because he's a brute ..." She sighed as if annoyed about something.

Tonks said quickly, "Did he harm you, is that it?"

"Let's just say he got over enthusiastic – I reckon he's capable of doing a great deal of harm and that's why I didn't want any more to do with him – but he wasn't the prowler, not the right build, far too big."

Tonks changed tack. "Now tell me Sasha, do you recognise this man?" He took a photograph of Dr McNally from his briefcase and held it up.

Sasha looked at the photograph carefully, her drugged brain trying to identify the image, "Yes, that's McNally, my doctor at the Health Clinic – what's he got to do with anything?"

Tonks returned the photo back into the briefcase. "He was caught attacking another, um, women of your profession, shortly after your assault, off the Euston Road, same patch as yours I reckon, a certain Gale Edwards to be exact, do you know her?"

Sasha was amazed at this news and laid there aghast, unable to take it all in. "What? McNally attacked Gale? I can't believe it, My God – not Gale?" She stared at Tonks, a state of complete disbelief clearly discernable despite the heavy bandage.

"Well, that's how it is, funny old world ain't it? What can you tell me about Dr McNally?"

She sipped the water more rapidly than before. "Well, he's a funny one alright, good at his job and everything, always so precise, but he was on some sort of crusade to clean up the area and get all us girls off the game – he always gave me a lecture at the end of each check-up and told me to do something else for a living, what the hell it had to do with him I don't know, but he was dead serious about it, in fact at the last check up he told me to, 'change before it's too late …' or words to that effect – I thought that was right out of order and a bit creepy, yeh, he's a creepy sort of man for sure – but you said he attacked Gale? Gale Edwards? I can't get my head around that, is she OK?"

Tonks squinted at the memory of Gale Edwards' battered face. "She was badly beaten about the face with a cosh of some sort, had several stitches over her eye, knocked unconscious, bit like you, but thankfully she's OK, traumatised but OK."

"I just can't believe all this business with Gale and McNally, it's all so bloody unbelievable." Then slowly, through her foggy brain the thought suddenly occurred, "And you think it was McNally who was the prowler, who attacked me, is that it?" Sasha's eyes widened completely filling the slits of her head bandage.

"Look Sasha, you and Gale Edwards are amongst five women who have been attacked in recent weeks, all of them like yourself, badly knocked about, broken jaws, cheekbones, stitches, and all at night near or close to where they live – circumstantial evidence suggests it's the same person but we only have one victim who can identify the attacker and that's Gale – all the others, like yourself, never saw his face, always hidden behind that wretched hoodie – so, when you think of Dr McNally, his shape and size, do you think it could be him? You said your attacker was only a bit taller than you – what do you think?"

Sasha extracted an image of McNally's from her memory files – she closed her eyes and concentrated on him standing in his clinic, walking over to his desk, leaning over her, and examining her wearing his head-torch – then she thought of the person standing on the pavement below her bedsit and tried to superimpose the first image over the second.

"Well, yes, I suppose so, it's difficult to be sure, I mean, I'm five foot five, how tall is McNally, not much more I reckon?"

She felt confused and was getting tired; the strong pain-reducing medication was beginning to numb her brain. She put the glass of water back onto the cabinet and rested her head on the pillow with a sigh. Tonks waited for her to regain her composure.

She looked at Tonks and said softly, "The hoodie – was he wearing a dark grey hoodie when he attacked Gale, is that right?"

Tonks squinted, "He was wearing a hoodie yes …" He checked his notebook, flicking the pages back and forth until he found what he was looking for, "Two of the other girls said it was dark blue, one said it was dark red and the other said grey like yourself – of course, it's difficult to tell the colour in the middle of the night down a dim back street."

Sasha was getting weary, her feeble strength being drained by all the questions and the burden they put on her memory. She thought about her attacker that first time he had appeared standing in the rain in the middle of the road – there was something about his hoodie and she tried with all her fading strength to remember the detail.

"The hoodie, it made him look like a badger." She took a deep breath and sighed.

The nurse came over and felt her forehead, poured some more water into the glass and pressed it to Sasha's lips. "She's exhausted Chief Inspector, not much longer if you don't mind."

"What do you mean Sasha, why did he look like a badger exactly?" Tonks realised she was becoming comatose.

"It was the stripes, going over the head, two stripes – couldn't tell the colour, maybe yellow, don't know for sure, but they made him look like a badger from above."

Just then the small wall-mounted TV opposite that had been quietly minding its own business showing some forgettable gardening programme switched to a news bulletin. Sasha looked across to see what was being broadcast, pleased for the unscheduled break in the official proceedings; Tonks too looked around hearing the Prime Minister's voice who was responding to questions about the Miners' strike and the recent Battle of Orgreave:

"Look, in the Falklands we had to fight the enemy from without. Here is the enemy within. And it is much more difficult to fight and just as dangerous to liberty." The Prime Minister's fake mollified tone and exoteric choice of words were deliberately pitched to gain maximum empathy from viewers.

The screen then switched to pictures of police officers with head injuries and blood running down their faces. There was no caption nor explanation to clarify where and how their injuries had been obtained.

The news bulletin went back to the Prime Minister:

"Look, Scargill has replaced democracy with thuggery and if the Government gives in to the violence and intimidation shown by the striking miners then there was no future for trades unionism, or, even democracy."

Then more pictures, this time of miners throwing missiles at police lines, possibly stones, but it was not clear.

Tonks looked back to Sasha, conscious time was passing. "That's fine Sasha, I'll check out the hoodie, very useful observation, could prove a vital link between McNally and you and then who knows, maybe with the other girls too."

Sasha kept looking at the TV and seemed mesmerised by the news coverage, "Getting a bit serious this Miners' strike business – funny though, some bloke I know, Theo, asked me what I thought of it, about whether the Government was right to take them on, said he had all the information I need about it – I didn't know what he meant."

Tonks squinted. "Really? Would that be Theo Harrison by any chance? What did you say?"

Sasha looked at Tonks, "Said I didn't get involved in that stuff, that I didn't understand it – but that was just to keep him from getting too familiar – but I read the papers and keep up with things, these miners are getting a hiding, the Prime Minister wants to finish 'em, Scargill and the unions, once and for all."

Tonks was amazed at this observation. "Very interesting Sasha – had no idea you were a keen political observer." He squinted and smiled at his sardonic remark.

"We should all be political observers Chief Inspector, otherwise they'll run rings around us."

"That reminds me, do you recognise this brooch?" He took out a photograph from his bag of the silver brooch of the helmeted winged St Michael.

Sasha recognised the brooch straightaway. "Yeh, that Theo bloke gave it to me, said it would protect me, you know, against all these attacks."

"But I thought you said you didn't think you would be attacked, that it was all 'a bit remote' is what you said, why would he give you a brooch to protect you if you weren't bothered about the attacks I wonder?" Tonks spoke slowly and calmly and squinted again in a dramatic gesture to demonstrate he was earnestly seeking the truth.

Sasha closed her eyes and spoke softly, almost as a mimic of Tonks tone, "I suppose he was just being over caring for some reason, who knows – the punters give me all sorts of stuff, but he gave it as a present – what's the big deal with the brooch anyway?"

"Well Sasha, it was found on the kerb where you were attacked, got your prints on it, got Mr Harrison's prints too, but he has not confirmed giving you the brooch – I must ask you therefore, did you take it without his permission, think carefully now before you answer?"

She kept her eyes closed and longed for peace and solitude, sitting by the river in late spring when the kingfisher flashes blue and gold darting from the lime, willow and hazel perched above the gurgling river swelled by winter rain its twisting eddies playful with the trapped fallen moss. Then she saw little Vana running by the seashore chasing gulls, skipping and jumping, happy as the sun that warmed her heart.

"I'm tired now, so tired – he gave me the brooch." She drifted off back to the river and the seashore.

The nurse responded, "That's enough now Inspector, you will have to come again tomorrow if you wish to pursue these matters but right now Sasha needs sleep and rest.

Outside the recovery room Tonks asked the doctor how Sasha was doing and she answered, "Very well, we were concerned there might be intracranial haemorrhage but the tests show there is none – we are giving her strong pain-killers whilst she recovers from the fractured cheekbone – she should be ready to go home in a week, hopefully, but rest is the most important thing for her right now."

Chapter Fourteen

Monday morning eventually came round like a slow train coming out of the long, dreary tunnel of Sunday. Sundays were always the same for Theo, a seemingly worthless drift of time that paralysed the spirit, locked in the jaws of another looming week of work; and if the spirit did manage to flap its wings it was met with a barren waste of bleak ghost-towns, one after another, strewn across the land, where every shop and cafe was firmly bolted shut and pubs reluctantly opened for limited time. He loathed Sundays to the core of his heart and if he ever found the fabled genie in a bottle with one wish to be granted, he would surely wish for the week to be reconfigured to four working days and a three-day weekend.

He spent little time thinking about the Sunday just passed, for it was not conspicuous in any sense, and the only moment when he managed to break its tiresome monotony was when he trod up and down Packington street hoping to come across the elusive Jenny – he knew the odds were stacked against him but he believed his dogged determination would be rewarded. The mission seemed doomed to fail and his heart slid down the greasy pole of despair, a familiar journey of late.

After an unsatisfactory sleep, where the difficult pending duties of awaiting Monday kept tripping awake his lightly poised state of unconsciousness with stubborn regularity, he got up late and sat sipping coffee and munching toast at the kitchen table.

He spent half an hour going over in his mind what he was going to say to Tubby at the office. Then he took out his resignation letter, carefully so as not to crease the envelope, and read it once more:

Dear Mr Trubshaw

I am hereby giving you notice of my resignation of PR Executive with immediate effect. I understand I am obliged to work out a four-week notice period but would ask you to consider waiving that commitment and instead pay me for the four weeks in lieu of notice.

I have enjoyed my two years working at the Government's Central Office under your stewardship and trust I have made a worthwhile contribution to the advancement and general communications of the Government's policies in that time.

However, due to recent events concerning the Miners' Strike in general, and the Battle of Orgreave in particular, I have come to the conclusion that I can no longer support, in all consciousness, the Government in its endeavours to defeat the miners and bring about the wholesale decimation of the UK Mining industry as a means to fulfil the wider aim of diminishing trade union powers in order to put into practice quasi monetarism theory.

I trust you will understand that under the circumstances, and in order not to perpetrate negative feelings around the office, it would be counter-productive for me to work out the four-week notice and agree to pay me for this period in lieu of notice.

I wish both you and my colleagues in the Government's Central PR Office every success for the future.

Sincerely,
Theobald Harrison

He read it again, and then again, wanting to make sure he was conveying his reasons honestly, but not too negatively, and certainly not disrespectfully – after all, he was only too aware that the day would come when he would need a positive testimonial from Tubby.

He finally put the letter in his jacket pocket, took one last gulp of coffee, and left to get the tube to Westminster Station and the short walk to the office on Smith's Square.

On arrival at about eleven-thirty he went straight to Imogen's office where he found her stretched out on the floor behind her desk.

"Imogen? Is that you?" Theo could see her feet poking out and the lower part of her slim legs covered in navy-blue tights.

"Theo? Yes, it's me, my back is playing up again – hang on."

There were some heavy grunts and puffs from behind the desk as she manoeuvred herself to her feet. "There, that's better." She sat down at her desk holding her lower back with one hand and pulling the report in the typewriter up through the roller with the other; she studied the report and the extent of her progress thus far.

"Crikey, I've got to finish typing this wretched Monday report for Tubby – you know, he insists on two reports now, one on Friday telling him what we've achieved that week and another on Monday telling him what the week's new PR objectives are – doesn't want much does he? Tubby seems to spend all his time on reports these days – makes him a bit grumpy, well, you know, even more grumpy than usual, ha, ha." Her laugh was restrained with soft high notes that Theo found endearing.

"It's all about accountability Imogen, and behind that is the issue of trust – no one trusts anyone anymore so they get you to spend half your time telling them what you've done when you're not writing reports – goodness knows what they actually do with the information, stick it up their … well, you know what I mean?" He took out the envelope from his inside pocket. "Here, Imogen, can you make sure Tubby gets this as soon as possible." He placed the envelope on her desk.

"What's this Theo, you after a pay rise? I reckon you might get one after all those ideas you came up with in Orgreave." She picked up the envelope and studied it as if it was something rare and fragile from the vaults of the Bodleian library.

"No, I'm handing in my notice – I'm leaving …"

Imogen was not known for any outward display of emotion and certainly not any form of histrionics, but on hearing Theo's announcement she opened her eyes so wide they protruded like two boiled eggs from their sockets and let out a low pitched gasp that would not have been out of place in a Hammer Horror movie.

"Ahhh. What? You're leaving? But why Theo?"

Just then a loud boom of laughter exploded from the open-plan office down the corroder.

Theo's ears twitched into alert state like a cat stalking a garden shrubbery, "What's going on? Sounds like a party or something?"

"Yes, they're all getting together for Olivia Darcie-Poots' birthday drink, Tubby's giving a little speech – trouble is she's still on reception duty and can't attend, so he's doing it over the internal phone – why don't you pop along and join them – but I must hear more about why you're leaving."

Theo slowly entered the open-plan office and stood as inconspicuously as possible by the door like a hat stand.

There was a good turn-out with representatives from all the departments gathered in the large work area like Emperor Penguins huddled together on an ice cap, nervous but keenly attentive; Poots was popular especially as she seemed to know everything about everyone and was more than willing to trade snippets of gossip for attention and a sense of comradeship. In the village, that is all office environments, she was the equivalent of the head post office clerk, the chief receiver, sorter and deliverer of all grades of rumour and minor tittle-tattle.

The group had been assembled for half an hour and were already tiddly after consuming two or three glasses of wine that caused them to sigh and giggle each time Tubby said something even remotely funny.

Tubby stood in the centre with the telephone handset held slightly away from his mouth to indicate they were all welcome to share the conversation:

"Well now Pooters, it was clear to me from the moment I saw you enter my office for interview that you were of excellent stock, an exemplary Brownie and an outstanding Girl Guide – I thought, 'This gal will make a first class Receptionist' ..."

Howls of laughter gusted outwards from wall to wall and upwards into the ceiling.

"And I have been proved right Pooters. Look at the marvellous way you connect one caller whilst putting several others on hold, talk about never getting your wires crossed, your switchboard skills are the envy of Westminster ..."

Guffaws boomed across the room like waves drumming a sea cave.

"And Pooters, who can forget that memorable day you sat down the three-man delegation from Swaziland in Reception underneath those rather enormous ferns you had insisted on installing just at the time they were releasing bellows of irritating spores from the undersides of their leafy fronds – spreading an instant pink spotty rash across the Swazilanders' faces – they all ended up looking like they had been flicked with pink paint by Jackson Pollock ..."

A young clerk from Accounts and an elderly gentleman from Research both choked beetroot red with laughter.

Tubby slowly looked around to signal the end of his speech.

"And so Pooters it just leaves me the great pleasure to wish you an exceedingly happy ..." He covered the telephone mouthpiece with his hand whilst raising his left eyebrow in anticipation, "What's her bloody age anyone?"

Penton-Fox who, hitherto, had been keenly engaged in an earnest conversation with Penelope Janners-Smith, during which he had cast several indiscreet glances down her opened top blouse, suddenly turned towards Tubby and shouted out, "She's twenty-three Sir."

Tubby nodded his appreciation and continued with evident relief, "An exceedingly happy twenty-third birthday, hip, hip …"

Everyone shouted with unrestrained enthusiasm and impeccable unison, "Hurrah!"

The door through which Theo had entered opened and Imogen put her head round, caught Tubby's eye, and beckoned him over. As he passed Theo he said, "Ah Harrison, good to see you again, wondered where you were – come and see me in a few minutes will you? Just got to see Imogen about something." He disappeared through the door.

Before Theo could settle and take in the scene around him Suzanne came over looking flushed and anxious, holding two glasses of white wine.

"I say Theo, thought you weren't coming back to us, Ooogh"

Her mouth squeaked with her customary saucy laugh and her breath smelt of mustard and cigarettes. "Here, have a drink, you look as if you could do with it."

He took the wine but held the glass at waist height having already decided not to drink alcohol before his meeting with Tubby.

"So what do you think about old Cadgers getting promotion – you sounded a bit pissed-off on the phone when I told you – have you had time to reflect Theo, are you going to march off and thump Tubby's enormous desk in protest or are you going to take it lying down, Ooogh?" She was playful and a little merry with wine.

He looked at her eyes glinting with mischief and wondered why she kept throwing herself at him, as if her desire was somehow geared to the rate at which he remained elusive – the more he resisted her advances the more she turned on the seductress allure.

"You'll find out pretty soon Suzie." He stood there straight and sober and felt decidedly alien amongst his fellow colleagues gaily chatting and laughing in the Conservative Central Office.

"Ooogh, a mystery eh? Tell me more Mr Harrison, you know I'll do anything to find out what you have planned, Ooogh." She sipped more wine and he thought he could see her eyes go boss-eyed, like someone momentarily losing consciousness.

"Tell me how your interview went with Ian MacGregor last week – what's happening with this new Union, the UDM?" He knew he sounded too serious for the occasion, but that was where his interest was pinned as far as Suzanne was concerned.

"Oh Theo, and there I was hoping you'd tell me how you feel about Cadgers' promotion – Oh well, if you must know, it went OK, he's a decent chap, really wants to get behind the Nottingham and Derby miners and promote their Union – actually, what I think he really wants is to end the NUM's closed shop rule and he sees this breakaway union as a way to do it – I'm working on the publicity right now, of course all the usual newspapers will get behind it, they always do don't they, I mean, you know, get behind us … Ooogh, we can always rely on them, like having our own newspaper business, dedicated just to us, Ooogh."

"Yes, that's part of the problem isn't it?" Then he noticed Imogen with her head around the door scanning the room for someone.

"Theo please don't get all leftie again – promise me you'll have a drink with me after work today, ya? I want to run my publicity ideas past you, ya? I want to see if they stand up, Ooogh" She sipped more wine and a trickle ran along her lip that she tried to lick with her tongue. She peered at him with the most licentious hint in her eyes. "What do you say Theo, Ooogh?"

"I'm not sure Suzie, got a lot on my mind at the moment and I've got to see Tubby, I'm not sure how things will pan out."

"Oh don't worry about him Theo, he's just an old softie – actually, I think he's a bit odd, did you hear what happened last week when he visited Ralph Lancaster-Brooks, you know, the Director of Tonbridge Wells' Conservative Club, he's so well off and gives the Party pots of money, well, anyway, he stayed overnight in the Royal Spa Hotel and next morning phoned Ralph at home at 07.00 am, would you sodding believe it, ordering him most precisely to bring two three and a half-minute boiled eggs over to his hotel room tout-suite – said they always get his boiled eggs hopelessly wrong at the Spa – either hard as bullets or so rare they practically run out of their shells – and so poor Ralph had to jump in the old Land Rover and hoof it across town with Tubby's bloody boiled eggs on the back seat wrapped in foil – absolute riot, bloody priceless, Ooogh." Suzanne leaned back and laughed until tears appeared in her eyes.

"Ah there you are Theo, Mr Trubshaw wants to see you now." Imogen held open the door.

Suzanne quickly said, "Don't forget Theo – drinks after work Ooogh."

Theo put the glass of wine on a side table and entered Tubby's office to find him sitting at his huge desk puffing away at one of his large Havana cigars. The mid-day sun was pouring through the window behind him and highlighting the trails of thick bluish smoke that gave the impression he was smouldering like a bag of old autumn leaves.

Tubby looked up, "What the hell is the meaning of this Harrison?" He waved Theo's resignation letter in the air as if he was an Exchange Teller on the Stock Market's trading floor.

"It's my resignation letter, I'm leaving …"

"I can read Harrison, I know that, but what I don't know is why, why are you resigning? It doesn't make sense Harrison, it's got to make sense. You did a great job up there in, um, in that mining place, um, yes, in Orgreave, that's it – came up with some excellent slogans, just what we wanted, you've seen the news haven't you, the Prime Minster has been using those slogans left, right and centre, it's all helped to move public opinion our way Harrison."

"What way is that exactly?" Theo stepped a little closer to Tubby's desk.

"Look, sit down Harrison, no point standing up like that, this is not some bloody public school head teacher's office."

Theo sat down in Tubby's guest chair, a low-standing, hard-seated affair that was both uncomfortable and forced the sitter to look up to Tubby sitting opposite in his lofty extra padded swivel chair. A plume of acrid cigar smoke engulfed him and stung his eyes as he tried to get comfortable on the unyielding chair. As he looked across and upwards he was reminded of Napoleon Bonaparte's grandiose tomb of green granite resting on a solid block of black marble beneath the towering dome of Les Invalides in Paris – carefully and most particularly designed for all visitors to crane their necks to look up to the imperial sarcophagus containing the remains of the petit taille Emperor and by so doing reinforce his high ranking status and historical importance – his facade of grandeur. So it was that all visitors sitting in front of Tubby's desk were forced to look up to him, for any meaningful conversation to take place, and be under no allusion as to who was superior and who was not.

"Look Harrison, we, the Conservative Party, which you represent as a well remunerated Public Relations Officer, are at war, there's no two ways about it, we are at war with those bloody pain-in-the-neck trade unions – this is an epic struggle Harrison, a struggle of ideology, we want to smash the buggers once and for all, never again see them beat our Party like they did under that weakling Heath back in the 70s – the Unions have held us back, we as a nation, they have been responsible for Britain's post-war decline with all their restrictive practices and strikes and pickets – crippling our progress at every turn

Harrison, and we, you and me, are engaged in a battle to stop them – that's what this miners' strike is all about, do you understand what I'm saying? It's got to make sense Harrison, you know that." He puffed at his cigar whilst staring at Theo trying to read his mind.

"I understand what you're saying Sir but it's a question of tactics and …"

"Nonsense Harrison, the only tactics are to reduce their power base by whatever means possible – turn the people against them, make them see trade unions as the enemy, as anti-democratic, as traitors Harrison – that's why your slogans were so spot on – you got it completely right my boy, what was it – oh yes, 'the Enemy Within' and 'the Rule of the Mob' – brilliant Harrison."

Theo recognised he was now held captive by Tubby's rant and all he could do was to wait for the storm to pass.

"But I never meant it like that …"

"It doesn't matter one jot what you meant Harrison, who cares what you meant, no one, the fact is those slogans have helped us shift public opinion – look …" He shuffled some papers around on his desk, " … here it is, before Orgreave 15% approved and 79% disapproved of the miners' strike methods, that's pretty good but not good enough – and now Harrison those statistics have changed to just 7% approval and 88% disapproval – that's the right direction and we'll keep at it until the only people who approve of the miners' behaviour are Scargill and his bunch of Marxist henchmen, a pernicious mob of has-beens if ever there was – we've got them on the run Harrison – soon the Unions will be nothing but a pack of toothless hecklers that everyone will ignore and then Harrison we can move on to the big prize, first we break the unions then we destabilise and finally eradicate Socialism – that's what we're working for Harrison, then we can really start to change things for the better – bring about the free market economy and do away with all these inefficient nationalised industries, how about that for a vision, with no Unions and a half-baked Opposition Party we can really get the free market going, isn't that wonderful Harrison, you see it's got to make sense – sell off all the electricity, steel, water, railways, post office, everything – it's all in Friedrich Hayek's book, *The Road to Serfdom*, our Party's Bible you might say, read it Harrison, do yourself a favour, then you'll see why we must win over Socialism and the Unions, they're the enemy to our cause, for a better future …"

Theo thought he ought to make some attempt at interjection. "Has this really been thought through Sir? What about all the unemployment that it brings, has anyone worked out the cost, the real cost to the taxpayer and the cost to human dignity and resulting poverty – have you been for a walk through the Waterloo Underpass recently, it's like a refugee camp down there – no point in talking to them about Hayek's philosophy of liberalism, they're more interested in how to get bits of cardboard for a mattress and a bowl of soup for supper, they won't be interested in this new vision nor will all the thousands of ex-public sector workers lined up in the dole queue, nor all the thousands thrown on the scrap heap by industries who can't compete with ever rising costs …" Theo could not see Hayek's vision working in practical terms, only the misery of the scorched land it would bring in its wake.

"Don't be so naïve Harrison – who cares a monkey's elbow about high unemployment and a few homeless sods, we've got all this lovely North Sea Oil lolly haven't we, barrels of the stuff locked in the vaults of the Bank of England, more dosh than you can imagine, then there'll be all the extra revenue from selling off the rest of the privatised industries, millions and millions of easy wonga will come pouring into the coffers, and we'll have no more nationalisation overhead, no more liability, and the beauty is that all the responsibility will be with the private sector, they'll have to put in the investment and sort out the strikes, if there are any, because the workers who are left won't feel like striking when there's so much unemployment, they'll know where they're better off, no more strikes Harrison, think about it – that's the vision we're talking about here, it has to make sense you see, imagine the Utopia rising up before you, no more inefficiency and over-employment and those wretched restrictive practices that have stifled productivity and increased running costs, all done away with at a stroke, not to mention making thousands of ordinary people shareholders overnight, thousands and thousands of little capitalists Harrison jumping up and down in their semi-detached houses or better still, in their newly bought council houses, all jumping up and down waving their share certificates and laughing all the way to the bank, now tell me who do you think they'll vote for at the next general election, eh?" Tubby's eyes squinted with egregious mischievousness at the mental image of his Party's triumph.

"But none of it is proven, is it? It's just one big social and economic experiment conducted on the people – it may not work, Government's plans rarely work out the way they're intended …" He thought again about the squalor of the homeless encampment at Waterloo Underpass and a strong hatred for everything Tubby stood for surged through him.

Tubby puffed away at his cigar and stretched out his enormous red braces with his thumbs. "No, no Harrison, that's all too weak and defeatist – of course it will work, we've already started it haven't we, selling off Jaguar, British Telecom, Cable & Wireless, British Aerospace, Britoil and recently British Gas – it's a Brave New World Harrison, and you are part of it, you can help make the country great again, move it to new glorious heights, break the Unions, smash Socialism, turn the ordinary hard working people into share-owning capitalists, Popular Capitalism is the new catch phrase Harrison that you'll soon hear coming from every public bar in the land, and you can be part of it, spreading it around, but instead you hand in your notice – why, tell me why Harrison? It just doesn't make any sense." Tubby's ample jowls wobbled with incomprehension.

Theo held his ground. "Because I just don't believe in it, it's all a lie, look at what's happened with all those shares, most people sold them straightaway and the majority fell into corporate ownership, the whole enterprise hasn't brought about the intended miracle of turning working people into capitalists has it – all it's done is made the large corporations richer and more powerful – and most of them are foreign and most of those are nationalised, what an irony that is, it's all one big sham isn't it, all gloss and no substance, just so many lies – and meanwhile the number of unemployed stack up and the poor are out there with no food or a pot to piss in …"

Tubby stubbed out his cigar, took a quick glance out the window, checked the clock on the wall and then looked at Theo with a cold stare, "So you really don't want to be part of this revolution Harrison, that's disappointing, had hopes for you, but I still don't understand it, what's really changed you?"

The scenes he witnessed in Orgreave came back to him in vivid Technicolor and he clenched his fists at the injustice of it all. "I saw the reality up there in Orgreave – I saw ordinary miners, young lads most of them, having their heads bashed in mercilessly by British policeman acting like Storm-Troopers, deliberately charging at them for no reason, with absolutely no provocation whatsoever, charging at them on horseback and cracking their heads with truncheons – it was a bloody rout pure and simple, and it had been planned in advance, no doubt between the police and the Government, you should have seen the way those young lads were herded into that field, like sheep, rounded up for the slaughter, and it was slaughter, a massacre of the innocents, they didn't stand a chance, and then, when some of them started to throw a few things in retaliation, bread rolls, tufts of grass, and yes, a few stones, they were charged at again, chased all the way into the backstreets of Orgreave village and beaten up on the pavements – it was a bloody disgrace, and I witnessed it first hand, but what trumped everything, what really got my blood boiling, was the contemptuous clap-trap I saw in the media coming from the Prime Minister and her Ministers that evening, and practically everyday since, all the lies and distortions, blaming the miners for the violence when it was the police that started it, and what topped it all was the BBC actually editing the news film to show the miners throwing missiles first and the police charging second – the truth was not like that, it was a lie, probably a collusion between the media and the Prime Minister's office – or was it this office, were you part of that lie Mr Trubshaw I wonder?"

After he lobbed this grenade there was a long silence during which the cold chill of uncertainty crept along the nerves down Theo's spine whilst he waited for the expected explosion.

To Theo's surprise Tubby remained calm. "I've told you Harrison, we are at war, and when you're at war you launch propaganda campaigns, that's what you do, you shouldn't be shocked at that, it's usual tactics – look, we have to get more miners back to work, that's all part of the campaign, an important part, and we've got the equipment, the forces and the organisation to stop these unlawful pickets from blocking the strike-breakers, or scabs as they call them, from going about their lawful duties at work – we have to continue our propaganda campaign to convince striking miners that there's no point in them staying out any longer – although frankly it beats me why anyone would want to work down a sodding mine, filthy, back breaking work – anyway, do you get the picture Harrison, you understand our tactics, and they're working – and you can lend your expertise to help the cause."

"Ah, and those tactics include withdrawing welfare benefit payments for the miners' wives and dependents do they? Anything to force them back to work is that it? See families suffer just for your ideology to succeed? Those tactics are immoral as are all the lies we put out – and what's this all costing I wonder? This campaign of yours must be running up a huge bill eh? Funny how the Government can clobber people with all these welfare cuts and unemployment on the one hand but then splash out thousands on all this 'organisation' as you call it …"

Tubby took a deep breath and began to look bored, "Now you're being naïve again, you see it's got to make sense Harrison, look, we have to move public opinion against the NUM, whatever the cost, that's our job Harrison, you have helped for goodness sake with those brilliant slogans of yours, we want to create animosity towards the NUM and vilify Scargill, yes, at any cost, because this is war, do you really think those striking miners are as innocent as you say, you know they have caused plenty of violence, maybe not directly at Orgreave last week but there have been other occasions when they have acted like leftie thugs – you can't blame the police for all the violence Harrison, and when the police do intervene and retaliate, well, they are just trying to uphold the law and safeguard individual civil rights, the rights of those miners who want to return to work – and that tide is turning, looks like about fifty-odd thousand will be back to work by the end of the month – that means our tactics are working Harrison – it's all making perfect sense, do you still really want to leave this successful campaign? Remember, it has to make sense Harrison."

Outside a roar went up like a football crowd exulting at their team's winning goal and amidst the din could be heard an inebriated Suzanne shouting down the internal phone to Olivia Darcie-Poots in what was clearly a take-off of Tubby's earlier performance complete with an exaggerated mimicking of his voice.

"Now look here dear old Pooters my girl, you know we all love you to bits, so we must take off our hats and not stand on ceremony, no, mustn't do that, out of the question, anyway, you know what, it's your birthday, haven't got a bloody clue how old you are, who cares, but here's wishing you all the best of wishes for a long, happy day on Reception – Happy Birthday Poots!" Then everyone shouted, 'Happy Birthday Poots' at the vacant receptionist still detained by her duties two floors down.

A faint trace of agitation was visible on Tubby's plump face as he looked again at the clock and was clearly getting ready to bring the meeting to a close.

Theo sensed the moment and hurried his response, "I don't want to be part of all this deceit and distortion – if you can't play it straight then you're a cheat, and I'm not a cheat, I didn't see any miners trying to stop other miners from crossing the picket at Orgreave – a few of them did try and stop the coke lorries but that's not the same thing is it, those drivers were drafted in and aren't members of the NUM – the miners at Orgreave didn't deserve what happened to them, it was wrong and you shouldn't try and defend the indefensible and you certainly shouldn't launch a tirade of lies to the public just to move your approval percentage points a few notches in your favour – and by the way, all those slogans you picked up on, they were meant to describe my reactions to the police and the Prime Minister for what happened at Orgreave, but I was half delirious when I made the phone call to you, practically passing out with heat stroke and dehydration, didn't know what I was saying, and you misunderstood and misreported what I said – and that certainly didn't make sense Sir!"

Tubby sighed, mostly with boredom but with a hint of regret. "Very well Harrison, I understand, it doesn't matter now does it? We have to beg to differ do we not? So yes, I will have to accept your resignation." Tubby was not listening properly and was clearly hijacked by some other pressing matter that had come to his mind.

Theo felt he had not made his case very well and quickly added, "It's a matter of integrity Sir, if we lose that we lose trust and if we lose that we do not deserve to govern."

This was met with a blank look of indifference from Tubby, no more so than if Theo had just recited the Lord's Prayer.

Theo quickly changed tack, "OK Sir, but under the circumstances, for the sake of office morale, it's best if I leave straightaway and not work out the four-week notice – so, get paid in lieu of notice I mean, I hope you agree Sir?"

Tubby stood up and brushed some cigar ash off his trousers.

"Yes, yes, you're probably right on that score Harrison – see Imogen about the details and she will organise the cheque and the paper work – so it's goodbye then, sorry we can't see things eye to eye, thought you would make a first class PR Officer but there you are …" He moved around his enormous desk and went over to Theo with an outstretched hand.

Theo shook Tubby's hand and as he got to the door leading to Imogen's connecting office he turned and said, "It's been good working for you Sir these past two years, but I could never have reported to Cadgers, although that was not my main reason for leaving …"

Tubby, who was already back at his desk studying some papers, said without looking up, "Yes, OK, good luck then Harrison."

Imogen was finishing the Monday report when Theo entered her office. She stopped typing immediately and asked in her soft, emotionless way, "Theo, so why are you leaving, can't believe it, what did Tubby say, I knew something was wrong when I telephoned you in that Sheffield hotel – you didn't sound right, you said you were tired of it all – didn't know what you meant, when are you leaving?" She gazed at him with a genuine look of concern.

"Oh, you know Imogen, I've just had enough of all this …" Theo moved his hand in a broad sweep around the office, "I fancy a bit of a change, something different, might take up teaching."

"Teaching? Really? Gosh!" Imogen kept looking at him trying to figure out what was in his mind. "You're a strange one Theo, silent waters run deep and all that."

"Imogen, I need you to work out my pay, for the days worked so far this month and to cover the four weeks notice period, starting today – Tubby has agreed to that and he also said something about drawing up the necessary papers, but I don't know what he's talking about."

"What? Are you leaving straightaway then? You don't hang around do you? Yeh, OK, as soon as I've finished this report I'll work out your money and the papers, he's referring to the termination of your contract, normal procedure, and your P45, have them ready by five o'clock, is that OK?"

"Yes, can you post them to me, first class please, I'm going to need the money." He had been distracted by the noise of a jet plane through the open window, flying low over Westminster, Heathrow bound, and as he looked back to Imogen he just caught her staring at his crotch. She diverted her gaze in the blink of an eye and a light blush was visible on her cheeks.

"Well, I can bring them round to your place after work if you like, or we could meet up somewhere, if it's really urgent I mean?" Now she kept her eyes level with his and waited for the response.

He quickly had a vision of her turning up at his bedsit and knew where that path would lead; he saw her naked on his bed, waiting for him warm and eager and breathing heavily with quick short panting sounds like a dog on heat; these lurid images were suddenly concluded with a picture of the two of them afterwards full of guilt and shame with nothing to say and heavy with remorse. The phrase, 'Post coitum omne animalium triste est' came to his mind like an SOS message.

"No, really it's OK Imogen, no need to put yourself out, just put them in the last post and that'll do fine. Thanks anyway, I appreciate the offer, really do."

He went to the door and turned, "Thanks Imogen, thanks for all your help, take care of yourself. Bye."

"Goodbye Theo, good luck."

He could hear the sound of her typewriter thundering away as he walked down the corridor. As he reached the main door he met Eldred 'Cadgers' Cadgington returning from some errand to the local shop. He looked absurdly adolescent holding a bar of KitKat like a naughty schoolboy sneaking back from the tuck shop.

"Well, well, so here you are Harrison, I suppose you've heard the news of my promotion, eh?" Cadgers' eagle eyes looked devious and glowed with a nasty dose of smugness, "Look, there's going to be some changes around here, some tightening up, long overdue in my opinion, I want more accountability, more targets and of course a proper procedure of measuring those targets, it will mean tighter control and more work and more commitment – there's a new broom now Harrison and you'll have to change and move with the times or, to put it frankly old bean, move on – look, why don't we have a chat about what I have in mind for you, we can look at your performance in general and see where you can make improvements, I'll write up some meaningful KPIs for you, put you on a proper navigational course, don't want you just wandering around do we, sort of meandering without purpose, without a rudder, no, must make sure you have a rudder Harrison, there's a lot to do to defeat those Trotsky miners and I want to make sure you're properly motivated for the job and not all at sea – look, can't fit you in today I'm afraid but come and see me first thing tomorrow morning, OK? You know where my new office is ya?"

Theo could see Cadgers at his shiny modern desk, setting work targets for everyone and demanding individual weekly reports, the ultimate clockwork task-master, completely lacking empathy and not a smidgen of interpersonal skills, just a heartless, imperious autocrat insisting on complete obedience and hiring and firing at whim.

Theo opened the door and said, "No Cadgers, it's not OK – I've handed in my notice and I'm leaving – frankly, I wouldn't work for you if you trebled my pay, you're a nasty spoilt brat Cadgers and you represent everything I loathe about this lousy Government and this absurd obsession the country has with toffs and the privileged class – you only got the job because your father pulled strings and bent Tubby's arm up his back, you are completely unfit for the task and the fact that did not come into the equation speaks volumes of what is wrong with your kind and the Party you represent – it's all built on deceit and thrives within the old-boy network, individual merit doesn't come into it, all of you helping each other up the ladder so you can get your snouts in the gravy trough – it's all corrupt and dishonest, nothing but a pack of lies – I'm off Cadgers and you know where you can stick your targets and KPIs and that clipboard you carry everywhere – up your arse, ya?"

It took several swings for the main door to finally shut and in that time the only part of Cadgers to move was the single motion of his eyelids as they opened ever wider in utter disbelief.

Coming towards him by St John's church on the opposite side of Smith's Square was Suzanne who had gone to get a sandwich. "Well, look who it isn't? It's Theo the Champion of the North Ooogh..." Theo detected she was still squiffy from too much wine. "Off to lunch then?"

He noticed her wickedly sparkling eyes and cheeks rosy like Worcester apples. "No Suzie, I'm off, for good, I've handed in my notice, so it's au revoir."

"You're kidding – you can't leave Theo, you're the toast of the office..."

"No, I'm certainly not, all that slogan stuff was all one big mistake – I don't believe in it anymore, what we're doing as a department and what the Government is doing to the country – I've lost trust Suzie – and it's impossible to believe in what you're doing in this game without trust …"

"Oh Theo, you're too sensitive, I do that all the time."

She looked at Theo's long serious face and changed her stance, "Is this all about those silly miners, for God's sake Theo they started this strike business, didn't they – and they can jolly well take the consequences – they're all a bunch of commies anyway, traitors the lot of 'em, I wouldn't get so worked up about a load of working class lefties from up north – why can't they see the whole country's against them, especially that Scargill creature, we all know he's a Trotskyist – look at what the Daily Express says about him, the man's hell bent on anarchy – look Theo, come back to the office and have a coffee, we can talk this through and you can always go and see Tubby to tell him it was all a mistake – you mustn't get so worked up over such trivial things. What do you say?"

He went over to her and kissed her on the forehead, "I say goodbye Suzie, stop reading the Daily Express, it's bad for your health and watch out for Cadgers, power has gone to his head, and there's nothing worse than a little upstart with too much power and so little knowledge – he'll have you drowning in reports and paperwork before you know it." He turned and started to walk away.

She looked abandoned and alone, "But Theo, what about that drink after work?"

Without looking back he said, "Goodbye Suzie, thanks for the dance."

Chapter Fifteen

Whether it was the slow realisation that Earl did indeed lack fun, was lazy and uncouth around the flat, revealed a secret gambling addiction and had decidedly gone off the boil in the sex department was difficult to ascertain – but nevertheless, all these factors did come together in Beverly's mind and conspire to turn her off pursuing a future with her young lover.

The veneer of their hastily arranged tryst had lost its lustre in a surprisingly short space of time; she reasoned that she could tolerate the odd idiosyncrasy and annoying habit such as not washing before bed or chewing food with his mouth open or snoring like a rhinoceros, but spending most of her spare time cleaning and ironing an endless heap of his socks and underwear whilst he disappeared to the betting shop and pub made her concentrate her mind most particularly on the enjoyment value of their new enterprise. Thus it was that she had found herself thinking more and more of Reggie, sitting alone in the family house with nothing but his box kite to keep him company; she kept going over what he had said the last time they had met, all those wonderful memories of their honeymoon and the laughs they had shared, and of course the magical years bringing up Jenny, the irreplaceable moments watching her develop and grow that produced a strong bond between them that now resurfaced in the wake of the harsh realities of living with Earl.

So it was that one Sunday afternoon when Earl was absent, presumed preoccupied at the pub, she decided to pay Reggie a visit to test the waters for a grand reconciliation.

The decision had not been taken lightly and in fairness to Beverly she had spent much time mentally preparing herself for what she knew would be a testing moment standing before the man she had so cruelly abandoned, asking him to take her back and eating large portions of humble pie in the process.

Working on the principle that needs must when the devil rides, she took her time to restore a certain staid retro look that she believed Reggie would appreciate and find reassuringly familiar; off went the short black skirt, the close-hugging white cotton top, the acai purple 100 denier tights, the mascara and heavily rouged lipstick and on went the grey slacks, the brown blouse and the no-frills make-up together with straight brushed hair of no particular style. If on the scale of such things she had dared to adopt the trimmings of an alluring seductress she was now firmly restored to the unremarkable blandness of a hospital receptionist. In short, she looked as if she was Reggie Rennes' wife once again.

She arrived at the family home at three o'clock and calculated that Reggie would have finished his Sunday lunch and was already relaxing in the garden or fiddling with his kite in the shed; she had brought his favourite cherry cake and was planning a pleasant reunion up to and including teatime.

She rang the doorbell and tried to relax her face muscles wanting to present a chaste and repentant demeanour. She waited but there were no sounds of any movement inside, just the hushed stillness of an empty house. She rang the bell again. Still there was no response or signs of movement from within. She rang the bell for the third time and stepped three paces back along the path.

She glanced upwards and noticed the bedroom curtains were drawn – she wondered whether Reggie might be sick or confined to his bed for some reason or was taking a nap; she kept looking at the window curious as to what might be wrong when she saw the curtains move, slightly but decidedly, they fluttered indicating someone was peeking out, not wanting to be noticed.

She rang the doorbell again and kept it pressed for longer than was polite. Faint bumping sounds came from within, feet against the floorboards, someone was on the move. Then a shadowy shape appeared behind the glass panel of the door followed by the sound of the latch being released. The door opened slowly, as if the person on the other side didn't mean it.

Betty stood there with one of Reggie's old towelling dressing gowns hastily wrapped around her. She peered at Beverly with penetrating eyes whilst she clasped the dressing gown tightly together over her bare chest with both hands.

"Yes? Can I help you?" Betty's face was full of curiosity as she searched for hidden clues in Beverly's eyes.

"I'm Beverly, Reggie's wife, who the hell are you?"

Betty's eyes widened with alarm. "Oh, I see – can you wait here a minute please?" The door closed with a thud behind the scampering Betty.

She disappeared and there were sounds of rapid movement and urgent conversation upstairs.

The front door opened again and Reggie stood there with a smug smile pinned on his face.

"Hello Bev – what can I do for you then?"

Beverly was speechless, she sucked air through her nose.

"What do you mean? I thought we could have a chat, you know, about us and the future …"

Reggie looked at his wife and in that moment all that could be detected in his eyes was the impenetrable sign of indifference.

"We don't have any future – you lied and deceived me."

She felt pain rising through her, like she had trodden on a piece of glass. "But we can talk this through, you and me Reg, like we always do, I can explain …"

He looked at her with resentment where love had once dwelled, "You forgot about the consequences – there's always consequences."

He closed the door.

Beverley turned and walked back down the road humiliated and broken, the Sunday silence sliced only by the sound of the latch being firmly shut behind her.

Chapter Sixteen

Detective Chief Inspector Tonks leant back in his chair and tapped the edge of his desk with both thumbs. He looked up at Detective Sergeant Whithers and started to squint his eyes, as was his habit when his mind raced and he was bedevilled by a complexity.

"So Detective Sergeant what have you got for me – did you check McNally's clothes?"

Whithers looked tired with dark semi-circles beneath his eyes and did his best to stifle a yawn, "Yes Guv – we went back to his place and searched it from top to bottom – he's got two hoodies, both dark blue but neither had stripes going over the hood – we looked everywhere, even in his and his neighbours' bins but couldn't find anything – we checked a small patch of grass at the back but there was no sign of the earth being dug up and no sign of a bonfire."

"Bugger it – so we've got nothing to link him to Ms Phillips and the other three, what are their names?" He checked some papers on his desk, "Um – Ms McDonald, Ms Tyler and Ms Patcham? Bugger it. What about the weapon, the Forensic boys thought it was some kind of cosh?"

"Nothing Gov – he probably chucked it somewhere – we never found it on him when he was caught at the scene with Gale Edwards – funny that, must have tossed it just before Crow and Noads arrived, but God knows where – Forensic said that all five victims' wounds were consistent with the same blunt instrument, but that's not conclusive I'm afraid."

This time Whithers could not hold back a long and deep yawn.

"You need a good night's sleep Detective Sergeant – and you're not the only one – well, all we've got then is a confession to the assault on Ms Edwards?"

"Yes Gov – and all he's got for an alibi for the other four assaults is that he was at home on each night – no one can verify it but no one prove otherwise either."

Tonks sighed and tapped his thumbs on the desk again, "He must have done all five, its got to be him – the coincidence is too great what with him being their doctor at the sex clinic and being a religious fanatic and all – it all adds up."

Whithers yawned again, "It does Gov but we just can't prove it, not yet any how …"

"OK – officially book him and let's get him in court – maybe a spell in prison will bring him round – at least we'll have him off the streets for a while, and that's something I suppose – but I haven't finished with this case Detective Sergeant."

Whithers yawned one more time.

* * * * * * * *

It had just turned six-thirty on Monday evening and Jenny sat in her comfy chair by the window in her little room on Packington Street. There had been a short, heavy downpour on her way back from work and she opened the window to let the cooler air alleviate the room's trapped stuffiness.

She had treated herself to some poached eggs and avocado spread over hot buttered toast and was feeling momentarily satisfied, an interlude of simple pleasure that was increasingly lacking in her humdrum life. She sipped tea from her favourite red mug with a fading picture of Mickey & Minnie Mouse dancing around in their clownish large shoes, Minnie's with high heels, and that absurd detail always cheered her up.

She reflected on her day's work at the office and her latest awkward case of young Edward who had lost his job as a fork-lift operator at the local timber merchant and slipped below the poverty line; shortly afterwards his wife had taken their eighteen month old baby and left him for a reason that was not clear. He could not find another job and, despite his best efforts, the rent arrears mounted up and became critical. He was issued with a final payment deadline but could not get the required money together in time and was given an immediate eviction notice.

His claim for housing assistance had been passed to Jenny for processing, along with hundreds of similar claims. Jenny had judged his case to be 'satisfactory' and marked his claim 'accepted' and then passed the recommendation for immediate housing assistance over to her new Head of Section, Justine Bavington. The claim was rejected by Justine on the basis that Edward had been living in a property owned by a member of his family and was therefore not without means – Jenny had gone back to Justine to point out that Edward's accommodation was not owned by a close relative but a distant one, a second cousin, and he was therefore not exempt from housing benefit under this rule; Justine had called Jenny into her office late that afternoon and told her to stop wasting time on inapt cases, that Edward did not qualify for the benefit and she should notify him of the decision and get on with more urgent cases.

Jenny reminded her of the rule at which point Justine became even more surly and shouted at Jenny that if she could not deal with her cases properly she would find someone who could, that she needed to know all her staff were competent and able to quickly finalise the high number of cases going through; this cut Jenny to the quick as she had poured her heart and soul into the job during the recent crisis period and her attainment record was exemplary; she returned to her desk feeling dejected and undervalued.

It was obvious to Jenny that Justine was trying to demotivate her to leave, and that this deliberate victimisation campaign came from some vengeful spite over Jenny having gone head to head with her for the Head of Section job. On that, Jenny knew she had little option but to grin and bear it or look for another position; but on the matter of Edward, she knew that Justine was wrong in her decision and that she had overlooked, or misunderstood or worse, was not aware, of the rules.

The working day had run out of time before she could decide what course of action was appropriate. So she went home and sat in her chair sipping tea and thinking about whether to go straight to her Director, Mr Bates, in the morning and get Justine's decision on Edward's claim revoked; she knew it was a risky enterprise, not least because of the strong rumours that Justine and Bates were having an affair.

She mulled over the details of the case and the likely consequences of her action. It was certain that Justine would make her life hell and she would be engaged in a battle of wills – but she was tough and, in any case, Justine relied on her experience around the office, especially as she had so little herself. It was a glaring injustice that Justine had been promoted above her and it continued to rankle her to the extent that she extrapolated the theory that all over the country, in every business and profession, similar injustices were being played out. She reflected that it was people who ruined things in the office, not the work itself; it was lack of leadership skills, cronyism and poor management acumen that led to dissatisfaction amongst staff. She also acknowledged that long before Edward's case she had felt the pressure of work mounting and was beginning to buckle under the strain – she knew that things were reaching a crisis point, but she would not cave in to the likes of Justine Bavington, never.

So her mind was made up and she felt more at ease, she had nothing to lose but to speak to Bates, hopefully Edward would get his housing assistance, Justine would get egg all over her face, and she would carry on helping the needy and displaced, because it was a decent job and she had right on her side.

She finished her tea and started to calm her mind. The evening sun had quickly replaced the rain clouds and she opened the window wider to let the warm glow enter the room. She leaned back in the armchair and closed her eyes letting her mind regain connection to the enchanting stillness of the little room, that seemed to be waiting for something to happen, the clock ticking on the bookcase, encapsulating each second as a rounded separate entity, like a precious jewel sparkling in its brief short moment of radiance, a butterfly movement of time, delicate and transient, then gone, tick-tocking to the next one, then the next, and the next, but how many jewels remained, how many seconds were left – she pondered these questions of great magnitude without conclusion.

Then her upstairs neighbour, Maggie McGuire, interrupted her thoughts, with her obsession of dragging an old wooden-chest across the floor, pushing and pulling the damn thing, as heavy and awkward as it was, to a new position that momentarily satisfied some quirk in her mind. She wondered, "How strange people are."

Maggie had met Jenny on the landing one day and invited her in for coffee which is when she noticed the ornate chest sitting in the corner, incongruous amongst the few worthless items and knick-knacks that defined her other possessions; Maggie was an Irish women, a curious mix of poverty and refinement, about fifty-six years old, but looked the wrong side of sixty-five, who had seen better days and who got by on a combination of gin, cigarettes, a sense of humour and the odd gentleman friend she enticed at her local pub, The Camden Head, where she often sat in her favourite chair in the snug bar omitting signals like a beacon to any man who was lost or desperate. She had asked Maggie what she kept in the chest and was told, "My photographs, my special photographs of my husband, our wedding, our holidays, all the times we were happy and together, they're all I have now, just my photos, my memories."

Jenny sat and waited for the sound of the heavy chest being dragged across Maggie's room to stop and sure enough, within a few minutes a temporary peace was restored.

The stillness returned and she pressed her head back into the armchair, letting her mind wander off again, along the thermals of drifting cloud, past the pillars that guarded her consciousness and the strains of her busy life, past the outrageous effrontery of her mother's behaviour and the sadness of her abandoned father, over the cares and woes of her daily routine, floating light beyond the injustices inflicted on ordinary people by an uncaring Government, drifting away from all the broken souls she tried to mend each day, on and on, soaring far away from it all, out beyond the limits of her experience, to where she had found peace and love that special day, that surreal moment she met Theo on Wissant dunes, the magic of his sudden appearance, sliding down and standing there in the late afternoon sun, mysterious and strange, standing there, from nowhere, with the sea at his back, as if Nereids and the sea nymphs had handed him over to Aphrodite who had placed him on the dunes near to where she had sat singing her sad lament of unrequited love, a gift from the gods meant just for her, a single blessing in her troublesome life, her heart torn by Danny but restored by Theo on that special afternoon, sweet it was like honey warmed by the sun, the sweet nectar of love, from no where it came, from the deep black mysterious sea, he had appeared and entered her life at the crucial moment, the moment of her despair, as if by fate, something ordained by God.

Her eyes became heavy as she started to drift further down the tunnel of time, back to that last evening with Theo at Wissant when she had ended up in his hotel room. The dream gathered around the edge of her subconscious as the warm Islington air wafted in through the window, scented by a delicate blend of geranium and hyacinth with an undertone of diesel, gas, coal, pump-outs, oils and greases from the canal. Off she went, the aromatic air fanning her memory of that special time when they had held each other close, exploring with their hands the bones and skin of each others' faces and then the long kisses, their tongues curled around each others' sending impulses of electric charge between nerve cells and out though their bodies like beams of candescent light flaming from a lighthouse across the sea; off she went, further and further, falling into the still rock pools left by the deep dark tide of time, down and down, her eyes closed as she swam warm and secure within the folds of sleep, back to Theo's darkened room, the luminous dial of the three-quartered moon lighting up a path to the huge four-poster bed and spotlighting the ivory white cotton covers of his feather down pillows. There they were, young and curious, falling onto the bed still holding each other, clasping and gripping like lovers ossified by molten lava from Mount Vesuvius, locked together on the big old bed, petrified by the strength and power of love, kissing and licking by impulse over noses, eyelids, ears and cheeks, on and on she sank into the sweet dream as if she was there re-enacting each special moment clear and real once again; the moonlight was radiant, she could smell the sea drifting in over the dunes, so real she could cup it in her hands and see the grains of sand trapped behind her nails, she could feel the ache in her heart to hold him and the tremble of her thighs to draw him closer; time pirouetted, spinning like a ballerina, she turned and writhed on that soft mattress, pulling away her clothes and unzipping his, the cold awkward belt strap, the exquisite softness of warm skin on warm skin, the deep searching kisses that never ended, the sense of heaven radiant all around, falling and turning, her body and his fingers clasped tight, sweaty and salty, lifted high into the dome of body fusion pleasure, sticky like syrup and sweet like honey, she arched her body with the electric charge of the holy union, total and final, the two bodies and minds melded by an endless sigh. "I love you." He had whispered. "I love you too." She had replied. The words hung in the air like incense, caressed their ears and restored their spirits, the Divine Liturgy complete, their blood and flesh shared, the Blessed Sacrament fulfilled.

A car went by outside sounding its horn and she opened her eyes to the living world once again, her mind slowly raised from the subconscious state like a pail being pulled from a well. She picked up her guitar and strummed a spontaneous jazz rift that carried off around the room and found the warm air thermals drifting through the open window – out it went across the street, escaping like a released wasp.

As she played she thought of that first time she had met Theo, when he had heard her singing across the dunes and set off to find her alone with her guitar; she could see him clearly in her mind's eye with his thick wavy hair, his grey-blue eyes and crooked Roman nose and full lips – his image pricked her memory, bringing back the tender sadness that sat like a thorn beneath the surface of her thoughts whilst he remained mysteriously absent.

"Where are you Theo, why haven't you phoned?" She felt both love and anger at the same time but the greater of these was love. She kept seeing him wrapped in her arms, staring into his eyes and touching his skin; she yearned to press her lips against his, as she had done that last night in Wissant, soft like a slice of warm peach.

"What happened, where are you Theo? Why does this keep happening to me, I find love then it vanishes for no reason, will I never be happy?"

She stopped strumming the guitar and gazed out the window across the Packington Street rooftops, peaceful and still on the June Monday evening, and started to well up with self-pity. True love, honest, real, true love, seemed to elude her and she doubted herself, she mistrusted her ability to make accurate character judgements. Ever since her early school days she had made bad decisions with people, wandering around the playground desperate for companionship, feeling feeble and vulnerable, she had allowed bullies to enlist her in their gangs and then manipulate her to perform minor misdemeanours, like smoking in the copse at the back of the playing fields. Then there was the run of post-puberty boyfriends, complete disasters the lot of them – always attracting the misfits and those damaged in some way, hopeless even desperate encounters that were marked by differences of language and meaning or void of abstract concepts. Even with Danny the imbalance had been there for all to see – he the charismatic, decadent John Falstaff of the King's Head and her the steadfast Social Worker devoted to caring for the dispossessed and limited by the moral codes of Folkestone's suburbia. Now the thought of Danny made her cringe with regret and shame at how he had used her for his own gratification. Ah, but then, just for once, the sun had come out and her sky turned blue with the bright warm love of Theo – how she had basked in the rays of that life-giving force, how she had rejoiced at the extraordinary chance gifted her on the Wissant dunes to share her love, real, true love, the likes of which she had never known before, and how it had transformed her, lifted her out of her tired old self and put a smile back in her eyes, as if she had been brought out of a coma. But alas, this one true love was now lost and the reason for the loss was a mystery, and so there she sat by the window complete in her bewilderment and dejection.

It was in this state of despair that the song, *Plaisir D'Amour*, drifted into her mind like flicks of dawn light through trees. She closed her eyes to recollect more clearly the lyrics of the haunting classical French love song, based on a poem by Jean-Pierre Claris de Florian; then started to strum the simple opening chords – finally she began to sing the sweet-sad poignant lines till they almost made her cry: -

"The joys of love
Are but a moment long
The pain of love
Endures the whole life long."

Unbeknown to her Theo was walking slowly along Packington Street at that very moment on what had become a daily ritual to find her. He had walked the entire length of one side and was halfway back along the other peering all around, studying each window and door on the off chance she would suddenly appear. He had now acquired a postman's familiarity with the Islington backstreet and could anticipate the detail of the next house before it was adjacent. As he walked, slithers of pink lightly shaded the thin tissue of cloud from the west and everything sat in stillness and sharp definition so typical of a mid-June evening.

Jenny kept thinking of Theo, she had no choice in the matter, driven by their own volition, her thoughts were invaded by a series of vivid, clear images of him as she continued singing the heart-rending love song:

"Your eyes kissed mine
I saw the love in them shine
You brought me heaven right there
When your eyes kissed mine."

Theo continued to walk slowly along, his mind blending sweet memories of Jenny interspersed with the awkward exchange earlier in the day with Tubby. It was nearly 07.15pm, that time in the evening when most commuters were either back home or sitting with friends in cafes and bars; the traffic too was lighter as the bustle of delivery vans and tradesmen's lorries inevitably petered out.

He peered into open windows as he walked, catching glimpses of people sitting on sofas or at dining tables and every now and then the faint crackle from a radio or television caught his ear. With only a quarter of the street left to walk he slowed down and eventually came to a halt by a lamppost. He was desperate to see Jenny again, to feel her and smell her skin once more; he wanted to tell her about his meeting with Tubby and to seek her counsel and the strength of her wisdom, to talk to her again, and the bliss of hearing her voice.

Standing by the lamppost he lit a cigarette and for some reason thought about Harry Lime in the film, *The Third Man*, standing alone in the shadows of a cobbled alleyway in post-war Vienna. It was then he heard the song, the beautiful drifting melody, the sad, evocative refrain of *Plaisir D'Amour* drifting out from one of the houses nearby:

"My love loves me,
A world of wonder I see
A rainbow shines through my window;
My love loves me."

He drew on his cigarette and looked left and right, his ears alert like a fox listening for prey. He walked on a few more steps and the song drifted closer, echoing from one side of the street to the other, it took off in looping rolls, rising and dipping like a lark:

"And now he's gone,
Like a dream that fades in the dawn
But the words stay locked in my heartstrings;
My love loves me."

He recognised the voice, the same stunning voice he had heard coming over the dunes at Wissant, the same sad, bittersweet, lovely voice of Jenny Rennes singing her beautiful love songs – his heart pumped hard against his chest and he felt dizzy with emotion, giddy with the huge surge of love that was waiting for release, waiting for her – he flicked the cigarette into a puddle and leapt into the middle of the street, his senses zigzagging around his febrile brain, the muscles in this throat went taught and the veins in his forehead stood out as he shouted at the top of his voice, "Jenny! Where are you? Jenny!" Two stock doves, summarily disturbed from their early evening liaison on a nearby chimney pot, flapped their wings and flew away in alarm.

A few seconds before Theo shouted out Jenny's name, Maggie McGuire decided it was time to move her old wooden chest once again across her bare wooden floor. The ensuing din created the usual bedlam of noise that blotted out all other sound from Jenny's ears; she stopped singing and waited for the brouhaha in the room above to stop. She stared at the ceiling and muttered underneath her breath, "This is getting bloody stupid, the silly cow must be off her rocker."

Theo ran across Packington Street from one pavement to the other, forward and back, turning in all directions, scrutinising the houses within the immediate vicinity, glaring at each open window, like a crazed person possessed by a demon. Alas, he could no longer hear the sweet sad song that signalled Jenny's elusive location. Frustrated he went over to the opposite pavement and assumed the same stance. A car went past and a front door opened and closed somewhere; but there was no longer any trace of Jenny's singing. He leant back, looking up to the heavens with closed eyes, angry and frustrated, he shouted at the top of his voice, "Jenny! Jenny!"

Peace was finally restored in Jenny's bedsit. She decided to go off down the corridor to the kitchen to make some more tea and stood up holding her faithful red mug and empty plate when she suddenly stopped in her tracks. There, quite clear, rising above the ordinary hum coming from Essex Street was the unmistakable voice of Theo shouting her name. She put the crockery down and pinned her ears to the open window with sharpened concentration – there it was again, no doubt about it, Theo was outside shouting out her name.

She bounded over to the window so fast she practically fell through it and, stretching her head out like a cuckoo from a clock, she scanned the street below – and there he was, twenty yards down on the opposite pavement looking the other way.

"Theo! Theo! Over here!" Her heart seemed to burst and tears flooded her eyes.

"Theo! I'm here, Theo!"

He looked around and saw her leaning out of the top floor window five houses down, "Jenny, Jenny …" He raised his arms as if to urge her to fly over to him, but she disappeared inside and for a moment he had to check himself that he had not hallucinated right there on the street.

He ran towards the house, his mind bouncing around scatty with expectation and impatience, and as he drew near the front door opened and there she was, her eyes beaming wide and moist and her mouth opened agog as if she had seen a ghost.

She cleared the six-step stoop in two strides and ran onto the pavement into his arms and there they stood, tight and secure like a padlock, in natural harmony, one breathing out and the other in:

We are twins – born within time, the same
You with your heart in rhythm with mine,
The same composure and sense of place
The same experience to touch and taste,
We are twins – the same eye, yours closing
Mine opening steady at the same pace.

She pulled away, her face feigning anger, and said sternly as if speaking a line from a Village Hall play:

"Where the hell have you been Mr Harrison? I thought I had lost you …"

Then she half-thumped his shoulder with her hand and immediately kissed him full on the lips, a long, long kiss that seemed to lift them both off the pavement, their souls fused and suspended in mid-air, held together by the unbreakable bond of love.

He was caught in the moment, choked with the pure joy of finding her again, as he whispered in her ear, "I looked everywhere for you Jenny Rennes, lost your phone number, been looking up and down the street …" She interrupted him with another kiss that melted their hearts and bled the tumour of their doubt.

She said softly as she led him up the stoop to the front door left ajar, "It's OK now, everything's OK now …" They tripped up the stoop so light, like children dancing with delight.

Half an hour later they lay naked on her bed, with its old brass headboard and mattress that dipped in the middle, staring at the ceiling. Both felt renewed and at peace once again, lying on their backs, he with his arm around her shoulder and she with her head nestled beneath his chin, her hand on his thigh, their contentment complete and without demands.

A fine and delicate stillness existed between them, a high state of peace, where both drifted in the soft evening light outside themselves, their out of body eye looking down on the other, standing guard over the priceless treasure. Time passed to the beat of her bedside alarm clock ticking like a regular drip of water. The light flecked and gradually faded, soft and fragile like a dandelion seed, and that special stillness of a June summer evening settled in the room. He took a lock of her long black hair between his thumb and forefinger and gently twiddled it as if he were sorting fibres of yarn for crocheting. She found a small but tangible scar along his thigh like a furrow in a field and followed its course with her finger as gentle as a fairy stroking a thread of silk. Like Psyche and Eros, their love bound them into one being, beyond words and other human limitations.

Finally she said, "I missed you Theo, thought you had changed your mind about us, I went and checked your flat by that old shop you mentioned, Schram and Scheddle, several times but couldn't work out whether you live to the right or left or right above it – but it didn't make any difference because I never saw you and you don't have a bell-name do you? Thought you had given me a wrong address deliberately."

She dug her nails into his thigh to vent the sense of anger and loss she had felt looking for him.

"I'm right above it." He whispered not wanting to end the dream like trance he was in. "But it was the same for me, I lost that bit of paper you wrote your phone number on – but remembered you lived in Packington Street – don't know how many times I went up and down on the off chance."

They squeezed each other's skin with their fingers to signify their understanding of each other's plight.

They both laid on their backs holding hands and staring at the ceiling; finally she asked, "So tell me how you got on with your job today – weren't you going to hand in your notice?"

He told her what happened, the chaotic drinks party for Olivia Darcie-Poots and the meeting with Tubby that followed.

"So he wanted you to stay? Well, that's a feather in your cap, were you tempted?"

"I've never been less tempted over anything." He paraphrased Tubby's comments on the Government's mission in general and Popular Capitalism in particular:

"They plan to crush the unions and socialism, sell off all the nationalised industries, sell off council houses, make little capitalists of us all whilst they bring in the so-called free market economy – some daft notion that if you load all the tax breaks towards the already rich and well-off they will 'Trickle Down' their wealth and boost the economy – what a load of bollocks, you just couldn't make it up – but it's clever too, the ordinary working people will swallow all the bullshit about buying shares in the nationalised industries and buying up their council houses for a fraction of the real cost – never mind about the shortage of council properties for generations to come – they will all leap at the chance to be little capitalists – for a day anyway, before they sell their damn shares to some foreign corporation – we won't have any industries left but we'll all be quasi capitalists working for the service industry and financial sector – God help us all –

but it will keep the Tories in power for years unless they cock up in some way."

She said, "They've already cocked up my world – I work for the needy and dispossessed and it's an ugly, hopeless world full of misery – and amongst all my other problems I've now got this little soot bag of a boss, the new Head of Section, Justine Bavington no less, who doesn't know her arse from her fanny and who dared to overturn my decision to grant housing assistance to this man, Edward, on the grounds that he lives in a place owned by a 'close relative' – but he doesn't, it's owned by a distant relative and that makes a difference – but Bavington is not a detail person, she's content to operate on the peripheral, away from the nitty-gritty, and skim over complexities – well tomorrow I'm going to talk to the Director and get him to change her decision – he'll have to, because I've got the rules on my side, but she won't like it, especially as she's screwing him."

"What will you do – tough it out?"

"Damn right I will – I've invested too much time and effort in this job to let some foxy, half-wit, dumb blonde like Justine Bavington come along and spoil things – you have to stand up to the likes of her, in the end they always fail because they've got no substance, no real experience, and they end up in some mess they can't clear up – I've got zero respect for her and I know it's only a matter of time before she leaves." She put her foot over his leg and clung onto him more tightly as if to draw strength from his body.

She continued in a soft, caring voice, like a nurse tending a wounded soldier in a field hospital, "So Theo, you've crossed the Rubicon, no turning back, and you're going to teach Marketing? That's exciting isn't it? You'll be good at it, I know you will."

"That's the plan but it doesn't feel too exciting right now, just scary – I'm going to have to get my B.Ed first – I enrolled this afternoon at Camden College, the course begins this

September – it's a year's course, I've got a bit saved up and the four weeks salary in lieu of notice but I'll have to get a part time job to see me through, working in a bar maybe for a few nights a week – it's all a bit of a gamble really, I've never been much of a gambler – I'm not as confident as I make out."

She slightly tilted her head towards him to give gravitas to her observation, "Yeh, most of us don't take risks do we, prefer staying in our comfort zone, who was it, that American women's lib activist, Mary Arlene Cruikshank Grefe, what a name eh? – it was her who asked, 'What Would You Attempt To Do If You Knew You Could Not Fail?' – you know, the path not taken and all that – where do we get all this hesitancy from – is it nurtured or is it nature?"

He thought about her question and said, "It's human to fail isn't it? That's how we get to succeed in the long run – we learn by doing, it's the best way. My father used to tell me that story of Robert the Bruce watching a spider trying to climb the cave wall where he was hiding during a battle, trying and failing six times but never giving up, always having belief in itself – and when the spider succeeded on the seventh attempt it inspired him to go out and try again to win the battle, which he did – that simple story really kindled my imagination as a kid, it's ironic seeing as my father gave up on us as a family without trying to keep things together ..." He stopped, something painful blocked his mind for a moment.

She stepped in, "I remember you saying, back in Wissant, you were only nine weren't you? Christ, that must have hurt you Theo."

He quickly recovered, "Well whatever the problem was, he just got up and left, abandoned us to our fate, saying marriage was difficult, living with someone was difficult, or some defeatist comment like that, I guess he didn't practice what he preached, a common failing amongst parents don't you think."

"We all have imperfections don't we? It's never wise to judge others just on surface evidence – you need to scratch away the surface, get right into the details, walk in their shoes and see how they fit." Now she paused and relaxed the grip of her legs around him.

"My father told me the other day that my mother has left him, gone off with a younger man from work – after thirty odd years – just like that, but it's not in his nature to fight for her back, even though he loves her, he'll just take it on the chin and grin – they're a funny lot aren't they, that Second World War generation, they just accept their destiny, like lemmings, never question, never explain, never show their pain – but then again, we don't know what it was like living through that bloody blitz do we? Imagine sitting all night in one of those pathetic tin-pot Anderson shelters with bombs falling all around you – imagine not knowing whether you and your family would be blown to bits at any moment, can you imagine it?"

Theo ignored the blitz and thought about her father, "No doubt your father has his pride – but this imperfection thing interests me, we're born innocent aren't we, and we learn to love before we learn to hate, so everything gets gradually buggered up during infancy – it's the small incremental changes that make a difference, bit by bit we absorb all the negativity, we learn guile to get our way over siblings, we learn to lie and cheat and worst of all we learn greed, to put ourselves first, not to share – you can try and teach kids to share but it's best to show them – I guess the biggest difference between Conservatism and Socialism is that fundamentally Socialism is about sharing, using the pooled wealth for the common good – that concept is such an anathema to the Tories, they believe in making your own individual wealth and let everyone else go hang, they just don't see that people aren't born equal, some struggle and need help – but they keep winning elections don't they, cutting public services and cutting taxes, the old Tory election formula – but people fall for it don't they, they can't see beyond the tax cut."

He reached over for his packet of cigarettes and lit one.

She said, "Most people are politically illiterate and easily duped, especially the working class, the saddest thing you'll ever see around election time is a member of the proletariat voting Tory, what the hell is that all about? Mind you, the Tory press do a good job on them don't they? They dominate the media and are highly skilled at controlling the message, they know that if the same slogan is banged out time and time again the gullible will believe it, repeat it like parrots, no matter how exaggerated or false – the Tories win elections with this collaborative effort with the press – look at the way they've tarnished Labour with the notion that they 'waste money' and 'can't manage the economy' – never mind that the Tories are ratcheting up huge interest rates, clobbering public services, taxing out business investment and seeing unemployment spiral out of control – the press don't mention that do they?"

He curled smoke rings up to the ceiling. "They've certainly been lying about the miners' strike, I know that first hand – so what makes some people caring and others not – my mother wouldn't hurt a fly or a spider, literally, she had an almost Buddhist nature for all living things – my father was indifferent and would take the practical route, if the fly was a threat or nuisance it had to go, whack it with a newspaper, used to cause arguments between them, arguing about flies and spiders would you believe?"

She giggled like a young girl and repositioned herself, turning over on her side with her head resting on his chest.

"All this talk about spiders is freaking me out ha, ha – Theo, tell me more about your mother and father – the biggest influences on our lives should be examined in more detail."

He took a deep drag on his cigarette. "Well, he had issues and that's for sure, a stickler for detail and correctness but he lacked imagination, he taught me to play chess, at least he thought he did, but really he only showed me where the pieces move but not how to apply game strategy – he was obsessed with how things worked but not their function – then there were his mood swings, an unpredictable, temperamental man, caring one minute and in a black rage the next – you had to read his mind and act accordingly – I suppose it was too much for my mother in the end, but it was him that got up and left, how strange it all is, this family trait puzzle – it never occurred to me before but maybe his decision to leave was a selfless act to rid my mother and me of the burden of his erratic self – although he never put it that way – my mother was some sort of saint, she put up with him, and he could be really nasty, but she would sit and take it, and then forgive him, however unjust, she never retaliated nor bore a grudge – I only knew her to cry once – he had shouted at her, over some ludicrous petty thing about his dinner, not being hot enough, and she went off to her room alone, as I passed her door I could hear her crying, soft little sobs from deep within her – it was the saddest thing … "

She touched his lips when he stopped speaking, gently squeezing them with her fingers, "We'll never fathom our parents' behaviour will we – too many unknowns, and they probably got their traits from their parents, and they from theirs, and so on, this whole personality thing comes down to a sort of huge DNA fruit machine – the moment of conception is the moment the handle is pulled and round goes all the DNA and nine months later, bang, you're born with a little bit of cherry from your dad, a little bit of lemon from your mum, a slice of apple from your grandma, an orange pip from your grandpa and if you are really lucky, and this would be pure fluke, you get four symbols the same and you're born a genius or a psychopath – just one big fusion of chance."

"You're right Jenny, we're all a bunch of fruit cakes – ha, ha. Or maybe it's just the act of being born that makes us crazy –

the pure life and death struggle to get out and breathe – that could explain a lot actually – ha, ha." She pinched his arm and tickled his stomach and they both laughed at the absurdity of the conversation.

She put on a tee shirt and jeans. "Let's have a glass of wine, I've got some in the kitchen, may not be chilled though, I'll get it." She went off down the corridor stepping lightly without a sound, like a cat on a carpet.

He got up and went over to the record player. Sitting on the turntable was Joan Baez's *Love Song* album. He put the stylus on the first track. The record wobbled and crackled showing its age and over-use. Then out into the room came that sweet, haunting song, *Come All Ye Fair and Tender Maidens*, that had captivated him back on the Wissant dunes on that memorable day he first heard Jenny sing it. He laid on the bed and listened to each line so beautifully sung, each word sharp and clear and sad:

"Oh don't you remember our days of courting
You told me that you would love me the best
You could make me believe by the fall of your eyes
That the sun rose in the west."

Then for a reason unknown to him he thought of Sasha, of his ordeal at the police station and being put in the cell for most of the night. He shuddered thinking of her injuries and wondered what had happened to her; a strong sense of guilt pressed down on him for not visiting her in hospital. Then he realised she represented his past, the old Theo who had lacked ambition, who believed he would fail at anything new he took on, shackled by his own lack of confidence, including his lack of confidence with women. Now everything had changed and he felt renewed, his life was transformed with Jenny by his side, he put behind him all the ghosts of his past, his father, Sandy, Angelina, his intolerable job and the need to pay for Sasha's pleasures when loneliness marred his better judgement – they were all part of his past and he now looked forward to the future with Jenny, strengthening his will with one look of her eye. He wondered whether to tell her the whole sorry story about Sasha but dismissed the idea – it was a hopeless imbroglio and irrelevant.

He was happy and content in the moment and let the lovely, sad song tease out a melancholy that although out of place nevertheless brought back the joy of his first meeting with Jenny.

She returned with two glasses full of ice and a bottle of warm Italian white wine. Her beaming face lit up the room delaying the sun now starting to retreat west. She handed him a glass of wine rattling with ice and laid down beside him.

"I like your choice of music – ha, ha. Hey, I've got something to say Theo Harrison – I've had an idea."

He sipped the cool white wine that tasted like spring flowers on a Tuscan hilltop. "Really? Take it easy, don't want you exhausting yourself."

"Stop it – listen, why don't you move in with me – here, right here, in this flat, you can concentrate on your college work without worrying about your rent and money and stuff – what do you say?"

The suggestion was genuine and made sense, he understood and appreciated its merits instantly and his eyes glowed as he quickly imagined himself living on Packington Street with Jenny.

"Do you mean it? Are you sure?" He ventured the trite questions just to give himself a few seconds to adjust. The idea had come from nowhere and struck him deep inside where all things gentle and affectionate were stored for release at moments like these – his mind swooned with the love wrapped around such a precious unexpected proposal.

"Do you mean it Jenny? I mean, won't it cramp your style or something – we've only known each other such a little while?"

"Don't be daft – we've known each other all our lives haven't we? Anyway, you'll have to do all the cleaning and washing up –

ha, ha." She rested her glass on the floor and put her arms around his neck pulling him close to her, "I love you and I want you near me all the time …"

His heart sang with joy, a deep joy of love and contentment and tears came into his eyes, welled up from years of inner confusion, disappointment and lack of identity.

"God, I love you too – so much." He kissed her, a long deep lasting kiss, a conduit for all the love he held for her to pass effortlessly from his heart to hers.

"And I love your singing, your wonderful songs brought us together, twice, the beautiful love songs of Jenny Rennes …"

They clung to each other, rolling over like children bundling down a meadow slope, they kissed each other's eyes and ears and licked each other's noses and lips, their minds and bodies fused into one, off they went, their hearts full, their thoughts shared by touch, off they went, into that warm meadow place, light as summer air, rolling amongst the flowers and grass, their skin tingling with each others' touch – off into nature's special place, heaven on earth, the colourful realm, the tended garden of scent, God sent, where real, honest love is found at last and tastes so sweet.

That we could hold these moments like ice in a glass
And amongst the torrid squalor confusion distil the
Crystal second before it melts into the past.

Chapter Seventeen

Sasha lay in bed, the wounds to her head still smarting from having the stitches removed. She had made a good recovery during the past week since the interview with Detective Inspector Tonks and although her consultant had advised her to stay in hospital under observation for a few more days she had insisted on returning home to sort out her affairs. She lay there thinking about the fragility of life, everyone dangling on thin threads, their lives altered in the wink of an eye by some unforeseen event. Vana's little face kept appearing before her, those big, brown eyes staring at her and reassuring her, giving her strength and resolve; she spoke to her image out loud every now and then, talking to her little miracle, her unique creation:

"It's alright Vana, everything's OK now, we will soon be in our new home in Weymouth, just the two of us, we will be so happy there by the seaside."

She thought about her parents and the love that flowed from them to her, natural and genuine, without conditions. They had wanted her and Vana to move in with them but she had convinced them she was well enough to return to Somers Town, just for a week, to gather her belongings and finalise her rent and other commitments; they had insisted on giving her the balance of what she had saved and the amount of deposit required for the Weymouth apartment, a sum totalling £560 that they rounded up to £750 to cover the cost towards a washing machine, carpet and bed. It was a huge amount for them, practically wiping out their life savings. She was forever in their debt and she swore, with tears in her eyes, that she would repay them one day.

The police had returned her savings, and the telephone answering machine, and now the cash was back in its metal box beneath her bed. Detective Inspector Tonks had charged Dr

McNally with Grievous Bodily Harm With Intent for the assault on Gale Edwards, an offence that carried a maximum life sentence, but Tonks was concerned it would not hold because the defence lawyer was pleading diminished responsibility for McNally due to excessive workload and resulting stress. Tonks thought McNally would only get four years and be out in two with good behaviour. Such was the dubious nature of the justice system with its inherent anomalies of sentencing for different severities of crime.

It was past midnight and she was feeling more tired than usual – a sort of inner exhaustion that sapped her energy. She applied some antibacterial cream to the wounds on her face, sipped the last mouthful of cocoa and turned off the light.

The weather had dramatically changed, a summer storm was starting to break the long hot spell that had dominated during the past few days, the temperature had dropped and the rain swirled around the rooftops. Outside the storm beat up everything it could get its hands on, like the scene in John Martin's painting, *The Deluge*, with a bully of a westerly wind whistling through the chimney stacks and pushing against front doors and bending back shrubs and trees close to breaking point. Every now and then a torn off twig clawed against the window as if it were seeking refuge from the Apocalypse raging outside and the constant dripping of rain onto the dustbins below assumed a rhythmic quality like African drum beats.

Sasha felt warm and secure snuggled up beneath the duvet – a reassuring contentment she had not experienced for weeks. Every now and then the huge wind seemed to abate and a momentary lull held the drama still for a few moments but it was quickly followed by new gusts that seemed rejuvenated and more powerful than the last. The storm's grand symphony and the warm sanctuary of her bed started to combine their mystical powers and carry her away, drifting off to the sweet oblivion of sleep – she pulled the end of the duvet tight beneath her chin and held it there, cocooned and airtight safe, like a conker in its case, snug and tightly fit, she closed her eyes and they stayed closed, the postural muscles worn down by fatigue and trauma, she released her grip on the duvet and fell back, back through the void, falling backwards like a parachutist into the cushion of space, back she fell, further and further down, the echoes of the raging storm grew fainter and fainter, down, and down she fell, past the day-to-day cares and obstructions, she succumbed to the wondrous wonderings of the time-traveller that is sleep –

Vana appeared, dressed in a white linen frock going to and fro on a garden swing by the Weymouth seaside, smiling her big brown eyes, up and down, beneath the lumbering ash tree, carefree and happy in the endless day, long and warm, in the summer garden smelling of earth and heat, up and down she went, gently pushing herself forward on the downward strokes, effortlessly, light as air, the bees and insects making way for her, the flowers and border plants saluting as she glided above, every blade of grass waiting patiently for her soft feet to pass.

The dream fragmented and spiralled further down into the underworld, now Sasha was Vana's age, riding piggyback on her father's shoulders, clinging to his ears, her head bobbing as he trotted along the country lane, discovering the secret places over the hedges, the lambs bleating, the silent brook, out towards the caravan park, her mother behind on the yellow bike with milk and bread in the basket, the dust pushed up from the passing tractor, the tobacco smoke from the old man's pipe sitting by the stream, the rickety five-bar gate by the stile, wafts of early morning bacon, the secret pull-down caravan bed, the passing train in the distance, the Sunday church bells, the smell of orchard apples, the flotsam and jetsam left on the shore by the outgoing tide, the wind and swift waters – down she went past the playground and the outlawed electric pylon, past the abandoned warehouse, past the padlocked school gates, past the grey winter streets, past the wicked spinney between the housing estates where the big boys and girls coalesced, past the fearful joyless Sunday nights and tummy-ache dread of Monday mornings, past the chewing gum and acne, past the make-up lipstick and the wonder of bodily discoveries, out into the long summer holidays flirting with the bad boys, roaming all day in the endless woods, and there, right there, was the day she unexpectedly returned home, there, right there, was the scorching of her eyes, the forbidden sight of her father leaving the house with a strange woman, the wicked mystery, never discussed, ignored, pushed deep into the compost at the back of the garden, the back of beyond, past the chicken coop and discarded things, something wrong, an indelible stain on her innocence, something lodged in the psyche of her youth, a hindrance against natural development, an immovable thorn in her innocence, something distorting her proclivity for loving relationships and its gift of sexual activity, her father with another women, everything up side down and wrong, corrupting her social identity and her place in the family, all those Sunday afternoon gatherings, how confused and alienated she had felt then, the phony concerns over news topics, the ready-made opinions, regurgitated from the tabloid press, the exaggerated intrigues, the spurious laughter and melodramatic story telling, the pitiful vacuousness that only she could detect and her affable father effortlessly exuberant, loquacious, and falsely earnest, a sickening display of lies and deceit. How she had wanted to disappear, to take flight from that contemptuous moment in her young life, straight through the open window, like Peter Pan, to fly from rooftop to treetop and have the moon and stars as honest companions.

Her disturbing dream then faltered, stopped by something nudging her back into consciousness, back up the fading slope of closing dream where dull perception awaits – a noise, outside, faint then loud, something against the windowpane – she rolled and turned like a butterfly from its chrysalis, out she came from her cossetted cave, from deep down below, like Eurydice coming out of the underworld, towards the upper world of cognisance, she could hear the land of the living above, something turning her upwards and outwards, she was finally pulled out into the dark little bedsit room and her eyes popped open wide.

The storm was spent and now only beads of rain thread down the window like tears. Her head ached slightly around the left hand side that had taken the full brunt against the kerb. She got up to take an Aspirin still groggy from her dream. Then she heard it again, something striking the window, not the rain nor a twig, but something harder, more definite and purposeful like a stone.

She moved slowly across to the window and pulled back the curtain, colourless in the darkened room. She looked out into the dark wet night, to the familiar scene of parked cars and vans, the pavement lined with lime trees, the little patches of garden in front of the houses with their clusters of shrub and the odd laburnum, the old lock-up storage units on the other side with their alleyways and parking areas, all unadorned macadam. A fox let out a high-pitched shriek into the night somewhere in the nearby shrubbery, a haunting, sad cry that wasn't quite human nor quite animal. The moon suddenly appeared from behind a cloud, a huge creamy vanilla disk irradiating the fathomless dark, black-crape sky.

The scene, so familiar to her for its loathsome taupe ugliness, sapped her will. Her head throbbed and she rubbed her eyes to shake out remnants of the dream. She felt weak, an early fever was gathering in her spinal nerves climbing up the vertebral column like a spider from hell. She longed to return to the sanctuary of her warm bed. A small shiver went through her arms and legs. She looked towards Euston station, out through the drizzle-sprinkled night to where that huge industrial cathedral stood lighting up the space above it, mysterious and promising, beckoning the traveller to escape the impersonal metropolis; she glanced down the line of houses to her left that faded away into repetitious monotony. She sighed, "It won't be long now Vana, we'll be away from all this …"

Then she looked straight ahead, and there it was, the hooded figure in the shadows near the parked cars, standing obscure in the middle of the storm brushed street, it shuffled and looked up pulling down the hood, the hood without stripes.

Sasha's eyes froze with utter disbelief as she stared through the window heavy with rain and dirt. She wiped the glass with her hand and strained her eyes to see clearly shouting out full throttle at the figure below:

"Yusuf – is that you Yusuf – is it really you?"

She struggled to see properly. Her heart an electric shock of anticipation. A car headlamp suddenly flooded the gloomy heavy night.

"Yusuf – is it really you?"

She felt faint with expectation and her chest heaved against her ribs. She clenched her fists and gasped.

"Yusuf – Yusuf!"

The car's beam picked up a broad smiling face of a young man caught in the dazzling light – he shielded his eyes turning his head to the right, the glare spotlighting his left ear, its shape irregular from a mutilated lobe.

She pressed her nose against the cold windowpane and stared with eyes so wide they almost popped onto her cheeks; the man lowered his hands and looked straight up at her, his mouth grinning with teeth lit up in the car's headlight, his face glowing as if he had found a perfect pearl lost in the sea of time.

END

A selection of poems
by Robert Creffield

Flowering love

In those distant days of precious youth
When I roamed the woodlands and valleys
And trod the soft grasslands light of foot over
The cowslip verges my heart singing with the
Skylark soaring under wisps of watchful clouds
That witnessed my fitful searches for the love
Invading my boyhood mind heady and strong
As the red-rum honeysuckle sipping my senses.

I saw you there before I met you as in spirit you
Came to me morphed from all that was natural
In every shrub and plant and tree I held you in my
Mind as sacred treasure, the Holy Grail for a Knight
Templar, where we lay in cosy nooks beside the
Silent stickleback stream our skin touching soft as a
Dandelion our hearts quivering as an Aspen sapling
Your beautiful self surreal and serene as any dream.

Through golden fern meadows and purple foxglove
Gates we ran dizzy down the wood sorrel slopes
Roly-poly over wild garlic and daisy florets whispering
Forget-me-not promises rare as ghost orchids cowling
In the scrubby tufts and guarded by the dog violets we
Tickled each others' chins with buttercups and there
I garlanded you my princess with peony sweet as scent
And thanked the Lord for your heavenly-blue love sent.

Gordon's wine bar

In the toffee-brown shade of candle wax light
The stone cloistered walls moist and dark
Silent whispers from the past
Sealed beneath Villiers Street
The lonely watery veins of your eyes
Reflected the space between you and I
Between the hard porn of our desires
And the soft recitals of our measured poise
Your hand loose in the vaulted light
The moment missed and the chance released
Like curling smoke drifting onto the street
Dispersing amongst the Embankment crowd
Silently gone like the cold passing gargle
Of the brown-black Thames
On its way to the sea.

Your beauty caught me with its smile

Not much hope was there before you
Just a boy in a bedroom vacant place
Unsettled by wet-the-bed blanket trace
The dread of Sunday lamppost flare of
Headlamps across the wall everywhere
And the cold frost of Monday after all.

Not much joy was there before you
Just an ethereal change from earth to clay
A growing sense that nothing was new
In the lonesome night and the empty day
Delicate sensibilities looked the other way.

Not much commitment was there before you
Just feckless love daring to go or stay
Shallow intensities that blew in then flew
In the lonesome night and the empty day
Impetuous youth rolled amongst the hay.

Not much integrity was there before you
Just a Knight unable to serve and obey
A chivalric Gawain his honour cut to sinew
In the lonesome night and the empty day
Prohibited violations of virtue castaway.

Not much love was there before you
Just an ache trying to reduce its pain
Then your beauty caught me with its smile
A blinding light of love gilded the sky
The fountain of joy began to flow, our loose
Souls tightly fused, the fire kindled to glow.

Like a long forgotten scent

Through short reluctant days of winter-lude
When grey cinder skies imprison the sun
And storms and gales embitter their feud
Reeking havoc on what the other has done

Then these tyrant winds do scorch the flanks
Enticing Nimbus into raging precipitous cloud
And Thor beats his breast and bursts the banks
Covering fields and groves in a watery shroud

Now all winter long beneath this sodden earth
The silk fine primroses patiently wait in queue
And by Nature's silent signal they break the turf
Revealing all their beauty dire winter has subdued

Like a long forgotten scent
From a garden in our youth
The fragrance of our love remains
Distilled in every touch and look.

My brown-eyed girl

Into your dark eyes I fell that night
along Beckenham's High Street in the cold wet
mists of March when the day was as long as the
night and the night vanished quick as a star.

Into your dark eyes I slipped that night
along the valley slopes that danced in flower and
the poppy-dotted meadows hushed in quaking grass
out to the crystal clear mystery of your beautiful self.

Into your dark eyes I drifted that night
along the dizzy path giddy in first love and the
newness of touch hot with the pulse of young blood
calming the colour of my trembling dreams.

Into your dark eyes I soared that night
along the rising thermals light as love in maiden
flight a lark ascending the troubled skies to the
warm feathered shelter nestled in your smile.

Into your dark eyes I swooned that night
along the penumbra of your golden moon that
eclipsed the shadowed ache of my heart with
radiant love for you my brown-eyed girl.

Dusk

Along those wooded valley slopes so high
The air winged by kingfisher and damselfly
Wisps of apple green and iridescent blue
Dazzled our love with wings that flew.

Now the valley stretches into the plain
And youthful variances all look the same
Involuntarily we sit more than we walk
Unwittingly we stare mute instead of talk.

Hebe's golden sun wrinkles into sunset mists
She curses Gēras with raging clenched fists
At the foreordained image that awaits ahead
Wreaths tied to her hair and eyes bloodshed.

Those flowing days of endless summer sun
When our youth unharnessed did run and run
Now strains the will to turn it slow and lusk
We fight the fading day as it ghosts to dusk.

Come sit by me and let me touch your eyes
By the transfer of thought I am mesmerised
To where our aging hearts be welded anew
Back to the valley slopes I will walk with you.

Only a woman knows

Only a woman knows the limits of pain
Only a woman bears the sinew stretching strain
The ripping flesh splitting tear of birth
And remain
Loving, caring and the same.

About The Author

Robert Creffield has worked for various academic and professional publishing companies managing their marketing operations. He is now retired and lives in north Cornwall.

He has had poems published in two national anthologies:-

'Pussies and Tigers' Young people's writings selected by Vanessa Redgrave
Published by NASM – The National Association of School Magazines
(One poem was read out by Tom Courtney in a national radio broadcast.)

'From Under The Desk' Poetry and prose from school magazines
Edited by Melville Hardiment
Published by Max Parrish London

Also by Robert Creffield

Days of Hope and Broken Dreams

The author's first novel introduces Theo as a young man in 1977 when he and his friends, Sandy, Katrina, Izzy, Mavis and Joe get caught up in the mayhem of the National Front march dubbed, The Battle of Lewisham.

They struggle to find meaning in their lives whilst searching for love and happiness in a turbulent era that witnessed the rise of fascism and all its forms of racism and bigotry. Some on this journey will find love, others will not, but all will see their lives changed by the march.

Paperback. Available from Amazon and can also be bought in download Kindle format.

Printed in Great Britain
by Amazon